I have edited Clive Gilson's books for over a decade now – he's prolific and can turn his hand to many genres. poetry, short fiction, contemporary novels, folklore and science fiction – and the common theme is that none of them ever fails to take my breath away. There's something in each story that is either memorably poignant, hauntingly unnerving or sidesplittingly funny.

Lorna Howarth, The Write Factor

Tales From The World's Firesides is a grand project. I've collected '000's of traditional texts as part of other projects, and while many of the original texts are available through channels like Project Gutenberg, some of the narratives can be hard to read by modern readers, & so the Fireside project was born. Put simply, I collect, collate & adapt traditional tales from around the world & publish them as a modern archive. *Part 1* covers a host of nations & regions across Europe. I'm not laying any claim to insight or specialist knowledge, but these collections are born out of my love of story-telling & I hope that you'll share my affection for traditional tales, myths & legends.

Cover image by:

Enrique Meseguer from Pixabay

Tales From Gallia

Traditional tales, fables and sagas from the Gallic tradition

Compiled & Edited by Clive Gilson

"Tales from the World's Firesides"

Book 18 in Part 1 of the series: Europe

Tales From Gallia, edited by Clive Gilson, Solitude, Bath, UK

www.boyonabench.com

First published as an eBook in 2019

This hard cover edition © 2020 Clive Gilson

All rights reserved. No portion of this book may be reproduced in any form without permission from the publisher, except as permitted by United Kingdom copyright law.

This is a work of fiction. Names, characters, places, and incidents either are the products of the author's imagination or are used fictitiously. Any resemblance to actual persons, living or dead, businesses, companies, events, or locales is entirely coincidental.

Printed by IngramSpark

ISBN 978-1-913500-96-2

 SOLITUDE

Contents

PREFACE

A FAIRY'S BLUNDER

COMORRE

PRINCESS BELLE-ETOILE

BEAUTY AND THE BEAST

RICKY OF THE TUFT

THE GREEN SERPENT

WHY THE ANIMALS NO LONGER FEAR THE SHEEP

PRINCESS ROSETTA

A FRENCH PUCK

THE STORY OF BLONDINE, BONNE-BICHE, AND BEAU-MINON

DONKEY SKIN

PERONNIK THE IDIOT

THE HIND OF THE WOOD

THE LITTLE GREY MOUSE

THE STONES OF PLOUVINEC

THE YELLOW DWARF

PRINCE FEATHERHEAD AND THE PRINCESS CELANDINE

ROBIN REDBREAST

THE FAIRIES

THE SEVEN CONQUERORS OF THE QUEEN OF THE MISSISSIPPI

THE ADVENTURES OF COVAN THE BROWN-HAIRED

THE WHITE INN

GRACIOSA AND PERCINET

HISTORICAL NOTES

ABOUT THE EDITOR

PREFACE

French, or Gallic, folklore encompasses the fables, folklore, fairy tales and legends of the French speaking people and their ancestors. Traditions of storytelling have a long and distinguished history, and in the Gallic tradition we can date back at least as far as Occitan literature in the Middle Ages. Occitan examples often include songs, poetry and literature from the South of France from the 11th and 12th centuries, much of which inspired vernacular literature throughout medieval Europe.

These early recorded songs and poetry reached their highest development in the 12th century and included the well-known *Songs of the Troubadours*. The songs, poetry and narratives of the troubadours, who were composers and performers travelling across the European continent during the High Middle Ages, flourished from the 11th century and spread throughout Europe from Southern France. Their songs dealt mainly with themes of chivalry and courtly love.

Songs of the Trouvère are songs and poetry that stemmed from poet-composers who were roughly contemporary with and influenced by the troubadours but who composed their works in the northern dialects of France.

A second form of legend in France during the Middle Ages was epic poetry, partly historical and partly legend with themes covering the formation of France, war, kingship, and important battles. This genre was known as *chansons de geste* which is Old French for "songs of heroic deeds." Pieces in this oeuvre are also often referred to as the epics of the *Matter of France*. *Chanson de geste* or *Matter of France* works were part history and part legendary heroic epic tales of Charlemagne and the history and founding of France by the Franks.

Another folkloric medium in the Middle Ages were fables, mock epics and animal folk tales, notably tales such as *Reynard Le Roman de Renart* by Perrout de Saint Cloude from the late eighteenth century.

French fairy tales are particularly known by their literary rather than their folk, oral variants. Charles Perrault derived almost all his tales from folk sources, but rewrote them for an upper-class audience, removing some of the more rustic elements.

In this collection we have tales collected by Andrew Lang, Charles Perrault, Jeanne-Marie Le Prince de Beaumont, Comtesse de Sophie Ségur, Marie-Catherine Le Jumel de Barneville, Baroness d'Aulnoy, Katharine Pyle and Edmund Dulac, some of the finest collectors working from the seventeenth century onwards.

As ever it's been a delight working with these tales. You'll see from the contents list that some of the more obviously famous French tales, such as *Cinderella* and *Puss in Boots* have been left out. I have so many tales of French origin that I wanted to re-tell some of the lesser known examples here. I'm sure, however, that we'll revisit those remaining classic tales before too long.

Clive,

Bath 2019

A FAIRY'S BLUNDER

This adaptation is taken from a story collected by Andrew Lang in his Grey Fairy Book, published in 1900. The original is taken from the Cabinet des Fées (The Cabinet of fairies), a collection of stories compiled by Knight Charles Joseph Mayer, which appeared in Amsterdam between 1785 and 1789. It included forty-one volumes, presenting the texts of about forty storytellers, including Charles Perrault, Madame d'Aulnoy, Mademoiselle Leprince de Beaumont, Mademoiselle de La Force, Miss Lheritier & Jean-Jacques Rousseau, the knight of Mailly.

ONCE UPON A TIME THERE LIVED a fairy whose name was Dindonette. She was the best creature in the world, with the kindest heart, but she had not much sense, and was always doing things, to benefit people, which generally ended in causing pain and distress to everybody concerned. No one knew this better than the inhabitants of an island far off in the midst of the sea, which, according to the laws of fairyland, she had taken under her special protection, thinking day and night of what she could do to make the isle the pleasantest place in the whole world, as it was already the most beautiful.

As the fairy went about, unseen, from house to house, she heard everywhere children longing for the time when they would be "grown-up," and able, they thought, to do as they liked. She heard old people talking about the past, and sighing to be young again.

"Is there no way of satisfying these poor things?" she thought. And then one night an idea occurred to her. "Oh, yes, of course! It has been tried before, but I will manage better than the rest, with their old Fountain of Youth, which, after all, only made people young again. I will enchant the spring that bubbles up in the middle of the orchard, and the children that drink of it shall at once become grown men and women, and the old people return to the days of their childhood."

And without stopping to consult one single other fairy, who might have given her good advice, off rushed Dindonette, to cast her spell over the fountain.

It was the only spring of fresh water in the island, and at dawn was crowded with people of all ages, come to drink at its source. Delighted at her plan for making them all happy, the fairy hid herself behind a thicket of roses, and peeped out whenever footsteps came that way. It was not long before she had ample proof of the success of her enchantments. Almost before her eyes the children put on the size and strength of adults, while the old men and women instantly became helpless, tiny babies. Indeed, so pleased was she with the result of her work, that she could no longer remain hidden, and went about telling everybody what she had done, and enjoying their gratitude and thanks.

But after the first outburst of delight at their wishes being granted, people began to be a little frightened at the rapid effects of the magic water. It was delicious to feel yourself at the height of your power and beauty, but you would wish to keep so always! Now this was exactly what the fairy had been in too much of a hurry to arrange, and no sooner had the children become grown up, and the men and women become babies, than they all rushed on to old age at an appalling rate! The fairy only found out her mistake when it was too late to set it right.

When the inhabitants of the island saw what had befallen them, they were filled with despair, and did everything they could think of to escape from such a dreadful fate. They dug wells in their places, so that they should no longer need to drink from the magic spring, but the sandy soil yielded no water, and the rainy season was already past. They stored up the dew that fell, and the juice of fruits and of herbs, but all this was as a drop in the ocean of their wants. Some threw themselves into the sea, trusting that the current might carry them to other shores, for they had no boats, and a few, still more impatient, put themselves to death on the spot. The rest submitted blindly to their destiny.

Perhaps the worst part of the enchantment was, that the change from one age to another was so rapid that the person had no time to prepare himself for it. It would not have mattered so much if the man who stood up in the assembly of the nation, to give his advice as to peace or war, had looked like a baby, as long as he spoke with the knowledge and sense of a full-grown man. But, alas! With the outward form of an infant, he had taken on its helplessness and foolishness, and there was no one who could train him to better things. The end of it all was, that before a month had passed the population had died out, and the fairy Dindonette, ashamed and grieved at the effects of her folly, had left the island for ever.

Many centuries after, the fairy Selnozoura, who had fallen into bad health, was ordered by her doctors to make the tour of the world twice a week for change of air, and in one of these journeys she found herself at Fountain Island. Selnozoura never made these trips alone, but always took with her two children, of whom she was very fond. Cornichon was a boy of fourteen, bought in his childhood at a slave-market, and Toupette was a few months younger, and had been entrusted to the care of the fairy by her guardian, the jinni Kristopo. Cornichon and Toupette were intended by Selnozoura to become husband and wife, as soon as they were old enough. Meanwhile, they travelled with her in a little vessel, whose speed through the air was just a thousand nine hundred and fifty times greater than that of the swiftest of our ships.

Struck with the beauty of the island, Selnozoura ran the vessel to ground, and leaving it in the care of the dragon which lived in the hold during the voyage, she stepped on shore with her two companions. Surprised at the sight of a large town whose streets and houses were absolutely desolate, the fairy resolved to put her magic arts in practice to find out the cause. While she was thus engaged, Cornichon and Toupette wandered away by themselves, and by-and-by arrived at the fountain, whose bubbling waters looked cool and delicious on such a hot day. Scarcely had they each drunk a deep draught, when the fairy, who by this time had discovered all she wished to know, hastened to the spot.

"Oh, beware! beware!" she cried, the moment she saw them. "If you drink that deadly poison you will be ruined for ever!"

"Poison?" answered Toupette. "It is the most refreshing water I have ever tasted, and Cornichon will say so too!"

"Unhappy children, then I am too late! Why did you leave me? Listen, and I will tell you what has befallen the wretched inhabitants of this island, and what will befall you too. The power of fairies is great," she added, when she had finished her story, "but they cannot destroy the work of another fairy. Very shortly you will pass into the weakness and silliness of extreme old age, and all I can do for you is to make it as easy to you as possible, and to preserve you from the death that others have suffered, from having no one to look after them. But the charm is working already! Cornichon is taller and more manly than he was an hour ago, and Toupette no longer looks like a little girl."

It was true, but this fact did not seem to render the young people as miserable as it did Selnozoura.

"Do not pity us," said Cornichon. "If we are fated to grow old so soon, let us no longer delay our marriage. What matter if we anticipate our decay, if we only anticipate our happiness too?"

The fairy felt that Cornichon had reason on his side, and seeing by a glance at Toupette's face that there was no opposition to be feared from her, she answered, "Let it be so, then. But not in this dreadful place. We will return at once to Bagota, and the festivities shall be the most brilliant ever seen."

They all returned to the vessel, and in a few hours the four thousand five hundred miles that lay between the island and Bagota were passed. Everyone was surprised to see the change which the short absence had made in the young people, but as the fairy had promised absolute silence about the adventure, they were none the wiser, and busied themselves in preparing their dresses for the marriage, which was fixed for the next night.

Early on the following morning the jinni Kristopo arrived at the Court, on one of the visits he was in the habit of paying his ward from time to time. Like the rest, he was astonished at the sudden improvement in the child. He had always been fond of her, and in a moment he fell violently in love. Hastily demanding an audience of the fairy, he laid his proposals before her, never doubting that she would give her consent to so brilliant a match. But Selnozoura refused to listen, and even hinted that in his own interest Kristopo had better turn his thoughts elsewhere. The jinni pretended to agree, but, instead, he went straight to Toupette's room, and flew away with her through the window, at the very instant that the bridegroom was awaiting her below.

When the fairy discovered what had happened, she was furious, and sent messenger after messenger to the jinni in his palace at Ratibouf, commanding him to restore Toupette without delay, and threatening to make war in case of refusal.

Kristopo gave no direct answer to the fairy's envoys, but kept Toupette closely guarded in a tower, where the poor girl used all her powers of persuasion to induce him to put off their marriage. All would, however, have been quite vain if, in the course of a few days, sorrow, joined to the spell of the magic water, had not altered her appearance so completely that Kristopo was quite alarmed, and declared that she needed amusement and fresh air, and that, as his presence seemed to distress her, she should be left her own mistress. But one thing he declined to do, and that was to send her back to Bagota.

In the meantime both sides had been busily collecting armies, and Kristopo had given the command of his to a famous general, while Selnozoura had placed Cornichon at the head of her forces. But before war was actually declared, Toupette's parents, who had been summoned by the jinni, arrived at Ratibouf. They had never seen their daughter since they parted from her as a baby, but from time to time travellers to Bagota had brought back accounts of her beauty. What was their amazement, therefore, at finding, instead of a lovely girl, a middle-aged woman, handsome indeed, but quite faded, looking, in fact, older than themselves. Kristopo, hardly less astonished than they were at the sudden change, thought that it was a joke on the part of one of his courtiers, who had hidden Toupette away, and put this elderly lady in her place. Bursting with rage, he sent instantly for all the servants and guards of the town, and inquired who had the insolence to play him such a trick, and what had become of their prisoner. They replied that since Toupette had been in their charge she had never left her rooms unveiled, and that during her walks in the surrounding gardens, her food had been brought in and placed on her table, and as she preferred to eat alone no one had ever seen her face, or knew what she was like.

The servants were clearly speaking the truth, and Kristopo was obliged to believe them. "But," thought he, "if they have not had a hand in this, it must be the work of the fairy," and in his anger he ordered the army to be ready to march.

On her side, Selnozoura of course knew what the jinni had to expect, but was deeply offended when she heard of the base trick which she was believed to have invented. Her first desire was to give battle to Kristopo at once, but with great difficulty her ministers induced her to pause, and to send an ambassador to Kristopo to try to arrange matters.

So the Prince Zeprady departed for the court of Ratibouf, and on his way he met Cornichon, who was encamped with his army just outside the gates of Bagota. The prince showed him the fairy's written order that for the present peace must still be kept, and Cornichon, filled with longing to see Toupette once more, begged to be allowed to accompany Zeprady on his mission to Ratibouf.

By this time the jinni's passion for Toupette, which had caused all these troubles, had died out, and he willingly accepted the terms of peace offered by Zeprady, though he informed the prince that he still believed the fairy to be guilty of the dreadful change in the girl. To this the prince only replied that on that point he had a witness who could prove, better than anyone else, if it was Toupette or not, and desired that Cornichon should be sent for.

When Toupette was told that she was to see her old lover again, her heart leapt with joy, but soon the recollection came to her of all that had happened, and she remembered that Cornichon would be changed as well as she. The moment of their meeting was not all happiness, especially on the part of Toupette, who could not forget her lost beauty, and the jinni, who was present, was at last convinced that he had not been deceived, and went out to sign the treaty of peace, followed by his attendants.

"Ah, Toupette, my dear Toupette!" cried Cornichon, as soon as they were left alone, "now that we are once more united, let our past troubles be forgotten."

"Our past troubles!" answered she, "and what do you call our lost beauty and the dreadful future before us? You are looking fifty years older than when I saw you last, and I know too well that fate has treated me no better!"

"Ah, do not say that," replied Cornichon, clasping her hand. "You are different, it is true, but every age has its graces, and surely no woman of sixty was ever handsomer than you! If your eyes had been as bright as of yore they would have matched badly with your faded skin. The wrinkles which I notice on your forehead explain the increased fulness of your cheeks, and your throat in withering is elegant in decay. Thus the harmony shown by your features, even as they grow old, is the best proof of their former beauty."

"Oh, monster!" cried Toupette, bursting into tears, "is that all the comfort you can give me?"

"But, Toupette," answered Cornichon, "you used to declare that you did not care for beauty, as long as you had my heart."

"Yes, I know," said she, "but how can you go on caring for a person who is as old and plain as I?"

"Toupette, Toupette," replied Cornichon, "you are only talking nonsense. My heart is as much yours as ever it was, and nothing in the world can make any difference."

At this point of the conversation the Prince Zeprady entered the room, with the news that the jinni, full of regret for his behaviour, had given Cornichon full permission to depart for Bagota as soon as he liked, and to take Toupette with him, adding that, though he begged they would excuse his taking leave of them before they went, he hoped, before long, to visit them at Bagota.

Neither of the lovers slept that night. Cornichon was full of joy at returning home, while Toupette was filled with dread of the blow to her vanity which awaited her at Bagota. It was hopeless for Cornichon to try to console her during the journey with the reasons he had given the day before. She only grew worse and worse, and when they reached the palace went straight to her old apartments, entreating the fairy to allow both herself and Cornichon to remain concealed, and to see no one.

For some time after their arrival the fairy was taken up with the preparations for the rejoicings which were to celebrate the peace, and with the reception of the jinni, who was determined to do all in his power to regain Selnozoura's lost friendship. Cornichon and Toupette were therefore left entirely to themselves, and though this was only what they wanted, still, they began to feel a little neglected.

At length, one morning, they saw from the windows that the fairy and the jinni were approaching, in state, with all their courtiers in attendance. Toupette instantly hid herself in the darkest corner of the room, but Cornichon, forgetting that he was now no longer a boy of fourteen, ran to meet them. In so doing he tripped and fell, bruising one of his eyes severely. At the sight of her lover lying helpless on the floor, Toupette hastened to his side, but her feeble legs gave way under her, and she fell almost on top of him, knocking out three of her loosened teeth against his forehead. The fairy, who entered the room at this moment, burst into tears, and listened in silence to the jinni, who hinted that by-and-by everything would be put right.

"At the last assembly of the fairies," he said, "when the doings of each fairy were examined and discussed, a proposal was made to lessen, as far as possible, the mischief caused by Dindonette by enchanting the fountain. And it was decided that, as she had meant nothing but kindness, she should have the power of undoing one half of the spell. Of course she might always have destroyed the fatal fountain, which would have been best of all, but this she never thought of. Yet, in spite of this, her heart is so good, that I am sure that the moment she hears that she is wanted she will fly to help. Only, before she comes, it is for you, Madam, to make up your mind which of the two shall regain their former strength and beauty."

At these words the fairy's soul sank. Both Cornichon and Toupette were equally dear to her, and how could she favour one at the cost of the other? As to the courtiers, none of the men were able to understand why she hesitated a second to declare for Toupette, while the ladies were equally strong on the side of Cornichon.

But, however undecided the fairy might be, it was quite different with Cornichon and Toupette.

"Ah, my love," exclaimed Cornichon, "at length I shall be able to give you the best proof of my devotion by showing you how I value the beauties of your mind above those of your body! While the most charming women of the court will fall victims to my youth and strength, I shall think of nothing but how to lay them at your feet, and pay heart-felt homage to your age and wrinkles."

"Not so fast," interrupted Toupette, "I don't see why you should have it all. Why do you heap such humiliations upon me? But I will trust to the justice of the fairy, who will not treat me so."

Then she entered her own rooms, and refused to leave them, in spite of the prayers of Cornichon, who begged her to let him explain.

No one at the court thought or spoke of any other subject during the few days before the arrival of Dindonette, whom everybody expected to set things right in a moment. But, alas! She had no idea herself what was best to be done, and always adopted the opinion of the person she was talking to. At length a thought struck her, which seemed the only way of satisfying both parties, and she asked the fairy to call together all the court and the people to hear her decision.

"Happy is she," she began, "who can repair the evil she has caused, but happier she who has never caused any."

As nobody contradicted this remark, she continued, "To me it is only allowed to undo one half of the mischief I have wrought. I could restore you your youth," she said to Cornichon, "or your beauty," turning to Toupette. "I will do both and I will do neither."

A murmur of curiosity arose from the crowd, while Cornichon and Toupette trembled with astonishment.

"No," went on Dindonette, "never should I have the cruelty to leave one of you to decay, while the other enjoys the glory of youth. And as I cannot restore you both at once to what you were, one half of each of your bodies shall become young again, while the other half goes on its way to decay. I will leave it to you to choose which half it shall be. Should I draw a line round the waist or a line straight down the middle of the body."

She looked about her proudly, expecting applause for her clever idea. But Cornichon and Toupette were shaking with rage and disappointment, and everyone else broke into shouts of laughter. In pity for the unhappy lovers, Selnozoura came forward.

"Do you not think," she said, "that instead of what you propose, it would be better to let them take it in turns to enjoy their former youth and beauty for a fixed time? I am sure you could easily manage that."

"What an excellent notion!" cried Dindonette. "Oh, yes, of course that is best! Which of you shall I touch first?"

"Touch her," replied Cornichon, who was always ready to give way to Toupette. "I know her heart too well to fear any change."

So the fairy bent forward and touched her with her magic ring, and in one instant the old woman was a girl again. The whole court wept with joy at the sight, and Toupette ran up to Cornichon, who had fallen down in his surprise, promising to pay him long visits, and tell him of all her balls and water parties.

The two fairies went to their own apartments, where the jinni followed them to take his leave.

"Oh, dear!" suddenly cried Dindonette, breaking in to the farewell speech of the jinni. "I quite forgot to fix the time when Cornichon should in his turn grow young. How stupid of me! And now I fear it is too late, for I ought to have declared it before I touched Toupette with the ring. Oh, dear! oh, dear! Why did nobody warn me?"

"You were so quick," replied Selnozoura, who had long been aware of the mischief the fairy had again done, "and we can only wait now till Cornichon shall have reached the utmost limits of his decay, when he will drink of the water, and become a baby once more, so that Toupette will have to spend her life as a nurse, a wife, and a caretaker."

After the anxiety of mind and the weakness of body to which for so long Toupette had been a prey, it seemed as if she could not amuse herself enough, and it was seldom indeed that she found time to visit poor Cornichon, though she did not cease to be fond of him, or to be kind to him. Still, she was perfectly happy without him, and this the poor man did not fail to see, almost blind and deaf from age though he was.

But it was left to Kristopo to undo at last the work of Dindonette, and give Cornichon back the youth he had lost, and this the jinni did all the more gladly, as he discovered, quite by accident, that Cornichon was in fact his son. It was on this plea that he attended the great yearly meeting of the fairies, and prayed that, in consideration of his services to so many of the members, this one boon might be granted him.

Such a request had never before been heard in fairyland, and was objected to by some of the older fairies, but both Kristopo and Selnozoura were held in such high honour that the murmurs of disgust were set aside, and the latest victim to the enchanted fountain was pronounced to be free of the spell. All that the jinni asked in return was that he might accompany the fairy back to Bagota, and be present when his son assumed his proper shape.

They made up their minds they would just tell Toupette that they had found a husband for her, and give her a pleasant surprise at her wedding, which was fixed for the following night. She heard the news with astonishment, and many pangs for the grief which Cornichon would certainly feel at his place being taken by another, but she did not dream of disobeying the fairy, and spent the whole day wondering who the bridegroom could be.

At the appointed hour, a large crowd assembled at the fairy's palace, which was decorated with the sweetest flowers, known only to fairyland. Toupette had taken her place, but where was the bridegroom?

"Fetch Cornichon!" said the fairy to her chamberlain.

But Toupette interposed, "Oh, Madam, spare him, I entreat you, this bitter pain, and let him remain hidden and in peace."

"It is necessary that he should be here," answered the fairy, "and he will not regret it."

And, as she spoke, Cornichon was led in, smiling with the foolishness of extreme old age at the sight of the gay crowd.

"Bring him here," commanded the fairy, waving her hand towards Toupette, who started back from surprise and horror.

Selnozoura then took the hand of the poor old man, and the jinni came forward and touched him three times with his ring, when Cornichon was transformed into a handsome young man.

"May you live long," the jinni said, "to enjoy happiness with your wife, and to love your father."

And that was the end of the mischief wrought by the fairy Dindonette!

COMORRE

This adaptation is taken from a collection called Breton Legends, although the original author or collector remains unknown.

In the old times, it is said that the city of Vannes was far larger and finer than it is in our days, and that instead of a prefect, it was ruled by a king, whose will was law. I do not know what his name was, but from all I have heard, it seems that he was a man who lived in the fear of God, and of whom no one had ever found occasion to speak an evil word.

He had been early left a widower, and he lived happily with his only daughter, said to be the most beautiful creature in the whole world. She was called Tryphyna, and those who knew her have asserted that she came of age unsullied by a single mortal sin. So that the king her father would have willingly sacrificed his horses, castles, and farms, rather than see Tryphyna made unhappy.

However, it came to pass, that one day ambassadors from Cornouaille were announced. They came on the part of Comorre, a powerful prince of those times, who ruled over the land of Black-Wheat as Tryphyna's father ruled that of the White.

After offering presents of honey, flax, and a dozen little pigs, to the king, they informed him that their master had visited the last fair at Vannes disguised as a soldier, and there beholding the beauty and modesty of the young princess, he had determined at all hazards to have her in marriage.

This proposal filled both the king and Tryphyna with great grief, for the Count Comorre was a giant, and said to be the wickedest man that had ever been on the earth since the days of Cain.

From his earliest youth he had been used to find his only pleasure in working mischief, and so malicious was he, that his mother herself had been accustomed to run and ring the alarm-bell whenever he left the castle, to warn the country people to take care of themselves. When older, and his own master, his cruelty was greater still. It was said that one morning, on his way out, he tried his gun upon a lad tending a colt at pasture, and killed him. And at other times, when returning unsuccessful from the chase, he would let loose his dogs upon the poor peasants in the fields, and suffer them to be pulled down like beasts of prey. But, most horrible of all, he had married four wives in succession, each of whom had died off suddenly without receiving the last Sacraments. It was even said that he had made away with them by the knife, fire, water, or poison.

So the King of Vannes replied to the ambassadors that his daughter was too young and too weak in health to think of marrying. But Comorre's people answered roughly, after their manner, that the Count Comorre would listen to no such excuses, and that they had received orders, if the young princess was not sent back with them, to declare war against the King of Vannes. The king replied, that they must do as they liked about that. Then the most aged among the envoys lighted a handful of straw, which he flung to the winds, declaring that thus should the anger of Comorre pass over the country of White-Wheat, and so they departed.

Tryphyna's father, being a courageous man, did not allow himself to be disheartened by this threat, and called together all the soldiers he could muster to defend his territories.

But in a few days he heard that the Count of Cornouaille was advancing upon Vannes with a powerful army, and it was not long before he came in sight with trumpets and cannons. Then the king put himself at the head of his people, and the battle was on the point of beginning, when St. Veltas came to find Tryphyna, who was praying in her oratory.

The saint wore the cloak which had served him as a vessel for crossing the sea, and carried the walking-staff which he had fastened to it as a mast to catch the wind. A halo of glory hovered round his brow. He announced to the young princess that the men of Vannes and Cornouaille were on the point of shedding each other's blood, and asked her whether she would not stay the death of so many Christians by consenting to become the wife of Count Comorre.

"Alas, then, God demands from me the death of all my peace and happiness," cried the young girl, weeping. "Why am I not a beggar? I could then at least be wedded to the beggar of my choice. Ah, if it is indeed the will of God that I espouse this giant, whom I dread so much, say for me, holy man, the Office for the Dead, for the count will kill me, as he has his other wives."

But St. Veltas replied, "Fear nothing, Tryphyna. See here this ring of silver, white as milk. It shall serve you as a warning, for so surely as Comorre is plotting anything against you, it will become as black as the crow's wing. Take courage, then, and save the Bretons from death."

The young princess, reassured by this present of the ring, consented to St. Veltas's request.

Then the saint hurried without loss of time towards the opposed armies, that he might announce the good tidings to their chiefs. The King of Vannes, notwithstanding his daughter's resolution, was very unwilling to consent to the marriage, but Comorre promised so fairly, that at last he accepted him as son-in-law.

The nuptials were celebrated with such festivities as have never been seen since within the two dioceses. The first day six thousand noble guests sat down to table, and on the second they received as many poor, whom the bride and bridegroom, forgetful of their rank, waited on at table, with napkins on their arms. Then there was dancing, at which all the musicians of Lower Brittany were engaged and wrestling-matches, in which the men of Brévelay contended with those of Cornouaille.

At last, when all was over, everyone went home to his own country, and Comorre carried off with him his young bride, as a sparrow-hawk that has pounced upon a poor little yellow-hammer.

However, during the first few months his affection for Tryphyna softened him more than might have been expected. The castle-dungeons remained empty, and the gibbets held no pasture for foul birds of prey.

The count's people whispered low,"What ails our lord, then, that he thirsts no more for tears and blood?"

But those who knew him better waited and said nothing. Tryphyna herself, notwithstanding the count's kindness towards her, could never feel easy or happy in her mind. Every day she went down to the castle-chapel, and there, praying on the tombs of Comorre's four dead wives, she besought God to preserve her from a violent death.

About this time a grand assembly of Breton princes took place at Rennes, and Comorre was obliged to join it. He gave into Tryphyna's keeping all the castle keys, even those of the cellars. He told her to amuse herself as she liked best, and set out with a great retinue.

It was five months before he returned, full of anxiety to see Tryphyna, of whom he had thought often during his absence. And in his haste, unwilling to lose time by announcing his arrival, he rushed up into her room, where she was at that moment engaged in making an infant's cap, trimmed with silver-lace.

On seeing the cap, Comorre turned pale, and asked for what it was designed. The countess, thinking to rejoice his heart, assured him that they would shortly have a child, but at this news the Prince of Cornouaille drew back in horror, and after looking at Tryphyna with a dreadful countenance, went suddenly out, not speaking a word.

The princess might have taken this for one of the count's frequent caprices, had she not perceived, on casting down her eyes, that the silver ring had turned black. She uttered a cry of terror, for she remembered the words of St. Veltas, and knew that she must be in imminent peril. But she knew not wherefore, neither could she tell how to escape it. Poor woman! All day long, and during part of the night, she employed herself in pondering what could be the reason for the count's displeasure, and at last, her heart growing heavier, she went down into the chapel to pray.

But scarcely had she finished her rosary, and risen to depart, when the hour of midnight struck. At that instant she beheld the four grave-stones of Comorre's four wives rise slowly up, and they themselves come out swathed in their funeral shrouds.

Tryphyna, more dead than alive, would have escaped, but the phantoms called to her, "Take care, poor lost one. Comorre waits to kill you."

"Me!" cried the countess, "and how have I offended, that he seeks my death?"

"You have told him you will shortly be a mother, and he knows, thanks to the evil one, that his first child will be his destroyer. Therefore it was that he took our lives also."

"My God! And have I fallen into hands so cruel?" cried Tryphyna, weeping. "If it is so, what hope remains for me? What can I do?"

"Go back to your father in the land of White-Wheat," said the phantoms.

"How can I fly?" returned the countess. "The giant dog of Comorre guards the gate."

"Give to him this poison, which killed me," said the first.

"How can I get down the high wall?" asked the young wife.

"Let yourself down by this cord, which strangled me," replied the second.

"But who will direct me through the darkness?" asked the princess.

"This fire, which consumed me," replied the third.

"How can I take so long a journey?" once more asked Tryphyna.

"Make use of this staff, which crushed my temples," said the last.

Comorre's wife took the staff, the torch, the cord, and the poison. She silenced the dog, she scaled the lofty wall, she penetrated the darkness, and took the road to Vannes, where her father dwelt.

Comorre, not being able to find her the next morning when he rose, sent his page to search for her in every chamber, but the page returned with the tidings that Tryphyna was no longer in the castle.

Then the count went up the donjon-tower, and looked out to the four winds.

To the north he saw a raven that croaked, to the sunrise a swallow on the wing, to the south a wailing sea-mew, and to the west a turtle-dove that sped away.

He instantly exclaimed that Tryphyna was in that direction, and having his horse saddled, set out in pursuit.

His unfortunate wife was still upon the border of the wood which surrounded the count's castle, but she was warned of his approach by seeing the ring grow black. Then she turned aside over the common, and came to the cabin of a poor shepherd, whose sole possession was an old magpie hanging in a cage.

The poor lady lay concealed there the whole day, bemoaning herself and praying. When night came on, she once more set forth along the paths which skirt the fields of flax and corn.

Comorre, who had kept to the high road, could not find her, and after travelling two days, he returned the same way as far as the common. But there, as ill-luck would have it, he entered the shepherd's hut, and heard the magpie trying to recall the melancholy wailings it had listened to, and murmuring, "Poor Tryphyna! Poor Tryphyna!" Then Comorre knew the countess had passed by that way, and calling his hunting-dog, set him on the track, and began to pursue her.

Meanwhile Tryphyna, pressed by terror, had walked on unresting, and was already drawing near to Vannes. But at last she felt herself unable to proceed, and turning into a wood, lay down upon the grass, where she gave birth to a miraculously lovely son, who was afterwards called St. Trever.

As she held him in her arms, and wept over him, half sorrowfully and half in joy, she perceived a falcon ornamented with a collar of gold. He was perched upon a neighbouring tree, and she knew him for her father's bird, the king of the land of White-Wheat. Calling him quickly by his name, the bird came down upon her knees, and giving him the warning-ring she had received from St. Veltas, she said, "Fly, falcon, hasten to my father's court, and carry him this ring. When he sees it, he will know I am in urgent danger, and will order his soldiers to horse. It is for you to lead them here to save me."

The bird understood, and taking the ring, flew like a flash of lightning in the direction of Vannes.

But almost at the same instant Comorre came in sight with his stag-hound, who had incessantly tracked Tryphyna, and as she had no longer the ring to forewarn her of approaching danger, she remained unconscious of it till she heard the tyrant's voice cheering on his dog.

Terror froze the marrow in her bones, and she had only just time to wrap the infant in her mantle and hide it in the hollow of a tree, when Comorre appeared upon his horse at the entrance of the pathway.

Seeing Tryphyna, he uttered a cry like that of a wild-beast, and throwing himself upon the unhappy victim, who had sunk upon her knees, he severed her head from her shoulders by one stroke of his hunting-knife.

Believing himself now at once rid of mother and child, he whistled back his dog, and set off on his return to Cornouaille.

Now the falcon arrived at the court of the King of Vannes, who was then dining, and hovering over the table, let fall the silver ring into his master's cup. He had no sooner recognised it, than he exclaimed, "Woe is me, some misfortune must have befallen my daughter, since the falcon brings me back her ring. Let the horses be made ready, and let St. Veltas be our companion, for I fear we shall but too soon stand in need of his assistance."

The servants obeyed promptly, and the king set forth with the saint, who had come at his prayer, and a numerous retinue. They put their horses to their full speed, and followed the course of the flying falcon, who led them to the glade where lay the dead Tryphyna and her living child.

The king then threw himself from his horse, and uttered cries that might have made the very oaks weep, but St. Veltas silenced him.

"Hush!" said he, "and join with me in prayer to God. He can even yet repair all."

With these words, he knelt down with all those who were present, and after addressing a fervent prayer to Heaven, he said to the dead body, "Arise!"

Tryphyna obeyed.

"Take your head and your child," added the saint, "and follow us to the castle of Comorre."

It was done as he commanded.

Then the terrified escort took horse once more, and spurred onwards towards Cornouaille. But however rapidly they rode, Tryphyna was ever in advance, holding her son upon her left arm, and her head on her right.

And thus they came before the castle of the murderer. Comorre, who saw them coming, caused the drawbridge to be raised. St. Veltas drew near the moat, and exclaimed, with a loud voice,"Count of Cornouaille, I bring you back your wife, such as your wickedness has made her, and your son, as God has bestowed him on you. Will you receive them beneath your roof?"

Comorre was silent. St. Veltas repeated the same words a second, then a third time, but still no voice replied. Taking, therefore, the infant from his mother's arms, he placed him on the ground.

Then was beheld a miracle which proved the Omnipotence of God, for the child walked alone, and boldly, to the edge of the moat, where he gathered a handful of the sand and flung it towards the castle, crying out, "God is just!"

At that instant the towers shook with a great tumult, the walls gaped open, and the whole castle sank down in ruins, burying the Count of Cornouaille, and all those who had abetted him in sin.

St. Veltas then replaced the head of Tryphyna on her shoulders, and laying his hands upon her, the holy woman came back to life, to the great content of the King of Vannes, and of all who were there present.

Tales From Gallia

PRINCESS BELLE-ETOILE

This adaptation is taken from a collection called Breton Legends, although the original author or collector remains unknown.

ONCE UPON A TIME THERE WERE three Princesses, named Roussette, Brunette, and Blondine, who lived in retirement with their mother, a Princess who had lost all her former grandeur. One day an old woman called and asked for a dinner, as this Princess was an excellent cook. After the meal was over, the old woman, who was a fairy, promised that their kindness should be rewarded, and immediately disappeared.

Shortly after, the King came that way, with his brother and the Lord Admiral. They were all so struck with the beauty of the three Princesses, that the King married the youngest, Blondine, his brother married Brunette, and the Lord Admiral married Roussette.

The good Fairy, who had brought all this about, also caused the young Queen Blondine to have three lovely children, two boys and a girl, out of whose hair fell fine jewels. Each had a brilliant star on the forehead, and a rich chain of gold around the neck. At the same time Brunette, her sister, gave birth to a handsome boy. Now the young Queen and Brunette were much attached to each other, but Roussette was jealous of both, and the old Queen, the King's mother, hated them. Brunette died soon after the birth of her son, and the King was absent on a warlike expedition, so Roussette joined the wicked old Queen in forming plans to injure Blondine. They ordered Feintise, the old Queen's waiting-woman, to strangle the Queen's three children and the son of Princess Brunette, and bury them secretly.

But as she was about to execute this wicked order, she was so struck by their beauty, and the appearance of the sparkling stars on their foreheads, that she shrank from the deed.

So she had a boat brought round to the beach, and put the four babes, with some strings of jewels, into a cradle, which she placed in the boat, and then set it adrift. The boat was soon far out at sea. The waves rose, the rain poured in torrents, and the thunder roared. Feintise could not doubt that the boat would be swamped, and felt relieved by the thought that the poor little innocents would perish, for she would otherwise always be haunted by the fear that something would occur to betray the share she had had in their preservation.

But the good Fairy protected them, and after floating at sea for seven days they were picked up by a Corsair. He was so struck by their beauty that he altered his course, and took them home to his wife, who had no children. She was transported with joy when he placed them in her hands. They admired together the wonderful stars, the chains of gold that could not be taken off their necks, and their long ringlets. Much greater was the woman's astonishment when she combed them, for at every instant there rolled out of their hair pearls, rubies, diamonds, and emeralds. She told her husband of it, who was no less surprised than herself.

"I am very tired," said he, "of a Corsair's life, and if the locks of those little children continue to supply us with such treasures, I will give up roaming the seas." The Corsair's wife, whose name was Corsine, was enchanted at this, and loved the four infants so much the more for it. She named the Princess, Belle-Etoile, her eldest brother, Petit-Soleil, the second, Heureux, and the son of Brunette, Cheri.

As they grew older, the Corsair applied himself seriously to their education, as he felt convinced there was some great mystery attached to their birth.

The Corsair and his wife had never told the story of the four children, who passed for their own. They were exceedingly united, but Prince Cheri entertained for Princess Belle-Etoile a greater affection than the other two. The moment she expressed a wish for anything, he would attempt even impossibilities to gratify her.

One day Belle-Etoile overheard the Corsair and his wife talking. "When I fell in with them," said the Corsair, "I saw nothing that could give me any idea of their birth."

"I suspect," said Corsine, "that Cheri is not their brother. He has neither star nor neck-chain."

Belle-Etoile immediately ran and told this to the three Princes, who resolved to speak to the Corsair and his wife, and ask them to let them set out to discover the secret of their birth. After some remonstrance they gained their consent. A beautiful vessel was prepared, and the young Princess and the three Princes set out. They determined to sail to the very spot where the Corsair had found them, and made preparations for a grand sacrifice to the fairies, for their protection and guidance. They were about to immolate a turtle-dove, but the Princess saved its life, and let it fly.

At this moment a syren issued from the water, and said, "Cease your anxiety, let your vessel go where it will, and land where it stops."

The vessel now sailed more quickly. Suddenly they came in sight of a city so beautiful that they were anxious their vessel should enter the port. Their wishes were accomplished. They landed, and the shore in a moment was crowded with people, who had observed the magnificence of their ship. They ran and told the King the news, and as the grand terrace of the Palace looked out upon the sea-shore, he speedily repaired there.

The Princes, hearing the people say, "There is the King," looked up, and made a profound obeisance. He looked earnestly at them, and was as much charmed by the Princess's beauty, as by the handsome mien of the young Princes. He ordered his equerry to offer them his protection, and everything that they might require.

The King was so interested in these four children, that he went into the chamber of the Queen, his mother, to tell her of the wonderful stars which shone upon their foreheads, and everything that he admired in them. She was thunderstruck at it, and was terribly afraid that Feintise had betrayed her, and sent her secretary to enquire about them. What he told her of their ages confirmed her suspicions. She sent for Feintise, and threatened to kill her. Feintise, half dead with terror, confessed all, but promised, if she spared her, that she would still find means to do away with them. The Queen was appeased, and, indeed, old Feintise did all she could for her own sake.

Taking a guitar, she went and sat down opposite the Princess's window, and sang a song which Belle-Etoile thought so pretty that she invited her into her chamber.

"My fair child," said Feintise, "Heaven has made you very lovely, but you yet want one thing. You need the dancing-water. If I had possessed it, you would not have seen a white hair upon my head, nor a wrinkle on my face. Alas! I knew this secret too late, and my charms had already faded."

"But where shall I find this dancing-water?" asked Belle-Etoile.

"It is in the luminous forest," said Feintise. "You have three brothers. Does not anyone of them love you sufficiently to go and fetch some?"

"My brothers all love me," said the Princess, "but there is one of them who would not refuse me anything."

The perfidious old woman retired, delighted at having been so successful. The Princes, returning from the chase, found Belle-Etoile engrossed by the advice of Feintise. Her anxiety about it was so apparent, that Cheri, who thought of nothing but pleasing her, soon found out the cause of it, and, in spite of her entreaties, he mounted his white horse, and set out in search of the dancing-water. When supper-time arrived, and the Princess did not see her brother Cheri, she could neither eat nor drink, and desired he might be sought for everywhere, and sent messengers to find him and bring him back.

The wicked Feintise was very anxious to know the result of her advice, and when she heard that Cheri had already set out, she was delighted, and reported to the Queen-Mother all that had passed. "I admit, Madam," said she, "that I can no longer doubt that they are the same four children, but one of the Princes is already gone to seek the dancing-water, and will no doubt perish in the attempt, and I shall find similar means to do away with all of them."

The plan she had adopted with regard to Prince Cheri was one of the most certain, for the dancing-water was not easily to be obtained. It was so notorious from the misfortunes which occurred to all who sought it, that everyone knew the road to it. Cheri was eight days without taking any repose but in the woods. At the end of this period he began to suffer very much from the heat, but it was not the heat of the sun, and he did not know the cause of it, until from the top of a mountain he perceived the luminous forest. All the trees were burning without being consumed, and casting out flames to such a distance that the country around was a dry desert.

At this terrible scene he descended, and more than once gave himself up for lost. As he approached this great fire he was ready to die with thirst, and perceiving a spring falling into a marble basin, he alighted from his horse, approached it, and stooped to take up some water in the little golden vase which he had brought with him. As he did so he saw a turtle-dove drowning in the fountain. Cheri took pity on it, and saved it.

"My Lord Cheri," said the turtle-dove, "I am not ungrateful. I can guide you to the dancing-water, which, without me, you could never obtain, as it rises in the middle of the forest, and can only be reached by going underground."

The Dove then flew away, and summoned a number of foxes, badgers, moles, snails, ants, and all sorts of creatures that burrow in the earth. Cheri got off his horse at the entrance of the subterranean passage they made for him, and groped his way after the kind turtle-dove, which safely conducted him to the fountain. The Prince filled his golden vase, and returned the same way he came.

He found Belle-Etoile sorrowfully seated under some trees, but when she saw him she was so pleased that she scarcely knew how to welcome him.

Old Feintise learned from her spies that Cheri had returned, and that the Princess, having washed her face with the dancing-water, had become more lovely than ever. Finding this, she lost no time in artfully making the Princess sigh for the wonderful singing-apple. Prince Cheri again found her unhappy, and again found out the cause, and once more set out on his white horse, leaving a letter for Belle-Etoile.

In the meanwhile, the King did not forget the lovely children, and reproached them for never going to the Palace. They excused themselves by saying that their brother's absence prevented them.

Prince Cheri at break of day perceived a handsome young man, from whom he learned where the singing-apple was to be found, but after travelling some time without seeing any sign of it, he saw a poor turtle-dove fall at his feet almost dead.

He took pity on it, and restored it, when it said, "Good-day, handsome Cheri. You are destined to save my life, and I to do you signal service. You are come to seek for the singing-apple. It is guarded by a terrible dragon."

The Dove then led him to a place where he found a suit of armour, all of glass, and by her advice he put it on, and boldly went to meet the dragon. The two-headed monster came bounding along, fire issuing from his throat, but when he saw his alarming figure multiplied in the Prince's mirrors he was frightened in his turn. He stopped, and looking fiercely at the Prince, apparently laden with dragons, he took flight and threw himself into a deep chasm. The Prince then found the tree, which was surrounded with human bones, and breaking off an apple, prepared to return to the Princess. She had never slept during his absence, and ran to meet him eagerly.

When the wicked Feintise heard the sweet singing of the apple, her grief was excessive, for instead of doing harm to these lovely children, she only did them good by her perfidious counsels. She allowed some days to pass by without showing herself, and then once more made the Princess unhappy by saying that the dancing-water and the singing-apple were useless without the little green bird that tells everything.

Cheri again set out, and after some trouble learnt that this bird was to be found on the top of a frightful rock, in a frozen climate. At length, at dawn of day, he perceived the rock, which was very high and very steep, and upon the summit of it was the bird, speaking like an oracle, telling wonderful things. He thought that with a little dexterity it would be easy to catch it, for it seemed very tame. He got off his horse, and climbed up very quietly. He was so close to the green bird that he thought he could lay hands on it, when suddenly the rock opened and he fell into a spacious hall, and became as motionless as a statue. He could neither stir, nor utter a complaint at his deplorable situation. Three hundred knights, who had made the same attempt, were in the same state. To look at each other was the only thing permitted them.

The time seemed so long to Belle-Etoile, with still no signs of her beloved Cheri, and she fell dangerously ill. In the hopes of curing her, Petit-Soleil resolved to seek him.

But he too was swallowed up by the rock and fell into the great hall. The first person he saw was Cheri, but he could not speak to him, and Prince Heureux, following soon after, met with the same fate as the other two.

When Feintise was aware that the third Prince was gone, she was exceedingly delighted at the success of her plan, and when Belle-Etoile, inconsolable at finding not one of her brothers return, reproached herself for their loss, and resolved to follow them, Feintise was quite overjoyed.

The Princess was disguised as a cavalier, but had no other armour than her helmet. She was dreadfully cold as she drew near the rock, but seeing a turtle-dove lying on the snow, she took it up, warmed it, and restored it to life.

The dove reviving, gaily said, "I know you, in spite of your disguise. Follow my advice. When you arrive at the rock, remain at the bottom and begin to sing the sweetest song you know. The green bird will listen to you. You must then pretend to go to sleep, for when it sees me, it will come down to peck me, and at that moment you will be able to seize it."

All this fell out as the Dove foretold. The green bird begged for liberty. "First," said Belle-Etoile, "I wish that you wouldst restore my three brothers to me."

"Under my left wing there is a red feather," said the bird. "Pull it out, and touch the rock with it."

The Princess hastened to do as she was instructed. The rock split from the top to the bottom. She entered with a victorious air the hall in which stood the three Princes with many others. She ran towards Cheri, who did not know her in her helmet and male attire, and could neither speak nor move. The green bird then told the Princess she must rub the eyes and mouth of all those she wished to disenchant with the red feather, which good office she did to all.

The three Princes and Belle-Etoile hastened to present themselves to the King, and when Belle-Etoile showed her treasures, the little green bird told him that the Princes Petit-Soleil and Heureux and the Princess Belle-Etoile were his children, and that Prince Cheri was his nephew. Queen Blondine, who had mourned for them all these years, embraced them, and the wicked Queen-Mother and old Feintise were justly punished. And the King, who thought his nephew Cheri the handsomest man at Court, consented to his marriage with Belle-Etoile. And lastly, to make everyone happy, the King sent for the Corsair and his wife, who gladly came.

BEAUTY AND THE BEAST

This adaptation is taken from Jeanne-Marie Le Prince de Beaumont's book, Magasin des Enfants (A tale for the entertainment of juvenile readers), published in 1756.

THERE WAS ONCE A VERY RICH MERCHANT, who had six children, three sons, and three daughters. Being a man of sense, he spared no cost for their education, but gave them all kinds of masters. His daughters were extremely handsome, especially the youngest, and when she was little, everybody admired her, and called her The little Beauty, so that, as she grew up, she still went by the name of Beauty, which made her sisters very jealous. The youngest, just as she was beautiful, was also better than her sisters. The two eldest had a great deal of pride, because they were rich. They gave themselves ridiculous airs, and would not visit other merchants' daughters, nor keep company with any but persons of quality. They went out every day upon parties of pleasure, balls, plays and concerts, and laughed at their youngest sister, because she spent the greatest part of her time in reading good books. As it was known that they were to have great fortunes, several eminent merchants made their addresses to them, but the two eldest said they would never marry, unless they could meet with a Duke, or an Earl at least. Beauty very civilly thanked them that courted her, and told them she was too young yet to marry, but chose to stay with her father a few years longer.

All at once the merchant lost his whole fortune, excepting a small country-house at a great distance from town, and told his children, with tears in his eyes, they most go there and work for their living. The two eldest answered, that they would not leave the town, for they had several lovers, who they were sure would be glad to have them, though they had no fortune, but in this they were mistaken, for their lovers slighted and forsook them in their poverty.

As they were not beloved on account of their pride, everybody said, "They do not deserve to be pitied, we are glad to see their pride humbled. Let them go and give themselves quality airs in milking the cows and minding their dairy. But", they added, "we are extremely concerned for Beauty. She was such a charming, sweet-tempered creature, spoke so kindly to poor people, and was of such an affable, obliging disposition."

Nay, several gentlemen would have married her, though they knew she had not a penny, but she told them she could not think of leaving her poor father in his misfortunes, but was determined to go along with him into the country to comfort and attend him.

Poor Beauty at first was sadly grieved at the loss of her fortune, "but", she said to herself, "were I to cry ever so much, that would not make things better, so I must try to make myself happy without a fortune."

When they came to their country-house, the merchant and his three sons applied themselves to husbandry and tillage, and Beauty rose at four in the morning, and made haste to have the house clean, and breakfast ready for the family. In the beginning she found it very difficult, for she had not been used to work as a servant, but in less than two months she grew stronger and healthier than ever. After she had done her work, she read, played on the harpsichord, or else sung whilst she spun. On the contrary, her two sisters did not know how to spend their time. They got up at ten, and did nothing but saunter about the whole day, lamenting the loss of their fine clothes and acquaintance.

"Do but see our youngest sister! What a poor, stupid mean-spirited creature she is, to be contented with such an unhappy situation."

The good merchant was of a quite different opinion, he knew very well that Beauty out-shone her sisters, in her person as well as her mind, and admired her humility, industry, and patience, for her sisters not only left her all the work of the house to do, but insulted her every moment.

The family had lived about a year in this retirement, when the merchant received a letter, with an account that a vessel, on board of which he had effects, was safely arrived. This news have turned the heads of the two eldest daughters, who immediately flattered themselves with the hopes of returning to town, for they were quite weary of a country life, and when they saw their father ready to set out, they begged him to buy them new gowns, caps, rings, and all manner of trifles, but Beauty asked for nothing, for she thought to herself, that all the money her father was going to receive would scarce be sufficient to purchase everything her sisters wanted. "What will you have, Beauty?" said her father.

"Since you are so kind as to think of me", answered she, "be so kind as to bring me a rose, for as none grow hereabouts, they are a kind of rarity." Not that Beauty cared for a rose, but she asked for something, lest she should seem by her example to condemn her sisters' conduct, who would have said she did it only to look particular. The good man went on his journey, but when he came to town, the other merchants went to law with him about the merchandise, and after a great deal of trouble and pains to no purpose, he came back as poor as before.

He was within thirty miles of his own house, thinking on the pleasure he should have in seeing his children again, when going through a large forest he lost himself. It rained and snowed terribly, and besides, the wind was so high, that it threw him twice off his horse, and with night coming on, he began to fear being either starved to death with cold and hunger, or else devoured by the wolves, whom he heard howling all around him. Then, on a sudden, looking through a long walk of trees, he saw a light at some distance, and going on a little farther, perceived it came from a palace illuminated from top to bottom. The merchant returned God thanks for this happy discovery, and hasted to the palace, but was greatly surprised at not meeting with anyone in the outer courtyards. His horse followed him, and seeing a large stable open, went in, and finding both hay and oats, the poor beast, who was almost famished, fell to eating very heartily. The merchant tied him up to the manger, and walked towards the house, where he saw no one, but entering into a large hall, he found a good fire, and a table plentifully set out, with but one cover laid. As he was wet quite through with the rain and snow, he drew near the fire to dry himself. "I hope", said he, "the master of the house, or his servants, will excuse the liberty I take. I suppose it will not be long before some of them appear."

He waited a considerable time, till it struck eleven, and still nobody came. At last he was so hungry that he could starve no longer, but took a chicken and ate it in two mouthfuls, trembling all the while. After this, he drank a few glasses of wine, and growing more courageous, he went out of the hall, and crossed through several grand apartments with magnificent furniture, till he came into a chamber, which had an exceedingly good bed in it. As he was very much fatigued, and it was past midnight, he concluded it was best to shut the door, and go to bed.

It was ten the next morning before the merchant waked, and as he was going to rise, he was astonished to see a good suit of clothes in the room instead of his own, which were quite spoiled. "Certainly", said he, "this palace belongs to some kind fairy, who has seen and pitied my distress." He looked through a window, but instead of snow saw the most delightful arbours, interwoven with the most beautiful flowers that ever were beheld. He then returned to the great hall, where he had supped the night before, and found some chocolate ready made on a little table.

"Thank you, good Madam Fairy", he said aloud, "for being so careful as to provide me a breakfast. I am extremely obliged to you for all your favours."

The good man drank his chocolate, and then went to look for his horse, but passing through an arbour of roses, he remembered Beauty's request to him, and gathered a branch on which were several. Immediately he heard a great noise, and saw such a frightful beast coming towards him, that he was ready to faint away.

"You are very ungrateful", said the beast to him, in a terrible voice. "I have saved your life by receiving you into my castle, and, in return, you steal my roses, which I value beyond anything in the universe, and you shall die for it. I give you but a quarter of an hour to prepare yourself, and to say your prayers."

The merchant fell on his knees, and lifted up both his hands, "My Lord", he said, "I beseech you to forgive me, indeed I had no intention to offend in gathering a rose for one of my daughters, who desired me to bring her one."

"My name is not My Lord", replied the monster, "but Beast. I don't love compliments, not I. I like people to speak as they think, and so do not imagine I am to be moved by any of your flattering speeches. But you say you have got daughters? I will forgive you, on condition that one of them comes here willingly, and suffers for you. Let me have no words, but go about your business, and swear that if your daughter refuses to die in your stead, you will return within three months."

The merchant had no mind to sacrifice his daughters to the ugly monster, but he thought, in obtaining this respite, he should have the satisfaction of seeing them once more, so he promised upon oath, he would return, and the Beast told him he might set out when he pleased, "but", he added, "you shall not depart empty handed. Go back to the room where you lay, and you will see a great empty chest. Fill it with whatever you like best, and I will send it to your home," and at the same time Beast withdrew.

"Well", said the good man to himself, "if I must die, I shall have the comfort, at least, of leaving something to my poor children."

He returned to the bed-chamber, and finding a great quantity of broad pieces of gold, he filled the great chest the Beast had mentioned, locked it, and afterwards took his horse out of the stable, leaving the palace with as much grief as he had entered it with joy. The horse, of his own accord, took one of the roads of the forest, and in a few hours the good man was at home. His children came around him, but, instead of receiving their embraces with pleasure, he looked on them, and, holding up the branch he had in his hands, he burst into tears. "Here, Beauty", he said, take these roses, but little do you think how dear they are like to cost your unhappy father." Then related his fatal adventure, and immediately the two eldest set up lamentable outcries, and said all manner of ill-natured things to Beauty, who did not cry at all.

"Do but see the pride of that little wretch", they said. "She would not ask for fine clothes, as we did, but no, truly, Miss wanted to distinguish herself, so now she will be the death of our poor father, and yet she does not so much as shed a tear."

"Why should I?" answered Beauty, "It would be very needless, for my father shall not suffer upon my account. Since the monster will accept of one of our father's daughters, I will deliver myself up to all his fury, and I am very happy in thinking that my death will save my father's life, and be a proof of my tender love for him."

"No, sister", said her three brothers. "That shall not be, we will go find the monster, and either kill him, or perish in the attempt."

"Do not imagine any such thing, my sons", said the merchant. "Beast's power is so great, that I have no hopes of your overcoming him. I am charmed with Beauty's kind and generous offer, but I cannot yield to it, for I am old, and have not long to live, so can only lose a few years, which I regret for your sakes alone, my dear children."

"Indeed, father", said Beauty, "you shall not go to the palace without me. You cannot hinder me from following you."

It was to no purpose with anything that they could say, for Beauty still insisted on setting out for the fine palace, and her sisters were delighted at it, for her virtue and amiable qualities made them envious and jealous.

The merchant was so afflicted at the thoughts of losing his daughter, that he had quite forgot the chest full of gold, but at night, when he retired to rest, no sooner had he shut his chamber-door, than, to his great astonishment, he found it by his bedside. He was determined, however, not to tell his children that he was grown rich, because they would have wanted to return to town, and he was resolved not to leave the country. But he trusted Beauty with the secret, who informed him, that two gentlemen came in his absence, and courted her sisters. She begged her father to consent to their marriage, and give them fortunes, for she was so good, that she loved them, and forgave them heartily all their ill-usage. These wicked creatures rubbed their eyes with an onion, to force some tears when they parted with their sister, but her brothers were really concerned. Beauty was the only one who did not shed tears at parting, because she would not increase their uneasiness.

The horse took the direct road to the palace, and towards evening they perceived it illuminated as at first. The horse went of himself into the stable, and the good man and his daughter came into the great hall, where they found a table splendidly served up, and two covers. The merchant had no heart to eat, but Beauty endeavoured to appear cheerful, sat down to table, and helped him. Afterwards, thought she to herself, "Beast surely has a mind to fatten me before he eats me, since he provides such a plentiful entertainment."

When they had supped, they heard a great noise, and the merchant, all in tears, bade his poor child farewell, for he thought Beast was coming. Beauty was sadly terrified at his horrid form, but she took courage as well as she could, and the monster having asked her if she came willingly?

"Y-e-e-e-s..." said she, trembling.

"You are very good, and I am greatly obliged to you, honest man. You shall go on your way tomorrow morning, but never think of returning here again. Farewell for now, Beauty."

"Farewell, Beast," answered she, and immediately the monster withdrew.

"Oh, daughter", said the merchant, embracing Beauty, "I am almost frightened to death. Believe me, you had better go back, and let me stay here."

"No, father", said Beauty, in a resolute tone, "you shall set out tomorrow morning, and leave me to the care and protection of Providence."

They went to bed, and thought they should not close their eyes all night, but scarce were they laid down, than they fell fast asleep, and Beauty dreamed that a fine lady came and said to her, "I am content, Beauty, with your good will. This good action of yours, in giving up your own life to save your father's, shall not go unrewarded." Beauty waked, and told her father her dream, and though it helped to comfort him a little, yet he could not help crying bitterly, when he took leave of his dear child.

As soon as he was gone, Beauty sat down in the great hall, and fell a crying likewise, but as she was mistress of a great deal of resolution, she recommended herself to God, and resolved not to be uneasy in the little time she had yet to live, for she firmly believed Beast would eat her up that night.

However, she thought she might as well walk about till then, and view this fine castle, which she could not help admiring. It was a delightfully pleasant place, and she was extremely surprised at seeing a door, over which was written; "BEAUTY'S APARTMENT." She opened it hastily, and was quite dazzled with the magnificence that reigned throughout, but what chiefly took up her attention, was a large library, a harpsichord, and several music books. "Well", she said to herself, "I see they will not let my time hang heavy on my hands for want of amusement." Then she reflected, "Were I but to stay here a day, there would not have been all these preparations." This consideration inspired her with fresh courage, and opening the library, she took a book, and read these words in letters of gold:

"Welcome, Beauty, banish fear,

You are queen and mistress here;

Speak your wishes, speak your will,

Swift obedience meets them still."

"Alas", she said with a sigh. "There is nothing I desire so much as to see my poor father, and to know what he is doing."

She had no sooner said this, when casting her eyes on a great looking-glass, to her great amazement she saw her own home, where her father arrived with a very dejected countenance. Her sisters went to meet him, and, notwithstanding their endeavours to appear sorrowful, their joy, felt for having got rid of their sister, was visible in every feature. A moment after, everything disappeared, and Beauty's was very afraid at this proof of Beast's magical abilities and willingness to please her.

At noon she found dinner ready, and while at table, was entertained with an excellent concert of music, though without seeing any body. But at night, as she was going to sit down to supper, she heard the noise Beast made, and could not help being sadly terrified.

"Beauty", said the monster, "will you give me leave to see you sup?"

"That is as you please," answered Beauty, trembling.

"No", replied the Beast, "you alone are mistress here. You need only bid me be gone, if my presence is troublesome, and I will immediately withdraw. But tell me, do not you think me very ugly?"

"That is true", said Beauty, "for I cannot tell a lie, but I believe you are very good-natured."

"So I am", said the monster, "but then, besides my ugliness, I have no sense, I know very well that I am a poor, silly, stupid creature."

"It's no sign of folly to think so", replied Beauty, "for never did a fool know this, or have so humble a conceit of his own understanding."

"Eat then, Beauty", said the monster, "and endeavour to amuse yourself in your palace, for everything here is yours, and I should be very uneasy if you were not happy."

"You are very obliging", answered Beauty. "I own I am pleased with your kindness, and when I consider that, your deformity scarce appears."

"Yes, yes", said the Beast. "My heart is good, but still I am a monster."

"Among mankind", said Beauty, "there are many that deserve that name more than you, and I prefer you, just as you are, to those, who, under a human form, hide a treacherous, corrupt, and ungrateful heart."

"If I had sense enough", replied the Beast, "I would make a fine compliment to thank you, but I am so dull, that I can only say, I am greatly obliged to you."

Beauty ate a hearty supper, and had almost conquered her dread of the monster, but she almost fainted away, when he said to her, "Beauty, will you be my wife?"

She was some time before she dare answer, for she was afraid of making him angry, if she refused. At last, however, she said, trembling, "No, Beast."

Immediately the poor monster began to sigh, and hissed so frightfully, that the whole palace echoed. But Beauty soon recovered her fright, for Beast having said, in a mournful voice, "then farewell, Beauty," left the room, and only turned back, now and then, to look at her as he went out.

When Beauty was alone, she felt a great deal of compassion for poor Beast. "Alas", she said "it's a thousand pities anything so good-natured should be so ugly."

Beauty spent three months very contentedly in the palace. Every evening Beast paid her a visit, and talked to her during supper, very rationally, with plain good common sense, but never with what the world calls wit, and Beauty daily discovered some valuable qualifications in the monster. Seeing him often, had so accustomed her to his deformity, that, far from dreading the time of his visit, she would often look on her watch to see when it would be nine, for the Beast never missed coming at that hour. There was but one thing that gave Beauty any concern, which was, that every night, before she went to bed, the monster always asked her, if she would be his wife.

One day she said to him, "Beast, you make me very uneasy. I wish I could consent to marry you, but I am too sincere to make you believe that will ever happen. I shall always esteem you as a friend, endeavour to be satisfied with this."

"I must ask", said the Beast, "for, alas! I know too well my own misfortune, but then I love you with the tenderest affection. However, I ought to think myself happy that you will stay here. Promise me never to leave my side."

Beauty blushed at these words. She had seen in her glass, that her father had pined himself sick for the loss of her, and she longed to see him again.

"I could", answered she, "indeed promise never to leave you entirely, but I have so great a desire to see my father, that I shall fret to death, if you refuse me that satisfaction."

"I had rather die myself", said the monster, "than give you the least uneasiness. I will send you to your father. You shall remain with him, and poor Beast will die with grief."

"No", said Beauty, weeping, "I love you too well to be the cause of your death, I give you my promise to return in a week. You have shown me that my sisters are married, and my brothers gone to the army. Only let me stay a week with my father, as he is alone."

"You shall be there tomorrow morning", said the Beast, "but remember your promise. You need only lay your ring on the table before you go to bed, when you have a mind to come back. Farewell, Beauty."

Beast sighed as usual, bidding her good night, and Beauty went to bed very sad at seeing him so afflicted. When she waked the next morning, she found herself at her father's, and having rang a little bell, that was by her bed-side, she saw the maid come, who, the moment she saw her, gave a loud shriek, at which the good man ran upstairs, and thought he should have died with joy to see his dear daughter again. He held her fast locked in his arms above a quarter of an hour. As soon as the first transports of joy were over, Beauty began to think of rising, and was afraid she had no clothes to put on, but the maid told her, that she had just found, in the next room, a large trunk full of gowns, covered with gold and diamonds. Beauty thanked good Beast for his kind care, and taking one of the plainest of them, she intended to make a present of the others to her sisters. She scarce had said so, when the trunk disappeared. Her father told her, that Beast insisted on her keeping them herself, and immediately both gowns and trunk came back again.

Beauty dressed herself, and in the mean time they sent to her sisters, who hasted there with their husbands. They were both of them very unhappy. The eldest had married a gentleman, extremely handsome indeed, but so fond of his own person, that he was full of nothing but his own dear self, and neglected his wife. The second had married a man of wit, but he only made use of it to plague and torment everybody, and his wife most of all. Beauty's sisters sickened with envy, when they saw her dressed like a Princess, and more beautiful than ever. Nor could all her obliging affectionate behaviour stifle their jealousy, which was ready to burst when she told them how happy she was. They went down into the garden to vent it in tears, and said one to the other, "In what is this little creature better than us, that she should be so much happier?"

"Sister", said the eldest, "a thought just strikes my mind. Let us endeavour to detain her above a week, and perhaps the silly monster will be so enraged at her for breaking her word, that he will devour her."

"Right, sister", answered the other. "Therefore, we must show her as much kindness as possible."

After they had taken this resolution, they went up, and behaved so affectionately to their sister, that poor Beauty wept for joy. When the week was expired, they cried and tore their hair, and seemed so sorry to part with her, that she promised to stay a week longer.

In the meantime, Beauty could not help reflecting on herself for the uneasiness she was likely to cause poor Beast, whom she sincerely loved, and really longed to see again. The tenth night she spent at her father's, she dreamed she was in the palace garden, and that she saw Beast extended on the grass-plot, who seemed just expiring, and, in a dying voice, reproached her with her ingratitude.

Beauty started out of her sleep and bursting into tears cried out, "Am not I very wicked to act so unkindly to Beast, who has worked so much to please me in everything? Is it his fault that he is so ugly, and has so little sense? He is kind and good, and that is sufficient. Why did I refuse to marry him? I should be happier with the monster than my sisters are with their husbands. It is neither wit nor a fine person in a husband, that makes a woman happy, but virtue, sweetness of temper, and complaisance, and Beast has all these valuable qualifications. It is true, I do not feel the tenderness of affection for him, but I find I have the highest gratitude, esteem, and friendship, and I will not make him miserable. Were I to be so ungrateful, I should never forgive myself."

Beauty having said this, rose, put her ring on the table, and then laid down again. Scarce was she in bed before she fell asleep, and when she waked the next morning, she was overjoyed to find herself in the Beast's palace. She put on one of her richest suits to please him, and waited for evening with the utmost impatience. At last the wished-for hour came, the clock struck nine, yet no Beast appeared. Beauty then feared she had been the cause of his death.

She ran crying and wringing her hands all about the palace, like one in despair. After having sought for him everywhere, she recollected her dream, and flew to the canal in the garden, where she dreamed she saw him. There she found poor Beast stretched out, quite senseless, and, as she imagined, dead. She threw herself upon him without any dread, and finding his heart beat still, she fetched some water from the canal, and poured it on his head.

Beast opened his eyes, and said to Beauty, "You forgot your promise, and I was so afflicted for having lost you, that I resolved to starve myself, but since I have the happiness of seeing you once more, I die satisfied."

"No, dear Beast", said Beauty, "you must not die. Live to be my husband. From this moment I give you my hand, and swear to be none but yours. Alas! I thought I had only a friendship for you, but, the grief I now feel convinces me, that I cannot live without you."

Beauty scarcely had pronounced these words, when she saw the palace sparkle with light, and fireworks, and instruments of music. Everything, seemed to give notice of some great event, but nothing could fix her attention, so she turned to her dear Beast, for whom she trembled with fear, but how great was her surprise! Beast had disappeared, and she saw, at her feet, one of the loveliest Princes that eye ever beheld, who returned her thanks for having put an end to the charm, under which he had so long resembled a Beast. Though this Prince was worthy of all her attention, she could not forbear asking where Beast was.

"You see him at your feet", said the Prince. "A wicked fairy had condemned me to remain under that shape till a beautiful virgin should consent to marry me. The fairy likewise enjoined me to conceal my understanding. There was only you in the world generous enough to be won by the goodness of my temper, and in offering you my crown, I can't discharge the obligations I have to you."

Beauty, agreeably surprised, gave the charming Prince her hand to rise, and they went together into the castle. Beauty was overjoyed to find, in the great hall, her father and his whole family, whom the beautiful lady, that appeared to her in her dream, had conveyed there.

"Beauty", said this lady, "come and receive the reward of your judicious choice. You have preferred virtue before either wit or beauty, and deserve to find a person in whom all these qualifications are united. You are going to be a great Queen. I hope the throne will not lessen your virtue, or make you forget yourself.

"As to you, ladies, said the Fairy to Beauty's two sisters, "I know your hearts, and all the malice they contain. Become two statues, but, under this transformation, still retain your reason. You shall stand before your sister's palace gate, and be it your punishment to behold her happiness, and it will not be in your power to return to your former state till you own your faults, but I am very much afraid that you will always remain statues. Pride, anger, gluttony, and idleness, are sometimes conquered, but the conversion of a malicious and envious mind is a kind of miracle."

Immediately the fairy gave a stroke with her wand, and in a moment all that were in the hall were transported into the Prince's palace. His subjects received him with joy, and he married Beauty, and lived with her many years, and their happiness, as it was founded on virtue, was complete.

Tales From Gallia

RICKY OF THE TUFT

This adaptation is taken from Charles Perrault's book, Old-time Stories, published by Dodd, Mead & Company, New York in 1921.

ONCE UPON A TIME THERE WAS a queen who bore a son so ugly and misshapen that for some time it was doubtful if he would have human form at all. But a fairy who was present at his birth promised that he should have plenty of brains, and added that by virtue of the gift which she had just bestowed upon him he would be able to impart to the person whom he should love best the same degree of intelligence which he possessed himself.

This somewhat consoled the poor queen, who was greatly disappointed at having brought into the world such a hideous brat. And indeed, no sooner did the child begin to speak than his sayings proved to be full of shrewdness, while all that he did was somehow so clever that he charmed everyone.

I forgot to mention that when he was born he had a little tuft of hair upon his head. For this reason he was called Ricky of the Tuft, Ricky being his family name.

Some seven or eight years later the queen of a neighbouring kingdom gave birth to twin daughters. The first one to come into the world was more beautiful than the dawn, and the queen was so overjoyed that it was feared her great excitement might do her some harm. The same fairy who had assisted at the birth of Ricky of the Tuft was present, and, in order to moderate the delights of the queen she declared that this little princess would have no sense at all, and would be as stupid as she was beautiful.

The queen was deeply mortified, and a moment or two later her chagrin became greater still, for the second daughter proved to be extremely ugly.

"Do not be distressed, Madam," said the fairy, "your daughter shall be recompensed in another way. She shall have so much good sense that her lack of beauty will scarcely be noticed."

"May Heaven grant it!" said the queen, "but is there no means by which the elder, who is so beautiful, can be endowed with some intelligence?"

"In the matter of brains I can do nothing for her, Madam," said the fairy, "but as regards beauty I can do a great deal. As there is nothing I would not do to please you, I will bestow upon her the power of making beautiful any person who shall greatly please her."

As the two princesses grew up their perfections increased, and everywhere the beauty of the elder and the wit of the younger were the subject of common talk.

It is equally true that their defects also increased as they became older. The younger grew uglier every minute, and the elder daily became more stupid. Either she answered nothing at all when spoken to, or replied with some idiotic remark. At the same time she was so awkward that she could not set four china vases on the mantelpiece without breaking one of them, nor drink a glass of water without spilling half of it over her clothes.

Now although the elder girl possessed the great advantage which beauty always confers upon youth, she was nevertheless outshone in almost all company by her younger sister. At first everyone gathered round the beauty to see and admire her, but very soon they were all attracted by the graceful and easy conversation of the clever one. In a very short time the elder girl would be left entirely alone, while everybody clustered round her sister.

The elder princess was not so stupid that she was not aware of this, and she would willingly have surrendered all her beauty for half her sister's cleverness. Sometimes she was ready to die of grief, for the queen, though a sensible woman, could not refrain from occasionally reproaching her with her stupidity.

The princess had retired one day to a wood to bemoan her misfortune, when she saw approaching her an ugly little man, of very disagreeable appearance, but clad in magnificent attire.

This was the young prince Ricky of the Tuft. He had fallen in love with her portrait, which was everywhere to be seen, and had left his father's kingdom in order to have the pleasure of seeing and talking to her.

Delighted to meet her thus alone, he approached with every mark of respect and politeness. But while he paid her the usual compliments he noticed that she was plunged in melancholy.

"I cannot understand, madam," he said, "how anyone with your beauty can be so sad as you appear. I can boast of having seen many fair ladies, and I declare that none of them could compare in beauty with you."

"It is very kind of you to say so, sir," answered the princess, and stopped there, at a loss what to say further.

"Beauty," said Ricky, "is of such great advantage that everything else can be disregarded, and I do not see that the possessor of it can have anything much to grieve about."

To this the princess replied, "I would rather be as plain as you are and have some sense, than be as beautiful as I am and at the same time stupid."

"Nothing more clearly displays good sense, madam, than a belief that one is not possessed of it. It follows, therefore, that the more one has, the more one fears it to be wanting."

"I am not sure about that," said the princess, "but I know only too well that I am very stupid, and this is the reason of the misery which is nearly killing me."

"If that is all that troubles you, madam, I can easily put an end to your suffering."

"How will you manage that?" said the princess.

"I am able, madam," said Ricky of the Tuft, "to bestow as much good sense as it is possible to possess on the person whom I love the most. You are that person, and it therefore rests with you to decide whether you will acquire so much intelligence. The only condition is that you shall consent to marry me."

The princess was dumbfounded, and remained silent.

"I can see," pursued Ricky, "that this suggestion perplexes you, and I am not surprised. But I will give you a whole year to make up your mind to it."

The princess had so little sense, and at the same time desired it so ardently, that she persuaded herself the end of this year would never come. So she accepted the offer which had been made to her. No sooner had she given her word to Ricky that she would marry him within one year from that very day, than she felt a complete change come over her. She found herself able to say all that she wished with the greatest ease, and to say it in an elegant, finished, and natural manner. She at once engaged Ricky in a brilliant and lengthy conversation, holding her own so well that Ricky feared he had given her a larger share of sense than he had retained for himself.

On her return to the palace amazement reigned throughout the Court at such a sudden and extraordinary change. Whereas formerly they had been accustomed to hear her give vent to silly, pert remarks, they now heard her express herself sensibly and very wittily.

The entire Court was overjoyed. The only person not too pleased was the younger sister, for now that she had no longer the advantage over the elder in wit, she seemed nothing but a little fright in comparison.

The king himself often took her advice, and several times held his councils in her apartment.

The news of this change spread abroad, and the princes of the neighbouring kingdoms made many attempts to captivate her. Almost all asked her in marriage. But she found none with enough sense, and so she listened to all without promising herself to any.

At last came one who was so powerful, so rich, so witty, and so handsome, that she could not help being somewhat attracted by him. Her father noticed this, and told her she could make her own choice of a husband, she had only to declare herself.

Now the more sense one has, the more difficult it is to make up one's mind in an affair of this kind. After thanking her father, therefore, she asked for a little time to think it over.

In order to ponder quietly what she had better do she went to walk in a wood, indeed, the very one, as it happened, where she encountered Ricky of the Tuft.

While she walked, deep in thought, she heard beneath her feet a thudding sound, as though many people were running busily to and fro. Listening more attentively she heard voices.

"Bring me that boiler," said one.

Then another saying, "Put some wood on that fire!"

At that moment the ground opened, and she saw below what appeared to be a large kitchen full of cooks and scullions, and all the train of attendants which the preparation of a great banquet involves. A gang of some twenty or thirty spit-turners emerged and took up their positions round a very long table in a path in the wood. They all wore their cook's caps on one side, and with their basting implements in their hands they kept time together as they worked, to the lilt of a melodious song.

The princess was astonished by this spectacle, and asked for whom their work was being done.

"For Prince Ricky of the Tuft, madam," said the foreman of the gang, "his wedding is tomorrow."

At this the princess was more surprised than ever. In a flash she remembered that it was a year to the very day since she had promised to marry Prince Ricky of the Tuft, and was taken aback by the recollection. The reason she had forgotten was that when she made the promise she was still without sense, and with the acquisition of that intelligence which the prince had bestowed upon her, all memory of her former stupidities had been blotted out.

She had not gone another thirty paces when Ricky of the Tuft appeared before her, gallant and resplendent, like a prince upon his wedding day.

"As you see, madam," he said, "I keep my word to the minute. I do not doubt that you have come to keep yours, and by giving me your hand to make me the happiest of men."

"I will be frank with you," replied the princess. "I have not yet made up my mind on the point, and I am afraid I shall never be able to take the decision you desire."

"You astonish me, madam," said Ricky of the Tuft.

"I can well believe it," said the princess, "and undoubtedly, if I had to deal with a clown, or a man who lacked good sense, I should feel myself very awkwardly situated. 'A princess must keep her word,' he would say, 'and you must marry me because you promised to!' But I am speaking to a man of the world, of the greatest good sense, and I am sure that he will listen to reason. As you are aware, I could not make up my mind to marry you even when I was entirely without sense, so how can you expect that today, possessing the intelligence you bestowed on me, which makes me still more difficult to please than formerly, I should take a decision which I could not take then? If you wished so much to marry me, you were very wrong to relieve me of my stupidity, and to let me see more clearly than I did."

"If a man who lacked good sense," replied Ricky of the Tuft, "would be justified, as you have just said, in reproaching you for breaking your word, why do you expect, madam, that I should act differently where the happiness of my whole life is at stake? Is it reasonable that people who have sense should be treated worse than those who have none? Would you maintain that for a moment, madam, who so markedly now has sense, and desired so ardently to have it? But, pardon me, let us get to the facts. With the exception of my ugliness, is there anything about me which displeases you? Are you dissatisfied with my breeding, my brains, my disposition, or my manners?"

"In no way," replied the princess, "I like exceedingly all that you have displayed of the qualities you mention."

"In that case," said Ricky of the Tuft, "happiness will be mine, for it lies in your power to make me the most attractive of men."

"How can that be done?" asked the princess.

"It will happen of itself," replied Ricky of the Tuft, "if you love me well enough to wish that it be so. To remove your doubts, madam, let me tell you that the same fairy who on the day of my birth bestowed upon me the power of endowing with intelligence the woman of my choice, gave to you also the power of endowing with beauty the man whom you should love, and on whom you should wish to confer this favour."

"If that is so," said the princess, "I wish with all my heart that you may become the handsomest and most attractive prince in the world, and I give you without reserve the boon which it is mine to bestow."

No sooner had the princess uttered these words than Ricky of the Tuft appeared before her eyes as the handsomest, most graceful and attractive man that she had ever set eyes on.

Some people assert that this was not the work of fairy enchantment, but that love alone brought about the transformation. They say that the princess, as she mused upon her lover's constancy, upon his good sense, and his many admirable qualities of heart and head, grew blind to the deformity of his body and the ugliness of his face, that his hump back seemed no more than was natural in a man who could make the courtliest of bows, and that the dreadful limp which had formerly distressed her now betokened nothing more than a certain diffidence and charming deference of manner. They say further that she found his eyes shine all the brighter for their squint, and that this defect in them was to her but a sign of passionate love, while his great red nose she found nought but martial and heroic.

However that may be, the princess promised to marry him on the spot, provided only that he could obtain the consent of her royal father.

The king knew Ricky of the Tuft to be a prince both wise and witty, and on learning of his daughter's regard for him, he accepted him with pleasure as a son-in-law.

The wedding took place upon the morrow, just as Ricky of the Tuft had foreseen, and in accordance with the arrangements he had long ago put in train.

Tales From Gallia

THE GREEN SERPENT

This adaptation is taken from Charles Perrault's book, Old-time Stories, published by Dodd, Mead & Company, New York in 1921.

THERE WAS ONCE UPON A TIME a very great Queen who gave birth to little twin girls. She immediately sent out invitations to twelve fairies in the neighbouring countries to come to the feast according to the custom of the country - a custom that was never by any means overlooked, because it was such a great advantage to have the fairies as guests.

When the twelve fairies were all assembled in the great hall where the feast was to be held, they took their seats at the table, a very big table laden with such good things to eat, and so rich, that it was past all comprehension. No sooner had all the guests seated themselves, than who should enter but the wicked fairy Magotine!

Now the Queen, when she saw her, felt that some disaster would follow because she had omitted to send this fairy an invitation, but she hid the thought deep in her mind, and off she went and found a beautiful soft seat all embroidered in gold and inlaid with sapphires. Then all the other fairies moved up and made room for Magotine to seat herself, saying at the same time, "Hurry up, sister, and make your wish for the little Princesses, and then come and sit down."

But, before Magotine came to table, she said rudely that she was quite big enough to eat standing. There she made a great mistake, because the table was very high and Magotine was very small, and, in reaching up, she fell. This misfortune only increased her bad temper.

"Madam," said the Queen, "I beg you to be seated at table."

"If you had so much wished to see me here," replied the fairy, "you would have sent me an invitation the same as the others. You have only invited to your court the most beautiful, well-dressed and good-tempered fairies, like my sisters here. With them I have no fault to find. I, however, have one advantage over them, as you will see!"

Then all the fairies begged her to seat herself with them, and she did so. In front of each fairy was placed a beautiful bouquet made of all kinds of precious stones. Each took the bouquet immediately in front of her, and there remained none at all for Magotine, and she growled furiously between her teeth.

The Queen, quickly noticing the awful error, ran to her cabinet and came back with a large cup all perfumed and studded outside with rubies, and inside full of diamonds that gave forth a thousand different colours. Going up to Magotine, she begged her to receive the present. But Magotine only shook her head and replied, "Keep your jewels, madam, I do not want them. I came simply to see if you had thought of me, and I find that you have forgotten me altogether." And with this she gave a tap with her wand on the table and at once all the good things were turned into serpents, which wriggled about and hissed viciously. The other fairies, seeing this, were filled with horror, and they threw down their serviettes and quitted the table.

While they were leaving the table the wicked little fairy Magotine, who had come to disturb the peace, made her way to the room where the little Princesses were asleep in a golden cot covered with a canopy studded with diamonds, the most beautiful ever seen in the world. The other fairies followed her to watch. Magotine stopped beside the cot, and, taking out her wand quickly, she touched one of the little Princesses, saying at the same time, "I wish that you become the most ugly person that it would be possible to find." Then she turned to the other little Princess, but, before she could do anything further, the other fairies interfered, and taking a great pan full of vitriol, threw it over the wicked Magotine. But not a drop touched her, for, before it splashed upon the floor, she had disappeared before their very eyes.

The Queen then made her way to the cot and took out the little Princess that Magotine had wished to be so ugly, and the Queen cried with sorrow because, every minute as she looked at it, the child was becoming uglier and uglier, until at last anyone could see she was the ugliest baby in the world.

Now the other good fairies consulted amongst themselves as to how they could lighten this great sorrow, so they turned to the Queen and said, "Madam, it is not possible to undo the evil that the fairy Magotine has put upon your child, but we will wish for her something that will help to balance that evil." And then they told the Queen that one day her daughter would be extremely happy. With this the fairies took their departure, but not before the Queen had given them all some beautiful presents, for this custom goes on amongst all the peoples of the earth, and will continue when other customs are forgotten.

The Queen called her ugly daughter Laideronnette, and the beautiful daughter Bellote, and these names suited them perfectly, because Laideronnette was frightfully ugly, and her sister was equally charming and beautiful.

When Laideronnette was twelve years old, she went and threw herself at the feet of the King and Queen, and begged them to allow her to go and shut herself up in a castle far away near the Light of Dawn, and to let her take the necessary servants and food to live there. She reminded them that they still had Bellote, and that she was enough to console them.

After a long while they agreed, and Laideronnette went away to her castle near the Light of Dawn. On one side of the castle the sea came right up to the window, and on another there was a great canal, while from still another view was a vast forest as far as the eye could see, and beyond again a great desert.

The little Princess played musical instruments beautifully, and also had a sweet voice just like a bird, and sang divinely, and so, with these delights, she lived for two whole years in perfect solitude. Then, at the end of the two years, she began to feel homesick and wished to see her father and mother, the King and Queen, so she started on the journey home at once, and arrived just as her sister the Princess Bellote was going to be married.

Now as soon as they saw Laideronnette, they did not offer to kiss her or say they were pleased to see her, and they told her she was not to come to the marriage feast, nor to the ball afterwards. Poor little Laideronnette said she had not come to dance and be merry, neither had she come to the marriage feast, she had come because she felt homesick and wanted to see her father and mother. However, she would go away back to her castle near the Light of Dawn, for there the desert, the trees, and the fountains never reproached her with her ugliness when she came near them.

The King and Queen were sorry that they had been so unkind, and asked Laideronnette to remain two or three days, but Laideronnette was so upset that she refused. Then her sister Bellote gave her some silk, and Bellote's betrothed gave her some ribbons. Now, if Laideronnette had been like some people she would have thrown the silk and the ribbons at the Princess and her future husband. But Laideronnette was not like that, and she only felt a great sorrow in her little heart, and turned away and took her faithful nurse with her, and all the way home towards the Light of Dawn, Laideronnette never spoke a single word.

One day, when Laideronnette was walking in a very shaded valley in the forest, she saw on a tree a big green serpent, who lifted his head and said to her, "Laideronnette, you are not the only unhappy person, look at my horrible form, and I was born more beautiful than you." The Princess was so terrified to hear a serpent talk that she fled away and remained in her room for days, in case she should see or meet the green serpent again.

Eventually Laideronnette got tired of being shut up in her room all day alone, so one evening she came down and went to the edge of the sea, bewailing all the time her awful loneliness and her sad destiny, when suddenly she saw coming towards her over the waves a little barque of a thousand different colours and designs on its sides. The sail was beautifully embroidered in gold, and the Princess became very curious to see all the beauties that the barque must contain inside.

She made her way aboard. Inside she found it lined with lovely velvet, the seats of pure gold and the walls studded with diamonds. Then, all of a sudden, the barque turned and went out to sea. The Princess ran up and caught hold of the oars, thinking to get back to her castle, but it was no use, for she could do nothing at all. On and on went the barque and the poor little Princess wept bitterly at this new sorrow that had come to her.

"Magotine is doing me a bad turn again," she thought, so she abandoned herself to her fate, hoping that she would die. "Just after I was looking forward to a little pleasure in seeing my parents yesterday, comes one catastrophe on another, and now my sister is going to be married to a great Prince. What have I done that I should have to live alone in a desert spot because of my ugliness? Alas! For my company I have only a serpent, who speaks!'

These reflections brought tears from the Princess, and she gazed on every side to see which way death was coming for her. While looking and gazing she saw, approaching on the waves, a serpent, flashing green in the sunlight. He came up to the side of the barque and said, "If you are good enough to receive help from a poor Green Serpent, tell me, for I am in a position to save your life."

"Death is nothing to me compared to the sight of you," cried the Princess, "and, if you really want to do me a favour, never show yourself before my eyes again."

The Green Serpent gave a big sigh (for that is the way of serpents in love), and, without replying at all, he dived to the bottom of the sea.

"What a horrible monster!" said the Princess to herself. "His body is of a thousand green colours, and he has eyes like fire. I would rather die than that he should save my life. What love can he have for me, and by what right does he speak like a human being?"

Suddenly a voice replied to her thoughts, and it said, "Listen, Laideronnette, it is not my fault that I am a Green Serpent, and it will not be for ever. I assure you, I am less ugly in my special way than you are in yours. All the same, it is not my wish to pain you, for I would comfort you if you would only let me!"

The voice surprised the Princess very much, and so sweet was it that she could not hold back her tears. "I am not crying because I am afraid to die", she answered, "but I am hurt enough to weep over my ugliness. I have nothing to live for, why should I cry for fear of dying?"

While she was thus moralising, the little barque that floated with the wind ran into a rock and broke up into pieces, and, when all else had sunk, there remained of the wreck only two little pieces of wood. The poor Princess caught hold of these two little pieces and kept herself afloat, until, happily, her feet touched a rock and she scrambled up on to it.

Alas! What was that coming towards her now but the Green Serpent! As if he knew that she was afraid, he moved away a little, and said, "You would be less afraid of me, Laideronnette, if you knew what advantages can be had through me. It is one of the punishments of my destiny, however, that I should frighten everyone in the world."

And with this he threw himself back into the sea, and Laideronnette remained alone on the rock in the middle of the ocean. On whichever side she looked she saw nothing but what would cause her despair, and darkness began to fall, and she had no food to eat, and Laideronnette did not know where to sleep.

"I thought," said she sadly, "that I should end my days at the bottom of the sea, but without a doubt this is to be the end, what sea-monster will come to eat me up?"

She crept higher and higher up the rock, and looked out over the sea. Darkness was falling fast, so she took off her dress and covered her head and face in it, so that she could not see the awful things that would pass in the night.

After a long time she fell asleep, and dreamt that she heard the most melodious music, and she tried to persuade herself that she was awake, but in a second she heard a voice singing, as if to her alone:

"Suffer the love that wounds you,

It is a tender fire.

The love that follows and surrounds you

To your love would aspire.

Banish fear, forgo all grieving,

Love hath joys past all believing.

Suffer the love that wounds you,

It is a tender fire."

At the end of this song she woke up at once. "What happiness or what misfortune threatens me?" said she. She opened her eyes very carefully, for she was full of fear, expecting to find herself surrounded by monsters from the sea, but, imagine her surprise to find herself in a chamber all glittering with gold! The bed on which she lay was perfect, and the most beautiful to be seen anywhere in the wide world. Laideronnette got up and went out on to a wide balcony, where she saw all the beauties of nature before her. The gardens were full of flowers, flowers that gave out the rarest perfume, fountains splashed everywhere, and were surmounted by lovely figures, and outside the gardens was a wonderful forest green with verdure. The palace and the walls were encrusted with precious stones, the roofs and ceilings were made of pearls, and so beautifully done that it was a perfect work of art. From the tower of the palace could be seen beyond the forest a sea calm and placid, just like a sheet of glass, and on the sea floated thousands of little boats with all kinds of different sails, which, when caught by the wind, had the most lovely effect imaginable.

"Gods, sweet gods!" cried Laideronnette, "What do I see? Where am I? Is it possible that I am in heaven, I who yesterday was in peril in a barque?"

She walked as she spoke, then she stopped, what noise was that she heard in her apartment? She turned and entered her room, and, coming towards her, she saw a hundred little animated pagodas, all of different designs. Some were very beautiful, while others were extremely ugly. In fact there was hardly any difference between the little pagodas and the people who inhabit the world.

The pagoda which now presented itself before Laideronnette was the deputy of the King. It said that sometimes it went travelling all over the world, but was allowed to do so only on one condition, namely, that it did not talk to anyone, otherwise the King would not give the necessary permission. On its return it entertained the King by recounting all that it had heard and seen. Moreover, it held the most precious secrets of the court.

"It will be a pleasure to serve you, madam," it went on, "and everything you want we shall be delighted to get for you. In the meantime we will play for you and dance so that you will have plenty to make you happy." And they all began to dance and sing, and play on castanets and tambourines.

When they had finished, the principal pagoda said to the Princess, "Listen, madam, these hundred pagodas are here expressly to serve you, and any mortal thing you want in the world you have only to ask for it and it shall be yours at once."

The little pagodas paused in their movements and came near to Laideronnette, and she saw at a glance that they were simply lovely.

Looking inside, she saw that they contained presents for her, some useful and others so beautiful that she could only cry out with joy.

The biggest pagoda, which was a little figure of pure diamonds, then came up to Laideronnette and asked her if she would now like her bath in the little grotto. The Princess walked, between a guard of honour, to the place it pointed to, and there she saw two beautiful baths of crystal, and from them came such a lovely fragrance that Laideronnette could not help remarking about it. Then she asked why there were two bathing places, and they told her that one was for her and the other for the King of the Pagodas.

"But where is he, then?" cried Laideronnette. "Madam," said they, "at present he is at the war, but you shall see him on his return."

The Princess asked them if he was married, and they shook their little top turrets, meaning that he was not. Then they told her that he was so good and kind that he had never found anyone good enough to marry.

Laideronnette then undressed herself and got into the bath, and at once the pagodas began to sing and play. Then, when the Princess was ready to come out of her bath, she was given a dress of shining colours, and they all walked before her to her room, where her toilet was made by maids, all of them quaint little pagodas.

The Princess was astounded, and expressed her delight at her great good fortune.

There was not a day that the pagodas did not come and tell her all the news of the courts where they had been in different parts of the world. People plotting for war, others seeking for peace, wives who were unfaithful, old widowers who married wives a thousand times more unsuitable than those they had lost, discovered treasures, favourites at court, and out of it, who had fallen from the coveted seat they occupied, jealous wives, to say nothing at all about husbands, women who flirted, and naughty children; in fact they told her everything that was going on, to make her happy and to help to pass the time away.

Now one night it happened that the Princess could not sleep, and she lay awake, thinking. At last she said, "What is going to happen to me? Shall I always be here? My life is passed more happily than I ever could wish, but, all the same, there is a feeling in my heart that there is something missing."

"Ah! Princess," said a voice, "is it not your own fault? If you would only love me, you would recognise at once that it would be possible to remain in this palace for ever, alone with the one you loved, without ever wishing to leave it."

"Which little pagoda is speaking to me now?" she asked. "What dreadful counsel to give me, contrary to all I have been taught in my life!"

"It is not a pagoda who is talking to you, it is the unhappy King who loves you, madam."

"A King who loves me!" replied the Princess. "Has this King eyes, or does he need glasses? Has he not seen that I am the ugliest person in the world?"

"Yes, I have seen you, madam. All that you are, and all that you may have been, make not the least difference to me. I repeat, I love you."

The Princess did not speak again, but she spent the rest of the night thinking over this adventure.

Every day on getting up she found new clothes and fresh jewels, it was too much homage, considering she was so ugly.

One night, and it must have been the darkest night of the whole year, Laideronnette was asleep, and, on awakening, she felt that someone sat near her bed. The Princess put out her hand to feel, but somebody took her hand and kissed it, and in so doing let teardrops fall upon it. She knew full well that it must be the invisible King.

"What do you want with me?" she said. "Can I love somebody I have never seen and do not know?"

"Ah! Madam," replied he, "what pleasure it would give me to be able to fulfil your wish! But the wicked Magotine, who played you such a cruel trick, has done the same to me, for I am condemned to remain thus for seven years, five have already gone by and there remain another two years. You could, if you would, lessen the time and make it pass quickly for me if you would marry me. You will think that what I ask is impossible, but, madam, if you only knew how deep my love is for you, you would never refuse me the favour I ask of you."

Laideronnette, as I have already said, thought that this invisible King was very sweet, and the love he offered was without a doubt genuine. And, in a moment of pity, she replied that she would like a few days to think over his proposal. So the days passed, and all the time the music went on and the pagodas danced and new presents arrived for her, better than those she had received before. And in the end the Princess made up her mind to marry the invisible King, and she promised to wait to see him until his time of punishment was over and he could take visible shape again.

Then the voice said, "The consequences will be terrible for you and for me if your curiosity should overcome you, and I shall have to commence my punishment all over again. But, should you, on the other hand, stay your desire to see me, you will receive that beauty that the wicked Magotine took away from you."

The Princess, full of this new hope, promised to keep her word to him. But after a while she had a deep desire to see her father and mother again, also her sister and her husband. The pagodas, who knew the road well, conducted the royal family to the castle of Laideronnette's father and mother, and when she saw them she nearly died of joy.

Her mother and her sister questioned Laideronnette about her husband, and Laideronnette remembered what her husband had told her. She did not like to tell her people the truth, so she told them that he was at the war fighting, and that he did not like seeing people. But her mother and sister chaffed her about him, and at last Laideronnette said that the wicked Magotine had punished him for seven years, that two remained to be finished, and that she had married him without ever having seen him, but that he was a charming person and his conversation proved the fact, and that if she held her curiosity until the two years were up, she would regain all the beauty that the fairy Magotine had taken from her.

"Ah!" replied her mother, "is it possible that you are such a simpleton as to believe all those tales? Your husband is a huge monster, he is the King of monkeys truly."

"I know full well," replied Laideronnette, "that he is the god of Love himself."

"What a terrible mistake!" screamed the Queen Bellote.

The poor Princess was so confused and upset that, after giving them the presents, she resolved to go and see her husband. Ah, fatal curiosity! She took a little lamp with her that she might be able to see him the better. What was her surprise when, instead of Love, she saw the Green Serpent! He drew himself up in rage and sorrow, crying, "O wicked one! Is this the return for all my love for you?'

Now Magotine, knowing that Laideronnette and the Green Serpent were in trouble, came to add to their sorrow and taunt them. She took away, with one wave of her wand, all the lovely castles and fountains and gardens. And Laideronnette, seeing all that she had done, was very troubled. So, during the night, Laideronnette deplored her sad fate. Then, high up near the stars, she saw coming towards her the Green Serpent.

"I always make you afraid," he cried, "but you are infinitely dear to me."

"Is it you, Serpent, dear lover, is it you?" cried Laideronnette. "Can you forgive me for my fatal curiosity?"

"Ah! How the sorrow of absence troubles this loving heart!" replied the Serpent, with never a word of reproach to Laideronnette for her broken promise.

Magotine, now, was one of those fairies who never slept at all. The wish to do harm and never to miss the chance kept her awake, and she did not fail to hear the conversation between the King Serpent and his spouse, and she came down upon them in a fury.

"Now then, Green Serpent," said she, "I order you for your punishment to go right to the good Proserpine, and give her my compliments."

The poor Green Serpent went at once with great sighs, leaving the Queen in sorrow. And Laideronnette cried out, "What crime have we committed now, you wicked Magotine? I am certain that the poor King, whom you have sent to the bottomless pit of hell, was as innocent as I myself am, but let me die, it is the least you can do."

"You would be too happy," said Magotine, "were I to listen and grant you your wish. I will send you to the bottom of the sea." So saying, she took the poor Princess to the top of the highest mountain and tied a mill-stone about her neck, telling her that she was to go down and bring enough Water of Discretion to fill up her great big glass. The Princess said that it was absolutely impossible to carry all that water.

"If you do not," said Magotine, "you may rest assured that your Green Serpent will suffer more."

This threat caused the Queen to think of her utter feebleness. She began to walk, but, alas, it was useless. Oh! If the Fairy Protectress would only help her! Loudly she called, and lo! there stood the good fairy by her side.

"See," said she, "to what a pass your fatal curiosity has brought you!" So saying, she took her to the top of the mountain, where she gave her a little carriage drawn by two white mice and told them to descend the mountain. Then she gave the little mice a vessel to fill up with the Water of Discretion for Magotine, and produced a little pair of iron shoes for Laideronnette to put on. She counselled her not to remain on the mountain and not to stay by the fountain, but to go into a little wood and to remain there three years, for then Magotine would think that she was getting the water or that she had perished in the awful perils of the voyage.

Laideronnette kissed and embraced the good Fairy Protectress, and thanked her a thousand times for her great favours. "But, madam," said

Laideronnette, "all the joys that you have given me will not lessen the sorrow of not having my Green Serpent."

"He will come to you after you have been three years in the wood in the mountain," said the fairy, "and on your return you can give the water to Magotine."

Laideronnette promised the fairy not to forget anything she had told her. So, when she got into her carriage, the mice took her to get the water, and afterwards they went to the wood that the fairy had told them about. There never was a more lovely place. Fruit hung on all the branches, and there were long avenues where the sun could not pierce, where thousands of little fountains splashed, but the most wonderful thing of all was, that all the animals could speak.

Three years passed, and the time had now arrived for her departure with the water for Magotine. So Laideronnette told all the animals that she was sorry to leave them, and tears fell from her eyes, because she was so touched with the kindness they all had shown her.

She did not forget the vessel full of the Water of Discretion, nor the little shoes of iron that the good fairy had given her, and, just when Magotine thought her dead, she presented herself all of a sudden before her, the stones around her neck, the shoes of iron on her feet, and the vessel full of water in her hand.

Magotine on seeing her cried out in surprise. Where had she come from?

"Madam," said Laideronnette, "I passed three years in trying to get this water for you."

Magotine roared with laughter when she thought of the awful job this poor Queen must have had to get it, but she regarded her attentively.

"What is it that I see?" she cried to Laideronnette, who had changed greatly. "How did you become so beautiful?"

Laideronnette told her that she had washed in the Water of Discretion, and that was how she had become beautiful.

Magotine, on hearing this, threw the water on the ground. "I will be avenged," said she. "Go down to the bottomless pit and ask Proserpine to give you the Essence of Long Life for me. I am always afraid of falling ill and dying. When you have done this you will be free. But mind you do not upset any, neither may you drink the tiniest drop."

The poor Queen, on hearing this new order, was terribly cut up. She began to cry, and Magotine, seeing this, was delighted. "Go on, get away!" said she. "Do not lose one moment."

Laideronnette walked for a long time without finding the right path, turning first one way and then the other, then suddenly she saw the Fairy Protectress, who said to her, "Do you know, beautiful Queen, that by the orders of Magotine your husband is to remain as he is until you take the Essence of Life to that wicked fairy?"

"I am yet a long way away," said Laideronnette.

"Here," said the Fairy Protectress, "see, here is a branch of a tree. Touch the earth and repeat this verse distinctly."

The Queen once again kissed the knees of this really good and generous fairy, and at the same time repeated after her:

'You who all malice canst disarm,

Protect me as I rove!

Deliver me from all who harm,

But not from him I love.

For, if devoured I am to be,

He is my monster - none but he!'

And immediately, in answer to her prayer, a little boy more beautiful than any in heaven or earth came up to her. On his head was a garland of flowers, and in his hand a bow and arrow. The Queen knew at once that it was Love. He said to her, "You appeal to me so tenderly that I deserted the heavens."

Love, who sang beautifully in verse, gave three knocks while singing this song:

"Earth, listen and my voice obey.
It is Love who speaks, reveal the way!"

The earth obeyed, a path opened up, and Love took Laideronnette under his protection, and so they arrived at the mouth of hell. She expected to see her husband in the form of a serpent, but he had just finished his terrible punishment. The first thing that Laideronnette saw was indeed her husband, but she had never seen such a charming figure, nor anyone so handsome, and neither had he seen anyone so beautiful as she had become. Then the Queen said with extreme tenderness:

"Destiny! I bend the knee
To you and your decree,
If he must dwell in deepest hell
He dwells there with me,
For even in hell I'll love him well
For all eternity."

The King was full of joy and love, and showed it by the way he kissed her. Love, however, never did believe in wasting time, so he took the Queen to Proserpine. The Queen gave the compliments of the fairy Magotine, and begged her to give her the Essence of Long Life. Love took it and handed it to her, telling her not to forget the penalty that she had paid for her curiosity, and to take every care this time. He would never leave them again. He conducted them to the fairy Magotine, and then, so that Magotine should not see him, he hid in their hearts.

During this time the fairy Magotine was so impressed with the beauty of human feelings, that she received the poor unfortunate King and Queen with some feeling of generosity. She gave them back the lovely palace with all the good things that they had before, and made the King head of the pagodas again. So they went home, and all the great sorrows that they had passed through they soon forgot in the greater joy of each other.

Tales From Gallia

Tales From Gallia

WHY THE ANIMALS NO LONGER FEAR THE SHEEP

Originally a French Creole story, this adaptation is taken from Katharine Pyle's book, Wonder Tales From Many Lands, published by George G. Harrap & Company Ltd, London, in 1920.

LONG, LONG AGO, WHEN THE ANIMALS were not as wise as they are now, they were all very much afraid of the sheep. Even the lion and tiger were afraid of him. They had never seen him angry, but he had such a solemn look, and his beard was so long, and his horns so strong and curly, that they were sure he would be very dangerous indeed if he were once roused.

One day old Papa Sheep invited Mr Tiger to come and spend the day with him, and he also invited him to bring Little Tiger along to play with Little Sheep, for Mr Tiger's little boy was just the same age as Papa Sheep's little boy.

Mr Tiger was very pleased at this invitation. He was glad to come himself, and he was glad to have Little Tiger become friendly with Little Sheep, for after a while Little Sheep would probably grow up and be just as big and strong and dangerous as his father was.

Mr Tiger and his little boy arrived quite early in the morning at the sheep's house, and they brought a present with them, so that Papa Sheep would feel pleased with them. The present they brought was a basket of nice fresh green things such as all sheep like.

Papa Sheep thanked them for the present, and patted Little Tiger on the head, and then he told the two children to run out of doors and play, because he and Mr Tiger wanted to talk big talk together.

The little ones were very glad to do this, for it was bright and pleasant outside, and they liked it better than staying in the house.

Little Tiger was very frisky and frolicsome, and Little Sheep was too. At first they ran about and chased each other, and tried which could jump highest, but after a while they grew rougher in their play. Little Sheep butted Little Tiger with his forehead, and then Little Tiger raised his paw and gave Little Sheep a blow on the side of the head.

Though the Tiger was young and small, he was also very strong, and his blow sent Little Sheep tumbling heels over head. Little Sheep was not angry however. He got up and laughed and laughed. When he laughed he opened his mouth wide, and Little Tiger was very much surprised to see what little teeth the sheep had. He did not say anything at the time, however, but only went on with his play.

But when Little Tiger and his father were walking home together that evening, Little Tiger said, "Papa, I saw Little Sheep's teeth today, and he only has little, little bits of teeth. They do not look as though they could bite anyone."

"Hush, hush," cried the Tiger. "You mustn't talk in that way. Someone might hear you."

"But it is true," said Little Tiger. "Why, I wouldn't be afraid of Little Sheep now, even if he did get angry."

"Will you be quiet?" cried the Tiger angrily. "If you ever say such a thing again I will box you so hard that you will forget whether you ever saw his teeth or not."

All the same Mr Tiger could not help wondering whether what Little Tiger had said was true. How strange it would be if Little Sheep only had little weak teeth, and stranger still if Papa Sheep's teeth were just the same!

That night, after all the Tiger family had gone to bed, Mr Tiger began to talk to his wife in a low tone. "Do you know what Little Tiger said today?"

"No, how should I know? Some nonsense, no doubt."

"He said he saw Little Sheep's teeth, and that they were so small and weak he did not believe he could bite anybody."

"Oh! Oh! Be quiet," cried his wife. "Are you crazy to talk so? Suppose someone heard you, and went and told Papa Sheep what you had been saying. He certainly would come and tear us all to pieces."

Mr Tiger said nothing in answer to this, but the less he said, the more he thought. At last he made up his mind to find out for a certainty whether Papa Sheep had biting teeth or no. For this purpose he in his turn invited Papa Sheep and Little Sheep to come and spend the day with him and his family.

Papa Sheep accepted the invitation, and on the day named he and Little Sheep arrived bright and early at the tiger's house.

As before, the little ones went out of doors to play, and the big animals sat and talked inside the house.

Presently Mr Tiger brought out a bottle of wine and set it on the table, and he and the sheep began to drink together. The more Papa Sheep drank, the merrier he grew. He quite lost his solemn look. He began to laugh loudly, and he threw back his head and opened his mouth so wide that the tiger could see every tooth he had. And very poor teeth they were too. They were so small and weak that they were not fit for biting anything tougher than grass.

When Mr Tiger saw how small the sheep's teeth were, he became very angry. He was in a rage to think he had ever been afraid of Papa Sheep, and had treated him with respect. With a roar he sprang at the old sheep, and gave him such a blow with his paw that the sheep fell down dead.

Little Tiger, outside, heard the noise, and he ran and looked in at the window. As soon as he saw what had happened, he called to Little Sheep,

"Run, Little Sheep! Run away, quick! My papa is biting your papa, and if you do not run away he will bite you next."

When Little Sheep heard this he was very much frightened. He did not stop to ask any questions. He took to his heels and ran home, crying bitterly all the way.

Old Mother Sheep saw him coming and hurried out to meet him. "What is the matter?" she cried. "Where is your father, and why are you crying so bitterly?"

"Oh! Oh!" wept Little Sheep. "The Tiger! He has bitten Papa to pieces, and I'm afraid he'll come and bite me too."

When Mother Sheep heard this, she too began to weep and lament. "What shall we do now?" she cried. "Where shall we go? The Tiger will certainly come in search of us next, and tear us to pieces as he did your father."

At this the Little Sheep raised his voice and wept more bitterly than ever.

Now it so chanced that when Mother Sheep ran out to meet Little Sheep she met him under a tall tree, and in this tree the Queen of the Birds was sitting. The Queen heard everything the two below her said, and she felt very sorry for them because they were in such distress and terror. She flew down to a branch just over their heads and spoke to them in a soothing manner. "I have overheard all that you have been saying. This Tiger that you speak of is indeed a very wicked animal. You are in great danger, but do not be afraid. I will help you. I have a plan that may rid us of him for ever. Go back to your home. Shut yourself in and remain there quietly until I send you further word."

When Mother Sheep heard this she was comforted, for she saw at once that it was a queen that was speaking to her. She promised to do as she was told, and with Little Sheep at her side she returned quickly to the house. There they shut themselves in and sat down to wait for what might happen.

Meanwhile the Queen flew away to the forest where she lived, and called all the birds together. "Listen now," she said to them. "Do you know what the wicked Tiger has done? He has killed poor old Papa Sheep, who never did harm to anyone. We all know how cruel the Tiger is, but this is the worst thing he has done yet. It is time for us to rid the forest of him."

The Queen then told them that she was going to give a grand ball. To this ball she intended to invite the Tiger. And not only should he be invited, but he should be her own partner for the dance. "When the music begins, you also must take partners," said she. "We will all stand up to dance, and then I will give a sign, and all the herons must clap their wings together. When they do this, the rest of you must instantly hide your heads under your wings. When I make another sign, they will again clap their wings, and then you must take your heads out again. If the plan I have in my mind works out well, we will soon put an end to this Tiger."

The birds promised to obey their Queen exactly in everything, and then she sent several of them away to the Tiger's house to invite him to the ball.

The Tiger was at home when the birds arrived, and he was very much flattered when he heard that the Queen wished him to come to her ball. He was even more delighted when he found that he was to be the Queen's own partner in the dance.

He at once began to make himself ready, smoothing his whiskers, and brushing his coat until it shone.

The Tiger's wife, however, was not at all pleased. "What nonsense is this?" cried she. "Why should you want to go to a ball? You have never been to court before, and you will not know how to act. You will be sure to do something foolish, and then everyone will laugh at you."

The Tiger became very angry when she said this. "Of course I shall go," he cried. "I know how to behave as well as anyone. You only talk this way because you are jealous at not being asked. If you had been invited too, you would have been eager enough to go. But you cannot dissuade me, whatever you say." The Tiger then hurried away through the forest to the place where the ball was to be held.

As soon as the Queen of the Birds saw him coming, she made haste to welcome him. A fine feast was already spread, and the Queen made the Tiger sit down at her right hand, and she offered him so many delicious things that he ate and drank a great deal more than was good for him. She also flattered him until he hardly knew what he was doing.

After the feast was ended the music began to play, and the birds all stood up to dance. Each one had a partner, but the Queen's partner was the Tiger himself, as she had promised him. When all were in position, the Queen gave a sign, and the great herons clapped their wings together with a loud noise. The noise was so very loud and so very sudden that it made the Tiger blink, and in that moment that the Tiger blinked all the birds hid their heads under their wings.

When the Tiger looked about him again he was very much surprised to see all the birds standing there apparently without any heads. The Queen alone held her head high, and she looked at him with an angry air.

"How is this?" said she. "Are these your court manners? Do you not know that at court no one except the Queen ever dances without removing his head? Look about you. Do you see even a single one of the birds with his head on?"

"But…but…" stammered the Tiger, "after the dance is over, what will they do without their heads? Your Majesty, how could I take care of my wife and family without a head?"

"Oh," said the Queen smiling, "after the dance is over they will have their heads again. It is only while they dance that they are without them. I will show you."

With these words the Queen again gave a sign. At once all the herons clapped their wings, and in the instant when the Tiger blinked the birds drew their heads from under their wings. The Tiger looked about him. There the birds all stood just as before, only now their heads were in their proper places, and they were all looking at him with a scornful air.

"Oh, your Majesty," cried the Tiger, "I am very much ashamed. I have never been to court before, and I did not know what was expected of me. If you will excuse me, I will run home and get rid of my head, and then I will return at once to dance with you."

"Very well," answered the Queen, "only do not be gone long", and she smiled upon him sweetly.

At once the Tiger bounded away, but the Queen bade a little sparrow follow him and bring her word of what happened to him.

The Tiger hurried on, leaping over logs and breaking through bushes, while the sparrow fluttered overhead unnoticed.

He reached his home, and scarcely had he crossed the threshold before he began to bawl for his wife. "Wife! Wife! Come here, quick! Bring an axe and chop off my head."

"Are you crazy?" cried his wife. "Chop off your head! Why should I do that?"

"You do not understand. I am to dance with the Queen, and no one may do that as long as he has a head on his shoulders."

"All the better for you. Why should you dance with her? And I certainly shall not kill you, Queen or no Queen."

When his wife said this, Mr Tiger fell into a terrible rage. "Am I the master of the house, or am I not?" he cried. "Do as I tell you, or I will tear you to pieces, as I did the poor silly Sheep." He looked so fierce that his wife was terrified. She ran out and got the axe. When she returned with it, however, she again began to argue with him. "Think, husband, think well what you would have me do. If your head is once off, there will be no putting it on again. That will be the end of you."

"You do not understand," cried the Tiger. "The Queen will see to that. She will see that my head is put back again after the dance." Then, as his wife still hesitated, he began to roar in such a terrible manner that she almost lost her wits, and seizing the axe, she cut off his head in a hurry. And that was the end of him, for even if the Queen had been able to do it, she would not have restored the head of such a wicked beast.

As soon as the sparrow had seen the end of the Tiger, he flew back to carry the news to the Queen. Then there was the greatest rejoicing all through the forest. Not a single bird or beast but was glad the Tiger was dead. No one, however, rejoiced as heartily as Mother Sheep and Little Sheep, for they were the ones who had been in most danger. Now they could come out from their house again and go about their usual business.

After a while, as time passed by, Little Sheep played so hard and ate so much that he grew up to be Big Sheep. He was larger and stronger than his father had ever been. His beard was longer, and his horns were curlier, and yet nobody was afraid of him. Word had gone to all the animals that the sheep's teeth were too small and weak to hurt anyone. And so it has been ever since. Not one of the animals has been afraid of the sheep from that day to this.

Tales From Gallia

PRINCESS ROSETTA

This adaptation is taken from Katharine Pyle's book, Wonder Tales From Many Lands, published by George G. Harrap & Company Ltd, London, in 1920.

THERE WERE ONCE A KING AND Queen who had three of the most beautiful children in the world. They loved all the children tenderly, one no better than the others, but the youngest, who was a girl, was always kept locked up in a strong tower. She was allowed to see no one but her attendants, and her parents and her two brothers, who went every day to visit her.

No one knew why she was kept shut up in this way except the King and Queen. Even her brothers did not know, and they often grieved to think that their sister Rosetta should be a prisoner all her life.

The fact was that when Rosetta was born a fairy had appeared to her parents and had told them that at some future time the princess would bring a great misfortune upon her brothers. Because of her they would be cast into a dungeon and perhaps even lose their lives. These misfortunes would happen when the Princess Rosetta was about to be married.

The royal parents were greatly troubled at hearing this, and they immediately caused a high tower to be built, and in this they placed the child. Every luxury was hers, the most beautiful clothes and jewels, and the most delicious and delicately cooked food. Her furniture was of gold and was carved in strange and wonderful shapes, and the hangings were all woven of gold and silver thread and richly embroidered.

No one, however, as was said, ever came to the tower, or saw her, except her father and mother and her brothers and the ladies who waited upon her.

The royal parents intended to tell their sons the reason for this imprisonment when Rosetta should have reached the age of eighteen. Her brothers would then understand that it was not through any cruelty that their sister was kept prisoner, but to protect their own lives.

Unfortunately, just before Rosetta's eighteenth birthday the King and Queen both died, and so suddenly that they had no time to reveal to anyone what the fairy had told them.

The keys of the tower were given to the elder prince, and one of his first acts was to set Rosetta free.

The princess was delighted to be able to see at last what the world outside of her tower was like. Everything was a wonder to her—the trees, the grass, the flowers and fountains. She wished to know the names of everything.

At one spot in the gardens a peacock sat sunning itself.

"What is that beautiful creature called?" she asked.

"That, dear sister, is a peacock," answered the princes.

"A peacock!" cried Rosetta. "Never in my life did I dream that such a beautiful thing existed. I am sure that in all the world there can be nothing else that is quite so beautiful. Dear brothers, if you love me, find the King of the Peacocks and bring him here, for he, and he alone, shall be my husband. Moreover, unless you find him and bring him to me, I shall certainly die of grief."

The princes loved their sister so dearly that they could refuse nothing that she asked of them. They at once began to make ready to set out into the world in search of the country of the peacocks. Before starting they caused a portrait of their sister to be painted. This they intended to take with them to the Peacock country, for they were sure that if the king of that country could only know how beautiful Rosetta was, he would never be contented until he had her for his queen.

As soon as their preparations had been made and the portrait was finished, the two princes set out upon their travels. They journeyed on and on, over many seas and many mountains and through many strange lands, until at last they came to a country where there were nothing but peacocks. There were peacock bakers and peacock tradesmen. Peacocks went in and out of the houses, and drove through the streets in magnificent coaches shining with gold and precious stones. Everywhere were only peacocks spreading their tails and parading in all their magnificence. Strangely enough, however, the King who ruled over this country was not a peacock at all, but a young man so handsome and graceful that even the peacocks could not equal him in beauty.

The princes, who had not taken long in finding the castle, were brought before the King by the peacocks who attended him. The brothers at once told him that they too were sons of a king, and that they were travelling through the world upon a secret errand of great importance. They did not tell him what their errand was, but after they had been talking with him for a short time, they began to speak of their sister, and of her beauty and sweetness. The young King became quite eager to see such a lovely creature, and the brothers sent for the portrait they had brought with them and showed it to him.

The King of the Peacocks had no sooner seen it than he fell violently in love with Rosetta, and begged them to promise her to him for a bride. The brothers were the more ready to do this because they had found that the Peacock King was not only singularly handsome, but that he was one of the richest and most powerful kings in the whole world.

Messengers were appointed to go to the princes' country and to bring Rosetta back with them. They were urged to make all the speed they could, for the young King was so eager to see the Beauty that he was ready to die with impatience.

After they had gone, the King had the portrait put where he could see it constantly, and feast his eyes upon it, and he was only happy when he was with it. The more he looked at it, however, the more he doubted whether any human being could be as beautiful as the painting. The brothers were obliged to assure him every day that when he saw Rosetta he would find her even more lovely than her portrait.

"Very well," said the Peacock King at last, "if I find all that you tell me is true, I will load you with wealth and honours, but if you have deceived me, I will surely put you to death."

The brothers were not dismayed at this threat, for they knew that it was impossible that he should be disappointed in the beauty of their sister.

Meanwhile the messengers, after many days, reached the country where Rosetta lived. They at once were brought before her, and when she heard that they had come to take her to the King of the Peacocks, she was wild with joy. She determined to set out at once, and as the journey was shorter by way of the sea, she made up her mind to go in a ship rather than in a coach and by land. She took with her only an old nurse and her foster-sister, and her little dog Fifine. This little dog was very wonderful, and had been given to her by a fairy. He was of a bright green colour and had only one ear, but he understood everything the princess said to him, and he knew a hundred pretty tricks.

The old nurse and her daughter pretended to be very fond of Rosetta, but in truth they hated her because she was so beautiful and beloved, and would have been glad to injure her in any way.

After they had sailed along for several days, and were almost within sight of the kingdom of the Peacocks, the old nurse brought to Rosetta a drink that she had mixed, and in which she had put a sleeping potion. Rosetta suspected nothing, and she drank all the old woman had brought her, except for a small part that she gave to Fifine.

Rosetta had scarcely swallowed the potion before she became very drowsy. Her eyelids weighed like lead, and before long she fell into a deep sleep. Fifine also became very sleepy. He crawled in under the silken covering that the princess had drawn over her, and lay there as though dead.

As soon as the old nurse saw that Rosetta was asleep, and that nothing could awaken her, she went to the sailors, and by means of bribes and threats she obliged them to do exactly as she bade them. Under her directions they carried the mattress upon which Rosetta lay up to the deck. The nurse looked about for Fifine, but could not find the little dog anywhere, for it was hidden under the coverlet. "No matter," said she. "I wished to keep the little animal for my daughter, but it is probably hiding somewhere about the ship, and I will find it later."

She then made the sailors take up the mattress and throw it overboard into the sea. This they did without awakening either Rosetta or Fifine. They then set all sail and sped on toward the shores of the Peacock country, which could already be seen before them. The wicked nurse felt sure that it would not be long before the mattress would become heavy with water and would sink, so she and her daughter need trouble themselves no more about the hated Rosetta.

Meanwhile the King of the Peacocks was growing more and more impatient to see his bride. Watchers had been placed upon the seashore to bring him news the moment the sails of the returning ship were seen.

It was on the twenty-first day after the messengers had departed that these watchers hastened to the palace, all out of breath, and told the King that the ship was approaching.

The King called his attendants about him, and hurried down to the seashore.

The vessel had already come to land. The wicked nurse had dressed her daughter in the most magnificent of Rosetta's clothes, which she wore as a toad might wear the dress of a fairy. The nurse had also bedecked her with the jewels belonging to the princess, and last of all she had thrown a silver veil over her, as though to guard her beauty from the sun.

As the prince saw this magnificently dressed person approaching him, he assumed it must be his bride. He hastened to meet her, and threw back the veil that covered her face, but when he saw the ugliness beneath the veil he almost fainted. He at once decided that the two princes had deceived him, that they had tricked him into sending for their sister and promising to marry her because no other king had been willing to take such a hideous creature for his wife.

Filled with rage, he sent his guards to take the princes and throw them into the deepest and darkest of the palace dungeons. He had given his word that he would marry their sister, and this word he could not break, but he promised himself that upon the day when he was married to this creature the two brothers should die.

The princes, meanwhile, had also heard that the ship had returned. They had no doubt that their sister was on board, and they had at once made ready to appear before the King, to be loaded with wealth and honours as he had promised them.

It was not long, indeed, before they heard a loud knock on their door, but instead of smiling courtiers coming to congratulate them, a guard of soldiers had arrived, and the two brothers were carried away, not to a grateful king, but to a horrible dungeon where their only companions were snakes and toads and slimy crawling things. The princes could not understand it. They could not imagine what had happened, nor why they were treated in this way. The soldiers would not answer their questions, and after they were shut in the dungeon no living soul came near them except the jailer, who unlocked the door to throw in to them a few vile crusts, and he was both deaf and dumb.

While the princes were lying thus imprisoned, preparations for the wedding were being made. A magnificent apartment had been set apart for the bride. Everything she asked for was given her, jewels and dresses of every kind, but the King she never saw. He had fallen ill with rage and disappointment, and no one could come near him except his attendants and the doctors.

The old nurse and her daughter were well content, however. The ugly girl was to become a queen, and one of the greatest queens in all the world, and that was enough for them. As for Rosetta, they were sure that she had been drowned, and that there was no need to trouble themselves about her.

The princess had not been drowned however. She was alive and well, and even more beautiful than ever, and she was at that very moment living in a poor hut in the outskirts of the city, and within sight of the very castle itself.

After the ship had sailed away and left her, the mattress upon which she lay had floated on and on until at last it had stranded upon a rock not far out from the shore.

The jar of striking the rock woke Fifine, for the little dog had only swallowed a small portion of the sleeping potion. He crawled out from under the silken coverlet, which was trailing in the sea, and when he saw the water all about him and his mistress still asleep, he began to bark as loudly as he could. The noise he made attracted the attention of a poor old beggar who lived in a hut not far away.

The old man hastened down to the water's edge, and with the aid of a boat-hook soon managed to draw the mattress to shore. What was his amazement to see a beautiful lady lying upon it fast asleep, and a little green dog keeping guard over her.

The old man tried to arouse Rosetta, but for a long time he was unsuccessful. At length, however, she opened her eyes and sat up and looked about her. She was amazed to find herself stranded upon an unknown shore and with only an old man and Fifine for her attendants instead of safely aboard her ship, with her nurse and foster-sister in attendance upon her.

"Where am I?" she cried. "Where is the ship and where are my attendants? And who are you, old man?"

The old man told her he was only a poor beggar, and of how he had seen her mattress stranded upon a rock and had drawn it to shore, and that this country where she found herself was the kingdom of the Peacocks. As to any ship, he knew nothing of it.

Rosetta could not wonder enough when she learned she was already in the Peacock country. The old man even pointed out to her a shining castle and a town not far away, and told her that was the place where the King of the Peacocks lived.

Seeing she was now able to raise herself and move about, the old man invited her to come with him to his hut. "It is but a poor place for a great princess," he said (for it was easy for him to see that Rosetta was a princess), "but at least it will be a safe shelter for you."

Rosetta gladly accepted his invitation. His hut was indeed poor and mean, but the old man was so kind and eager to please her that she could not but be grateful. He was greatly distressed because he could offer her nothing to eat but a piece of black bread and a cup of water.

"Do not grieve over that," said the princess. "Only give me a basket and we shall soon be supplied with a fine feast."

Wondering, the old man gave her a basket. Rosetta tied it round the neck of Fifine.

"Fifine," said she, "run to the palace of the King and bring us from there a part of the dinner that has been prepared for him."

Fifine understood every word perfectly. He at once set out, and made such good speed that he quickly reached the palace. He slipped into the kitchen without being seen. The King's dinner was done to a turn, and waiting to be carried to him. Fifine, slipping about here and there, managed to steal a part of everything, and the best part at that, of the meat, the poultry, the pastries and sweetmeats—he took some of each, and hid it in the basket.

Then he ran away, still without being noticed, and was soon back at the old man's hut.

The old man was filled with amazement when he saw what the dog had brought. Never had he seen such delicious food before. The princess sat down and he served her, and after she had finished he ate his fill, and still there was some left.

The next day Rosetta wished for some fresh food. She had no love for cold dishes. Again she tied the basket round the neck of the little dog. "Fifine," she said, "you did very well yesterday. Today you must again bring me a portion of all that the King is to have for dinner."

Fifine bounded away with the basket, and it was not long before he returned, bringing a part of all that was to have been served to the King.

So it went on for some time. Every day the best part of the King's dinner was stolen just before it was ready to be carried to him. Rosetta and the old man feasted finely every day, and the poor young King was like to die of hunger, because every day his dinner was stolen. A guard was set about the palace kitchen to prevent anyone except the cook and his assistants from going in and out, but still the food continued to disappear, for Fifine was so small and quick that he managed to escape the notice of the guard.

At last one day a little scullion, who had grown very curious about the matter, hid himself behind the kitchen door, determined to watch for himself. The dinner was cooked, and ready to be put into the dishes, when the scullion saw a little green dog, with a basket tied about his neck, slip into the room. The dog looked about to make sure that no one was watching. Seeing no one, he hastened to take the best part of the dinner and put it in the basket. As soon as he had done this, he slipped silently from the kitchen and ran off as fast as he could toward the old man's hut. The scullion followed him and saw where he went. Then he returned to the palace and told the cook what he had seen. The cook found it hard to believe such a strange tale, but still he repeated it to the Captain of the Guard, the Captain told it to the Grand Councillor, the Grand Councillor told it to the King's favourite, and so in time it reached the ears of the King himself.

"This is a curious thing if it is true," said the King. "I would like to see it for myself." So the next day he arose, and just before dinner-time he went down to the kitchen and hid himself behind the door. He had not been there long when the door was pushed open, and a little green dog slipped into the room. The little animal went from dish to dish, just as the scullion had said, and helped himself until his basket was full. Then he slipped away and ran home to the old man's hut, and the King followed him without being observed.

His Majesty did not go as far as the hut, however. He waited until the little dog had been admitted and the door closed behind him, and then he returned to his palace, very thoughtful.

The next day he sent to the hut for Rosetta and the old man to appear before him. The beggar was greatly alarmed when he received the message.

"See what you have brought upon us," he cried to the princess. "No doubt they have discovered that it is your dog that has been stealing the King's dinner, and now we shall be punished for it. Perhaps we may even lose our lives."

Rosetta, however, was not troubled. She was, indeed, only too glad to be brought before the King. It was what she had been hoping for. She waited only to draw a veil over her face, and then she was ready to go with the guard to the palace.

As soon as Rosetta, with the beggar and Fifine, entered the room where the young King was, he was struck by the grace and dignity with which she moved. He called her close to him and began to question her.

"Who are you," he asked, "and where do you come from? And is it you who have caused my dinners to disappear?"

To all this Rosetta answered nothing. The King then leaned forward and drew the veil aside from her face. As soon as he did so, the beauty of the princess shone forth like the sun. Everyone was amazed at it. As for the King, he was overcome with joy and wonder, for he at once recognized her as the original of the portrait that the princes had shown him, only her living face was far more beautiful than the painting, even as the sun surpasses the moon in brightness.

"Beautiful princess, where have you come from?" he cried. "Why have you hidden from me for all these days and allowed another to take your place? And one so hideous as she who claims to be my bride?"

Rosetta told him her story as far as she knew it, and the King listened attentively. He at once guessed that it was the treachery of the old nurse and her daughter that had placed Rosetta in this situation. He sent for them to appear before him, and while he waited for them to come, he and the princess talked together, and so wise she was and so witty that with every word she said he loved her better.

The nurse and her daughter, when they received the King's message, made sure that he had sent for them in order to arrange the time for the wedding. They were overjoyed, and at once put on their finest clothes. But no sooner had they entered the audience-room, and seen Rosetta seated on the throne beside the King, than they almost swooned with terror. They knew that now all had been discovered, and they fell on their knees before him and began to beseech him to pardon them.

The King was so angry at the wrong they had done the princess that he would have sent them to some miserable dungeon for the rest of their lives. But Rosetta was as tender-hearted as she was beautiful. She pleaded with him to have mercy, so the two wicked women were spared that fate.

Instead, their fine clothes were taken from them, and they were dressed in rags and driven from the palace, and as they were too ugly and wicked for anyone but Rosetta to pity them, no doubt they ended their lives in misery.

The two princes were brought from their dungeons and given all the wealth and honours the King had promised them, and when they learned how he had been deceived, they could not but forgive him his ill-treatment of them.

As for the old beggar-man, he was made rich for life.

The King and the princess were married, and lived in mutual love and happiness to the end of their days, and as for Fifine, he slept on satin cushions and ate the daintiest fare, and lived long enough to play with Rosetta's children and show them the hundred pretty tricks he knew.

A FRENCH PUCK

This adaptation is taken from a story collected by Andrew Lang in his Lilac Fairy Book, published in 1910. The original is taken from Litterature Orale de l'Auvergne, a collection of stories compiled by Paul Sebillot in 1898.

AMONG THE MOUNTAIN PASTURES AND VALLEYS that lie in the centre of France there dwelt a mischievous kind of spirit, whose delight it was to play tricks on everybody, and particularly on the shepherds and the cowherds. They never knew when they were safe from him, as he could change himself into a man, woman or child, a stick, a goat, a ploughshare. Indeed, there was only one thing whose shape he could not take, and that was a needle. At least, he could transform himself into a needle, but try as he might he never was able to imitate the hole, so every woman would have found him out at once, and this he knew.

Now the hour oftenest chosen by this naughty sprite (whom we will call Puck) for performing his pranks was about midnight, just when the shepherds and cowherds, tired out with their long day's work, were sound asleep. Then he would go into the cowsheds and unfasten the chains that fixed each beast in its own stall, and let them fall with a heavy clang to the ground. The noise was so loud that it was certain to awaken the cowherds, however fatigued they might be, and they dragged themselves wearily to the stable to put back the chains. But no sooner had they returned to their beds than the same thing happened again, and so on till the morning. Or perhaps Puck would spend his night in plaiting together the manes and tails of two of the horses, so that it would take the grooms hours of labour to get them right in the morning, while Puck, hidden among the hay in the loft, would peep out to watch them, enjoying himself amazingly all the time.

One evening more than eighty years ago a man named William was passing along the bank of a stream when he noticed a sheep who was bleating loudly. William thought it must have strayed from the flock, and that he had better take it home with him till he could discover its owner. So he went up to where it was standing, and as it seemed so tired that it could hardly walk, he hoisted it on his shoulders and continued on his way. The sheep was pretty heavy, but the good man was merciful and staggered along as best he could under his load.

"It is not much further," he thought to himself as he reached an avenue of walnut trees, when suddenly a voice spoke out from over his head, and made him jump.

"Where are you?" said the voice, and the sheep answered, "Here on the shoulders of a donkey."

In another moment the sheep was standing on the ground and William was running towards home as fast as his legs would carry him. But as he went, a laugh, which yet was something of a bleat, rang in his ears, and though he tried not to hear, the words reached him, "Oh, dear! What fun I have had, to be sure!"

Puck was careful not always to play his tricks in the same place, but visited one village after another, so that everyone trembled lest they should be the next victim. After a bit he grew tired of cowherds and shepherds, and wondered if there was no one else to give him some sport. At length he was told of a young couple who were going to the nearest town to buy all that they needed for setting up house. Quite certain that they would forget something which they could not do without, Puck waited patiently till they were jogging along in their cart on their return journey, and changed himself into a fly in order to overhear their conversation.

For a long time it was very dull, all about their wedding day next month, and who were to be invited. This led the bride to her wedding dress, and she gave a little scream. "Just think! Oh! How could I be so stupid! I have forgotten to buy the different coloured reels of cotton to match my clothes!"

"Dear, dear!" exclaimed the young man. "That is unlucky, and didn't you tell me that the dressmaker was coming in tomorrow?"

"Yes, I did," and then suddenly she gave another little scream, which had quite a different sound from the first. "Look! Look!"

The bridegroom looked, and on one side of the road he saw a large ball of thread of all colours, of all the colours, that is, of the dresses that were tied on to the back of the cart.

"Well, that is a wonderful piece of good fortune," cried he, as he sprang out to get it. "One would think a fairy had put it there on purpose."

"Perhaps she has," laughed the girl, and as she spoke she seemed to hear an echo of her laughter coming from the horse, but of course that was nonsense.

The dressmaker was delighted with the thread that was given her. It matched the stuffs so perfectly, and never tied itself in knots, or broke perpetually, as most thread did. She finished her work much quicker than she expected and the bride said she was to be sure to come to the church and see her in her wedding dress.

There was a great crowd assembled to witness the ceremony, for the young people were immense favourites in the neighbourhood, and their parents were very rich. The doors were open, and the bride could be seen from afar, walking under the chestnut avenue.

"What a beautiful girl!" exclaimed the men. "What a lovely dress!" whispered the women. But just as she entered the church and took the hand of the bridegroom, who was waiting for her, a loud noise was heard.

"Crick! Crack! Crick! Crack!" and the wedding garments fell to the ground, to the great confusion of the wearer.

Not that the ceremony was put off for a little thing like that! Cloaks in profusion were instantly offered to the young bride, but she was so upset that she could hardly keep from tears. One of the guests, more curious than the rest, stayed behind to examine the dress, determined, if she could, to find out the cause of the disaster.

"The thread must have been rotten," she said to herself. "I will see if I can break it." But search as she would she could find none.

The thread had vanished!

Tales From Gallia

THE STORY OF BLONDINE, BONNE-BICHE, AND BEAU-MINON

This adaptation is taken from a story collected by Comtesse de Sophie Ségur in Old French Fairy Tales, published by The Penn Publishing Company, Philadelphia, in 1920.

Blondine

THERE WAS ONCE A KING CALLED Benin. He was good and all the world loved him, for he was just and the wicked feared him. His wife, the Queen Doucette, was also good, and much beloved.

This happy pair had a daughter called the Princess Blondine, because of her superb fair hair, and she was as amiable and charming as her father the king and her mother the queen.

Unfortunately, the poor queen died a short time after the birth of Blondine and for a long time the king wept bitterly at his great loss. Blondine was too young to understand her mother's death, and she did not weep but continued to laugh, to play and to sleep peacefully. The king loved her tenderly and she loved him more than all the world. He gave his little daughter the most beautiful jewels, the finest bonbons, and the most rare and delicious fruits. Blondine was very happy.

One day it was announced to the king, that all his subjects demanded that he should marry again in order to have a son who should reign after him. He refused at first but finally yielded to the pressing desires of his people and said to his minister Leger, "My dear friend, my subjects wish me to marry again but my heart is so sad because of the death of my cherished queen Doucette that I cannot undertake the task of seeking another wife. Go, then, my good Leger and find me a princess who will make my sweet Blondine happy. Go, I ask for nothing more. When you have found a perfect woman, you will demand her hand in marriage and conduct her to my court."

Leger set off immediately, visited many courts and saw innumerable princesses, most of them ugly, humpbacked and wicked.

At last he arrived at the kingdom of the monarch Turbulent, who had a lovely daughter, bright, winning and apparently good. Leger found her so charming, that he asked her hand in marriage for his king Benin, without sufficiently inquiring into her real character.

Turbulent was enchanted at the prospect of getting rid of his daughter who was jealous, proud and wicked. Also, her presence often interfered with his excursions for pleasure, with the chase and with his various entertainments at the palace.

Without a moment's hesitation, he acceded to the Prime Minister's request, and Leger returned with the princess to the kingdom of the good king Benin.

The princess Fourbette was accompanied by four thousand mules, loaded with the jewels and wardrobe of the charming bride.

King Benin had been apprised of their approach by a courier and went forward to receive the princess Fourbette. He found her beautiful but he noted the absence of the mild and attractive expression of the poor lost Doucette.

When Fourbette's eyes fell upon Blondine her glance was so cruel, so wicked, that the poor child, who was now three years old, was greatly terrified and began to weep bitterly.

"What is the matter?" said the king. "Why does my sweet and sensible Blondine weep like a bad little girl?"

"Papa! Dear papa!" cried Blondine, throwing herself into the arms of the king, "do not give me into the hands of this princess. I am afraid of her. Her eyes are cruel!"

The king was much surprised. He turned so suddenly towards the princess Fourbette that she had no time to control herself and he perceived the terrible glance with which she regarded the little Blondine.

Benin immediately resolved that Blondine should be wholly separated from the new queen and remain as before under the exclusive protection of the nurse who had taken care of her and who loved her tenderly.

The queen thus saw Blondine rarely, and when she met her by chance she could not wholly dissimulate the hatred she felt for her.

About a year from that time a daughter was born to the queen Fourbette. She was named Brunette, because of her dark hair which was black as the raven's wing.

Brunette was pretty but not so lovely as Blondine, moreover she was as wicked as her mother. She detested Blondine and played all sorts of cruel tricks upon her, bit her, pinched her, pulled her hair, broke her toys and tore her beautiful dresses.

The good little Blondine was never in a passion with her sister but always tried to make excuses for her conduct.

"Oh, papa!" she said to the king, "do not scold Brunette. She is so little! She does not know that she grieves me when she breaks my toys! It is only in play that she bites me, pulls my hair and pinches me."

The good king embraced his little daughter, and was silent but he knew that Brunette was cruel and wicked, and that Blondine was too gentle and good to accuse her. He loved Blondine, therefore, more and more from day to day and his heart grew cold to Brunette.

The ambitious queen Fourbette saw all this clearly and hated intensely the innocent and gentle Blondine. If she had not feared the rage of the king she would have made Blondine the most wretched child in the world.

Benin had commanded that Blondine should never be left alone with the queen. He was known to be just and good but he punished disobedience severely and the queen herself dared not defy his commands.

Blondine Lost

Blondine grew to be seven years old and Brunette three.

The king had given Blondine a charming little carriage drawn by ostriches, and a little coachman ten years of age, who was the nephew of her nurse.

The little page, who was called Gourmandinet, loved Blondine tenderly. He had been her playmate from her birth and she had shown him a thousand acts of kindness.

But Gourmandinet had one terrible fault, for he was a gourmand, and was so fond of dainties and sweet things, that for a paper of bonbons he would commit almost any wicked action. Blondine often said to him, "I love you dearly, Gourmandinet, but I do not love to see you so greedy. I entreat you to correct this villainous fault which will make you despised by all the world."

Gourmandinet kissed her hand and promised to reform. But, alas, he continued to steal cakes from the kitchen and bonbons from the store-room. Often, indeed, he was whipped for his disobedience and gluttony.

The queen Fourbette heard on every hand the reproaches lavished upon the page and she was cunning enough to think that she might make use of this weakness of Gourmandinet and thus get rid of poor Blondine.

The garden in which Blondine drove in her little carriage, drawn by ostriches and guided by her little coachman, Gourmandinet, was separated by a grating from an immense and magnificent forest, called the Forest of Lilacs because during the whole year these lilacs were always covered with superb flowers.

No one, however, entered these woods. It was well known that it was enchanted ground and that if you once entered there you could never hope to escape.

Gourmandinet knew the terrible secret of this forest. He had been severely forbidden ever to drive the carriage of Blondine in that direction lest by some chance Blondine might pass the grating and place her little feet on the enchanted ground.

Many times the king Benin had sought to build a wall the entire length of the grating or to secure it in some way so as to make an entrance there impossible. But the workmen had no sooner laid the foundation than some unknown and invisible power raised the stones and they disappeared from sight.

The queen Fourbette now sought diligently to gain the friendship of Gourmandinet by giving him every day some delicious dainties. In this way she made him so complete a slave to his appetite that he could not live without the jellies, bonbons and cakes which she gave him in such profusion. At last she sent for him to come to her, and said, "Gourmandinet, it depends entirely upon yourself whether you shall have a large trunk full of bonbons and delicious dainties or never again eat one during your life."

"Never again eat one! Oh, madam, I should die of such punishment. Speak, madam, what must I do to escape this terrible fate?"

"It is necessary," said the queen, looking at him fixedly, "that you should drive the princess Blondine near to the Forest of Lilacs."

"I cannot do it, madam, the king has forbidden it."

"Ah! You cannot do it? Well, then, adieu. No more dainties for you. I shall command everyone in the house to give you nothing."

"Oh, madam!" said Gourmandinet, weeping bitterly, "Do not be so cruel. Give me some order which it is in my power to execute."

"I can only repeat that I command you to lead the princess Blondine near to the Forest of Lilacs, and that you encourage her to descend from the carriage, to cross the grating and enter the enchanted ground."

"But, madam," replied Gourmandinet, turning very pale, "if the princess enters this forest she can never escape from it. You know the penalty of entering upon enchanted ground. To send my dear princess there is to give her up to certain death."

"For the third and last time," said the queen, frowning fearfully, "I ask if you will take the princess to the forest? Choose! Either you'll receive an immense box of bonbons, which I will renew every month, or never again will you taste the delicacies which you love."

"But how shall I escape from the dreadful punishment which his majesty will inflict upon me?"

"Do not be disquieted on that account. As soon as you have induced Blondine to enter the Forest of Lilacs, return to me. I will send you off out of danger with your bonbons, and I charge myself with your future fortune."

"Oh, madam, have pity upon me. Do not compel me to lead my dear princess to destruction. She who has always been so good to me!"

"You still hesitate, miserable coward! Of what importance is the fate of Blondine to you? When you have obeyed my commands I will see that you enter the service of Brunette and I declare to you solemnly that the bonbons shall never fail."

Gourmandinet hesitated and reflected a few moments longer and, alas, at last resolved to sacrifice his good little mistress to his gluttony.

The remainder of that day he still hesitated and he lay awake all night weeping bitter tears as he endeavoured to discover some way to escape from the power of the wicked queen, but the certainty of the queen's bitter revenge if he refused to execute her cruel orders, and the hope of rescuing Blondine at some future day by seeking the aid of some powerful fairy, conquered his irresolution and decided him to obey the queen.

In the morning at ten o'clock Blondine ordered her little carriage and entered it for a drive, after having embraced the king her father and promised him to return in two hours.

The garden was immense. Gourmandinet, on starting, turned the ostriches away from the Forest of Lilacs. When, however, they were entirely out of sight of the palace, he changed his course and turned towards the grating which separated them from the enchanted ground. He was sad and silent. His crime weighed upon his heart and conscience.

"What is the matter?" said Blondine, kindly. "You say nothing Are you ill, Gourmandinet?"

"No, my princess, I am well."

"But how pale you are! Tell me what distresses you, poor boy, and I promise to do all in my power to make you happy."

Blondine's kind inquiries and attentions almost softened the hard heart of Gourmandinet, but the remembrance of the bonbons promised by the wicked queen, Fourbette, soon chased away his good resolutions. Before he had time to reply, the ostriches reached the grating of the Forest of Lilacs.

"Oh! the beautiful lilacs!" exclaimed Blondine, "how fragrant, how delicious! I must have a bouquet of those beautiful flowers for my good papa. Get down, Gourmandinet and bring me some of those superb branches."

"I cannot leave my seat, princess, the ostriches might run away with you during my absence."

"Do not fear," replied Blondine, "I could guide them myself to the palace."

"But the king would give me a terrible scolding for having abandoned you, princess. It is best that you go yourself and gather your flowers."

"That is true. I should be very sorry to get you a scolding, my poor Gourmandinet."

While saying these words she sprang lightly from the carriage, crossed the bars of the grating and commenced to gather the flowers.

At this moment Gourmandinet shuddered and was overwhelmed with remorse. He wished to repair his fault by calling Blondine but although she was only ten steps from him, although he saw her perfectly, she could not hear his voice, and in a short time she was lost to view in the enchanted forest.

For a long time Gourmandinet wept over his crime, cursed his gluttony and despised the wicked queen Fourbette.

At last he recalled to himself that the hour approached at which Blondine would be expected at the palace. He returned to the stables through the back entrance and ran at once to the queen, who was anxiously expecting him.

On seeing him so deadly pale and his eyes inflamed from the tears of awful remorse, she knew that Blondine had perished.

"Is it done?" said she.

Gourmandinet bowed his head. He had not the strength to speak.

"Come," said she, "behold your reward!"

She pointed to a large box full of delicious bonbons of every variety. She commanded a valet to raise the box and place it upon one of the mules which had brought her jewellery.

"I confide this box to Gourmandinet, in order that he may take it to my father," she said. "Go, boy, and return in a month for another." She placed in his hand at the same time a purse full of gold.

Gourmandinet mounted the mule in perfect silence and set off in full gallop. The mule was obstinate and wilful and soon grew restive under the weight of the box and began to prance and kick. He did this so effectually that he threw Gourmandinet and his precious box of bonbons upon the ground.

Gourmandinet, who had never ridden upon a horse or mule, fell heavily with his head upon the stones and died instantly.

Thus he did not receive from his crime the profit which he had hoped, for he had not even tasted of the bonbons which the queen had given him.

No one regretted him. No one but the poor Blondine had ever loved him.

The Forest of Lilacs

When Blondine entered the forest she commenced gathering the beautiful branches of lilacs. She rejoiced in their profusion and delighted in their fragrance.

As she made her selection, it seemed to her that those which were more distant were still more beautiful so she emptied her apron and her hat, which were both full and filled them again and again.

Blondine had been thus busily occupied for about an hour. She began to suffer from the heat and to feel great fatigue. She found the branches of lilacs heavy to carry and thought it was time to return to the palace. She looked around and saw herself surrounded with lilacs. She called Gourmandinet but no one replied.

"I have wandered further than I intended," said Blondine. "I will return at once, though I am very weary. Gourmandinet will hear me and will surely come to meet me."

Blondine walked on rapidly for some time but she could not find the boundaries of the forest.

Many times she called anxiously upon Gourmandinet but he did not respond and at last she became terribly frightened.

"What will become of me, all alone in this vast forest? What will my poor papa think when I do not return? And Gourmandinet, how will he dare go back to the palace without me? He will be scolded, perhaps beaten and all this is my fault because I would leave my carriage to gather lilacs?

Unfortunate girl that I am! I shall die of hunger and thirst in this forest if the wolves do not eat me up this night."

Weeping bitterly, Blondine fell on the ground at the foot of a large tree. She wept a long time. At last her great fatigue mastered her grief. She placed her little head upon her bundle of lilacs, and slept peacefully.

Blondine's Awakening & Beau-Minon

Blondine slept calmly all night. No ferocious beast came to trouble her slumbers. She did not suffer from the cold and awakened at a late hour in the morning. She rubbed her eyes, much surprised to see herself surrounded by trees, in place of being in her own room in the palace, and upon her own bed.

She called her nurse and a soft mewing was the only response. Astonished and almost frightened, she looked around and saw at her feet a superb white cat, looking gently upon her and continuing to mew plaintively.

"Ah! Pretty puss! How beautiful you are!" cried Blondine, placing her little hand caressingly upon the soft fur, white as snow. "I am so happy to see you, pretty puss, for you will conduct me to your home. I am indeed very hungry and I have not the strength to walk much further without food."

Blondine had scarcely uttered these words, when the white pussy mewed again and pointed with her little paw to a small package lying near her, wrapped neatly in fine white linen. She opened the parcel and found it contained bread and butter which she found delicious. She gave the crumbs to pussy, who munched them with seeming delight.

When they had finished their simple meal, Blondine leaned over towards her little companion, and said, caressingly, "Thanks, pretty puss, for the breakfast you have given me. Now, can you conduct me to my papa, who is certainly in despair because of my absence?"

Pussy, whom Blondine named Beau-Minon, shook her head and mewed plaintively.

"Ah! You understand me, Beau-Minon," said Blondine. "I entreat you to have pity upon me and lead me to some house before I perish with hunger, cold and terror in this vast forest!"

Beau-Minon looked at the princess fixedly and made a sign with her little graceful white head which seemed to say, "I understand you." She rose, advanced a few steps and paused to see if Blondine followed her.

"I am here, Beau-Minon, I am following you gladly," said Blondine, "but how can we pass through these bushy thickets? I see no path."

Beau-Minon made no reply but sprang lightly into the thicket which opened of itself to allow Blondine and Beau-Minon to pass, and then closed up immediately.

Blondine walked on for about half an hour. As she advanced, the forest became lighter, the grass was finer and the flowers more abundant. She saw many pretty birds singing melodiously and graceful squirrels, bounding along the branches of the trees.

Blondine, who had no doubt that she was about to leave the forest and see her dear father again, was enchanted with all that she saw. She wished to pause and gather the lovely wild flowers, but Beau-Minon advanced steadily and mewed plaintively whenever Blondine relaxed her speed.

In about an hour Blondine perceived an elegant castle. Beau-Minon led her to the gilded grating. However, Blondine did not know how to enter. There was no bell and the gate was closed. Beau-Minon had disappeared and Blondine was once more alone.

Bonne-Biche

Beau-Minon had entered by a little passage, which seemed made expressly for him and had probably given notice to someone at the castle, as the gate opened without Blondine having called. She entered the court-yard but saw no one.

The door of the castle opened of itself. Blondine entered the vestibule which was of rare white marble. All the doors of the castle now opened like the first and the princess passed through a suite of beautiful rooms.

At last, in the back part of a charming salon, furnished with blue and gold, she perceived a white hind, lying upon a bed of fine and fragrant grasses. Beau-Minon stood near her. The pretty hind saw Blondine, arose, and approached her.

"You are most welcome, Blondine," said she. "My son Beau-Minon and I have expected you for a long time."

At these words, Blondine was much frightened.

"Take courage, princess, you are with friends. I know the king your father and I love him and I love you also."

"Oh, madam," said Blondine, "if you know the king my father, I pray you to take me to him. My absence must make him very wretched."

"My dear Blondine," said the hind, whose name was Bonne-Biche, sighing, "it is not in my power to conduct you to your father. You are in the hands of the magician of the Forest of Lilacs. I myself am subject to his power which is superior to mine but I can send soft dreams to your father, which will reassure him as to your fate and let him know that you are safe with me."

"Oh, madam!" said Blondine, in an agony of grief, "shall I never again see my father whom I love so tenderly? My poor father!"

"Dear Blondine, do not distress yourself as to the future. Wisdom and prudence are always recompensed. You will see your father again but not now. In the meantime be good and docile. Beau-Minon and I will do all in our power to make you happy."

Blondine sighed heavily and shed a few tears. She then reflected that to manifest such grief was a poor recompense for all the goodness of Bonne-Biche. She resolved, therefore, to control herself and to be cheerful.

Bonne-Biche took her to see the apartment they had prepared for her. The bedroom was hung with rose-coloured silk embroidered with gold. The furniture was covered with white velvet worked with silks of the most brilliant hues. Every species of animal, bird and butterfly were represented in rare embroidery.

Adjoining Blondine's chamber was a small study. It was hung with sky-blue damask and embroidered with fine pearls. The furniture was covered with silver moiré and adorned with nails of turquoise. Two magnificent portraits, representing a young and superbly handsome woman and a strikingly attractive young man, hung on the walls. Their costumes indicated that they were of royal race.

"Whose portraits are these, madam?" said Blondine to Bonne-Biche.

"I am forbidden to answer that question, dear Blondine. You will know later, but this is the hour for dinner. Come, Blondine, I am sure you are hungry."

Blondine was in fact almost dying of hunger. She followed Bonne-Biche and they entered the dining-room where she saw a table strangely served.

An enormous cushion of black satin was placed on the floor for Bonne-Biche. On the table before her was a vase filled with the choicest herbs, fresh and nutritious and near this vase was a golden bucket, filled with fresh and limpid water.

Opposite Bonne-Biche was a little stool for Beau-Minon while before him was a little porringer in gold, filled with little fried fish and the thighs of snipes. At one side was a bowl of rich crystal full of fresh milk.

Between Beau-Minon and Bonne-Biche a plate was placed for Blondine. Her chair was of carved ivory covered with crimson velvet attached with nails of diamonds. Before her was a gold plate richly chased, filled with delicious soup made of a young pullet and fig-birds, her glass and water-bottle were of carved rock-crystal, a muffin was placed by her side, her fork and spoon were of gold and her napkin was of linen, finer than anything she had ever seen.

The table was served by gazelles who were marvellously adroit. They waited, carved and even divined the wishes of Blondine, Bonne-Biche and Beau-Minon. The dinner was exquisite. The chicken was splendid, the game and fish most delicate, and the pastry and bonbons superlative. Blondine was hungry so she ate of all and found all excellent.

After dinner, Bonne-Biche and Beau-Minon conducted the princess into the garden. She found there the most delicious fruits and lovely walks.

After a charming walk, Blondine entered the castle with her new friends, much fatigued. Bonne-Biche proposed that she retire, to which she agreed joyfully.

Blondine entered her chamber and found two gazelles waiting to attend her. They disrobed her with grace and adroitness, placed her in bed and seated themselves by her couch to watch over her.

Blondine was soon peacefully asleep, but not, however, without having first thought of her father and wept bitterly over her cruel separation from him.

Blondine's Second Awakening

Blondine slept profoundly, and on awaking she found herself entirely changed. Indeed, it seemed to her she could not be the same person. She was much taller, her intellect was developed, her knowledge enlarged. She remembered a number of books she thought she had read during her sleep. She was sure she had been writing, drawing, singing and playing on the piano and harp.

She looked around, however, and knew that the chamber was the same to which Bonne-Biche had conducted her and in which she had gone to sleep.

Agitated, disquieted, she rose and ran to the glass. She saw that she was much grown and she found herself charming, a hundred times more beautiful than when she retired the night before. Her fair ringlets fell to her feet, her complexion was like the lily and the rose, her eyes celestial blue, her nose beautifully formed, her cheeks rosy as the morn, and her form was erect and graceful. In short, Blondine thought herself the most beautiful person she had ever seen.

Trembling, almost frightened, she dressed herself hastily and ran to seek Bonne-Biche whom she found in the apartment where she had first seen her.

"Bonne-Biche, Bonne-Biche!" she exclaimed, "I entreat you to explain to me the change which I see and feel in myself. Last night I went to sleep a child. I awoke this morning, and found myself a young lady. Is this an illusion or have I indeed grown and developed thus during the night?"

"Yes, my dear Blondine, you are fourteen years old today. But you have slept peacefully seven years. My son Beau-Minon and I wished to spare you the weariness of all early studies. When you first entered the castle you knew nothing, not even how to read. I put you to sleep for seven years, and Beau-Minon and I have passed this time in instructing you during your sleep. I see by the wonder expressed in your eyes, sweet princess, that you doubt all this. Come into your study and reassure yourself on this point."

Blondine followed Bonne-Biche to the little room. She ran first to the piano, commenced playing and found that she played remarkably well. She then tried the harp and drew from it the most ravishing sounds, and she sang enchantingly.

She took her pencil and brushes and drew and painted with a facility which denoted a true talent. She wrote and found her handwriting clear and elegant. She looked at the countless books which were ranged round the room and knew that she had read them all.

Surprised, delighted, she threw her arms around the neck of Bonne-Biche, embraced Beau-Minon tenderly and said to them, "Oh! my dear true good friends, what a debt of gratitude do I owe you for having thus watched over my childhood and developed my intellect and my heart. I feel how much I am improved in every respect and I owe it all to you."

Bonne-Biche returned her caresses and Beau-Minon patted her hand delicately. After the first few happy moments had passed, Blondine cast down her eyes and said timidly, "Do not think me ungrateful, my dear good friends, if I wish you to add one more to the benefits you have already conferred upon me. Tell me something of my father. Does he still weep my absence? Is he happy since he lost me?"

"Dear Blondine, your anxiety on this point is most natural and shall be relieved. Look in this mirror, Blondine, and you shall see the king your father and all that has passed since you left the palace."

Blondine raised her eyes to the mirror and looked into the apartment of her father. The king seemed much agitated and was walking backwards and forwards. He appeared to be expecting someone. The queen, Fourbette, entered and related to him that notwithstanding the remonstrances of Gourmandinet, Blondine had herself seized the reins and guided the ostriches who becoming frightened dashed off in the direction of the Forest of Lilacs and overturned the carriage. Blondine was thrown over the grating which bounded the forest. She stated that Gourmandinet had become insane from terror and grief and she had sent him home to his parents.

The king was in wild despair at this news. He ran to the Forest of Lilacs and he had to be withheld by force from throwing himself across the boundary in order to search for his cherished Blondine. They carried him to the palace where he yielded to the most frightful sorrow and despair, calling unceasingly upon his dear Blondine, his beloved child. At last, overcome by grief, he slept and saw in a dream Blondine in the castle of Bonne-Biche and Beau-Minon. Bonne-Biche gave him the sweet assurance that Blondine should one day be restored to him and that her childhood should be calm and happy.

The mirror now became misty and everything disappeared. Then again it became clear as crystal and Blondine saw her father a second time. He had become old. His hair was white as snow and his countenance was sad. He held in his hand a little portrait of Blondine. His tears fell upon it and he pressed it often to his lips. The king was alone. Blondine saw neither the Queen nor Brunette.

Poor Blondine wept bitterly. "Alas!" said she, "why is my dear father alone? Where is the queen? Where is Brunette?"

"The queen," said Bonne-Biche, "showed so little grief at your death, my princess, that your father's heart was filled with hatred and suspicion towards her and he sent her back to the king Turbulent, her father, who confined her in a tower, where she soon died of rage and anger. All the world supposed you to be dead. As to your sister Brunette, she became so wicked, so insupportable, that the king hastened to give her in marriage last year to the prince Violent, who charged himself with the duty of reforming the character of the cruel and envious princess Brunette. The prince was stern and harsh. Brunette saw that her wicked heart prevented her from being happy and she commenced trying to correct her faults. You will see her again someday, dear Blondine and your example may complete her reformation."

Blondine thanked Bonne-Biche tenderly for all these details. Her heart prompted her to ask, "But when shall I see my father and sister?" But she feared to appear ungrateful and too anxious to leave the castle of her good friends. She resolved then to await another more suitable opportunity to ask this question.

The days passed away quietly and pleasantly. Blondine was much occupied, but was sometimes melancholy. She had no one to talk with but Bonne-Biche and she was only with her during the hours of lessons and repasts. Beau-Minon could not converse and could only make himself understood by signs. The gazelles served Blondine with zeal and intelligence but they had not the gift of speech.

Blondine walked every day, always accompanied by Beau-Minon, who pointed out to her the most lovely and sequestered paths and the rarest and richest flowers.

Bonne-Biche had made Blondine promise solemnly never to leave the enclosure of the park and never to enter the forest. Many times Blondine had asked Bonne-Biche the reason of this prohibition. Sighing profoundly, she had replied, "Ah, Blondine! Do not seek to penetrate the forest. It is a fatal spot. May you never enter there."

Sometimes Blondine mounted a pavilion which was built on an eminence near the boundary of the forest. She looked admiringly and longingly at the magnificent trees, the lovely and fragrant flowers, the thousand graceful birds flying and singing and seeming to call her name.

"Alas!" said she, "why will not Bonne-Biche allow me to walk in this beautiful forest? What possible danger can I encounter in that lovely place and under her protection?"

Whenever she was lost in these reflections, Beau-Minon, who seemed to comprehend what was passing in her heart, mewed plaintively, pulled her robe and tried to draw her from the pavilion. Blondine smiled sweetly, followed her gentle companion and recommenced her walk in the solitary park.

The Parrot

Six months had passed since Blondine awaked from her seven years' sleep. It seemed to the little princess a long time. The remembrance of her dear father often saddened her heart.

Bonne-Biche and Beau-Minon seemed to divine her thoughts. Beau-Minon mewed plaintively, and Bonne-Biche heaved the most profound sighs. Blondine spoke but rarely of that which occupied her thoughts continually. She feared to offend Bonne-Biche, who had said to her three or four times, "Dear Blondine, be patient. You will see your father when you are fifteen, if you continue wise and good. Trust me, dear child, do not trouble yourself about the future and above all do not seek to leave us."

One morning Blondine was alone and very sad. She was musing upon her singular and monotonous existence. Suddenly she was disturbed in her reverie by three soft little strokes upon her window. Raising her head, she perceived a parrot with beautiful green plumage and throat and breast of bright orange.

Surprised at the appearance of a bird entirely unknown to her, she opened the window and invited the parrot to enter.

What was her amazement when the bird said to her, in a fine sharp voice, "Good day, Blondine! I know that you sometimes have a very tedious time of it, because you have no one to talk to. I have taken pity upon you and come to have a chat with you. But I pray you do not mention that you have seen me, for Bonne-Biche would cut my throat if she knew it."

"Why so, beautiful Parrot? Bonne-Biche is good, she injures no one and only hates the wicked."

"Blondine, listen! If you do not promise to conceal my visit from Bonne-Biche and Beau-Minon, I will fly away at once and never return."

"Since you wish it so much, beautiful Parrot, I will promise silence. Let us chat a little. It is a long time since I have had an opportunity to converse. You seem to me gay and witty. I do not doubt that you will amuse me much."

Blondine listened with delight to the lively talk of the Parrot, who complimented extravagantly her beauty, her wit and her talents.

Blondine was enchanted. In about an hour the Parrot flew away, promising to return the next day. In short, he returned every day and continued to compliment and amuse her.

One morning he struck upon the window and said, "Blondine! Blondine! Open the window, quickly! I bring you news of your father. But above all make no noise unless you want my throat cut."

Blondine was overwhelmed with joy. She opened the window with alacrity and said, "Is it true, my beautiful Parrot, that you bring me news of my dear father? Speak quickly! What is he doing and how is he?"

"Your father is well, Blondine, but he weeps your loss always. I have promised him to employ all my power to deliver you from your prison but I can do nothing without your assistance."

"My prison!" said Blondine. "But you are ignorant of all the goodness which Bonne-Biche and Beau-Minon have shown me, of the pains they have lavished upon my education, of all their tenderness and forbearance. They will be enchanted to find a way of restoring me to my father. Come with me, beautiful Parrot and I will present you to Bonne-Biche. Come, I entreat you."

"Ah! Blondine," said the sharp voice of the Parrot, "it is you, Princess, who do not know Bonne-Biche and Beau-Minon. They detest me because I have sometimes succeeded in rescuing their victims from them. You will never see your father again, Blondine, you will never leave this forest, unless you yourself shall break the charm which holds you here."

"What charm?" said Blondine. "I know of no charm and what interest have Bonne-Biche and Beau-Minon in keeping me a prisoner?"

"Is it not to their interest to enliven their solitude, Blondine? There is a talisman which can procure your release. It is a simple Rose, which, gathered by yourself, will deliver you from your exile and restore you to the arms of your fond father."

"But there is not a single Rose in the garden. How then can I gather one?"

"I will explain this to you another day, Blondine. Now I can tell you no more, as I hear Bonne-Biche coming. But to convince you of the virtues of the Rose, entreat Bonne-Biche to give you one and see what she will say. Tomorrow, tomorrow, Blondine!"

The Parrot flew away, well content to have scattered in Blondine's heart the first seeds of discontent and ingratitude.

The Parrot had scarcely disappeared when Bonne-Biche entered. She appeared greatly agitated.

"With whom have you been talking, Blondine?" looking suspiciously towards the open window.

"With no one, madam," said the princess.

"I am certain I heard voices in conversation."

"I must have been speaking to myself."

Bonne-Biche made no reply. She was very sad and tears fell from her eyes.

Blondine was also engaged in thought. The cunning words of the Parrot made her look upon the kindness of Bonne-Biche and Beau-Minon in a totally different light.

In place of saying to herself that a hind which had the power to speak, to make wild beasts intelligent, to put an infant to sleep for seven years, to dedicate seven years to a tiresome and ignorant little girl, in short, a hind lodged and served like a queen, could be no ordinary criminal, in place of cherishing a sentiment of gratitude for all that Bonne-Biche had done for her. Blondine, alas, now believed blindly in the Parrot, the unknown bird of whose character and veracity she had no proof. She did not remember that the Parrot could have no possible motive for risking its life to render her a service. Blondine believed it though, implicitly, because of the flattery which the Parrot had lavished upon her. She did not even recall with gratitude the sweet and happy existence which Bonne-Biche and Beau-Minon had secured to her. She resolved to follow implicitly the counsels of the Parrot. During the course of the day she said to Bonne-Biche, "Why, madam, do I not see among your flowers the most lovely and charming of all flowers, the fragrant Rose?"

Bonne-Biche was greatly agitated and said in a trembling voice, "Blondine! Blondine! Do not ask for this most perfidious flower, which pierces all who touch it! Never speak to me of the Rose, Blondine. You cannot know what fatal danger this flower contains for you!"

The expression of Bonne-Biche was so stern and severe that Blondine dared not question her further.

The day passed away sadly enough. Bonne-Biche was unhappy and Beau-Minon very sad.

Early in the morning, Blondine ran to her window and the Parrot entered the moment she opened it.

"Well, my dear Blondine, did you notice the agitation of Bonne-Biche, when you mentioned the Rose? I promised you to point out the means by which you could obtain one of these charming flowers. Listen now to my counsel. You will leave this park and enter the forest. I will accompany you and I will conduct you to a garden where you will find the most beautiful Rose in the world!"

"But how is it possible for me to leave the park? Beau-Minon always accompanies me in my walks."

"Try to get rid of him," said the Parrot, "but if that is impossible, go in spite of him."

"If this Rose is at a distance, will not my absence be perceived?"

"It is about an hour's walk. Bonne-Biche has been careful to separate you as far as possible from the Rose in order that you might not find the means to escape from her power."

"But why does she wish to hold me captive? She is all-powerful and could surely find pleasures more acceptable than educating an ignorant child."

"All this will be explained to you in the future, Blondine, when you will be in the arms of your father. Be firm! After breakfast, in some way get away from Beau-Minon and enter the forest. I will expect you there."

Blondine promised, and closed the window, fearing that Bonne-Biche would surprise her.

After breakfast, according to her usual custom, she entered the garden. Beau-Minon followed her in spite of some rude rebuffs which he received with plaintive mews. Arrived at the alley which led out of the park, Blondine resolved to get rid of Beau-Minon.

"I wish to be alone," said she, sternly, "begone, Beau-Minon!"

Beau-Minon pretended not to understand. Blondine was impatient and enraged. She forgot herself so far as to strike Beau-Minon with her foot. When poor Beau-Minon received this humiliating blow, he uttered a cry of anguish and fled towards the palace. Blondine trembled and was on the point of recalling him, when a false shame arrested her. She walked on rapidly to the gate, opened it not without trembling and entered the forest. The Parrot joined her without delay.

"Courage, Blondine! In one hour you will have the Rose and will see your father, who weeps for you."

At these words, Blondine recovered her resolution which had begun to falter. She walked on in the path indicated by the Parrot, who flew before her from branch to branch. The forest, which had seemed so beautiful and attractive near the park of Bonne-Biche, became wilder and more entangled. Brambles and stones almost filled up the path, the sweet songs of the birds were no longer heard and the flowers had entirely disappeared. Blondine felt oppressed by an inexplicable restlessness. The Parrot pressed her eagerly to advance.

"Quick, quick, Blondine! time flies! If Bonne-Biche perceives your absence you will never again see your father."

Blondine, fatigued, almost breathless, with her arms torn by the briers and her shoes in shreds, now declared that she would go no further when the Parrot exclaimed, "We have arrived, Blondine. Look! That is the enclosure which separates us from the Rose."

Blondine saw at a turn in the path a small enclosure, the gate of which was quickly opened by the Parrot. The soil was arid and stony but a magnificent, majestic rose-bush adorned with one Rose, which was more beautiful than all the roses of the world grew in the midst of this sterile spot.

"Take it, Blondine!" said the parrot, "you deserve it. You have truly earned it!"

Blondine seized the branch eagerly and in spite of the thorns which pierced her fingers cruelly, she tore it from the bush.

The Rose was scarcely grasped firmly in her hand, when she heard a burst of mocking laughter. The Flower fell from her grasp, crying, "Thanks, Blondine, for having delivered me from the prison in which Bonne-Biche held me captive. I am your evil jinni! Now you belong to me!"

"Ha ha!" now exclaimed the Parrot. "Thanks, Blondine! I can now resume my form of magician. You have destroyed your friends for I am their mortal enemy!"

Saying these cruel words, the Parrot and the Rose disappeared, leaving Blondine alone in the forest.

Repentance

Blondine was stupefied! Her conduct now appeared to her in all its horror. She had shown a monstrous ingratitude towards the friends who had been so tenderly devoted to her, and who had dedicated seven years to the care of her education. Would these kind friends ever receive her, ever pardon her? What would be her fate, if they should close their doors against her? And then, what did those awful words of the wicked Parrot signify, "You have caused the destruction of your friends"?

Blondine turned round and wished to retrace her steps to the castle of Bonne-Biche. The briers and thorns tore her arms and face terribly. She continued however to force her way bravely through the thickets and after three hours of most painful walking she came before the castle of Bonne-Biche and Beau-Minon.

Horror seized upon her, when in place of the superb building she saw only an appalling ruin. In place of the magnificent trees and rare flowers which surrounded it, only briers and thorns, nettles and thistles, could be seen. Terrified and most desolate, she tried to force her way in the midst of the ruins, to seek some knowledge of her kind friends. A large Toad issued from a pile of stones, advanced before her, and said, "What are you seeking? Have you not occasioned the death of your friends by the basest ingratitude? Begone! Do not insult their memory by your unwelcome presence!"

"Alas! Alas!" cried Blondine, "My poor friends, Bonne-Biche and Beau-Minon, why can I not atone by my death for the sufferings I have caused them?" And she fell, sobbing piteously, upon the stones and nettles. Her grief and her repentance were so excessive that she did not feel their sharp points in her tender flesh. She wept profusely a long time. At last she arose and looked about her, hoping to find some shelter where she might take refuge. Ruin only stared her in the face.

"Well," said she, "let the wild beasts tear me to pieces. Let me die of hunger and thirst, if I can expiate my sins here upon the tomb of Bonne-Biche and Beau-Minon!"

As she uttered these words, she heard a soft voice saying, "True repentance can atone for the worst of crimes."

She raised her head and saw only an immense black Crow flying above her.

"Alas! Alas!" said Blondine, "My repentance, however true, however bitter it may be, can never give me back the lives of my dear Bonne-Biche and Beau-Minon!"

"Courage, courage, Blondine! Redeem your fault by your repentance and do not allow yourself to be utterly cast down by grief."

The poor princess arose and left the scene of desolation. She followed a little path, where the large trees seemed to have rooted out the brambles and the earth was covered with moss. She was utterly exhausted with grief and fatigue and fell at the foot of a large tree, sobbing piteously.

"Courage, Blondine!" said another voice, "Courage and hope!"

She saw near her only a Frog, which was looking at her compassionately.

"Oh, Frog!" said the princess, "You seem to pity my anguish! What will become of me now that I am alone and desolate in the world?"

"Courage and hope!" was the reply.

Blondine sighed deeply and looked around, hoping to discover some herb or fruit to appease her hunger and thirst. She saw nothing and her tears flowed freely. The sound of bells now somewhat dissipated her despairing thoughts. She saw a beautiful cow approaching her, gently and slowly. On arriving near her, the cow paused, bowed down, and showed her a silver porringer attached to her neck by a chain of beaten gold.

Blondine was very grateful for this unexpected succour. She detached the porringer, milked the cow and drank the sweet milk with delight. The pretty, gentle cow signed to her to replace the porringer. Blondine obeyed, kissed her on the neck and said, sadly, "Thanks, Blanchette, it is without doubt to my poor friends that I owe this sweet charity. Perhaps in another and better world they can see the repentance of their poor Blondine and wish to assist her in her frightful position."

"A true repentance will obtain pardon for all faults," said a kind voice.

"Ah!" exclaimed Blondine, "Years of sorrow and weeping for my crimes would not suffice! I can never pardon myself!"

In the meantime, night approached. Notwithstanding her anguish and repentance, Blondine began to reflect upon some means of securing herself from the ferocious wild beasts, whose terrible roars she already believed she heard in the distance. She saw some steps before her a kind of hut, formed by several trees growing near together and interlacing their branches. Bowing her head, she entered, and found that by carefully connecting some branches she could form a pretty and secure retreat. She employed the remainder of the day in arranging this little room and gathered a quantity of moss, with which she made herself a bed and pillow. She concealed the entrance to this little retreat by some broken branches and leaves and went to rest, utterly worn out with regret and fatigue.

When Blondine awoke it was broad daylight. At first she could scarcely collect her thoughts and understand her position but the sad realities of her lot were soon apparent to her and she commenced weeping as before.

Blondine was hungry, and she could not imagine how she was to secure food but soon she heard again the sound of the cow-bells. In a few moments, Blanchette stood near her. Blondine again loosened the porringer, drew the milk and drank till her hunger was appeased, then replaced the porringer and kissed Blanchette, hoping to see her again during the day. Every day, in the morning, at midday and in the evening, Blanchette came to offer Blondine her frugal repast.

Blondine passed the time in tears for her poor friends, and bitter self-reproach for her crimes.

"By my unpardonable disobedience," she said to herself, "I have caused the most terrible misfortunes, which it is not in my power to repair. I have not only lost my good and true friends but I am deprived of the only means of finding my father, my poor father, who perhaps still expects his Blondine, his most unhappy Blondine, condemned to live and die alone in this frightful forest where her evil jinni reigns supreme."

Blondine sought to amuse and employ herself in every possible way. Her little home was neatly arranged, and fresh moss and leaves composed her simple couch. She had tied some branches together and formed a seat and she made herself some needles and pins of the thorns and twisted some thread from the hemp which grew near her little hut, and with these implements she had mended the rents in her shoes.

In this simple way Blondine lived for six months. Her grief was always the same and it is just to say that it was not her sad and solitary life which made her unhappy but sincere regret for her fault. She would willingly have consented to pass her life in the forest if she could thus have brought to life Bonne-Biche and Beau-Minon.

The Tortoise

One day Blondine was seated at the entrance of her hut, musing sadly as usual, thinking of her lost friends and of her father, when she saw before her an enormous Tortoise.

"Blondine," said the Tortoise, "if you will place yourself under my protection, I will conduct you out of this forest."

"And why, Madam Tortoise, should I seek to leave this forest? Here I caused the death of my friends and here I wish to die."

"Are you very certain of their death, Blondine?"

"What do you mean? Is it possible I may be deceived? But, no, I saw the ruins of their castle. The Parrot and the Toad assured me of their death. You are kind and good and wish to console me without doubt but, alas, I do not hope to see them again. If they still lived they would not have left me alone with the frightful despair of having caused their death."

"But how do you know, Blondine, that this seeming neglect is not forced upon them? They may now be subjected to a power greater than their own. You know, Blondine, that a true repentance will obtain pardon for many crimes."

"Ah! Madam Tortoise, if they still live, if you can give me news of them, if you can assure me that I need no longer reproach myself with their death, assure me that I shall one day see them again, there is no price which I will not gladly pay to merit this great happiness."

"Blondine, I am not permitted to disclose to you the fate of your friends but if you have the courage to mount on my back, remain there for six months and not address a single question to me during the journey, I will conduct you to a place where all will be revealed."

"I promise all that you ask, Madam Tortoise, provided I can only learn what has become of my friends."

"Take care, Blondine! Reflect well. Six months without descending from my back and without asking me a single question! When once you have accepted the conditions, when we have commenced our journey, if you have not the courage to endure to the end, you will remain eternally in the power of the enchanter, Perroquet, and his sister Rose and I cannot even continue to bestow upon you the little assistance to which you owe your life during the last six months."

"Let us go, Madam Tortoise, let us be off immediately. I prefer to die of hunger and fatigue rather than of grief and uncertainty. Your words have brought hope to my poor heart, and I have courage to undertake even a more difficult journey than that of which you speak."

"Let it be according to your wish, Blondine. Mount my back. Fear neither hunger nor thirst nor cold nor sunshine nor any accident during our long journey. As long as it lasts you shall not suffer from any inconvenience."

Blondine mounted on the back of the Tortoise. "Now, silence!" said she, "And not one word till we have arrived and I speak to you first."

The Journey And Arrival

The journey of Blondine lasted, as the Tortoise had said, six months. They were three months passing through the forest. At the end of that time she found herself on an arid plain which it required six weeks to cross. Then Blondine perceived a castle which reminded her of that of Bonne-Biche and Beau-Minon. They were a full month passing through the avenue to this castle.

Blondine burned with impatience. Would she indeed learn the fate of her dear friends at the palace? In spite of her extreme anxiety, she dared not ask a single question. If she could have descended from the back of the Tortoise, ten minutes would have sufficed for her to reach the castle. But the Tortoise crept on slowly and Blondine remembered that she had been forbidden to alight or to utter a word. She resolved, therefore, to control her impatience. The Tortoise seemed rather to relax than to increase her speed. She consumed fourteen days still in passing through this avenue. They seemed fourteen centuries to Blondine. She never, however, lost sight of the castle or of the door. The place seemed deserted, she heard no noise, she saw no sign of life.

At last, after twenty-four days' journey, the Tortoise paused, and said to Blondine, "Now, princess, descend. By your courage and obedience you have earned the recompense I promised. Enter the little door which you see before you. The first person you will meet will be the fairy Bienveillante and she will make known to you the fate of your friends."

Blondine sprang lightly to the earth. She had been immovable so long she feared her limbs would be cramped but on the contrary she was as light and active as when she had lived so happily with her dear Bonne-Biche and Beau-Minon and ran joyously and gracefully gathering flowers and chasing butterflies.

After having thanked the Tortoise most warmly she opened the door which had been pointed out to her and found herself before a young person clothed in white, who asked in a sweet voice, whom she desired to see?

"I wish to see the fairy Bienveillante. Tell her, I pray you, miss, that the princess Blondine begs earnestly to see her without delay."

"Follow me, princess", replied the young girl.

Blondine followed in great agitation. She passed through several beautiful rooms and met many young girls clothed in white, like her guide. They looked at her as if they recognized her and smiled graciously.

At last Blondine arrived in a room in every respect resembling that of Bonne-Biche in the Forest of Lilacs. The remembrances which this recalled were so painful that she did not perceive the disappearance of her fair young guide.

Blondine gazed sadly at the furniture of the room. She saw but one piece which had not adorned the apartment of Bonne-Biche in the Forest of Lilacs. This was a wardrobe in gold and ivory, exquisitely carved. It was closed. Blondine felt herself drawn towards it in an inexplicable manner. She was gazing at it intently, not having indeed the power to turn her eyes away, when a door opened and a young and beautiful woman, magnificently dressed, entered and drew near Blondine.

"What do you wish, my child?" said she, in a sweet, caressing voice.

"Oh, madam!" said Blondine, throwing herself at her feet, "I have been assured that you could give me news of my dear, kind friends, Bonne-Biche and Beau-Minon. You know, madam, without doubt by what heedless disobedience I gave them up to destruction and that I wept for them a long time, believing them to be dead, but the Tortoise, who conducted me here, has given me reason to hope I may one day see them again. Tell me, madam, tell me if they yet live and if I may dare hope for the happiness of rejoining them?"

"Blondine", replied the fairy Bienveillante, sadly, "you are now about to know the fate of your friends, but no matter what you see or hear, do not lose courage or hope."

Saying these words, she seized the trembling Blondine and conducted her in front of the wardrobe which had already so forcibly attracted her attention.

"Blondine, here is the key to this wardrobe. Open it, and be brave!"

She handed Blondine a gold key. With a trembling hand the princess opened the wardrobe. What was her anguish when she saw the skins of Bonne-Biche and Beau-Minon fastened to the wardrobe with diamond nails! At this terrible sight the unfortunate princess uttered a cry of horror and fell insensible at the feet of the fairy. At this moment the door opened and a prince, beautiful as the day, sprang towards Blondine, saying, "Oh, my mother! This is too severe a trial for my sweet Blondine!"

"Alas! My son, my heart also bleeds for her. But you know that this last punishment was indispensable to deliver her for ever from the yoke of the cruel jinni of the Forest of Lilacs."

The fairy Bienveillante now with her wand touched Blondine, who was immediately restored to consciousness but despairing and sobbing convulsively, she exclaimed, "Let me die at once! My life is odious to me! No hope, no happiness, from this time forth for ever for poor Blondine! My friends! My cherished friends! I will join you soon in the land of shadows!"

"Blondine! Ever dear Blondine!" said the fairy, clasping her in her arms, "Your friends live and love you tenderly. I am Bonne-Biche and this is my son, Beau-Minon. The wicked jinni of the Forest of Lilacs, taking advantage of the negligence of my son, obtained dominion over us and forced us into the forms under which you have known us. We could not resume our natural appearance unless you should pluck the Rose, which I, knowing it to be your evil jinni, retained captive. I placed it as far as possible from the castle in order to withdraw it from your view. I knew the misfortune to which you would be exposed on delivering your evil jinni from his prison and Heaven is my witness, that my son and I would willingly have remained a Hind and a Cat for ever in your eyes in order to spare you the cruel tortures to which you have been subjected. The Parrot gained you over, in spite of all our precautions. You know the rest, my dear child. But you can never know all that we have suffered in witnessing your tears and your desolation."

Blondine embraced the Fairy ardently and addressed a thousand questions to her.

"What has become of the gazelles who waited upon us so gracefully?"

"You have already seen them, dear Blondine. They are the young girls who accompanied you. They also were changed when the evil jinni gained his power over us."

"And the good white cow who brought me milk every day?"

"We obtained permission from the Queen of the Fairies to send you this light refreshment. The encouraging words of the Crow came also from us."

"You, then, madam, also sent me the Tortoise?"

"Yes, Blondine. The Queen of the Fairies, touched by your repentance and your grief, deprived the Evil Jinni of the Forest of all power over us on condition of obtaining from you one last proof of submission, compelling you to take this long and fatiguing journey and inflicting the terrible punishment of making you believe that my son and I had died from your imprudence. I implored, entreated the Queen of the Fairies to spare you at least this last anguish but she was inflexible."

Blondine gazed at her lost friends, listened eagerly to every word and did not cease to embrace those she had feared were eternally separated from her by death. The remembrance of her dear father now presented itself. The prince Parfait understood her secret desire and made it known to his mother, the fairy Bienveillante.

"Prepare yourself, dear Blondine, to see your father. Informed by me, he now expects you."

At this moment, Blondine found herself in a chariot of gold and pearls, with the fairy Bienveillante seated at her right hand, and the prince Parfait at her feet, regarding her kindly and tenderly. The chariot was drawn by four swans of dazzling whiteness. They flew with such rapidity, that five minutes brought them to the palace of King Benin. All the court was assembled about the king. All were expecting the princess Blondine.

When the chariot appeared, the cries of joy and welcome were so tumultuous that the swans were confused and almost lost their way. Prince Parfait, who guided them, succeeded in arresting their attention and the chariot drew up at the foot of the grand stairway. King Benin sprang towards Blondine who, jumping lightly from the chariot, threw herself in her father's arms. They remained a long time in this position and everybody wept tears of joy.

When King Benin had somewhat recovered himself he kissed, respectfully and tenderly, the hand of the good fairy who, after having protected and educated the princess Blondine had now restored her to him. He embraced the prince Parfait whom he found most charming.

There were eight resplendent gala days in honour of the return of Blondine. At the close of this gay festival, the fairy Bienveillante announced her intention of returning home. But Prince Parfait and Blondine were so melancholy at the prospect of this separation that King Benin resolved they should never quit the place. He wedded the fairy and Blondine became the happy wife of Prince Parfait who was always for her the Beau-Minon of the Forest of Lilacs.

Brunette, whose character had entirely changed, came often to see Blondine. Prince Violent, her husband, became more amiable as Brunette became more gentle and they were very happy.

As to Blondine, she had no misfortunes, no griefs. She had lovely daughters, who resembled her, and good and handsome sons, the image of their manly father, Prince Parfait. Everybody loved them and everyone connected with them was happy ever after.

DONKEY SKIN

This adaptation is taken from a story collected by Charles Perrault in The Fairy Tales of Charles Perrault, published by George G. Harrap & Co. Ltd, Portsmouth Street, Kingsway, London. W.C.2, in 1922.

ONCE UPON A TIME THERE WAS a King, so great, so beloved by his people, and so respected by all his neighbours and allies that one might almost say he was the happiest monarch alive. His good fortune was made even greater by the choice he had made for wife of a Princess as beautiful as she was virtuous, with whom he lived in perfect happiness. Now, of this chaste marriage was born a daughter endowed with so many gifts that they had no regret because other children were not given to them.

Magnificence, good taste, and abundance reigned in the palace, where there were wise and clever ministers, virtuous and devoted courtiers, faithful and diligent servants. The spacious stables were filled with the most beautiful horses in the world, and coverts of rich caparison, but what most astonished strangers who came to admire them was to see, in the finest stall, a master donkey, with great long ears.

Now, it was not for a whim but for a good reason that the King had given this donkey a particular and distinguished place. The special qualities of this rare animal deserved the distinction, since nature had made it in so extraordinary a way that its litter, instead of being like that of other donkeys, was covered every morning with an abundance of beautiful golden crowns, and golden louis of every kind, which were collected daily.

Since the vicissitudes of life wait on Kings as much as on their subjects, and good is always mingled with ill, it so befell that the Queen was suddenly attacked by a fatal illness, and, in spite of science, and the skill of the doctors, no remedy could be found. There was great mourning throughout the land. The King who, notwithstanding the famous proverb, that marriage is the tomb of love, was deeply attached to his wife, was distressed beyond measure and made fervent vows to all the temples in his kingdom, and offered to give his life for that of his beloved consort, but he invoked the gods and the Fairies in vain.

The Queen, feeling her last hour approach, said to her husband, who was dissolved in tears, "It is well that I should speak to you of a certain matter before I die, if, perchance, you should desire to marry again...."

At these words the King broke into piteous cries, took his wife's hands in his own, and assured her that it was useless to speak to him of a second marriage. "No, my dear spouse," he said at last, "speak to me rather of how I may follow you."

"The State," continued the Queen with a finality which but increased the laments of the King, "the State demands successors, and since I have only given you a daughter, it will urge you to beget sons who resemble you, but I ask you earnestly not to give way to the persuasions of your people until you have found a Princess more beautiful and more perfectly fashioned than I. I beg you to swear this to me, and then I shall die content."

Perchance, the Queen, who did not lack self-esteem, exacted this oath firmly believing that there was not her equal in the world, and so felt assured that the King would never marry again. Be this as it may, at length she died, and never did husband make so much lamentation. The King wept and sobbed day and night, and the punctilious fulfilment of the rites of widower-hood, even the smallest, was his sole occupation.

But even great griefs do not last for ever. After a time the magnates of the State assembled and came to the King, urging him to take another wife. At first this request seemed hard to him and made him shed fresh tears. He pleaded the vows he had made to the Queen, and defied his counsellors to find a Princess more beautiful and better fashioned than was she, thinking this to be impossible. But the Council treated the promise as a trifle, and said that it mattered little about beauty if the Queen were but virtuous and fruitful. For the State needed Princes for its peace and prosperity, and though, in truth, the Princess, his daughter, had all the qualities requisite for making a great Queen, yet of necessity she must choose an alien for her husband, and then the stranger would take her away with him. If, on the other hand, he remained in her country and shared the throne with her, their children would not be considered to be of pure native stock, and so, there being no Prince of his name, neighbouring peoples would stir up wars, and the kingdom would be ruined.

The King, impressed by these considerations, promised that he would think over the matter. And so search was made among all the marriageable Princesses for one that would suit him. Every day charming portraits were brought him, but none gave promise of the beauty of his late Queen. Instead of coming to a decision he brooded over his sorrow until in the end his reason left him. In his delusions he imagined himself once more a young man, and he thought the Princess his daughter, in her youth and beauty, was his Queen as he had known her in the days of their courtship, and living thus in the past he urged the unhappy girl to speedily become his bride.

The young Princess, who was virtuous and chaste, threw herself at the feet of the King her father and conjured him, with all the eloquence she could command, not to constrain her to consent to his unnatural desire.

The King, in his madness, could not understand the reason of her desperate reluctance, and asked an old Druid-priest to set the conscience of the Princess at rest. Now this Druid, less religious than ambitious, sacrificed the cause of innocence and virtue to the favour of so great a monarch, and instead of trying to restore the King to his right mind, he encouraged him in his delusion.

The young Princess, beside herself with misery, at last bethought her of the Lilac-fairy, her godmother, and determined to consult her, she set out that same night in a pretty little carriage drawn by a great sheep who knew all the roads. When she arrived the Fairy, who loved the Princess, told her that she knew all she had come to say, but that she need have no fear, for nothing would harm her if only she faithfully fulfilled the Fairy's injunctions. "For, my dear child," she said to her, "it would be a great sin to submit to your father's wishes, but you can avoid the necessity without displeasing him. Tell him that to satisfy a whim you have, he must give you a dress the colour of the weather. Never, in spite of all his love and his power will he be able to give you that."

The Princess thanked her godmother from her heart, and the next morning spoke to the King as the Fairy had counselled her, and protested that no one would win her hand unless he gave her a dress the colour of the weather. The King, overjoyed and hopeful, called together the most skilful workmen, and demanded this robe of them, otherwise they should be hanged. But he was saved from resorting to this extreme measure, since, on the second day, they brought the much desired robe. The heavens are not a more beautiful blue, when they are girdled with clouds of gold, than was that lovely dress when it was unfolded. The Princess was very sad because of it, and did not know what to do.

Once more she went to her Fairy-godmother who, astonished that her plan had been foiled, now told her to ask for another gown the colour of the moon.

The King again sought out the most clever workmen and expressly commanded them to make a dress the colour of the moon, and woe betide them if between the giving of the order and the bringing of the dress more than twenty-four hours should elapse.

The Princess, though pleased with the dress when it was delivered, gave way to distress when she was with her women and her nurse. The Lilac-fairy, who knew all, hastened to comfort her and said, "Either I am greatly deceived or it is certain that if you ask for a dress the colour of the sun we shall at last baffle the King your father, for it would never be possible to make such a gown, and in any case we should gain time."

So the Princess asked for yet another gown as the Fairy bade her. The infatuated King could refuse his daughter nothing, and he gave without regret all the diamonds and rubies in his crown to aid this superb work, nothing was to be spared that could make the dress as beautiful as the sun. And, indeed, when the dress appeared, all those who unfolded it were obliged to close their eyes, so much were they dazzled. And, truth to tell, green spectacles and smoked glasses date from that time.

What was the Princess to do? Never had so beautiful and so artistic a robe been seen. She was dumb-founded, and pretending that its brilliance had hurt her eyes she retired to her chamber, where she found the Fairy awaiting her.

On seeing the dress like the sun, the Lilac-fairy became red with rage. "Oh! This time, my child," she said to the Princess, "we will put the King to terrible proof. In spite of his madness I think he will be a little astonished by the request that I counsel you to make of him. It is that he should give you the skin of that ass he loves so dearly, and which supplies him so profusely with the means of paying all his expenses. Go, and do not fail to tell him that you want this skin."

The Princess, overjoyed at finding yet another avenue of escape, for she thought that her father could never bring himself to sacrifice the ass, went to find him, and unfolded to him her latest desire.

Although the King was astonished by this whim, he did not hesitate to satisfy it. The poor ass was sacrificed and the skin brought, with due ceremony, to the Princess, who, seeing no other way of avoiding her ill-fortune, was desperate.

At that moment her godmother arrived. "What are you doing, my child?" she asked, seeing the Princess tearing her hair, her beautiful cheeks stained with tears. "This is the most happy moment of your life. Wrap yourself in this skin, leave the palace, and walk so long as you can find ground to carry you. When one sacrifices everything to virtue the gods know how to mete out reward. Go, and I will take care that your possessions follow you. In whatever place you rest, your chest with your clothes and your jewels will follow your steps, and here is my wand which I will give you. Tap the ground with it when you have need of the chest, and it will appear before your eyes, but haste to set forth, and do not delay."

The Princess embraced her godmother many times, and begged her not to forsake her. Then after she had smeared herself with soot from the chimney, she wrapped herself up in that ugly skin and went out from the magnificent palace without being recognised by a single person.

The absence of the Princess caused a great commotion. The King, who had caused a sumptuous banquet to be prepared, was inconsolable. He sent out more than a hundred gendarmes, and more than a thousand musketeers in quest of her, but the Lilac-fairy made her invisible to the cleverest seekers, and thus she escaped their vigilance.

Meanwhile the Princess walked far, far and even farther away, until, after a time, she sought for a resting place, but although out of charity people gave her food, she was so dishevelled and dirty that no one wanted to keep her. At length she came to a beautiful town, at the gate of which was a small farm. Now the farmer's wife had need of a wench to wash the dishes and to attend to the geese and the pigs, and seeing so dirty a vagrant offered to engage her. The Princess, who was now much fatigued, accepted joyfully. She was put into a recess in the kitchen where for the first days she was subjected to the coarse jokes of the men-servants, so dirty and unpleasant did the donkey-skin make her appear. At last they tired of their pleasantries, and moreover she was so attentive to her work that the farmer's wife took her under her protection. She minded the sheep, and penned them up when it was necessary, and she took the geese out to feed with such intelligence that it seemed as if she had never done anything else. Everything that her beautiful hands undertook was done well.

One day she was sitting near a clear fountain where she often repaired to bemoan her sad condition, when she thought she would look at herself in the water. The horrible donkey-skin which covered her from head to toe revolted her. Ashamed, she washed her face and her hands, which became whiter than ivory, and once again her lovely complexion took its natural freshness. The joy of finding herself so beautiful filled her with the desire to bathe in the pool, and this she did. But she had to don her unworthy skin again before she returned to the farm.

By good fortune the next day chanced to be a holiday, and so she had leisure to tap for her chest with the fairy's wand. She arranged her toilet, powdered her beautiful hair and put on the lovely gown which was the colour of the weather, but the room was so small that the train could not be properly spread out. The beautiful Princess looked at herself, and with good reason, admired her appearance so much that she resolved to wear her magnificent dresses in turn on holidays and Sundays for her own amusement, and this she regularly did. She entwined flowers and diamonds in her lovely hair with admirable art, and often she sighed that she had no witness of her beauty save the sheep and geese, who loved her just as much in the horrible donkey-skin after which she had been named at the farm.

One holiday when Donkey-skin had put on her sun-hued dress, the son of the King to whom the farm belonged alighted there to rest on his return from the hunt. This Prince was young and handsome, beloved of his father and of the Queen his mother, and adored by the people. After he had partaken of the simple collation which was offered him he set out to inspect the farm-yard and all its nooks and corners. In going thus from place to place, he entered a dark alley at the bottom of which was a closed door. Curiosity made him put his eye to the keyhole. Imagine his astonishment at seeing a Princess so beautiful and so richly dressed, and withal of so noble and dignified a mien, that he took her to be a divinity. The impetuosity of his feelings at this moment would have made him force the door, had it not been for the respect with which that charming figure filled him.

It was with difficulty that he withdrew from this gloomy little alley, intent on discovering who the inmate of the tiny room might be. He was told that it was a scullion called Donkey-skin because of the skin which she always wore, and that she was so dirty and unpleasant that no one took any notice of her, or even spoke to her. She had just been taken out of pity to look after the geese.

The Prince, though little satisfied by this information, saw that these dense people knew no more, and that it was useless to question them. So he returned to the palace of the King his father, beyond words in love, having continually before his eyes the beautiful image of the goddess whom he had seen through the keyhole. He was full of regret that he had not knocked at the door, and promised himself that he would not fail to do so next time. But the fervency of his love caused him such great agitation that the same night he was seized by a terrible fever, and was soon at death's door.

The Queen, who had no other child, was in despair because all remedies proved useless. In vain she promised great rewards to the doctors, though they exerted all their skill, nothing would cure the Prince. At last they decided that some great sorrow had caused this terrible fever. They told the Queen, who, full of tenderness for her son, went to him and begged him to tell her his trouble. She declared that even if it was a matter of giving him the crown, his father would yield the throne to him without regret, or if he desired some Princess, even though there should be war with the King her father and their subjects should, with reason, complain, all should be sacrificed to obtain what he wished. She implored him with tears not to die, since their life depended on his. The Queen did not finish this touching discourse without moving the Prince to tears.

"Madam," he said at last, in a very feeble voice, "I am not so base that I desire the crown of my father. Rather may Heaven grant him life for many years, and that I may always be the most faithful and the most respectful of his subjects! As to the Princesses that you speak of, I have never yet thought of marriage, and you well know that, subject as I am to your wishes, I shall obey you always, even though it be painful to me."

"Ah! My son," replied the Queen, "we will spare nothing to save your life. But, my dear child, save mine and that of the King your father by telling me what you desire, and be assured that you shall have it."

"Well, Madam," he said, "since you would have me tell you my thought, I obey you. It would indeed be a sin to place in danger two lives so dear to me. Know, my mother, that I wish Donkey-skin to make me a cake, and to have it brought to me when it is ready."

The Queen, astonished at this strange name, asked who Donkey-skin might be.

"It is, Madam," replied one of her officers who had by chance seen this girl, "It is the most ugly creature imaginable after the wolf, a slut who lodges at your farm, and minds your geese."

"It matters not," said the Queen, "my son, on his way home from the chase, has perchance eaten of her cakes, it is a whim such as those who are sick do sometimes have. In a word, I wish that Donkey-skin, since Donkey-skin it is, make him presently a cake."

A messenger ran to the farm and told Donkey-skin that she was to make a cake for the Prince as well as she possibly could. Now, some believe that Donkey-skin had been aware of the Prince in her heart at the moment when he had put his eye to the keyhole, and then, looking from her little window, she had seen him, so young, so handsome, and so shapely, that the remembrance of him had remained, and that often the thought of him had cost her some sighs. Be that as it may, Donkey-skin, either having seen him, or having heard him spoken of with praise, was overjoyed to think that she might become known to him. She shut herself in her little room, threw off the ugly skin, bathed her face and hands, arranged her hair, put on a beautiful corsage of bright silver, and an equally beautiful petticoat, and then set herself to make the much desired cake. She took the finest flour, and newest eggs and freshest butter, and while she was working them, whether by design or no, a ring which she had on her finger fell into the cake and was mixed in it. When the cooking was done she muffled herself in her horrible skin and gave the cake to the messenger, asking him for news of the Prince, but the man would not deign to reply, and without a word ran quickly back to the palace.

The Prince took the cake greedily from the man's hands, and ate it with such voracity that the doctors who were present did not fail to say that this haste was not a good sign. Indeed, the Prince came near to being choked by the ring, which he nearly swallowed, in one of the pieces of cake. But he drew it cleverly from his mouth, and his desire for the cake was forgotten as he examined the fine emerald set in a gold keeper-ring, a ring so small that he knew it could only be worn on the prettiest little finger in the world.

He kissed the ring a thousand times, put it under his pillow, and drew it out every moment that he thought himself unobserved. The torment that he gave himself, planning how he might see her to whom the ring belonged, not daring to believe that if he asked for Donkey-skin she would be allowed to come, and not daring to speak of what he had seen through the keyhole for fear that he would be laughed at for a dreamer, brought back the fever with great violence. The doctors, not knowing what more to do, declared to the Queen that the Prince's malady was love, whereupon the Queen and the disconsolate King ran to their son.

"My son, my dear son," cried the affected monarch, "tell us the name of her whom you desire, we swear that we will give her to you. Even though she were the vilest of slaves."

The Queen embracing him, agreed with all that the King had said, and the Prince, moved by their tears and caresses, said to them, "My father and my mother, I in no way desire to make a marriage which is displeasing to you." And drawing the emerald from under his pillow he added, "To prove the truth of this, I desire to marry her to whom this ring belongs. It is not likely that she who owns so pretty a ring is a rustic or a peasant."

The King and the Queen took the ring, examined it with great curiosity, and agreed with the Prince that it could only belong to the daughter of a good house. Then the King, having embraced his son, and entreated him to get well, went out. He ordered the drums and fifes and trumpets to be sounded throughout the town, and the heralds to cry that she whose finger a certain ring would fit should marry the heir to the throne.

First the Princesses arrived, then the duchesses, and the marquises, and the baronesses, but though they did all they could to make their fingers small, none could put on the ring. So the country girls had to be tried, but pretty though they all were, they all had fingers that were too fat. The Prince, who was feeling better, made the trial himself. At last it was the turn of the chamber-maids, but they succeeded no better. Then, when everyone else had tried, the Prince asked for the kitchen-maids, the scullions, and the sheep-girls. They were all brought to the palace, but their coarse red, short, fingers would hardly go through the golden hoop as far as the nail.

"You have not brought that Donkey-skin, who made me the cake," said the Prince.

Everyone laughed and said, "No," so dirty and unpleasant was she.

"Let someone fetch her at once," said the King, "it shall not be said that I left out the lowliest." And the servants ran laughing and mocking to find the goose-girl.

The Princess, who had heard the drums and the cries of the heralds, had no doubt that the ring was the cause of this uproar. Now, she loved the Prince, and, as true love is timorous and has no vanity, she was in perpetual fear that some other lady would be found to have a finger as small as hers. Great, then, was her joy when the messengers came and knocked at her door. Since she knew that they were seeking the owner of the right finger on which to set her ring, some impulse had moved her to arrange her hair with great care, and to put on her beautiful silver corsage, and the petticoat full of furbelows and silver lace studded with emeralds. At the first knock she quickly covered her finery with the donkey-skin and opened the door.

The visitors, in derision, told her that the King had sent for her in order to marry her to his son. Then with loud peals of laughter they led her to the

Prince, who was astonished at the garb of this girl, and dared not believe that it was she whom he had seen so majestic and so beautiful. Sad and confounded, he said, "Is it you who lodge at the bottom of that dark alley in the third yard of the farm?"

"Yes, your Highness," she replied.

"Show me your hand," said the Prince trembling, and heaving a deep sigh.

Imagine how astonished everyone was! The King and the Queen, the chamberlains and all the courtiers were dumb-founded, when from beneath that black and dirty skin came a delicate little white and rose-pink hand, and the ring slipped without difficulty on to the prettiest little finger in the world.

Then, by a little movement which the Princess made, the skin fell from her shoulders and so enchanting was her guise, that the Prince, weak though he was, fell on his knees and held her so closely that she blushed. But that was scarcely noticed, for the King and Queen came to embrace her heartily, and to ask her if she would marry their son. The Princess, confused by all these caresses and by the love of the handsome young Prince, was about to thank them when suddenly the ceiling opened, and the Lilac-fairy descended in a chariot made of the branches and flowers from which she took her name, and, with great charm, told the Princess's story.

The King and Queen, overjoyed to know that Donkey-skin was a great Princess redoubled their caresses, but the Prince was even more sensible of her virtue, and his love increased as the Fairy unfolded her tale. His impatience to marry her, indeed, was so great that he could scarcely allow time for the necessary preparations for the grand wedding which was their due. The King and Queen, now entirely devoted to their daughter-in-law, overwhelmed her with affection. She had declared that she could not marry the Prince without the consent of the King her father, so, he was the first to whom an invitation to the wedding was sent.

He was not, however, told the name of the bride. The Lilac-fairy, who, as was right, presided over all, had recommended this course to prevent trouble. Kings came from all the countries round, some in sedan-chairs, others in beautiful carriages, those who came from the most distant countries rode on elephants and tigers and eagles. But the most magnificent and most glorious of all was the father of the Princess. He had happily recovered his reason, and had married a Queen who was a widow and very beautiful, but by whom he had no child. The Princess ran to him, and he recognised her at once and embraced her with great tenderness before she had time to throw herself on her knees. The King and Queen presented their son to him, and the happiness of all was complete. The nuptials were celebrated with all imaginable pomp, but the young couple were hardly aware of the ceremony, so wrapped up were they in one another.

In spite of the protests of the noble-hearted young man, the Prince's father caused his son to be crowned the same day, and kissing his hand, placed him on the throne.

The celebrations of this illustrious marriage lasted nearly three months, but the love of the two young people would have endured for more than a hundred years, had they out-lived that age, so great was their affection for one another.

Tales From Gallia

PERONNIK THE IDIOT

This adaptation is taken from a collection called Breton Legends, although the original author or collector remains unknown.

YOU CANNOT SURELY HAVE FAILED, SOME time or other, to meet by chance some of those poor idiots, or innocents, whose utmost wisdom scarcely serves to lead them as beggars from door to door in quest of daily bread. One might almost fancy they were straying calves who have lost their way home. They stare all round with open eyes and mouth, as if in search of something, but, alas, what they seek is not plentiful enough in these parts to be found upon the highways, for it is common sense.

Peronnik was one of these poor idiots, to whom the charity of strangers had been in place of father or of mother. He wandered ever onwards unconscious of where he was going. When he was thirsty, he drank from wayside springs, and when hungry, he begged stale crusts from the women he saw standing at their doors. When in need of sleep, he looked out for a heap of straw, and hollowed himself out a nest in it like a lizard.

As to any knowledge of a trade, Peronnik had, indeed, never learnt one, but for all that he was skilful enough in many matters. He could go on eating as long as you desired him to do so, he could out sleep anyone for any length of time, and he could imitate with his tongue the song of larks. There is many a one now in these parts who cannot do so much as this.

At the time of which I am telling you (that is, many a hundred years ago and more), the land of White-Wheat was not altogether what you see nowadays. Since then many a gentleman has devoured his inheritance, and cut up his forests into wooden shoes. Thus the forest of Paimpont extended over more than twenty parishes. Some say it even crossed the river, and went as far as Elven. However that may be, Peronnik came one day to a farm built upon the border of the wood, and as the Benedicite bell had long since rung in his stomach, he drew near to ask for food.

The farmer's wife happened at that moment to be kneeling down on the door-sill to scrape the soup-bowl with her flint-stone, but when she heard the idiot's voice asking for food in the name of God, she stopped and held the kettle towards him.

"Here," she cried, "poor fellow, eat these scrapings, and say an 'Our Father' for our pigs, that nothing on earth will fatten."

Peronnik seated himself on the ground, put the kettle between his knees, and began to scrape it with his nails, but it was little enough he could succeed in finding, for all the spoons in the house had already done their duty upon it. However, he licked his fingers, and made an audible grunt of satisfaction, as if he had never tasted anything better.

"It is millet-flour," said he, in a low voice, "millet-flour moistened with the black cow's milk, and by the best cook in the whole Low Country."

The farmer's wife, who was going by, turned round delighted. "Poor innocent," said she, "there is little enough of it left, but I will add a scrap of rye-bread."

And she brought the lad the first cutting of a round loaf just out of the oven. Peronnik bit into it like a wolf into a lamb's leg, and declared that it must have been kneaded by the baker to his lordship the Bishop of Vannes.

The flattered peasant replied that this was nothing to the taste of it when spread with fresh-churned butter, and to prove her words, she brought him some in a little covered saucer. After taking this, the idiot declared that this was living butter, not to be excelled by butter of the White Week itself, and to give greater force to his words, he poured over his crust all that the saucer contained. But the satisfaction of the farmer's wife prevented her from noticing this, and she added to what she had already given him with a lump of dripping left from the Sunday soup.

Peronnik praised every mouthful more and more, and swallowed everything as if it had been water from a spring, for it was very long since he had made so good a meal.

The farmer's wife went and came, watching him as he ate, and adding from time to time sundry scraps, which he took, making each time the sign of the cross.

Whilst thus employed in recruiting himself, behold a knight appeared at the house-door, and addressing himself to the woman, asked her which was the road to Kerglas castle.

"Heavens! Good gentleman," exclaimed the farmer's wife, "are you going there?"

"Yes," replied the warrior, "and I have come from a land so distant for this purpose, that I have been travelling night and day these three months to get so far on my way."

"And what are you come to seek at Kerglas?" asked the Breton woman.

"I am come in quest of the golden basin and the diamond lance."

"These two are, then, very valuable things?" asked Peronnik.

"They are of more value than all the crowns on earth," replied the stranger, "for not only will the golden basin produce instantaneously all the dainties and the wealth one can desire, but it suffices to drink therefrom to be healed of every malady, and the dead themselves are raised to life by touching it with their lips. As to the diamond lance, it kills and overthrows all that it touches."

"And to whom do this diamond lance and golden basin belong?" asked Peronnik, bewildered.

"To a magician called Rogéar, who lives in the castle of Kerglas," answered the farmer's wife. "He is to be seen any day near the forest pathway, riding along upon his black mare followed by a colt of three months' old, but no one dares to attack him, for he holds the fearful lance in his hand."

"Yes," replied the stranger, "but the command of God forbids him to make use of it within the castle of Kerglas. So soon as he arrives there, the lance and the basin are deposited at the bottom of a dark cave, which no key will open. Therefore, it is in that place I propose to attack the magician."

"Alas, you will never succeed, my good sir," replied the peasant woman. "More than a hundred gentlemen have already attempted it, but not one amongst them has returned."

"I know that, my good woman," answered the knight, "but they had not been instructed as I have by the Hermit of Blavet."

"And what did the Hermit tell you?" asked Peronnik.

"He warned me of all that I shall have to do," replied the stranger. "First of all, I shall have to cross an enchanted wood, wherein every kind of magic will be put in force to terrify and bewilder me from my way. The greater number of my predecessors have lost themselves, and there died of cold, hunger, or fatigue."

"And if you succeed in crossing it?" said the idiot.

"If I get safely through it," continued the gentleman, "I shall meet a Korigan armed with a fiery sword, which lays all it touches in ashes. This Korigan keeps watch beside an apple-tree, from which it is necessary that I should gather one apple."

"And then?" said Peronnik.

"Then I shall discover the laughing flower, and this is guarded by a lion whose mane is made of vipers. This flower I must also gather, after which I must cross the lake of dragons to fight the black man, who flings an iron bowl that ever hits its mark and returns to its master of its own accord. Then I shall enter on the valley of delights, where everything that can tempt and stay the feet of a Christian will be arrayed before me, until finally I shall reach a river with one single ford. There I shall meet a lady clad in sable whom I shall take upon my horse's crupper, and she will tell me all that remains to be done."

The farmer's wife did her best to persuade the stranger that it would be impossible for him to go through so many trials, but he replied that women were incapable of judging in so weighty a matter, and after ascertaining correctly the forest entrance, he set off at full gallop, and was soon lost among the trees.

The farmer's wife heaved a deep sigh, declaring that here was another soul going before our Lord for judgment. Then giving some more crusts to Peronnik, she bade him go on his way.

He was about to follow her advice, when the farmer came in from the fields. He had just been turning off the lad who looked after his cows at the wood-side, and was revolving in his mind how his place should be supplied.

The sight of the idiot was to him as a ray of light, for he thought he had happened on the very thing he sought, and after putting a few questions to Peronnik, he asked him bluntly if he would stay at the farm to look after the cattle. Peronnik would have preferred having no one but himself to look after, for no one had a greater aptitude than he for doing nothing, but the taste of the lard, the fresh butter, the rye-bread, and the millet-flour hung still sweet upon his lips, so he suffered himself to be tempted, and accepted the farmer's proposal.

The good man forthwith conducted him to the edge of the forest, counted aloud all the cows, not forgetting the heifers, cut him a hazel-switch to drive them with, and bade him bring them safely home at set of sun.

Behold, Peronnik now established as a keeper of cattle, watching over them to see they did no mischief, and running from the black to the red, and from the red to the white, to keep them from straying out of the appointed boundary.

Now whilst he was thus running from side to side, he heard suddenly the sound of horse's hoofs, and saw in one of the forest-paths the giant Rogéar seated on his mare, followed by her three-months' colt. He carried from his neck the golden basin, and in his hand the diamond lance, which glittered like flame. Peronnik, terrified, hid himself behind a bush, while the giant passed close by him and went on his way. As soon as he was gone by, the idiot came out of his hiding-place, and looked down in the direction he had taken, but without being able to see which path he had followed.

Well, armed knights came on unceasingly in quest of the castle of Kerglas, and not one was ever seen to return. The giant, on the contrary, took his airing every day as usual. The idiot, who had at length grown bolder, no longer thought of concealing himself when he passed, but looked after him as long as he was in sight with envious eyes, for the desire of possessing the golden basin and the diamond lance grew stronger every day within his heart. But these things, alas, were more easily desired than obtained.

One day, when Peronnik was all alone in the pasture-land as usual, he saw a man with a white beard pausing at the entrance of the forest-path. The idiot took him for some fresh adventurer, and inquired if he did not seek the road to Kerglas.

"I seek it not, since I already know it," replied the stranger.

"You have been there, and the magician has not killed you?" exclaimed the idiot.

"Because he has nothing to fear from me," replied the white-bearded old man. "I am called the sorcerer Bryak, and am Rogéar's elder brother. When I wish to pay him a visit I come here, and as, in spite of all my power, I cannot cross the enchanted wood without losing my way, I call the black colt to carry me."

With these words, he traced three circles with his finger in the dust, repeated in a low tone such words as demons teach to sorcerers, and then cried, "Colt, wild, unbroken, and with footstep free, Colt, I am here, come quick, I wait for you."

The little horse speedily made his appearance. Bryak put him on a halter, shackled his feet, and then mounting on his back, allowed him to return into the forest.

Peronnik said nothing of this adventure to anyone, but he now understood that the first step towards visiting Kerglas was to secure the colt that knew the way. Unfortunately he knew neither how to trace the three circles, nor to pronounce the magic words necessary for the colt to hear the summons. Some other method, therefore, must be hit upon for making himself master of it, and, when once it was captured, of gathering the apple, plucking the laughing flower, escaping the black man's bowl, and of crossing the valley of delights.

Peronnik thought it all over for a long time, and at last he fancied himself able to succeed. Those who are strong go forth clad in their strength to meet danger, and too often perish in it, but the weak compass their ends sideways. Having no hope of braving the giant, the idiot resolved to try craft and cunning. As to difficulties, he suffered them not to scare him. He knew that medlars are hard as flint-stones when first gathered, and that a little straw and much patience softens them at length.

So he made all his preparations against the time when the giant usually appeared in the forest-path. First he made a halter and a horse-shackle of black hemp, then a springe for taking woodcocks, moistening the hairs of it in holy water. Next he made a cloth-bag full of birdlime and lark's feathers, a rosary, an elder-whistle, and a bit of crust rubbed with rancid lard. This done, he crumbled the bread given him for breakfast along the pathway in which Rogéar, his mare, and three months' colt would shortly pass.

They all three appeared at the usual hour, and crossed the pasture as on other days, but the colt, which was walking with hanging head, snuffing the ground, smelt out the crumbs of bread, and stopped to eat them, so that it was soon left alone out of the giant's sight. Then Peronnik drew gently near, threw his halter over it, fastened the shackle on two of its feet, jumped upon its back, and left it free to follow its own course, certain that the colt, which knew its way, would carry him to the castle of Kerglas.

And so it came to pass, for the young horse took unhesitatingly one of the wildest paths, and went on as rapidly as the shackle would permit.

Peronnik trembled like a leaf, for all the witchery of the forest was at work to scare him. One moment it seemed as if a bottomless pit yawned suddenly before his steed, the next all the trees appeared on fire, and he found himself surrounded by flames, while often whilst in the act of crossing a brook, it became as a torrent, and threatened to carry him away. At other times, whilst following a little footway beneath a gentle slope, he saw huge rocks on the point of rolling down and crushing him to pieces.

In vain he assured himself these were but magical delusions, for he felt his very marrow grow cold with dread. At last he resolutely pulled his hat down over his eyes, and let the colt carry him blindly onwards. Thus they both came safely to a plain where all enchantment ceased, and Peronnik pushed up his cap and looked about him.

It was a barren spot, and gloomier than a cemetery. Here and there might be seen the skeletons of gentlemen who had come in quest of Kerglas Castle. There they lay, stretched beside their horses, and the grey wolves still gnawing at their bones.

At length the idiot entered a meadow entirely overshadowed by one single apple-tree, and this was so heavily laden with fruit, that the branches hung to the ground. Before this tree the Korigan kept watch, grasping in his hand the fiery sword which would lay all it touched in ashes.

At sight of Peronnik, he uttered a cry like that of a wild bird, and raised his weapon, but, without betraying any emotion, the lad simply touched his hat politely, and said, "Don't disturb yourself, my little prince, I am only passing by on my way to Kerglas, according to an appointment the Lord Rogéar has made with me."

"With you?" replied the dwarf, "and who, then, may you be?"

"I am our master's new servant," said the idiot, "you know, the one he is expecting."

"I know nothing of it," replied the dwarf, "and you look to me uncommonly like a cheat."

"Excuse me," returned Peronnik, "such is by no means my profession, for I am only a catcher and trainer of birds. But, for God's sake, don't keep me now, for his lordship, the magician, is expecting me this very moment, and has even lent me his own colt, as you see, that I may the sooner reach the castle."

The Korigan saw, in fact, that Peronnik rode the magician's young horse, and began to consider whether he might not really be speaking truth. Besides, the idiot had so simple an air, that it was not possible to suspect him of inventing such a story. However, he still felt mistrust, and asked what need the magician had of a bird-catcher?

"The greatest need, it seems," said Peronnik, "for, according to his account, all that ripens, whether seed or fruit, in the garden at Kerglas, is just now eaten up by birds."

"And what can you do to hinder them?" asked the dwarf.

Peronnik showed the little snare which he had manufactured, and declared that no bird would be able to escape it.

"That is just what I will make sure of," said the Korigan. "My apple-tree is ravaged just as much by the blackbirds and thrushes. Set your snare, and if you can catch them, I will let you pass."

To this Peronnik agreed. He fastened his colt to a bush, and going up to the apple-tree, fixed therein one end of the snare, calling to the Korigan to hold the other whilst he got the skewers ready. He did as the idiot requested, and Peronnik hastily drew the running noose so that the dwarf found himself caught like a bird.

He uttered a cry of rage, and struggled to get free, but the springe, having been well steeped in holy water, bade defiance to all his efforts.

The idiot had time enough to run to the tree, pluck an apple from it, and remount his colt, which continued its onward course.

And so they came out of the plain, and behold, there lay a thicket before them, formed of the very loveliest plants. There were to be seen roses of every hue, Spanish brooms, rose-coloured honeysuckles, and, towering above all, the mysterious laughing flower, but round about the thicket stalked a lion, with a mane of vipers, rolling his eyes, and grinding his teeth like a couple of new mill-stones.

Peronnik stopped, and bowed over and over again, for he knew that in the presence of the powerful a hat is more serviceable in the hand than on the head. He wished all sorts of prosperities to the lion and his family, and requested to know if he was without mistake upon the road to Kerglas.

"And what are you going to do at Kerglas?" cried the ferocious beast with a terrible air.

"May it please your worship," replied the idiot timidly, "I am in the service of a lady who is a great friend of Lord Rogéar, and she has sent him something as a present to make a lark-pasty of."

"Larks!" repeated the lion, licking his moustache, "it is an age since I have tasted them. How many have you got?"

"This bagful, your lordship," replied Peronnik, showing the cloth-bag which he had stuffed with feathers and birdlime.

And in order to verify his words, he began to counterfeit the warbling of larks.

This song aggravated the lion's appetite.

"Let me see," said he, drawing near, "show me your birds, I should like to know if they are large enough to be served up at our master's table."

"I desire nothing so much," replied the idiot, "but if I open the bag, I am afraid they will fly away."

"Half open it, just to let me peep in," said the greedy monster.

This desire fulfilled Peronnik's highest hopes. He offered the bag to the lion, who poked in his head to seize the larks, and found himself smothered in feathers and birdlime. The idiot hastily drew the strings of the bag tight round his neck, making the sign of the cross over the knot, to keep it inviolable. Then, rushing to the laughing flower, he gathered it, and set off as fast as the colt could go.

But it was not long before he came to the dragons' lake, which he must needs cross by swimming, and scarcely had he plunged in, when the dragons came towards him from every side to devour him.

This time Peronnik troubled not to pull off his hat, but he began to throw out to them the beads of his rosary, as one would scatter black wheat to ducks, and at every bead swallowed one of the dragons turned over on its back and expired, so that he at length reached the opposite shore unharmed.

The valley guarded by the black man had now to be crossed. Peronnik soon perceived him, chained by one foot to the rock, and holding in his hand an iron bowl, which ever returned, of its own accord, so soon as it had struck the appointed mark. He had six eyes, ranged round his head, which generally took turns in keeping watch, but at this moment it so chanced that they were all open. Peronnik, knowing that if seen he should be struck by the iron bowl before he had the opportunity of speaking a word, resolved to creep along the brushwood. And by this means, hiding himself carefully behind the bushes, he soon found himself within a few steps of the black man, who had just sat down, and closed two of his eyes in repose. Peronnik, guessing that he was sleepy, began to chant in a drowsy voice the beginning of the High Mass. The black man at first, taken by surprise, started, and raised his head, but, as the murmur took effect upon him, a third eye closed. Peronnik then went on to intone the Kyrie eleison, in the tone of one possessed by the sleepy demon. The black man closed a fourth eye, and half the fifth. Peronnik then began Vespers, but before he had reached the Magnificat, the black man slept soundly.

Then the youth, taking the colt by the bridle, led it softly over mossy places, and so, passing close by the slumbering guardian, he came into the valley of delights.

This was the most-to-be-dreaded place of all, for it was no longer a question of avoiding positive danger, but of fleeing from temptation. Peronnik called all the saints of Brittany to his aid.

The valley through which he was now passing bore every appearance of a garden richly filled with fruits, with flowers, and with fountains, but the fountains were of wines and delicious drinks, the flowers sang with voices as sweet as those of cherubim in Paradise, and the fruits came of their own accord and offered themselves to the hand. Then at every turning of the path Peronnik beheld huge tables, spread as for a king. He could scent the tempting odour of pastry drawn fresh from the oven, and see the valets apparently expecting him, whilst further off were beautiful maidens coming to dance upon the turf, who called him by his name to come and lead the ball.

In vain the idiot made the sign of the cross, and insensibly he slackened the pace of his colt. Involuntarily he raised his face to snuff up the delicious odour of the smoking dishes, and to gaze more fixedly upon the lovely maidens. He would possibly have stopped altogether, and there would have been an end of him, if the recollection of the golden basin and the diamond lance had not all at once crossed his mind. Then he instantly began to blow his elder-whistle, that he might hear no more those soft appeals. He ate his bread well rubbed with rancid dripping to deaden the odour of the dainty meats, and he stared fixedly at his horse's ears, so that the lovely dancers might no more attract his eyes.

And so he came to the end of the garden quite safely, and caught sight at last of Kerglas Castle. But the river of which he had been told still lay between it and him, and he knew that this river could only be forded in one place. Happily the colt was familiar with this ford, and prepared to enter at the right spot.

Then Peronnik looked around him in quest of the lady who was to be his guide to the castle, and soon perceived her seated on a rock, clad in black satin, with her countenance as yellow as a Moor's.

The idiot pulled off his hat, and asked if it was her pleasure to cross the river.

"I expected you for that very purpose," replied the lady, "draw near, that I may seat myself behind you."

Peronnik approached, took her on his horse's crupper, and began to cross the ford. He had almost reached the middle of it, when the lady said to him, "Do you know who I am, poor innocent?"

"I beg your pardon," replied Peronnik, "but from your dress I clearly see that you are a noble and powerful lady."

"As to noble, I ought to be," replied the lady, "for I can trace back my origin to the first sin, and powerful I certainly am, for all nations give way before me."

"Then what is your name, may it please you, madam?" asked Peronnik.

"I am called the Plague," replied the yellow woman.

The idiot made a spring as if he would have thrown himself from his horse into the water, but the Plague said to him, "Rest easy, poor innocent, you have nothing to fear from me. On the contrary, I can be of service to you."

"Is it possible that you will be so benevolent, Madam Plague?" said Peronnik, taking his hat off, this time for good, "By the by, I now remember that it is you who are to teach me how to rid myself of the magician Rogéar."

"The magician must die," said the yellow lady.

"I should like nothing better," replied Peronnik, "but he is immortal."

"Listen, and try to understand," said the Plague. "The apple-tree guarded by the Korigan is a slip from the tree of good and evil, set in the earthly Paradise by God Himself. Its fruit, like that which was eaten by Adam and Eve, renders immortals susceptible of death. Try, then, to induce the magician to taste the apple, and from that moment he need only be touched by me to sink in death."

"I will try," said Peronnik, "but even if I succeed, how can I obtain the golden basin and the diamond lance, since they lie hidden in a gloomy cave, which cannot be opened by any key yet forged?"

"The laughing flower will open every door," replied the Plague, "and can illuminate the darkest night."

As she spoke these words they reached the further bank of the river, and the idiot went onwards to the castle.

Now there was before the entrance-hall a huge canopy, like that which is carried over his lordship the Bishop of Vannes at the processions of the Fête Dieu. Beneath this sat the giant, sheltered from the heat of the sun, his legs crossed, like a proprietor who has gathered in his harvest, and smoking a tobacco-pipe of virgin gold. On perceiving the colt, on which sat Peronnik and the lady clad in black satin, he lifted up his head, and cried in a voice which roared like thunder, "Why this idiot is mounted on my three-months' colt!"

"The very same, O greatest of all magicians," replied Peronnik.

"And how did you get possession of him?" asked Rogéar.

"I repeated what your brother Bryak taught me," replied the idiot. "On reaching the forest border I said, 'Colt, wild, unbroken, and with footstep free, Colt, I am here, come quick, I wait for you.' and the little horse came at once."

"Then you know my brother?" said the giant.

"As one knows his master," replied the youth.

"And what has he sent you here for?"

"To bring you a present of two curiosities he has just received from the country of the Moors. I bring this apple of delight, and the female slave whom you see there. If you eat the first, you will always have a heart as much at rest as that of a poor man who has found a purse of a hundred crowns in his wooden shoe, and if you take the second into your service, you will have nothing left you to desire in the world."

"Give me then the apple, and make the Moorish woman dismount," replied Rogéar.

The idiot obeyed, but the instant the giant had set his teeth into the fruit, the yellow lady laid her hand upon him, and he fell to the ground like a bullock in the slaughter-house.

Then Peronnik entered the palace, holding the laughing flower in his hand. He traversed more than fifty halls, one after the other, and came at length before the cavern with the silver door. This opened of its own accord before the flower, which also gave the idiot sufficient light to find the golden basin and the diamond lance.

But scarcely had he seized them when the earth shook under his feet. A terrible clap of thunder was heard, the palace disappeared, and Peronnik found himself once more in the midst of the forest, holding his two talismans, with which he set forward instantly to the court of the King of Brittany.

He only delayed long enough at Vannes to buy the richest costume he could find there, and the finest horse that was for sale in the diocese of White-Wheat.

Now when he came to Nantes, this town was besieged by the Franks, who had so mercilessly ravaged the surrounding country, that there were scarcely more trees left than would serve a single goat for forage, and more than that, famine was in the city, and those soldiers died of hunger whose wounds had spared their lives. And on the very day of Peronnik's arrival, a trumpeter proclaimed aloud in every street that the King of Brittany would adopt that man as his heir who could deliver the city, and drive the enemy out of the country.

Hearing this promise, Peronnik said to the trumpeter, "Proclaim no more, but lead me to the king, for I am able to do all he asks."

"You!" said the herald, seeing him so young and small, "Go on your way, fine goldfinch, the king has now no time for taking little birds from cottage-roofs."

By way of reply, Peronnik touched the soldier with his lance, and that very instant he fell dead, to the infinite terror of the crowd who looked on, and would have fled away, but the idiot cried, "You have just seen what I can do against my enemies. Know now what is in my power for my friends."

And having touched with his golden basin the dead man's lips, he rose up instantly, restored to life.

The king being informed of this wonder, gave Peronnik command of all the soldiers he had left, and as with his diamond lance the idiot killed thousands of the Franks, and with his golden basin restored to life the Bretons who were slain. A very few days sufficed him for putting an end to the enemy's army, and taking possession of all the goods their camp contained.

He then proposed to conquer all the neighbouring countries, such as Anjou, Poitou, and Normandy, which cost him but very little trouble, and finally, when all were in obedience to the king, he declared his intention of setting out to deliver the Holy Land, and embarked from Nantes in a magnificent fleet, with the first nobility of the land.

On reaching Palestine, he performed great deeds of valour, compelled many Saracens to be baptised, and married a fair maiden, by whom he had many sons and daughters, to each of whom he gave wealth and lands. Some even say that, thanks to the golden basin, he and his sons are living still, and reign in this land, but others maintain that Rogéar's brother, the magician Bryak, has succeeded in regaining possession of the two talismans, and that those who wish for them have only to seek them out.

Tales From Gallia

THE HIND OF THE WOOD

This adaptation is taken from Edmund Dulac's collection called Edmund Dulac's Fairy Book, published by George H. Doran Company, New York in 1916.

ONCE UPON A TIME THERE LIVED a King and a Queen whose marriage was as happy as happy could be, they loved each other tenderly, and, in turn, their subjects loved them, but one thing clouded their life, and that was that they had no children, no heir. The Queen thought that the King would love her much more if she had a child. So she made up her mind to drink of the water of a certain spring. People came there in thousands from afar to drink of this special kind of water, and one saw so many that it looked as though all the world and his wife were there.

Now there were many, many lovely fountains in the wood where the Queen and other people went to drink at the spring, so the Queen asked her ladies to lead the others away to these fountains to amuse themselves, and leave her alone. Then, when they had all withdrawn, she wailed in a plaintive voice, "Am I not unhappy," she said, "to have no children! The poor women, who can badly afford them, have plenty, but here it is now five years that I have begged heaven to give me one. Oh! Am I to die without ever having a little child? Never! Never! Nev…'

She broke off suddenly, for she saw that the water of the fountain was troubled. Then a big Crayfish came up and climbed on to the bank and spoke to her, "Great Queen, you shall have your desire. Near here is the grand palace which the fairies built, but it is impossible for you to find it, because it is surrounded by strong fairy barricades, through which no mortal eye could ever see, nor mortal footstep pass without a guide. But I am your humble servant, and, if you will trust yourself to me, I will take you there."

The Queen listened without interrupting, for hearing a big Crayfish talk, and talk so nicely too was a great surprise to her. But there was a still greater surprise in store. The Crayfish waved its feelers in the air, and, before she could count three, it had taken the form of a beautiful little old woman, with pretty snow-white hair and a dainty shepherdess costume. She bowed low, and then spoke, "Well, madam," said she, 'always look upon me as one of your friends, for I wish nothing but what would be for your good.'

She was so sweet and charming that the Queen kissed her, and then by common consent they went off hand in hand through the wood by a way which surprised the Queen. It was the way by which the fairies came from the palace to the fountains.

As they went the Queen paused to look at a strange thing which made her heart beat very fast. At a certain spot the bushes overhead were full of roses and orange blossoms, entwined and laced in such a way as to form a cradle covered with leaves. The earth beneath was a carpet of violets, and, in the giant cedars above, thousands of little birds, each one a different colour, sang their songs, and the meaning of their melody was that this cradle, woven by fairy fingers was not there for nothing.

The Queen had not got over this surprise before she saw in the distance a castle that dazzled her vision, so splendid did it shine. To tell the truth, the walls and the ceilings were of nothing but diamonds, and all the benches, even the balcony and terraces, all were pure diamonds scintillating with flashes beyond the strength of human eyes to bear. The Queen gave a great cry of joy as she covered her eyes with her hand. Then, as they came to the gate of the castle, she asked the little old woman if what she saw were real, or if she were dreaming?

"Nothing is more real, madam," the fairy replied. And at that moment the door of the castle opened and six other fairies came out. But what fairies! They were the most beautiful ever seen. They all made a low bow to the Queen, and each one presented her with a branch flowering with petals of precious stones, to make herself a bouquet. One bore roses, another tulips, another rare wild-flowers, and the rest budded with carnations and pomegranates.

"Madam," they said, "we could not give you a greater mark of our friendship for you, than to invite you here. We are pleased to be able to tell you that you shall have a lovely little Princess whom you shall call Désirée. Be sure not to forget that, when she is born, you summon us, because we wish to endow her with all the good qualities possible. All you will have to do is to take the branches of the bouquet, and, in naming each flower, think of the fairy of that name, and rest assured that we shall be in your room immediately.'

The Queen, full of joy, threw her arms around each one's neck in turn, and kissed them all, over and over again, for half an hour. After that they begged the Queen to go through their palace, and the diamonds were so bright that the Queen could not keep her eyes open. Then they took her through their garden. Never was there such lovely fruit. The apricots were larger than her head, and she could only eat a quarter of one, and the taste was so lovely that the Queen resolved never to eat anything else as long as she lived. She remained in the palace until the evening, and then, having thanked the fairies for all they had done for her, she returned with the Fairy of the Fountain.

Now, when the Queen went home, she found that they were all very upset, and had been searching for her, and could not think where she had gone. Some had thought that, as she was so beautiful and young, some stranger had taken her away, which was reasonable, for she spoke so nicely to everyone. But now at last they had found her, and the King was himself again.

The Queen soon found that what the fairies had said was true. On a certain day she had a little daughter, and she called her Désirée. Then, remembering their words, she at once took the bouquet and named each flower and thought of the fairies one after the other, and immediately they were all there. Their arms were crammed full of presents. And, after they had kissed the Queen and the little Princess, they began to distribute the presents. There was beautiful lace with the history of the world worked into it, then came a lovely cover all marked in gold representing all the toys that children play with. The cot was then shown, and the Queen went into raptures over it, it surely was the nicest ever made, it was of beautiful, rare wood, with a canopy of blue silk, inwrought with diamonds and rubies.

Then the fairies took the little Princess on their knees, and kissed her and hugged her because she was so good and beautiful. Each fairy wished her a good quality. One wished her to be wise, another wished that she might be good, another wished her to be virtuous, another to be beautiful, another to possess a good fortune, and the fifth asked for her a long life and good health. Then came the last, and she wished that Désirée might obtain all that she herself could ever wish for.

The Queen thanked them a hundred times for all the good things they had given her little daughter, and, while she was doing so, all gave a sudden start, for the door opened and a tremendous Crayfish, so large that it could hardly get through the door, came in, waving its feelers in the air.

"O ungrateful Queen!" said the Crayfish, "you did not trouble to ask me here. Is it possible that you have so soon forgotten the Fairy of the Fountain and the good services I did in taking you to my sisters. Why, you have invited all of them, and I am the only one forgotten."

The Queen was terribly upset at her error, and begged the Fairy to forgive her. She hastened to assure her that she had not for a moment forgotten her great obligation to her, and she begged her not to go back on her friendship, and particularly to be good to the little Princess.

The others thought that the Fairy of the Fountain would wish evil to the baby Princess, so they said to her, "Dear sister, do not be cross with the Queen, for she is good and never would offend you."

Now, as the Fairy of the Fountain liked to be spoken to nicely, this softened her a little, and she said, "Very well, I will not wish her all the harm I was going to, I will lessen it a little. But take care that she never sees the light of day until she is fifteen, or she and you will have reason to regret it. That is all I have to say."

Then, suddenly changing into the little old woman with the white hair and shepherdess dress, she pirouetted through the wall, staff in hand. And the cries of the Queen and the prayers of the good fairies did not matter a bit.

The Queen begged the other fairies to avert the terrible catastrophe, and besought them to tell her what to do. They consulted together, and at last told the Queen that they would build a palace without any windows or doors, and with an underground passage, so that the Princess's food could be brought to her. And she was to be kept there until she was fifteen.

Then, with a wave of their wands, they made a lovely, pure-white marble castle spring up, and, inside of this, all the chairs were made of jewels, and even the floors were no different. And here the little Princess dwelt and grew up a good and beautiful child, possessing all the good qualities that her fairy godmothers had wished for her, and from time to time they came to see how she was getting on. But, of all the fairy godmothers, Tulip was the favourite. She reminded the Queen never to forget the warning not to allow the Princess to see the light of day, lest the terrible fate that the Fairy of the Fountain had laid upon her would surely come to pass. The Queen, of course, promised never to forget so important a matter.

Now, just as her little daughter was nearing the age of fifteen, the Queen had her portrait taken and sent to all the great courts of the world. And so it happened that one Prince, when he saw it, took it and shut it up in his cabinet and talked to the portrait as though it was the Princess herself in the flesh.

The courtiers heard him and went and told his father that his son had gone mad, and that he was shut up in his room, talking all day long to something or somebody who wasn't there.

The King immediately sent for his son and told him what the courtiers had said about him. Then he asked him if it was true, and what had come over him to act like this.

The Prince thought this a favourable opportunity, so he threw himself at the feet of the King and said, "You have resolved, sire, to marry me to the Black Princess, but I love the Princess Désirée."

"You have not seen her," said the King. "How can you love her?"

"Neither have I seen the Black Princess, but I have both their portraits," replied the Warrior Prince (he was so named because he had won three great battles), "but I assure you that I have such a love for the Princess Désirée, that if you do not withdraw your word to the Black Princess and allow me to have Désirée, I shall die, and I shall be very glad to do so if I am unable to have the Princess I love."

"It is to her portrait, then, that you have been speaking?" said the King. "My son, you have made yourself the laughing-stock of the whole court. They think you are mad."

"You would be as much struck as I am if you saw her portrait," replied the Prince firmly.

"Fetch it and show it to me, then," said the King, equally firmly.

The Prince went, and returned with the Princess's portrait as requested, and the King was so struck with her beauty that he gave the Prince leave there and then to marry her, and promised to withdraw his word from the other Princess.

"My dear Warrior," said he, "I should love to have so beautiful a Princess in my court."

The Prince kissed his father's hand and bowed his knee, for he could not conceal his joy. He begged the King to send a messenger not only to the Black Princess but also to Princess Désirée, and he hoped that in regard to his own Princess, he would choose a man who would prove the most capable, and he must be rich, because this was a special occasion and called for all the elaborate preparation it was possible to show in such a diplomatic mission.

The King's choice fell on Prince Becafigue. He was a young Prince who spoke eloquently, and he possessed five millions of money. And, besides this, he loved the Warrior Prince very dearly.

When the messenger was taking his leave the Prince said to him, "Do not forget, my dear Becafigue, that my life depends on my marrying Princess Désirée, whom you are going to see. Do your best for me and tell the Princess that I love her." Then he handed Becafigue his photograph to give the Princess.

The young Prince Becafigue's cortège was so grand, and consisted of so many carriages, that it took them twenty-three hours to pass, and the whole world turned out to see him enter the gates of the palace where the King and Queen and Princess Désirée lived. The King and Queen saw him coming and were very pleased with all his grandeur, and commanded that he should be received in a manner befitting so great a personage.

Becafigue was taken before the King and Queen, and, after paying his respects to them, told them his message and asked to be introduced to the Princess Désirée. What was his surprise on being refused!

"I am very sorry to have to say no to your request, Prince Becafigue," said the King, "but I will tell you why. On the day the Princess was born a fairy took an aversion to her, and said that a great misfortune should befall her if she saw the light of day before she was fifteen years of age."

"And am I to return without her?" said Becafigue. "Here is a portrait of the Warrior Prince." Then, as he was handing it to the King, and was about to say something further about it, a voice came from the photograph, speaking with loving tones, "Dear Désirée, you cannot imagine with what joy I wait for you, come soon to our court, where your beauty will grace it as no other court will ever be graced."

The portrait said nothing more, and the King and the Queen were so surprised that they asked Becafigue to allow them to show it to the Princess.

Becafigue readily assented and the Queen took the portrait to the Princess and showed it to her, and the Princess was delighted. Although the Queen had told her nothing, the Princess knew that it meant a great marriage, and was not surprised when her mother asked, "Would you be cross if you had to marry this man?"

"Madam," said the Princess, "it is not for me to choose, I shall be pleased to obey whatever you wish."

"But," said the Queen, "if my choice should fall on this particular Prince, would you consider yourself happy?"

The Princess blushed and turned her eyes away and said nothing. Then the Queen took her in her arms and kissed her, for she loved the Princess very much and knew that she would soon lose her, for it wanted only three months to her fifteenth birthday.

When the Prince knew that he could not have his dear Princess Désirée until three months had passed, he became very sad, and could not sleep at night, until at last his strength gave way and he was near to death. Doctors were called in, but they could do nothing at all, and the King was in a dreadful state, for he loved his son very much.

Now the other messenger, who was sent to the Black Princess to tell her that the Prince had changed his mind and was going to marry another, was admitted to her presence and soon explained his errand.

"Mr. Messenger," she said when he had finished, "is it possible that your master does not think I am beautiful or rich enough? Look out over my broad lands and you will find that they are so vast that you cannot see where they end, and, as for money, I have large coffers full to the brim, as anyone will tell you."

"Madam," replied the messenger, "I blame my master as much as a humble subject may. Now if I were sitting on the greatest throne in the world, I would think it the highest favour from heaven if you would share it with me."

"That speech has saved your life," said the Black Princess, "you may go."

When the Fairy of the Fountain heard this she was extremely angry and she looked in her book to make sure that the Warrior Prince had really left the Black Princess in favour of the Princess Désirée. Yes, it was quite true.

"What!" cried the Fairy of the Fountain, "This ill-omened Désirée is always in some way upsetting my plans. No! I will not allow it to happen. Why should I?"

Now the messenger Becafigue hurried along to the court of Désirée's father and mother, and threw himself at their feet, and told them that his master was very ill and likely to die if he did not see the Princess.

The King and Queen agreed that it would be best to go and tell the Princess about the Prince, so the Queen went and told her daughter all she knew, not forgetting to mention the evil wish that had been laid upon her at the time of her birth. But the Princess asked her mother if it were not possible to defeat this wish by taking steps to send her to the Prince in a carriage with all the light shut out.

This was agreed upon and a carriage was made on a subtle plan, with a separate compartment for the Princess, and mouse-trap blinds through which food and drink could be inserted without admitting the light of day. In this she, with her two ladies-in-waiting, Long-Epine and Giroflée, set forth, and all the court wept together with the King and Queen at the going away of their little Princess.

Now Long-Epine did not care for Désirée very much, and, what is more, she loved the Warrior Prince, having seen his photograph and heard him speak.

The Queen's last words at parting were, "Take care of my little daughter, and do not on any account let her see the light of day. I have made all arrangements with the Prince that she is to be shut up in a room where she will not be able to see the light, and every care will be taken." And, with these words in their ears, they set off, having promised the Queen that all would be done as she wished.

Long-Epine told herself she would never let the Princess win the Warrior Prince, not if she could prevent it, so, at dinner time that day, when the sun was at its highest, she went as usual to the carriage with the Princess's food, and, with a big knife, slit the blind so that the light streamed in. No sooner had she done so than a strange thing happened. The Princess had been quite alone in the darkened compartment, so how was it that a white hind leapt out through the window and sped away into the forest? Long-Epine watched it, wondering. Then she looked in at the window, but the compartment was empty. The Princess had gone!

Immediately the Princess, in the form of a white hind, had disappeared into the forest, her good friend Giroflée began to chase after her. As soon as she had gone, Long-Epine took the clothes of her mistress and dressed herself up in them, and resolved to impersonate the Princess before the young Prince. Then the carriage drove on, and in it sat Long-Epine disguised as the Princess.

When they arrived she presented herself as Désirée, but the Prince looked at her with horror, for she was not at all like a real Princess. Désirée's dress, which she wore, came to her knees, and she had not noticed that her ugly legs showed below the dress.

"This is not the Princess of the portrait," said the Prince and his father together. "You took us for fools, no doubt!"

The false Princess said that it was a terrible thing to bring her away from her kingdom to be treated in this way, and to break the word that they had given. "How can you do this?" she cried.

At this the Prince and his father were so angry that they did not reply at all, but simply had the false Princess clapped in irons and put into prison.

The Prince was so heart-broken at this new trouble that he resolved to go and shut himself up for the remainder of his life, alone. At once he summoned the faithful Becafigue, and told him all. Then he wrote a letter to his father and sent it by Becafigue.

"If I never see my real Princess again," he wrote, "I beg of you that at least you will keep that sham one locked up, and guard her close."

Now all this time the Princess was in the wood, running here and there as hinds do. Once or twice she looked at herself in the water of the fountain, and saw herself so changed that she cried out, "Is it I? Am I this hind?" Then at last she got very hungry, and began to eat berries and herbs, and finally sought a quiet spot and went to sleep.

The Fairy Tulip had always loved the Princess, and said that if she left the castle before she was fifteen, she was sure that the Fairy of the Fountain would relent and do her no harm. But Giroflée was all this time wandering round looking for the little Princess. She had walked so much and now felt so tired that she lay down and went to sleep in the forest. The next morning the Princess, seeking moss among the ferns, found her. When she saw that it was Giroflée, she went up to her and caressed her with her nose, as hinds do, and looked into her eyes until at last Giroflée knew full well that it was the Princess turned into a White Hind. She watched the Hind attentively and saw two large tears fall from her eyes, and then there was not a single doubt that it was her dear little Princess, so she put her arms around her neck, and they wept together.

Then Giroflée told the Princess that she would never leave her, and that she would stay with her until the end.

The Hind understood, and, to show her gratitude, took Giroflée into the very deepest part of the forest to find her some luscious fruit which she had seen there, but on the way Giroflée called out in alarm, for she would die of fright if she had to spend the night in such a desolate spot, and then they both began to cry. Their cries were so pitiful that they touched the heart of the good Fairy Tulip, and she came to their aid.

Giroflée begged her to have pity on her young mistress, and to give her back her natural form, but the Fairy Tulip said that it was impossible to do that. She said that she would do what she could. She told Giroflée that if she went into the forest, she would come to the hut of an old woman. She was to speak her fair and ask her to take charge of both of them. Then when night came, the Princess would change back into her natural form, but as this could only happen at night in the hut, they must be very careful.

Now Giroflée thanked the fairy and went, as she had told her, far into the wood, and there, sure enough, she saw a hut and an old woman sitting outside on a bench. She went up to her at once.

"My dear mother," she said, "will you allow me to have a little room in your house for myself and my little Hind?"

"Yes, my dear daughter," she replied, "I will certainly give you a room." And she immediately took them into the hut, and then into the dearest little room it was possible to find. It contained two little beds all draped in pure white and beautifully clean.

As the night began to come in, Désirée changed her form and became the Princess again, and, seeing this, Giroflée kissed her and hugged her with delight. The old woman knocked at the door, and, without entering, she handed Giroflée some fresh fruit which they were very pleased to have to eat, and then they went to bed. But, as soon as day dawned, Désirée took again the shape and form of a White Hind.

Now Becafigue was in the very same wood, and came to the hut where the old woman lived. He begged her to give him something for his master to eat, but the old woman told him that if his master spent the night in the forest, harm would surely happen to him, because it was full of wild animals. Why should he not come to her hut? Why should he not accept the little room she could offer him? He was welcome to it and a good meal besides.

Then Becafigue went back and told the Prince all that the old woman had said and persuaded him to accept her offer. They put the Prince into the room next to the Princess, but neither of them knew anything of this arrangement.

The next morning the Prince called Becafigue, and told him that he was going into the forest and that he was not to follow him. The Prince had walked and walked for a long time in the forest, grieving over his loss, when suddenly in the distance he saw a lovely little White Hind, and gave chase and tried to catch it. The Hind, who was no other than the little Princess, ran and ran far away until the Prince, in utter fatigue, gave up the chase, but he resolved to look again the next day, and to be more careful this time, so as not to let the Hind get away. Then he went home and told the story to Becafigue, while the Princess on her side was telling her dear Giroflée that a young hunter had chased her and tried to kill her, but she was so fleet-footed that she got away.

Giroflée told her not to go out any more, but to stay in and read some books that she would find for her, but, after a little thought, the Princess found it too awful to be shut up in one little room all day long, so the next morning she went out again into the forest, and wandered through the beautiful dells and glades. After going some distance she saw a young hunter lying down on the mossy bank asleep, and, approaching him cautiously, she found that she was now so very close to him that it would be impossible to get away before he awoke. Then again, he was so handsome, that, instead of running away, she rubbed her little nose against the young hunter. What was her surprise to see that it was her dear Prince, for he, at her caress, opened his eyes, and she at once recognised him. And when he jumped up and stroked and patted her, she trembled with delight and raised her beautiful eyes to his in the dumb eloquence of love.

"Ah! Little White Hind," said he, "if you only knew how miserable I am, and what the cause of it is, you would not envy me! I love you, little Hind, and I will take care of you and look after you." And with this he went farther into the forest to find some green herbs for her.

Now the Hind with a sudden fright found its heels again, and, just because she wanted so much to stay, she bounded off as fast as she could go, and never stopped till she reached home, where in great excitement she told Giroflée all that had happened.

The Prince, when he returned and found that the Hind had disappeared, went back also to the hut, and told the old woman that the Hind had deserted him just when he had been so very kind to it and had gone in search of food for it. The Warrior Prince then explained to Becafigue that it was only to see the little Hind that he had remained so long, and that on the morrow he would depart and go away. But he did not.

The Princess in the meantime resolved to go a long way into the forest on the morrow, so as to miss the Prince, but he guessed her little trick, and so the next day he did the same as she. Then, suddenly, in the distance he saw the Hind so plainly that he let fly an arrow to attract its attention. What was his dismay to see the arrow pierce the flank of the poor little Hind! She fell down immediately on a mossy bank, and swiftly the Prince ran up. He was so upset at what had happened, that he flew and got leaves and stopped the bleeding. Then he said, "Is it not your fault, little flier? You ran away and left me yesterday, and the same would have happened today if this had not occurred."

The Hind did not reply at all, for what could she say? And besides, she was in too much pain to do anything but moan.

The Prince caressed her again and again. "What have I done to you?" he said. "I love you, and I cannot bear to think I have wounded you."

But her moaning went on. At last the Prince resolved to go to the hut and get something to carry her on, but before he went he tied her up with little ribbons, and they were tied in such a manner that the Princess could not undo them. As she was trying to free herself she saw Giroflée coming towards her, and made a sign to her to hasten, and, strange to say, Giroflée reached her exactly at the same moment as the Prince with Becafigue.

"I have wounded this little Hind, madam," said the Prince, "and she is mine."

"Sir," replied Giroflée, "this little Hind is well known to me, and, if you want to see how she recognises me, you will give her liberty."

The Prince then cut the ribbons in compliance with her request.

"Come along, my little Hind," said Giroflée, "kiss me!"

At this the little Hind threw herself on Giroflée's neck. "Nestle to my heart! Now give me a sigh!" The Hind obeyed, and the Prince could not doubt that what Giroflée said was true.

"I give her to you," said the Prince, "for I see she loves you."

Now when Becafigue saw Giroflée, he told the Prince that he had seen her in the castle with the Princess Désirée, and that he knew that Giroflée was staying in a part of their own hut. Why could they not find out if the Princess was staying there also? So the following night, the Prince having agreed, Becafigue listened through a chink in the wall of the hut, and what was his surprise to hear two voices talking!

One said, "Oh, that I might die at once! It would be better than to remain a Hind all the days of my life! What a fate! Only to be myself to you, and to all others a little White Hind! How terrible never to be able to talk to my Prince!"

Becafigue put his eye to the chink and this is what he saw.

There was the Princess in a beautiful dress all shining with gold. In her lovely hair were diamonds, but the tears in her eyes seemed to sparkle even more brightly. She was beautiful beyond words, and disconsolate beyond sorrow.

Becafigue nearly cried out with joy at sight of her. He ran off at once and told the Prince.

"Ah! Seigneur," said he, "come with me at once and you will see in the flesh the maiden you love."

The Prince ran with him, and when they came on tip-toe to the chink in the wall, he looked and saw his dear Princess.

Then so great was his joy that he could not be restrained. He went and knocked at the door, resolving to see his Princess at once.

Giroflée, thinking it was the old woman, opened the door, and the Prince immediately dashed into the room and threw himself at the feet of the Princess, and kissed her hand and told her how much he loved her.

"What! My dear little Princess, was it you that I wounded as a little Hind? What can I do to show my sorrow for so great a crime?"

The way in which he spoke put all the doubts out of the Princess's mind. The Prince, knowing all, loved her. She bade him rise, and then stood with downcast eyes, fearing the worst. Her fears were justified, for in a moment his arms were around her, and she was sobbing for joy on his breast.

They had stood a moment so, when suddenly the Prince started and listened. What sound was that? It was the tramp of armed men, and nearer and nearer came this threatening sound of an advancing host. He opened the window, and, on looking out, saw a great army approaching. They were his own soldiers, going up against Désirée's father to avenge the insult offered to their Prince. And the King his father was at their head, in a litter of gold.

When the Warrior Prince saw that his father was there he ran out to him and threw his arms round his neck and kissed him.

"Where have you been, my son?" said the King. "Your absence has caused me great sorrow!"

Then the Prince told him all about Long-Epine, and how the Princess had been changed into a Hind through her disregard of the Fairy's warning.

The King was terribly grieved at this news, and turned his eyes to heaven and clasped his hands. At this moment the Princess Désirée came out, mounted on a pure-white horse and looking more beautiful and lovely than she had ever been. Giroflée was also with her as her attendant. The spell had been removed for ever.

At sight of them the old King blessed them, and said that he would give his kingdom to his son as soon as he was married to the Princess Désirée. The Princess thanked him a thousand times for his goodness, and then the King ordered the army to return to the city, for there would be no war, but only rejoicing.

Back into the capital they went in a mighty procession, an army headed by its rulers, and victorious without striking a blow. Great was the joy of all the people to see the Prince and the Princess, and they showered upon them heaps of presents the like of which was never seen.

The faithful Becafigue begged the Prince to allow him to marry Giroflée. She was delighted to have such a great offer, and more than delighted to remain in a land where she would always be with her dear Princess.

Now the Fairy Tulip, when she heard all that had happened, resolved, out of the goodness of her heart, to give Giroflée a splendid present, so that her husband should not have the advantage of being the richer. It will astonish you to hear that she gave her four big gold mines in India, and you know what gold mines in India are worth.

And the marriage feasts lasted several months. Each day was a greater day than the one before, and every day the adventures of the little White Hind were sung throughout the country, even as they are still sung, in boudoir, fireside, and camp, to this very day.

THE LITTLE GREY MOUSE

This adaptation is taken from a story collected by Comtesse de Sophie Ségur in Old French Fairy Tales, published by The Penn Publishing Company, Philadelphia, in 1920.

The Little House

THERE WAS ONCE A MAN NAMED Prudent, who was a widower and he lived alone with his little daughter. His wife had died a few days after the birth of this little girl, who was named Rosalie.

Rosalie's father had a large fortune. He lived in a great house, which belonged to him. This house was surrounded by a large garden in which Rosalie walked whenever she pleased to do so.

She had been trained with great tenderness and gentleness but her father had accustomed her to the most unquestioning obedience. He forbade her positively to ask him any useless questions or to insist upon knowing anything he did not wish to tell her. In this way, by unceasing care and watchfulness, he had almost succeeded in curing one of Rosalie's great faults, a fault indeed unfortunately too common, that being the fault of curiosity.

Rosalie never left the park, which was surrounded by high walls. She never saw anyone but her father. They had no domestic in the house, and everything seemed to be done of itself. She always had what she wanted, be that clothing, books, work, and playthings. Her father educated her himself and although she was nearly fifteen years old, she was never weary and never thought that she might live otherwise and might see more of the world.

There was a little house at the end of the park without windows and with but one door, which was always locked. Rosalie's father entered this house every day and always carried the key about his person. Rosalie thought it was only a little hut in which the garden-tools were kept. She never thought of speaking about it but one day, when she was seeking a watering-pot for her flowers, she said to him, "Father, please give me the key of the little house in the garden."

"What do you want with this key, Rosalie?"

"I want a watering-pot and I think I could find one in that little house."

"No, Rosalie, there is no watering-pot there."

Prudent's voice trembled so much in pronouncing these words that Rosalie looked up with surprise, and saw that his face was pale and his forehead bathed in perspiration.

"What is the matter, father?" said she, alarmed.

"Nothing, daughter, nothing."

"It was my asking for the key which agitated you so violently, father. What does this little house contain which frightens you so much?"

"Rosalie, Rosalie! You do not know what you are saying. Go and look for your watering-pot in the green-house."

"But, father, what is there in the little garden-house?"

"Nothing that can interest you, Rosalie."

"But why do you go there every day without permitting me to go with you?"

"Rosalie, you know that I do not like to be questioned and that curiosity is the greatest defect in your character."

Rosalie said no more but she remained very thoughtful. This little house, of which she had never before thought, was now constantly in her mind.

"What can be concealed there?" she said to herself. "How pale my father turned when I asked his permission to enter! I am sure he thought I should be in some sort of danger. But why does he go there himself every day? It is no doubt to carry food to some ferocious beast confined there. But if it was some wild animal, would I not hear it roar or howl or shake the house? No, I have never heard any sound from this cabin. It cannot then be a beast. Besides, if it was a ferocious beast, it would devour my father when he entered alone. Perhaps, however, it is chained. But if it is indeed chained, then there would be no danger for me. What can it be? A prisoner? My father is good, he would not deprive any unfortunate innocent of light and liberty. Well, I absolutely must discover this mystery. How shall I manage it? If I could only secretly get the key from my father for a half hour! Perhaps some day he will forget it."

Rosalie was aroused from this chain of reflection by her father, who called to her with a strangely agitated voice.

"Here, father, I am coming."

She entered the house and looked steadily at her father. His pale, sad countenance indicated great agitation.

More than ever curious, she resolved to feign gaiety and indifference in order to allay her father's suspicions and make him feel secure. In this way she thought she might perhaps obtain possession of the key at some future time. He might not always think of it if she herself seemed to have forgotten it.

They seated themselves at the table. Prudent ate but little and was sad and silent, in spite of his efforts to appear gay. Rosalie, however, seemed so thoughtless and bright that her father at last recovered his accustomed good spirits.

Rosalie would be fifteen years old in three weeks. Her father had promised an agreeable surprise for this event. A few days passed peacefully away.

There remained but fifteen days before her birthday. One morning Prudent said to Rosalie, "My dear child, I am compelled to be absent for one hour. I must go out to arrange something for your birthday. Wait for me in the house, my dear. Do not yield yourself up to idle curiosity. In fifteen days you will know all that you desire to know, for I read your thoughts and I know what occupies your mind. Adieu, my daughter, and beware of curiosity!"

Prudent embraced his daughter tenderly and withdrew, leaving her with great reluctance.

As soon as he was out of sight, Rosalie ran to her father's room and what was her joy to see the key forgotten upon the table! She seized it and ran quickly to the end of the park. When she arrived at the little house, she remembered the words of her father, "Beware of curiosity!" She hesitated, and was upon the point of returning the key without having looked at the house, when she thought she heard a light groan. She put her ear against the door and heard a very little voice singing softly:

"A lonely prisoner I pine,

No hope of freedom now is mine;

I soon must draw my latest breath,

And in this dungeon meet my death."

"No doubt," said Rosalie to herself, "this is some unfortunate creature whom my father holds captive."

Tapping softly upon the door, she said, "Who are you, and what can I do for you?"

"Open the door, Rosalie! I pray you open the door!"

"But why are you a prisoner? Have you not committed some crime?"

"Alas, no, Rosalie. An enchanter keeps me here a prisoner. Save me and I will prove my gratitude by telling you truly who I am."

Rosalie no longer hesitated, for her curiosity was stronger than her obedience. She put the key in the lock, but her hand trembled so that she could not open it. She was about to give up the effort, when the little voice continued, "Rosalie, that which I have to tell you will teach you many things which will interest you. Your father is not what he appears to be."

At these words Rosalie made a last effort, the key turned and the door opened.

The Fairy Detestable

Rosalie looked in eagerly. The little house was dark, she could see nothing but she heard the little voice, "Thanks, Rosalie, it is to you that I owe my deliverance."

The voice seemed to come from the earth. She looked, and saw in a corner two brilliant little eyes gazing at her maliciously.

"My cunning trick has succeeded, Rosalie, and betrayed you into yielding to your curiosity. If I had not spoken and sung you would have returned with the key and I should have been lost. Now that you have set me at liberty, you and your father are both in my power."

Rosalie did not yet fully comprehend the extent of the misfortune she had brought about by her disobedience. She knew, however, that it was a dangerous foe which her father had held captive and she wished to retire and close the door.

"Stop, Rosalie! It is no longer in your power to keep me in this odious prison from which I never could have escaped if you had waited until your fifteenth birthday."

At this moment the little house disappeared entirely, and Rosalie saw with the greatest consternation that the key alone remained in her hand. She now saw at her side a small grey mouse who gazed at her with its sparkling little eyes and began to laugh in a thin, discordant voice.

"Ha ha ha! What a frightened air you have, Rosalie! In truth you amuse me very much. But it is lucky for me that you had so much curiosity. It has been nearly fifteen years since I was shut up in this frightful prison, having no power to injure your father, whom I hate, or to bring any evil upon you, whom I detest because you are his daughter."

"Who are you, then, wicked mouse?"

"I am the mortal enemy of your family, my pet. I call myself the fairy Detestable and the name suits me, I assure you. All the world hates me and I hate all the world. I shall follow you now for the rest of your life, wherever you go."

"Go away at once, miserable creature! A mouse is not to be feared and I will find a way to get rid of you."

"We shall see, my pet! I shall remain at your side wherever you go!"

Rosalie now ran rapidly towards the house, but every time she turned she saw the mouse galloping after her, and laughing with a mocking air. Arrived at the house, she tried to crush the mouse in the door, but it remained open in spite of every effort she could make and the mouse remained quietly upon the door-sill.

"Wait awhile, wicked monster!" cried Rosalie, beside herself with rage and terror.

She seized a broom and tried to dash it violently against the mouse but the broom was on fire at once, and blazed up and burned her hands, so she threw it quickly to the floor and pushed it into the chimney with her foot, lest it should set fire to the house. Then seizing a kettle which was boiling on the fire, she emptied it upon the mouse but the boiling water was changed into good fresh milk and the mouse commenced drinking it, saying, "How exceedingly amiable you are, Rosalie! Not content with having released me from captivity, you give me an excellent breakfast."

Poor Rosalie now began to weep bitterly. She was utterly at a loss as to what to do, when she heard her father entering.

"My father!" cried she, "My father! Oh, cruel mouse, I beseech you in pity to go away that my father may not see you!"

"No, I shall not go but I will hide myself behind your heels until your father knows of your disobedience."

The mouse had scarcely concealed herself behind Rosalie, when Prudent entered. He looked at Rosalie, whose paleness and embarrassed air betrayed her fear.

"Rosalie," said Prudent, with a trembling voice, "I forgot the key of the little garden-house, have you found it?"

"Here it is, father," said Rosalie, presenting it to him, and colouring deeply.

"How did this cream come to be upset on the floor?"

"Father, it was the cat."

"The cat? Impossible. The cat brought a vessel of milk to the middle of the room and upset it there?"

"No! No! Father, it was I that did it, in carrying it, I accidentally overturned it."

Rosalie spoke in a low voice, and dared not look at her father.

"Take the broom, Rosalie, and sweep up this cream."

"There is no broom, father."

"No broom! There was one when I left the house."

"I burned it, father, accidentally, by... by..."

She paused. Her father looked fixedly at her, threw a searching unquiet glance about the room, sighed and turned his steps slowly towards the little house in the garden.

Rosalie fell sobbing bitterly upon a chair, but the mouse did not stir. A few moments afterwards, Prudent entered hastily, his countenance marked with horror.

"Rosalie! Unhappy child! What have you done? You have yielded to your fatal curiosity and released our most cruel enemy from prison."

"Pardon me, father! Oh pardon me!" she cried, throwing herself at his feet, "I was ignorant of the evil I did."

"Misfortune is always the result of disobedience, Rosalie. Disobedient children think they are only committing a small fault, when they are doing the greatest injury to themselves and others."

"But, father, who and what then is this mouse, who causes you this terrible fear? How, if it had so much power, could you keep it so long a prisoner and why can you not put it in prison again?"

"This mouse, my unhappy child, is a wicked fairy, but very powerful. For myself, I am the jinni Prudent and since you have given liberty to my enemy, I can now reveal to you that which I should have concealed until you were fifteen years old.

"I am, then, as I said to you, the jinni Prudent. Your dear mother was a simple mortal but her virtues and her graces touched the queen of the fairies and also the king of the jinns and they permitted me to wed her. I gave a splendid festival on my marriage-day. Unfortunately I forgot to invite the fairy Detestable, who was already irritated against me for having married a princess, after having refused one of her daughters. She was so exasperated against me that she swore an implacable hatred against me, my wife and my children. I was not terrified at her threats, as I myself had a power almost equal to her own and I was much beloved by the queen of the fairies. Many times by the power of my enchantments, I triumphed over the malicious hatred of the fairy Detestable.

"A few hours after your birth your mother was thrown into the most violent convulsions which I could not calm. I left her for a few moments to invoke the aid of the queen of the fairies. When I returned your mother was dead.

"The wicked fairy Detestable had profited by my absence and caused her death. She was about to endow you with all the passions and vices of this evil world, when my unexpected return happily paralyzed her efforts. I interrupted her at the moment when she had endowed you with a curiosity sufficient to make you wretched and to subject you entirely to her power at fifteen years of age. By my power, united to that of the queen of the fairies, I counter-balanced this fatal influence and we decided that you should not fall under her power at fifteen years of age, unless you yielded three times under the gravest circumstances to your idle curiosity.

"At the same time the queen of the fairies, to punish the fairy Detestable, changed her into a mouse, shut her up in the little garden house, and declared that she should never leave it unless you voluntarily opened the door. Also, that she should never resume her original form of fairy unless you yielded three times to your criminal curiosity before you were fifteen years of age. Lastly, that if you resisted once the fatal passion you should be for ever released, as well as myself, from the power of the fairy Detestable.

"With great difficulty I obtained all these favours and only by promising that I would share your fate and become, like yourself, the slave of the fairy Detestable, if you weakly allowed yourself to yield three times to your curiosity. I promised solemnly to educate you in such a manner as to destroy this terrible passion, calculated to cause so many sorrows.

"For all these reasons I have confined myself and you, Rosalie, in this enclosure. I have permitted you to see no one, not even a domestic. I procured by my power all that your heart desired and I have been feeling quite satisfied in having succeeded so well with you. In three weeks you would have been fifteen, and for ever delivered from the odious yoke of the fairy Detestable.

"I was alarmed when you asked for the key of the little house, of which you had never before seemed to think. I could not conceal the painful impression which this demand made upon me. My agitation excited your curiosity. In spite of your gaiety and assumed thoughtlessness, I penetrated your thoughts, and you may judge of my grief when the queen of the fairies ordered me to make the temptation possible and the resistance meritorious by leaving the key at least once in your reach. I was thus compelled to leave it, that fatal key, and thus facilitate by my absence my own and your destruction.

"Imagine, Rosalie, what I suffered during the hour of my absence, leaving you alone with this temptation before your eyes and when I saw your embarrassment and blushes on my return, indicating to me too well that you had allowed your curiosity to master you.

"I was commanded to conceal everything from you, to tell you nothing of your birth or of the dangers which surround you, until your fifteenth birthday. If I had disobeyed, you would at once have fallen into the power of the fairy Detestable.

"And yet, Rosalie, all is not lost. You can yet repair your fault by resisting for fifteen days this terrible passion. At fifteen years of age you were to have been united to a charming prince, who is related to us, the prince Gracious. This union is yet possible.

"Ah, Rosalie! My still dear child, take pity on yourself, if you have no mercy for me and resist your curiosity."

Rosalie was on her knees before her father, her face concealed in her hands and weeping bitterly. At these words she took courage, embraced him tenderly and said to him, "Oh, father! I promise you solemnly that I will atone for this fault. Do not leave me, dear father! With you by me, I shall be inspired with a courage which would otherwise fail me. I dare not be deprived of your wise paternal counsel."

"Alas, Rosalie! It is no longer in my power to remain with you for I am now under the dominion of my enemy. Most certainly she will not allow me to stay by your side and warn you against the snares and temptations which she will spread at your feet. I am astonished at not having seen my cruel foe before this time. The view of my affliction and despair would have for her hard heart an irresistible charm."

"I have been near you all the time, at your daughter's feet," said the little grey mouse, in a sharp voice, stepping out and showing herself to the unfortunate jinni. "I have been highly entertained at the recital of all that I have already made you suffer, and the pleasure I felt in hearing you give this account to your daughter induced me to conceal myself till this moment. Now say adieu to your dear but curious Rosalie, for she must accompany me, and I forbid you to follow her."

Saying these words, she seized the hem of Rosalie's dress with her sharp little teeth and tried to draw her away. Rosalie uttered a piercing cry and clung convulsively to her father but an irresistible force bore her off. The unfortunate jinni seized a stick and raised it to strike the mouse but before he had time to inflict the blow the mouse placed one of her little paws on the jinni's foot and he remained as immovable as a statue.

Rosalie embraced her father's knees and implored the mouse to take pity upon her but the little wretch gave one of her sharp, diabolical laughs and said, "Come, come, my pretty! Pity it is not here that you will find the temptations to yield twice to your irresistible fault! We will travel all over the world together and I will show you many countries in fifteen days."

The mouse pulled Rosalie without ceasing. Her arms were still clasped around her father, striving to resist the overpowering force of her enemy. The mouse uttered a discordant little cry and suddenly the house was in flames. Rosalie had sufficient presence of mind to reflect that if she allowed herself to be burned there would be no means left of saving her father, who must then remain eternally under the power of Detestable. Whereas, if she preserved her own life there remained always some chance of rescuing him.

"Adieu, adieu, dear father!" she cried, "We will meet again in fifteen days. After having given you over to your enemy, your Rosalie will yet save you."

She then tore herself away, in order not to be devoured by the flames. She ran on rapidly for some time without knowing where she was going. She walked several hours but at last, exhausted with fatigue and half dead with hunger, she resolved to approach a kind-looking woman who was seated at her door.

"Madam," said she, "will you give me a place to sleep? I am dying with hunger and fatigue. Will you not be so kind as to allow me to enter and pass the night with you?"

"How is it that so beautiful a girl as yourself is found upon the highways and what ugly animal is that with the expression of a demon which accompanies you."

Rosalie turned round and saw the little grey mouse smiling upon her mockingly. She tried to chase it away but the mouse obstinately refused to move. The good woman, seeing this contest, shook her head and said, "Go on your ways, my pretty one. The Evil One and his followers cannot lodge with me."

Weeping bitterly, Rosalie continued her journey, and wherever she presented herself they refused to receive her and the mouse, who never quitted her side. She entered a forest where happily she found a brook at which she quenched her thirst. She found also fruits and nuts in abundance. She drank, ate and seated herself near a tree, thinking with agony of her father and wondering what would become of him during the fifteen days.

While Rosalie was thus musing she kept her eyes closed so as not to see the wicked little grey mouse. Her fatigue, and the silence and darkness around her, brought on sleep and she slept a long time profoundly.

The Prince Gracious

While Rosalie was thus quietly sleeping, the prince Gracious was engaged in a hunt through the forest by torch-light. The fawn, pursued fiercely by the dogs, came trembling with terror to crouch down near the brook by which Rosalie was sleeping. The dogs and gamekeepers sprang forward after the fawn. Suddenly the dogs ceased barking and grouped themselves silently around Rosalie. The prince dismounted from his horse to set the dogs again upon the trail of the deer but what was his surprise to see a lovely young girl asleep in this lonely forest! He looked carefully around but saw no one else. She was indeed alone and abandoned. On examining her more closely, he saw traces of tears upon her cheeks and indeed they were still escaping slowly from her closed eyelids.

Rosalie was simply clothed but the richness of her silk dress denoted wealth. Her fine white hands, her rosy nails, her beautiful chestnut locks, carefully and tastefully arranged with a gold comb, her elegant boots and necklace of pure pearls, indicated elevated rank.

Rosalie did not awake, notwithstanding the stamping of the horses, the baying of the dogs and the noisy tumult made by a crowd of sportsmen.

The prince was stupefied and stood gazing steadily at Rosalie. No one present recognized her. Anxious and disquieted by this profound sleep, Prince Gracious took her hand softly. Rosalie still slept. The prince pressed her hand lightly in his but even this did not awaken her.

Turning to his officers, he said, "I cannot thus abandon this unfortunate child, who has perhaps been led astray by some design, the victim of some cruel wickedness."

"But how can she be removed while she is asleep, prince?" said Hubert, his principal gamekeeper, "Can we not make a litter of branches and thus remove her to some hostel in the neighbourhood while your highness continues the chase?"

"Your idea is good, Hubert. Make the litter and we will immediately place her upon it, only you will not carry her to a hostel, but to my palace. This young maiden is assuredly of high birth, and she is beautiful as an angel. I will watch over her myself, so that she may receive the care and attention to which she is entitled."

Hubert, with the assistance of his men, soon arranged the litter upon which Prince Gracious spread his mantle. Then approaching Rosalie, who was still sleeping softly, he raised her gently in his arms and laid her upon the cloak. At this moment Rosalie seemed to be dreaming. She smiled and murmured, in low tones, "My father! My father! Saved for ever! The Queen of the Fairies! The Prince Gracious! I see him, he is charming!"

The prince, surprised to hear his name pronounced, did not doubt that Rosalie was a princess under some cruel enchantment. He commanded his gamekeepers to walk very softly so as not to wake her and he walked by the side of the litter.

On arriving at the palace, Prince Gracious ordered that the queen's apartment should be prepared for Rosalie. He suffered no one to touch her but carried her himself to her chamber and laid her gently upon the bed, ordering the women who were to wait upon and watch over her to apprise him as soon as she awaked. Then, casting a farewell look upon the sad, sweet face of the sleeper, he strode from the room.

Rosalie slept tranquilly until morning. The sun was shining brightly when she awoke. She looked about her with great surprise. The wicked mouse was not near her to terrify her for it had happily disappeared.

"Am I delivered from this wicked fairy Detestable?" said she, joyfully. "Am I in the hands of a fairy more powerful than herself?"

Rosalie now stepped to the window and saw many armed men and many officers, dressed in brilliant uniforms. More and more surprised, she was about to call one of the men, whom she believed to be either jinns or enchanters, when she heard footsteps approaching. She turned and saw the prince Gracious, clothed in an elegant and rich hunting-dress, standing before her and regarding her with admiration.

Rosalie immediately recognised the prince of her dream and cried out involuntarily, "The prince Gracious!"

"You know me then?" said the prince, in amazement. "How, if you have ever known me, could I have forgotten your name and features?"

"I have only seen you in my dreams, prince," said Rosalie, blushing. "As to my name, you could not possibly know it, since I myself did not know my father's name until yesterday."

"And what is the name, may I ask, which has been concealed from you so long?"

Rosalie then told him all that she had heard from her father. She frankly confessed her culpable curiosity and its terrible consequences.

"Judge of my grief, prince. I was compelled to leave my father in order to escape from the flames which the wicked fairy had lighted. I was rejected everywhere because of the wicked mouse, and I found myself exposed to death from hunger and thirst! Soon, however, a heavy sleep took possession of me, during which I had many strange dreams. I do not know how I came here or whether it is in your palace that I find myself."

Gracious then related to Rosalie how he had found her asleep in the forest and the words which he had heard her utter in her dream. He then added, "There is one thing your father did not tell you, Rosalie. The queen of the fairies, who is our relation, had decided that we should be married when you were fifteen years of age. It was no doubt the queen of the fairies who inspired me with the desire to go hunting by torchlight, in order that I might find you in the forest where you had wandered. Since you will be fifteen in a few days, Rosalie, deign to consider my palace as your own and command here in advance, as my queen. Your father will soon be restored to you and we will celebrate our happy marriage."

Rosalie thanked her young and handsome cousin heartily and then returned to her chamber, where she found her maids awaiting her with a wonderful selection of rich and splendid robes and head-dresses. Rosalie, who had never given much attention to her toilet, took the first dress that was presented to her. It was of rose-coloured gauze, ornamented with fine lace with a head-dress of lace and moss rosebuds. Her beautiful chestnut hair was arranged in bands, forming a crown. When her toilet was completed, the prince came to conduct her to breakfast.

Rosalie ate like a person who had not dined the day before. After the repast, the prince led her to the garden and conducted her to the green-houses, which were very magnificent. At the end of one of the hot-houses there was a little rotunda, ornamented with choice flowers, and in the centre of this rotunda there was a large case which seemed to contain a tree but a thick heavy cloth was thrown over it and tightly sewed together.

Through the cloth however could be seen a number of points of extraordinary brilliancy.

The Tree In The Rotunda

Rosalie admired all the flowers very much but she waited with some impatience for the prince to remove the cloth which enveloped this mysterious tree. He left the green-house, however, without having spoken of it.

"What then, my prince, is this tree which is so carefully concealed?"

"It is the wedding present which I destined for you but you cannot see it until your fifteenth birthday," said the prince, gayly.

"But what is it that shines so brilliantly under the cloth?" said she, importunately.

"You will know all in a few days, Rosalie, and I flatter myself that you will not find my present a common affair."

"And can I not see it before my birthday?"

"No, Rosalie. The queen of the fairies has forbidden me, under heavy penalties, to show it to you until after you become my wife. I do hope that you love me enough to control your curiosity till that time."

These last words made Rosalie tremble, for they recalled to her the little grey mouse and the misfortunes which menaced her and her father, if she allowed herself to fall under the temptation, which, without doubt, her enemy the fairy Detestable had placed before her. She spoke no more of the mysterious case, and continued her walk with the prince. The day passed most agreeably. The prince presented her to the ladies of his court and commanded them to honour and respect in her the princess Rosalie, whom the queen of the fairies had selected as his bride. Rosalie was very amiable to everyone and they all rejoiced in the idea of having so charming and lovely a queen.

The following days were passed in every species of festivity. The prince and Rosalie both saw with joyous hearts the approach of the birthday which was to be also that of their marriage, the prince, because he tenderly loved his cousin, and Rosalie because she loved the prince, because she desired strongly to see her father again, and also because she hoped to see what the case in the rotunda contained. She thought of this incessantly. She dreamed of it during the night and whenever she was alone she could with difficulty restrain herself from rushing to the green-house to try to discover the secret.

Finally, the last day of anticipation and anxiety arrived. In the morning Rosalie would be fifteen. The prince was much occupied with the preparations for his marriage, for it was to be a very grand affair. All the good fairies of his acquaintance were to be present as well as the queen of the fairies. Rosalie found herself alone in the morning and she resolved to take a walk. While musing upon the happiness of the morrow, she involuntarily approached the green-house. She entered, smiling pensively, and found herself face to face with the cloth which covered the treasure.

"Tomorrow," said she, "I shall at last know what this thick cloth conceals from me. If I wished, indeed I might see it today, for I plainly perceive some little openings in which I might insert my fingers and by enlarging just a little... In fact, who would ever know it? I would sew the cloth after having taken a glimpse. Since tomorrow is so near, when I am to see all, I may as well take a glance today."

Rosalie looked about her and saw no one, and, in her extreme desire to gratify her curiosity, she forgot the goodness of the prince and the dangers which menaced them all if she yielded to this temptation.

She passed her fingers through the little apertures and strained them lightly. The cloth was rent from the top to the bottom with a noise like thunder and Rosalie saw before her eyes a tree of marvellous beauty, with a coral trunk and leaves of emeralds. The seeming fruits which covered the tree were of precious stones of all colours; diamonds, sapphires, pearls, rubies, opals, topazes, all as large as the fruits they were intended to represent and of such brilliancy that Rosalie was completely dazzled by them.

But scarcely had she seen this rare and unparalleled tree, when a noise louder than the first drew her from her ecstasy. She felt herself lifted up and transported to a vast plain, from which she saw the palace of the king falling in ruins and heard the most frightful cries of terror and suffering issue from its walls. Soon Rosalie saw the prince himself creep from the ruins bleeding and his clothing almost torn from him. He advanced towards her and said sadly, "Rosalie! Ungrateful Rosalie! See what you have done to me, not only to me, but to my whole court. After what you have done, I do not doubt that you will yield a third time to your curiosity, and that you will complete my misfortunes, those of your unhappy father and your own. Adieu, Rosalie, adieu! May sincere repentance atone for your ingratitude towards an unhappy prince who loved you and only sought to make you happy!"

Saying these words, he withdrew slowly.

Rosalie threw herself upon her knees, bathed in tears and called him tenderly but he disappeared without ever turning to contemplate her despair. Rosalie was about to faint away, when she heard the little discordant laugh of the grey mouse and saw it before her.

"Your thanks are due to me, my dear Rosalie, for having assisted you so well. It was I who sent you those bewitching dreams of the mysterious tree during the night. It was I who nibbled the cloth, to help you in your wish to look in. Without this last artifice of mine, I believe I should have lost you, as well as your father and your prince Gracious. One more slip, my pet, and you will be my slave for ever!"

The cruel mouse, in her malicious joy, began to dance around Rosalie, but her words, wicked as they were, did not excite the anger of the guilty girl.

"This is all my fault," said she, "had it not been for my fatal curiosity and my base ingratitude, the grey mouse would not have succeeded in making me yield so readily to temptation. I must atone for all this by my sorrow, by my patience and by the firmness with which I will resist the third proof to which I am subjected, no matter how difficult it may be. Besides, I have but a few hours to wait and my dear prince has told me that his happiness and that of my dearly loved father and my own, depends upon myself."

Before her lay the smouldering ruins of the palace of the Prince Gracious. So complete had been its destruction that a cloud of dust and smoke hung over it, and hardly one stone remained upon another. The cries of those in pain were borne to her ears and added to her bitterness of feeling.

Rosalie continued to lie prone on the ground. The grey mouse employed every possible means to induce her to move from the spot. Rosalie, the poor, unhappy and guilty Rosalie, persisted in remaining in view of the ruin she had caused.

The Casket

Thus passed the entire day. Rosalie suffered cruelly with thirst.

"Ought I not suffer even more than I do?" she said to herself, "in order to punish me for all I have made my father and my cousin endure? I will await in this terrible spot the dawning of my fifteenth birthday."

The night was falling when an old woman who was passing by, approached and said, "My beautiful child, will you oblige me by taking care of this casket, which is very heavy to carry, while I go a short distance to see one of my relations?"

"Willingly, madam," replied Rosalie, who was very obliging.

The old woman placed the casket in her hands, saying, "Many thanks, my beautiful child! I shall not be absent long. But I entreat you not to look in this casket, for it contains things, things such as you have never seen, and as you will never have an opportunity to see again. Do not handle it rudely, for it is of very fragile ware and would be very easily broken and then you would see what it contains and no one ought to see what is there concealed."

The old woman went off after saying this. Rosalie placed the casket near her and reflected on all the events which had just passed. It was now night and the old woman did not return. Rosalie now threw her eyes on the casket and saw with surprise that it illuminated the ground all around her.

"What can there be in this casket which is so brilliant?" said she.

She turned it round and round and regarded it from every side but nothing could explain this extraordinary light and she placed it carefully upon the ground, saying, "Of what importance is it to me what this casket contains? It is not mine but belongs to the old woman who confided it to me. I will not think of it again for fear I may be tempted to open it."

In fact, she no longer looked at it and endeavoured not to think of it. She now closed her eyes and resolved to wait patiently till the dawn.

"In the morning I shall be fifteen years of age. I shall see my father and Gracious and will have nothing more to fear from the wicked fairy."

"Rosalie! Rosalie!" said suddenly the small voice of the little mouse, "I am near you once more. I am no longer your enemy and to prove that I am not, if you wish it, I will show you what this casket contains."

Rosalie did not reply.

"Rosalie, do you not hear what I propose? I am your friend, believe me."

No reply.

Then the little grey mouse, having no time to lose, sprang upon the casket and began to gnaw the lid.

"Monster!" cried Rosalie, seizing the casket and pressing it against her bosom, "if you touch this casket again I will wring your neck."

The mouse cast a diabolical glance upon Rosalie but it dared not brave her anger. While it was meditating some other means of exciting the curiosity of Rosalie, a clock struck twelve. At the same moment the mouse uttered a cry of rage and disappointment and said to Rosalie, "Rosalie, the hour of your birth has just sounded. You are now fifteen and you have nothing more to fear from me. You are now beyond my power and my temptations as are also your odious father and hated prince. As to myself, I am compelled to keep this ignoble form of a mouse until I can tempt some young girl as beautiful and well born as yourself to fall into my snares. Adieu, Rosalie! you can now open the casket."

Saying these words, the mouse disappeared.

Rosalie, wisely distrusting these words of her enemy, would not follow her last counsel, and resolved to guard the casket carefully till the dawn. Scarcely had she taken this resolution, when an owl, which was flying above her head, let a stone fall upon the casket, which broke into a thousand pieces. Rosalie uttered a cry of terror and at the same moment she saw before her the queen of the fairies, who said, "Come Rosalie, you have finally triumphed over the cruel enemy of your family. I will now restore you to your father but first you must eat and drink, as you are much exhausted."

The fairy now presented her with a rare fruit, of which a single mouthful satisfied both hunger and thirst. Then a splendid chariot, drawn by two dragons, drew up before the fairy. She entered and commanded Rosalie to do the same. Rosalie, as soon as she recovered from her surprise, thanked the queen of the fairies with all her heart for her protection and asked if she was not to see her father and the prince Gracious.

"Your father awaits you in the palace of the prince."

"But, madam, I thought that the palace of the prince was destroyed and he himself wounded sadly?"

"That, Rosalie, was only an illusion to fill you with horror and remorse at the result of your curiosity and to prevent you from falling before the third temptation. You will soon see the palace of the prince just as it was before you tore the cloth which covered the precious tree he destined for you."

As the fairy said this the chariot drew up before the palace steps. Rosalie's father and the prince were awaiting her with all the court. Rosalie first threw herself in her father's arms, then in those of the prince, who seemed to have no remembrance of the fault she had committed the day before. All was ready for the marriage ceremony which was to be celebrated immediately. All the good fairies assisted at this festival which lasted several days.

Rosalie's father lived with his child and she was completely cured of her curiosity. She was tenderly loved by Prince Gracious whom she loved fondly all her life. They had beautiful children, for whom they chose powerful fairies as godmothers in order that they might be protected against the wicked fairies and jinns.

Tales From Gallia

THE STONES OF PLOUVINEC

Originally a story from Brittany, this adaptation is taken from Katharine Pyle's book, Wonder Tales From Many Lands, published by George G. Harrap & Company Ltd, London, in 1920.

IN the little village of Plouvinec there once lived a poor stone-cutter named Bernet. Bernet was an honest and industrious young man, and yet he never seemed to succeed in the world. Work as he might, he was always poor. This was a great grief to him, for he was in love with the beautiful Madeleine Pornec, and she was the daughter of the richest man in Plouvinec.

Madeleine had many suitors, but she cared for none of them except Bernet. She would gladly have married him in spite of his poverty, but her father was covetous as well as rich. He had no wish for a poor son-in-law, and Madeleine was so beautiful he expected her to marry some rich merchant, or a well-to-do farmer at least. But if Madeleine could not have Bernet for a husband, she was determined that she would have no one.

There came a winter when Bernet found himself poorer than he had ever been before. Scarcely anyone seemed to have any need for a stone-cutter, and even for such work as he did get he was poorly paid. He learned to know what it meant to go without a meal and to be cold as well as hungry.

As Christmas drew near, the landlord of the inn at Plouvinec decided to give a feast for all the good folk of the village, and Bernet was invited along with all the rest.

He was glad enough to go to the feast, for he knew that Madeleine was to be there, and even if he did not have a chance to talk to her, he could at least look at her, and that would be better than nothing.

The feast was a fine one. There was plenty to eat and drink, and all was of the best, and the more the guests feasted, the merrier they grew. If Bernet and Madeleine ate little and spoke less, no one noticed it. People were too busy filling their own stomachs and laughing at the jokes that were cracked. The fun was at its height when the door was pushed open, and a ragged, ill-looking beggar slipped into the room.

At the sight of him the laughter and merriment died away. This beggar was well known to all the people of the village, though none knew where he came from nor where he went when he was away on his wanderings. He was sly and crafty, and he was feared as well as disliked, for it was said that he had the evil eye. Whether he had or not, it was well known that no one had ever offended him without having some misfortune happen soon after.

"I heard there was a great feast here tonight," said the beggar in a humble voice, "and that all the village had been bidden to it. Perhaps, when all have eaten, there may be some scraps that I might pick up."

"Scraps there are in plenty," answered the landlord, "but it is not scraps that I am offering to anyone tonight. Draw up a chair to the table, and eat and drink what you will. There is more than enough for all." But the landlord looked none too pleased as he spoke. It was a piece of ill-luck to have the beggar come to his house this night of all nights, to spoil the pleasure of the guests.

The beggar drew up to the table as the landlord bade him, but the fun and merriment were ended. Presently the guests began to leave the table, and after thanking their host, they went away to their own homes.

When the beggar had eaten and drunk to his heart's content, he pushed back his chair from the table.

"I have eaten well," said he to the landlord. "Is there not now some corner where I can spend the night?"

"There is the stable," answered the landlord grudgingly. "Every room in the house is full, but if you choose to sleep there among the clean hay, I am not the one to say you nay."

Well, the beggar was well content with that. He went out to the stable, and there he snuggled down among the soft hay, and soon he was fast asleep. He had slept for some hours, and it was midnight, when he suddenly awoke with a startled feeling that he was not alone in the stable. In the darkness two strange voices were talking together.

"Well, brother, how goes it since last Christmas?" asked one voice.

"Poorly, brother, but poorly," answered the other. "Methinks the work has been heavier these last twelve months than ever before."

The beggar, listening as he lay in the hay, wondered who could be talking there at this hour of the night. Then he discovered that the voices came from the stalls nearby, for the ox and the donkey were talking together.

The beggar was so surprised that he almost exclaimed aloud, but he restrained himself. He remembered a story he had often heard, but had never before believed, that on every Christmas night it is given to the dumb beasts in the stalls to talk in human tones for a short time. It was said that those who had been lucky enough to hear them at such times had sometimes learned strange secrets from their talk. Now the beggar lay listening with all his ears, and scarcely daring to breathe lest he should disturb them.

"It has been a hard year for me too," said the ox, answering what the donkey had just said. "I would our master had some of the treasure that lies hidden under the stones of Plouvinec. Then he could buy more oxen and more donkeys, and the work would be easier for us."

"The treasure! What treasure is that?" asked the donkey.

The ox seemed very much surprised. "Have you never heard? I thought everyone knew of the hidden treasure under the stones."

"Tell me about it," said the donkey, "for I dearly love a tale."

The ox was not loath to do this. At once it began, "You know the barren heath just outside of Plouvinec, and the great stones that lie there, each so large that it would take more than a team of oxen to drag it from its place?"

Yes, the donkey knew that heath, and the stones too. He had often passed by them on his journeys to the neighbouring town.

"It is said that under those stones lies hidden an enormous treasure of gold," said the ox. "That is the story, and it is well known. But none have seen that treasure, for jealously the stones guard it. Once in every hundred years, however, the stones go down to the river to drink. They are only away for a few minutes, then they come rolling back in mad haste to cover their gold again. But if anyone could be there on the heath for those few minutes, it is a wonderful sight that he would see while the stones are away. It is now a hundred years, all but a week, since the stones went down to drink."

"Then a week from tonight the treasure will be uncovered again?" asked the donkey.

"Yes, exactly a week from now, at midnight."

"Ah, if only our master knew this," and the donkey sighed heavily. "If only we could tell him! Then he might go to the heath and not only see the treasure, but gather a sack full of it for himself."

"Yes, but even if he did, he would never return with it alive. As I told you, the stones are very jealous of their treasure, and are away for only a few minutes. By the time he had gathered up the gold and was ready to escape, the stones would return and would crush him to powder."

The beggar, who had become very much excited at the story, felt a cold shiver creep over him at these words.

"No one could ever bring away any of it then?" asked the donkey.

"I did not say that. The stones are enchanted. If anyone could find a five-leaved clover, and carry it with him to the heath, the stones could not harm him, for the five-leaved clover is a magic plant that has power over all enchanted things, and those stones are enchanted."

"Then all he would need would be to have a five-leaved clover."

"If he carried that with him, the stones could not harm him. He might escape safely with the treasure, but it would do him little good. With the first rays of the sun the treasure would crumble away unless the life of a human being had been sacrificed to the stones there on the heath before sunrise."

"And who would sacrifice a human life for a treasure!" cried the donkey. "Not our master, I am sure."

The ox made no answer, and now the donkey too was silent. The hour had passed in which they could speak in human voices. For another year they would again be only dumb brutes.

As for the beggar, he lay among the hay, shaking all over with excitement. Visions of untold wealth shone before his eyes. The treasure of Plouvinec! Why, if he could only get it, he would be the richest man in the village. In the village? No, in the country. In the whole world! Only to see it and handle it for a few hours would be something. But before even that were possible and safe it would be necessary to find a five-leaved clover.

With the earliest peep of dawn the beggar rolled from the hay, and, wrapping his rags about him, stole out of the stable and away into the country. There he began looking about for bunches of clover. These were not hard to find, for they were everywhere, though the most of them were withered now. He found and examined clump after clump. Here and there he found a stem that bore four leaves, but none had five. Night came on, and the darkness made him give up the search, but the next day he began anew. Again he was unsuccessful. So day after day passed by, and still he had not found the thing he sought so eagerly.

The beggar was in a fever of rage and disappointment. Six days slipped by. By the time the seventh dawned he was so discouraged that he hunted for only a few hours. Then, though it was still daylight, he determined to give up the search. With drooping head he turned back toward the village. As he was passing a heap of rocks he noticed a clump of clover growing in a crevice. Idly, and with no hope of success, he stooped and began to examine it leaf by leaf.

Suddenly he gave a cry of joy. His legs trembled under him so that he was obliged to sink to his knees. The last stem of all bore five leaves. He had found his five-leaved clover!

With the magic plant safely hidden away in his bosom the beggar hurried back toward the village. He would rest in the inn until night. Then he would go to the heath, and if the story the ox had told were true, he would see a sight such as no one living had ever seen before.

His way led him past the heath. Dusk was falling as he approached it. Suddenly the beggar paused and listened. From among the stones sounded a strange tap-tapping. Cautiously he drew nearer, peering about among the stones. Then he saw what seemed to him a curious sight for such a place and such a time. Before the largest stone of all stood Bernet, busily at work with hammer and chisel. He was cutting a cross upon the face of the rock.

The beggar drew near to him so quietly that Bernet did not notice him. He started as a voice suddenly spoke close to his ear. "That is a strange thing for you to be doing," said the beggar. "Why should you waste your time in cutting a cross in such a lonely place as this?"

"The sign of the cross never comes amiss, wherever it may be," answered Bernet. "And as for wasting my time, no one seems to have any use for it at present. It is better for me to spend it in this way than to idle it away over nothing."

Suddenly a strange idea flashed into the beggar's mind, a thought so strange and terrible that it made him turn pale. He drew nearer to the stone-cutter and laid his hand upon his arm.

"Listen, Bernet," said he, "you are a clever workman and an honest one as well, and yet all your work scarcely brings you in enough to live on. Suppose I were to tell you that in one night you might become richer than the richest man in the village, so that there would be no desire that you could not satisfy. What would you think of that?"

"I would think nothing of it, for I would know it was not true," answered Bernet carelessly.

"But it is true, it is true, I tell you," cried the beggar. "Listen, and I will tell you."

He drew still nearer to Bernet, so that his mouth almost touched the stone-cutter's ear, and in a whisper he repeated to him the story he had heard the ox telling the donkey. But it was only a part of the story that he told after all, for he did not tell Bernet that anyone who was rash enough to seek the treasure would be crushed by the stones unless he carried a five-leaved clover, nor did he tell him that if the treasure were carried away from the heath it would turn to ashes unless a human life had been sacrificed to the stones. As Bernet listened to the story he became very grave. His eyes shone through the fading light as he stared at the beggar's face.

"Why do you tell me this?" he asked. "And why are you willing to share the treasure that might be all your own? If you make me rich, what do you expect me to do for you in return?"

"Do you not see?" answered the beggar. "You are much stronger than I. I, as you know, am a weak man and slow of movement. While the stones are away we two together could gather more than twice as much as I could gather myself. In return for telling you this secret, all I ask is that if we go there and gather all we can, and bring it away with us, you will make an even division with me, that you will give me half of all we get."

"That seems only just," said Bernet slowly. "It would be strange if this story of the hidden treasure proved to be true. At any rate, I will come with you to the heath tonight. We will bring with us some large bags, and if we manage to secure even a small part of the gold you talk of I shall never cease to be grateful to you."

The beggar could not answer. His teeth were chattering, half with fear and half with excitement. The honest stone-cutter little guessed that the beggar was planning to sacrifice him to the stones in order that he himself might become a rich man.

It was well on toward midnight when Bernet and the beggar returned to the heath with the bags. The moon shone clear and bright, and by its light they could see the stones towering up above them, solid and motionless. It seemed impossible to believe that they had ever stirred from their places, or ever would again. In the moonlight Bernet could clearly see the cross that he had carved upon the largest stone.

He and the beggar lay hidden behind a clump of bushes. All was still except for the faint sound of the river some short distance away. Suddenly a breath seemed to pass over the heath. Far off, in the village of Plouvinec, sounded the first stroke of twelve.

At that stroke the two men saw a strange and wonderful thing happen. The motionless stones rocked and stirred in their places. With a rending sound they tore themselves from the places where they had stood for so long. Then down the slope toward the river they rolled, bounding faster and faster, while there on the heath an immense treasure glittered in the moonlight.

"Quick! Quick!" cried the beggar in a shrill voice. "They will return! We have not a moment to waste."

Greedily he threw himself upon the treasure. Gathering it up by handfuls he thrust it hurriedly into a sack. Bernet was not slow to follow his example. They worked with such frenzy that soon the two largest sacks were almost full. In their haste everything but the gold was forgotten.

Some sound, a rumbling and crashing, made Bernet look up. At once he sprang to his feet with a cry of fear.

"Look! look!" he cried. "The stones are returning. They are almost on us. We shall be crushed."

"You, perhaps, but not I," answered the beggar. "You should have provided yourself with a five-leaved clover. It is a magic herb, and the stones have no power to touch him who holds it."

Even as the beggar spoke the stones were almost upon them. Trembling, but secure, he held up the five-leaved clover before them. As he did so the ranks of stones divided, passing around him a rank on either side, then, closing together, they rolled on toward Bernet.

The poor stone-cutter felt that he was lost. He tried to murmur a prayer, but his tongue clove to the roof of his mouth with fear.

Suddenly the largest stone of all, the one upon which he had cut the cross, separated itself from the others. Rolling in front of them, it placed itself before him as a shield. Grey and immovable it towered above him. For a moment the others paused as if irresolute, while Bernet cowered close against the protecting stone. Then they rolled by without touching him and settled sullenly into their places.

The beggar was already gathering up the sacks. He believed himself safe, but he wished to leave the heath as quickly as possible. He glanced fearfully over his shoulder. Then he gave a shriek, and, turning, he held up the five-leaved clover. The largest stone was rolling toward him. It was almost upon him.

But the magic herb had no power over a stone marked with a cross. On it rolled, over the miserable man, and into the place where it must rest again for still another hundred years.

It was morning, and the sun was high in the heavens when Bernet staggered into the inn at Plouvinec. A heavy, bulging sack was thrown over one shoulder, while he dragged a second sack behind him. Both of the sacks were full of gold, the treasure from under the stones of Plouvinec.

From that time Bernet was the richest man in Plouvinec. Madeleine's father was glad enough to call him son-in-law and to welcome him into his family. He and Madeleine were married, and lived in the greatest comfort and happiness all their days. But for as long as he lived Bernet could never be induced to go near the heath nor to look upon the stones that had so nearly caused his death.

THE YELLOW DWARF

This adaptation is taken from a story collected by Andrew Lang in his Blue Fairy Book, published in 1889. The original is taken from a collection of stories compiled by Marie-Catherine Le Jumel de Barneville, Baroness d'Aulnoy, a French writer known for her fairy tales. When she termed her works contes de fées (fairy tales), she originated the term that is now generally used for the genre.

ONCE UPON A TIME THERE LIVED a queen who had been the mother of a great many children, and of them all only one daughter was left. But then she was worth at least a thousand.

Her mother, who, since the death of the King, her father, had nothing in the world she cared for so much as this little Princess, was so terribly afraid of losing her that she quite spoiled her, and never tried to correct any of her faults. The consequence was that this little person, who was as pretty as possible, and was one day to wear a crown, grew up so proud and so much in love with her own beauty that she despised everyone else in the world.

The Queen, her mother, by her caresses and flatteries, helped to make her believe that there was nothing too good for her. She was dressed almost always in the prettiest frocks, as a fairy, or as a queen going out to hunt, and the ladies of the Court followed her dressed as forest fairies.

And to make her more vain than ever the Queen caused her portrait to be taken by the cleverest painters and sent it to several neighbouring kings with whom she was very friendly.

When they saw this portrait they fell in love with the Princess, every one of them, but upon each it had a different effect. One fell ill, one went quite crazy, and a few of the luckiest set off to see her as soon as possible, but these poor princes became her slaves the moment they set eyes on her.

Never has there been a gayer Court. Twenty delightful kings did everything they could think of to make themselves agreeable, and after having spent ever so much money in giving a single entertainment thought themselves very lucky if the Princess said "That's pretty."

All this admiration vastly pleased the Queen. Not a day passed but she received seven or eight thousand sonnets, and as many elegies, madrigals, and songs, which were sent her by all the poets in the world. All the prose and the poetry that was written just then was about Bellissima, for that was the Princess's name, and all the bonfires that they had were made of these verses, which crackled and sparkled better than any other sort of wood.

Bellissima was already fifteen years old, and every one of the Princes wished to marry her, but not one dared to say so. How could they when they knew that any of them might have cut off his head five or six times a day just to please her, and she would have thought it a mere trifle, so little did she care? You may imagine how hard-hearted her lovers thought her, and the Queen, who wished to see her married, did not know how to persuade her to think of it seriously.

"Bellissima," she said, "I do wish you would not be so proud. What makes you despise all these nice kings? I wish you to marry one of them, and you do not try to please me."

"I am so happy," Bellissima answered, "do leave me in peace, madam. I don't want to care for anyone."

"But you would be very happy with any of these Princes," said the Queen, "and I shall be very angry if you fall in love with anyone who is not worthy of you."

But the Princess thought so much of herself that she did not consider anyone of her lovers clever or handsome enough for her, and her mother, who was getting really angry at her determination not to be married, began to wish that she had not allowed her to have her own way so much.

At last, not knowing what else to do, she resolved to consult a certain witch who was called "The Fairy of the Desert." Now this was very difficult to do, as she was guarded by some terrible lions, but happily the Queen had heard a long time before that whoever wanted to pass these lions safely must throw to them a cake made of millet flour, sugar-candy, and crocodile's eggs. This cake she prepared with her own hands, and putting it in a little basket, she set out to seek the Fairy. But as she was not used to walking far, she soon felt very tired and sat down at the foot of a tree to rest, and presently fell fast asleep. When she awoke she was dismayed to find her basket empty. The cake was all gone, and, to make matters worse, at that moment she heard the roaring of the great lions, who had found out that she was near and were coming to look for her.

"What shall I do?" she cried, "I shall be eaten up," and being too frightened to run a single step, she began to cry, and leaned against the tree under which she had been asleep.

Just then she heard someone say, "H'm, h'm!"

She looked all round her, and then up the tree, and there she saw a little tiny man, who was eating oranges.

"Oh, Queen," said he, "I know you very well, and I know how much afraid you are of the lions, and you are quite right too, for they have eaten many other people, and what can you expect, as you have not any cake to give them?"

"I must make up my mind to die," said the poor Queen. "Alas! I should not care so much if only my dear daughter were married."

"Oh, you have a daughter," cried the Yellow Dwarf (who was so called because he was a dwarf and had such a yellow face, and lived in the orange tree). "I'm really glad to hear that, for I've been looking for a wife all over the world. Now, if you will promise that she shall marry me, not one of the lions, tigers, or bears shall touch you."

The Queen looked at him and was almost as much afraid of his ugly little face as she had been of the lions before, so that she could not speak a word.

"What! You hesitate, madam," cried the Dwarf. "You must be very fond of being eaten up alive."

And, as he spoke, the Queen saw the lions, which were running down a hill toward them.

Each one had two heads, eight feet, and four rows of teeth, and their skins were as hard as turtle shells, and were bright red.

At this dreadful sight, the poor Queen, who was trembling like a dove when it sees a hawk, cried out as loud as she could, "Oh! Dear Mr. Dwarf, Bellissima shall marry you."

"Oh, indeed!" said he disdainfully. "Bellissima is pretty enough, but I don't particularly want to marry her. You can keep her."

"Oh! Noble sir," said the Queen in great distress, "do not refuse her. She is the most charming Princess in the world."

"Oh, well," he replied, "out of charity I will take her, but be sure and don't forget that she is mine."

As he spoke a little door opened in the trunk of the orange tree, in rushed the Queen, only just in time, and the door shut with a bang in the faces of the lions.

The Queen was so confused that at first she did not notice another little door in the orange tree, but presently it opened and she found herself in a field of thistles and nettles. It was encircled by a muddy ditch, and a little further on was a tiny thatched cottage, out of which came the Yellow Dwarf with a very jaunty air. He wore wooden shoes and a little yellow coat, and as he had no hair and very long ears he looked altogether a shocking little object.

"I am delighted," said he to the Queen, "that, as you are to be my mother-in-law, you should see the little house in which your Bellissima will live with me. With these thistles and nettles she can feed a donkey which she can ride whenever she likes. Under this humble roof no weather can hurt her, she will drink the water of this brook and eat frogs, which grow very fat about here, and then she will have me always with her, as handsome, agreeable, and gay as you see me now. For if her shadow stays by her more closely than I do I shall be surprised."

The unhappy Queen, seeing all at once what a miserable life her daughter would have with this Dwarf could not bear the idea, and fell down insensible without saying a word.

When she revived she found to her great surprise that she was lying in her own bed at home, and, what was more, that she had on the loveliest lace night cap that she had ever seen in her life. At first she thought that all her adventures, the terrible lions, and her promise to the Yellow Dwarf that he should marry Bellissima, must have been a dream, but there was the new cap with its beautiful ribbon and lace to remind her that it was all true, which made her so unhappy that she could neither eat, drink, nor sleep for thinking of it.

The Princess, who, in spite of her wilfulness, really loved her mother with all her heart, was much grieved when she saw her looking so sad, and often asked her what was the matter, but the Queen, who didn't want her to find out the truth, only said that she was ill, or that one of her neighbours was threatening to make war against her. Bellissima knew quite well that something was being hidden from her, and that neither of these was the real reason of the Queen's uneasiness. So she made up her mind that she would go and consult the Fairy of the Desert about it, especially as she had often heard how wise she was, and she thought that at the same time she might ask her advice as to whether it would be as well to be married, or not.

So, with great care, she made some of the proper cake to pacify the lions, and one night went up to her room very early, pretending that she was going to bed, but instead of that, she wrapped herself in a long white veil, and went down a secret staircase, and set off all by herself to find the Witch.

But when she got as far as the same fatal orange tree, and saw it covered with flowers and fruit, she stopped and began to gather some of the oranges, and then, putting down her basket, she sat down to eat them. But when it was time to go on again the basket had disappeared and, though she looked everywhere, not a trace of it could she find. The more she hunted for it, the more frightened she got, and at last she began to cry. Then all at once she saw before her the Yellow Dwarf.

"What's the matter with you, my pretty one?" said he. "What are you crying about?"

"Alas!" she answered, "No wonder that I am crying, seeing that I have lost the basket of cake that was to help me to get safely to the cave of the Fairy of the Desert."

"And what do you want with her, pretty one?" said the little monster, "for I am a friend of hers, and, for the matter of that, I am quite as clever as she is."

"The Queen, my mother," replied the Princess, "has lately fallen into such deep sadness that I fear that she will die, and I am afraid that perhaps I am the cause of it, for she very much wishes me to be married, and I must tell you truly that as yet I have not found anyone I consider worthy to be my husband. So for all these reasons I wished to talk to the Fairy."

"Do not give yourself any further trouble, Princess," answered the Dwarf. "I can tell you all you want to know better than she could. The Queen, your mother, has promised you in marriage…"

"Has promised me!" interrupted the Princess. "Oh, no! I'm sure she has not. She would have told me if she had. I am too much interested in the matter for her to promise anything without my consent. You must be mistaken."

"Beautiful Princess," cried the Dwarf suddenly, throwing himself on his knees before her, "I flatter myself that you will not be displeased at her choice when I tell you that it is to me she has promised the happiness of marrying you."

"You!" cried Bellissima, starting back. "My mother wishes me to marry you! How can you be so silly as to think of such a thing?"

"Oh, it isn't that I care much to have that honour," cried the Dwarf angrily, "but here are the lions coming, they'll eat you up in three mouthfuls, and there will be an end of you and your pride."

And, indeed, at that moment the poor Princess heard their dreadful howls coming nearer and nearer.

"What shall I do?" she cried. "Must all my happy days come to an end like this?"

The malicious Dwarf looked at her and began to laugh spitefully. "At least," said he, "you have the satisfaction of dying unmarried. A lovely Princess like you must surely prefer to die rather than be the wife of a poor little dwarf like myself."

"Oh, don't be angry with me," cried the Princess, clasping her hands. "I'd rather marry all the dwarfs in the world than die in this horrible way."

"Look at me well, Princess, before you give me your word," said he. "I don't want you to promise me in a hurry."

"Oh!" cried she, "The lions are coming. I have looked at you enough. I am so frightened. Save me this minute, or I shall die of terror."

Indeed, as she spoke she fell down insensible, and when she recovered she found herself in her own little bed at home. How she got there she could not tell, but she was dressed in the most beautiful lace and ribbons, and on her finger was a little ring, made of a single red hair, which fitted so tightly that, try as she might, she could not get it off.

When the Princess saw all these things, and remembered what had happened, she, too, fell into the deepest sadness, which surprised and alarmed the whole Court, and the Queen more than anyone else. A hundred times she asked Bellissima if anything was the matter with her, but she always said that there was nothing.

At last the chief men of the kingdom, anxious to see their Princess married, sent to the Queen to beg her to choose a husband for her as soon as possible. She replied that nothing would please her better, but that her daughter seemed so unwilling to marry, and she recommended them to go and talk to the Princess about it themselves so this they at once did.

Now Bellissima was much less proud since her adventure with the Yellow Dwarf, and she could not think of a better way of getting rid of the little monster than to marry some powerful king, so she replied to their request much more favourably than they had hoped, saying that, though she was very happy as she was, still, to please them, she would consent to marry the King of the Gold Mines. Now he was a very handsome and powerful Prince, who had been in love with the Princess for years, but had not thought that she would ever care about him at all. You can easily imagine how delighted he was when he heard the news, and how angry it made all the other kings to lose for ever the hope of marrying the Princess, but, after all, Bellissima could not have married twenty kings. Indeed, she had found it quite difficult enough to choose one, for her vanity made her believe that there was nobody in the world who was worthy of her.

Preparations were begun at once for the grandest wedding that had ever been held at the palace. The King of the Gold Mines sent such immense sums of money that the whole sea was covered with the ships that brought it. Messengers were sent to all the gayest and most refined Courts, particularly to the Court of France, to seek out everything rare and precious to adorn the Princess, although her beauty was so perfect that nothing she wore could make her look prettier. At least that is what the King of the Gold Mines thought, and he was never happy unless he was with her.

As for the Princess, the more she saw of the King the more she liked him, he was so generous, so handsome and clever, that at last she was almost as much in love with him as he was with her. How happy they were as they wandered about in the beautiful gardens together, sometimes listening to sweet music! And the King used to write songs for Bellissima. This is one that she liked very much:

In the forest all is gay

When my Princess walks that way.

All the blossoms then are found

Downward fluttering to the ground,

Hoping she may tread on them.

And bright flowers on slender stem

Gaze up at her as she passes

Brushing lightly through the grasses.

Oh, my Princess, birds above

Echo back our songs of love,

As through this enchanted land

Blithe we wander, hand in hand.

They really were as happy as the day was long. All the King's unsuccessful rivals had gone home in despair. They said goodbye to the Princess so sadly that she could not help being sorry for them.

"Ah, madam," the King of the Gold Mines said to her "how is this? Why do you waste your pity on these princes, who love you so much that all their trouble would be well repaid by a single smile from you?"

"I should be sorry," answered Bellissima, "if you had not noticed how much I pitied these princes who were leaving me for ever. But for you, sire, it is very different, for you have every reason to be pleased with me, but they are going sorrowfully away, so you must not grudge them my compassion."

The King of the Gold Mines was quite overcome by the Princess's good-natured way of taking his interference, and, throwing himself at her feet, he kissed her hand a thousand times and begged her to forgive him.

At last the happy day came. Everything was ready for Bellissima's wedding. The trumpets sounded, all the streets of the town were hung with flags and strewn with flowers, and the people ran in crowds to the great square before the palace. The Queen was so overjoyed that she had hardly been able to sleep at all, and she got up before it was light to give the necessary orders and to choose the jewels that the Princess was to wear. These were nothing less than diamonds, even to her shoes, which were covered with them, and her dress of silver brocade was embroidered with a dozen of the sun's rays. You may imagine how much these had cost, but then nothing could have been more brilliant, except the beauty of the Princess! Upon her head she wore a splendid crown, her lovely hair waved nearly to her feet, and her stately figure could easily be distinguished among all the ladies who attended her.

The King of the Gold Mines was not less noble and splendid. It was easy to see by his face how happy he was, and everyone who went near him returned loaded with presents, for all round the great banqueting hall had been arranged a thousand barrels full of gold, and numberless bags made of velvet embroidered with pearls and filled with money, each one containing at least a hundred thousand gold pieces, which were given away to everyone who liked to hold out his hand, which numbers of people hastened to do, you may be sure. Indeed, some found this by far the most amusing part of the wedding festivities.

The Queen and the Princess were just ready to set out with the King when they saw, advancing toward them from the end of the long gallery, two great basilisks, dragging after them a very badly made box. Behind them came a tall old woman, whose ugliness was even more surprising than her extreme old age. She wore a ruff of black taffeta, a red velvet hood, and a farthingale all in rags, and she leaned heavily upon a crutch. This strange old woman, without saying a single word, hobbled three times round the gallery, followed by the basilisks, then stopping in the middle, and brandishing her crutch threateningly, she cried, "Ho, ho, Queen! Ho, ho, Princess! Do you think you are going to break with impunity the promise that you made to my friend the Yellow Dwarf? I am the Fairy of the Desert. Without the Yellow Dwarf and his orange tree my great lions would soon have eaten you up, I can tell you, and in Fairyland we do not suffer ourselves to be insulted like this. Make up your minds at once what you will do, for I vow that you shall marry the Yellow Dwarf. If you don't, may I burn my crutch!"

"Ah, Princess," said the Queen, weeping, "what is this that I hear? What have you promised?"

"Ah, my mother," replied Bellissima sadly, "what did you promise, yourself?"

The King of the Gold Mines, indignant at being kept from his happiness by this wicked old woman, went up to her, and threatening her with his sword, said, "Get away out of my country at once, and for ever, miserable creature, lest I take your life, and so rid myself of your malice."

He had hardly spoken these words when the lid of the box fell back on the floor with a terrible noise, and to their horror out sprang the Yellow Dwarf, mounted upon a great Spanish cat.

"Rash youth!" he cried, rushing between the Fairy of the Desert and the King. "Don't you dare lay a finger upon this illustrious Fairy! Your quarrel is with me only. I am your enemy and your rival. That faithless Princess who would have married you is promised to me. See if she has not upon her finger a ring made of one of my hairs. Just try to take it off, and you will soon find out that I am more powerful than you are!"

"Wretched little monster!" said the King, "do you dare to call yourself the Princess's lover, and to lay claim to such a treasure? Do you know that you are a dwarf, that you are so ugly that one cannot bear to look at you, and that I should have killed you myself long before this if you had been worthy of such a glorious death?"

The Yellow Dwarf, deeply enraged at these words, set spurs to his cat, which yelled horribly, and leaped here and there terrifying everybody except the brave King, who pursued the Dwarf closely, till he, drawing a great knife with which he was armed, challenged the King to meet him in single combat, before rushing down into the courtyard of the palace with a terrible clatter.

The King, quite provoked, followed him hastily, but they had hardly taken their places facing one another, and the whole Court had only just had time to rush out upon the balconies to watch what was going on, when suddenly the sun became as red as blood, and it was so dark that they could scarcely see at all. The thunder crashed, and the lightning seemed as if it must burn up everything. The two basilisks appeared, one on each side of the bad Dwarf, like giants, mountains high, and fire flew from their mouths and ears, until they looked like flaming furnaces.

None of these things could terrify the noble young King, and the boldness of his looks and actions reassured those who were looking on, and perhaps even embarrassed the Yellow Dwarf himself, but even his courage gave way when he saw what was happening to his beloved Princess. For the Fairy of the Desert, looking more terrible than before, mounted upon a winged griffin, and with long snakes coiled round her neck, had given her such a blow with the lance she carried that Bellissima fell into the Queen's arms bleeding and senseless. Her fond mother, feeling as much hurt by the blow as the Princess herself, uttered such piercing cries and lamentations that the King, hearing them, entirely lost his courage and presence of mind. Giving up the combat, he flew toward the Princess, to rescue or to die with her, but the Yellow Dwarf was too quick for him. Leaping with his Spanish cat upon the balcony, he snatched Bellissima from the Queen's arms, and before any of the ladies of the Court could stop him he had sprung upon the roof of the palace and disappeared with his prize.

The King, motionless with horror, looked on despairingly at this dreadful occurrence, which he was quite powerless to prevent, and to make matters worse his sight failed him, everything became dark, and he felt himself carried along through the air by a strong hand.

This new misfortune was the work of the wicked Fairy of the Desert, who had come with the Yellow Dwarf to help him carry off the Princess, and had fallen in love with the handsome young King of the Gold Mines directly she saw him. She thought that if she carried him off to some frightful cavern and chained him to a rock, then the fear of death would make him forget Bellissima and become her slave. So, as soon as they reached the place, she gave him back his sight, but without releasing him from his chains, and by her magic power she appeared before him as a young and beautiful fairy, and pretended to have come there quite by chance.

"What do I see?" she cried. "Is it you, dear Prince? What misfortune has brought you to this dismal place?"

The King, who was quite deceived by her altered appearance, replied, "Alas! Beautiful Fairy, the fairy who brought me here first took away my sight, but by her voice I recognized her as the Fairy of the Desert, though what she should have carried me off for I cannot tell you."

"Ah!" cried the pretended Fairy, "If you have fallen into her hands, you won't get away until you have married her. She has carried off more than one Prince like this, and she will certainly have anything she takes a fancy to."

While she was thus pretending to be sorry for the King, he suddenly noticed her feet, which were like those of a griffin, and knew in a moment that this must be the Fairy of the Desert, for her feet were the one thing she could not change, however pretty she might make her face.

Without seeming to have noticed anything, he said, in a confidential way, "Not that I have any dislike to the Fairy of the Desert, but I really cannot endure the way in which she protects the Yellow Dwarf and keeps me chained here like a criminal. It is true that I love a charming princess, but if the Fairy should set me free my gratitude would oblige me to love her only."

"Do you really mean what you say, Prince?" said the Fairy, quite deceived.

"Surely," replied the Prince, "how could I deceive you? You see it is so much more flattering to my vanity to be loved by a fairy than by a simple princess. But, even if I am dying of love for her, I shall pretend to hate her until I am set free."

The Fairy of the Desert, quite taken in by these words, resolved at once to transport the Prince to a pleasanter place. So, making him mount her chariot, to which she had harnessed swans instead of the bats which generally drew it, away she flew with him. But imagine the distress of the Prince when, from the giddy height at which they were rushing through the air, he saw his beloved Princess in a castle built of polished steel, the walls of which reflected the sun's rays so hotly that no one could approach it without being burnt to a cinder! Bellissima was sitting in a little thicket by a brook, leaning her head upon her hand and weeping bitterly, but just as they passed she looked up and saw the King and the Fairy of the Desert. Now, the Fairy was so clever that she could not only seem beautiful to the King, but even the poor Princess thought her the most lovely being she had ever seen.

"What!" she cried, "Was I not unhappy enough in this lonely castle to which that frightful Yellow Dwarf brought me? Must I also be made to know that the King of the Gold Mines ceased to love me as soon as he lost sight of me? But who can my rival be, whose fatal beauty is greater than mine?"

While she was saying this, the King, who really loved her as much as ever, was feeling terribly sad at being so rapidly torn away from his beloved

Princess, but he knew too well how powerful the Fairy was to have any hope of escaping from her except by great patience and cunning.

The Fairy of the Desert had also seen Bellissima, and she tried to read in the King's eyes the effect that this unexpected sight had had upon him.

"No one can tell you what you wish to know better than I can," said he. "This chance meeting with an unhappy princess for whom I once had a passing fancy, before I was lucky enough to meet you, has affected me a little, I admit, but you are so much more to me than she is that I would rather die than leave you."

"Ah, Prince," she said, "can I believe that you really love me so much?"

"Time will show, madam," replied the King, "but if you wish to convince me that you have some regard for me, do not, I beg of you, refuse to aid Bellissima."

"Do you know what you are asking?" said the Fairy of the Desert, frowning, and looking at him suspiciously. "Do you want me to employ my art against the Yellow Dwarf, who is my best friend, and take away from him a proud princess whom I can but look upon as my rival?"

The King sighed, but made no answer. Indeed, what was there to be said to such a clear-sighted person? At last they reached a vast meadow, gay with all sorts of flowers. A deep river surrounded it, and many little brooks murmured softly under the shady trees, where it was always cool and fresh. A little way off stood a splendid palace, the walls of which were of transparent emeralds. As soon as the swans which drew the Fairy's chariot had alighted under a porch, which was paved with diamonds and had arches of rubies, they were greeted on all sides by thousands of beautiful beings, who came to meet them joyfully, singing these words:

"When Love within a heart would reign,

Useless to strive against him 'tis.

The proud but feel a sharper pain,

And make a greater triumph his."

The Fairy of the Desert was delighted to hear them sing of her triumphs. She led the King into the most splendid room that can be imagined, and left him alone for a little while, just that he might not feel that he was a prisoner, but he felt sure that she had not really gone quite away, but was watching him from some hiding place. So walking up to a great mirror, he said to it, "Trusty counsellor, let me see what I can do to make myself agreeable to the charming Fairy of the Desert, for I can think of nothing but how to please her."

And he at once set to work to curl his hair, and, seeing upon a table a grander coat than his own, he put it on carefully. The Fairy came back so delighted that she could not conceal her joy.

"I am quite aware of the trouble you have taken to please me," said she, "and I must tell you that you have succeeded perfectly already. You see it is not difficult to do if you really care for me."

The King, who had his own reasons for wishing to keep the old Fairy in a good humour, did not spare pretty speeches, and after a time he was allowed to walk by himself upon the sea-shore. The Fairy of the Desert had by her enchantments raised such a terrible storm that the boldest pilot would not venture out in it, so she was not afraid of her prisoner's being able to escape, and he found it some relief to think sadly over his terrible situation without being interrupted by his cruel captor.

Presently, after walking wildly up and down, he wrote these verses upon the sand with his stick:

"At last may I upon this shore

Lighten my sorrow with soft tears.

Alas! Alas! I see no more

My Love, who yet my sadness cheers.

And you, O raging, stormy Sea,

Stirred by wild winds, from depth to height,

You hold my loved one far from me,

And I am captive to your might.

My heart is still more wild than thine,

For Fate is cruel unto me.

Why must I thus in exile pine?

Why is my Princess snatched from me?

O, lovely Nymphs, from ocean caves,

Who know how sweet true love may be,

Come up and calm the furious waves

And set a desperate lover free!"

While he was still writing he heard a voice which attracted his attention in spite of himself. Seeing that the waves were rolling in higher than ever, he looked all round, and presently saw a lovely lady floating gently toward him upon the crest of a huge billow, her long hair spread all about her. In one hand she held a mirror, and in the other a comb, and instead of feet she had a beautiful tail like a fish, with which she swam.

The King was struck dumb with astonishment at this unexpected sight, but as soon as she came within speaking distance, she said to him, "I know how sad you are at losing your Princess and being kept a prisoner by the Fairy of the Desert. If you like I will help you to escape from this fatal place, where you may otherwise have to drag on a weary existence for thirty years or more."

The King of the Gold Mines hardly knew what answer to make to this proposal. Not because he did not wish very much to escape, but he was afraid that this might be only another device by which the Fairy of the Desert was trying to deceive him. As he hesitated the Mermaid, who guessed his thoughts, said to him, "You may trust me. I am not trying to entrap you. I am so angry with the Yellow Dwarf and the Fairy of the Desert that I am not likely to wish to help them, especially since I constantly see your poor Princess, whose beauty and goodness make me pity her so much, and I tell you that if you will have confidence in me I will help you to escape."

"I trust you absolutely," cried the King, "and I will do whatever you tell me, but if you have seen my Princess I beg of you to tell me how she is and what is happening to her.

"We must not waste time in talking," said she. "Come with me and I will carry you to the Castle of Steel, and we will leave upon this shore a figure so like you that even the Fairy herself will be deceived by it."

So saying, she quickly collected a bundle of sea-weed, and, blowing it three times, she said, "My friendly sea-weeds, I order you to stay here stretched upon the sand until the Fairy of the Desert comes to take you away."

And at once the sea-weeds became like the King, who stood looking at them in great astonishment, for they were even dressed in a coat like his, but they lay there pale and still as the King himself might have lain if one of the great waves had overtaken him and thrown him senseless upon the shore. And then the Mermaid caught up the King, and away they swam joyfully together.

"Now," said she, "I have time to tell you about the Princess. In spite of the blow which the Fairy of the Desert gave her, the Yellow Dwarf compelled her to mount behind him upon his terrible Spanish cat, but she soon fainted away with pain and terror, and did not recover till they were within the walls of his frightful Castle of Steel. Here she was received by the prettiest girls it was possible to find, who had been carried there by the Yellow Dwarf, who hastened to wait upon her and showed her every possible attention. She was laid upon a couch covered with cloth of gold, embroidered with pearls as big as nuts."

"Ah!" interrupted the King of the Gold Mines, "If Bellissima forgets me, and consents to marry him, I shall break my heart."

"You need not be afraid of that," answered the Mermaid, "the Princess thinks of no one but you, and the frightful Dwarf cannot persuade her to look at him."

"Pray go on with your story," said the King.

"What more is there to tell you?" replied the Mermaid. "Bellissima was sitting in the wood when you passed, and saw you with the Fairy of the Desert, who was so cleverly disguised that the Princess took her to be prettier than herself. You may imagine her despair, for she thought that you had fallen in love with her."

"She believes that I love her!" cried the King. "What a fatal mistake! What is to be done to undeceive her?"

"You know best," answered the Mermaid, smiling kindly at him. "When people are as much in love with one another as you two are, they don't need advice from anyone else."

As she spoke they reached the Castle of Steel, the side next the sea being the only one which the Yellow Dwarf had left unprotected by the dreadful burning walls.

"I know quite well," said the Mermaid, "that the Princess is sitting by the brook-side, just where you saw her as you passed, but as you will have many enemies to fight with before you can reach her, take this sword. Armed with it you may dare any danger, and overcome the greatest difficulties. Only beware of one thing, that is, never to let it fall from your hand. Farewell, now. I will wait by that rock, and if you need my help in carrying off your beloved Princess I will not fail you, for the Queen, her mother, is my best friend, and it was for her sake that I went to rescue you."

So saying, she gave to the King a sword made from a single diamond, which was more brilliant than the sun. He could not find words to express his gratitude, but he begged her to believe that he fully appreciated the importance of her gift, and would never forget her help and kindness.

We must now go back to the Fairy of the Desert. When she found that the King did not return, she hastened out to look for him, and reached the shore, with a hundred of the ladies of her train, loaded with splendid presents for him. Some carried baskets full of diamonds, others golden cups of wonderful workmanship, and amber, coral, and pearls. Others, again, balanced upon their heads bales of the richest and most beautiful stuffs, while the rest brought fruit and flowers, and even birds. But what was the horror of the Fairy, who followed this gay troop, when she saw, stretched upon the sands, the image of the King which the Mermaid had made with the sea-weeds.

Struck with astonishment and sorrow, she uttered a terrible cry, and threw herself down beside the pretended King, weeping, and howling, and calling upon her eleven sisters, who were also fairies, and who came to her assistance. But they were all taken in by the image of the King, for, clever as they were, the Mermaid was still cleverer, and all they could do was to help the Fairy of the Desert to make a wonderful monument over what they thought was the grave of the King of the Gold Mines.

But while they were collecting jasper and porphyry, agate and marble, gold and bronze, statues and devices, to immortalize the King's memory, he was thanking the good Mermaid and begging her still to help him, which she graciously promised to do as she disappeared, and then he set out for the Castle of Steel.

He walked fast, looking anxiously round him, and longing once more to see his darling Bellissima, but he had not gone far before he was surrounded by four terrible sphinxes who would very soon have torn him to pieces with their sharp talons if it had not been for the Mermaid's diamond sword. For, no sooner had he flashed it before their eyes than down they fell at his feet quite helpless, and he killed them with one blow.

But he had hardly turned to continue his search when he met six dragons covered with scales that were harder than iron. Frightful as this encounter was the King's courage was unshaken, and by the aid of his wonderful sword he cut them in pieces one after the other. Now he hoped his difficulties were over, but at the next turning he was met by one which he did not know how to overcome. Four-and-twenty pretty and graceful nymphs advanced toward him, holding garlands of flowers, with which they barred the way.

"Where are you going, Prince?" they said, "It is our duty to guard this place, and if we let you pass great misfortunes will happen to you and to us. We beg you not to insist upon going on. Do you want to kill four-and-twenty girls who have never displeased you in any way?"

The King did not know what to do or to say. It went against all his ideas as a knight to do anything a lady begged him not to do, but, as he hesitated, a voice in his ear said, "Strike! Strike and do not spare, or your Princess is lost for ever!"

So, without reply to the nymphs, he rushed forward instantly, breaking their garlands, and scattering them in all directions, and then went on without further hindrance to the little wood where he had seen Bellissima. She was seated by the brook looking pale and weary when he reached her, and he would have thrown himself down at her feet, but she drew herself away from him with as much indignation as if he had been the Yellow Dwarf.

"Ah, Princess," he cried, "do not be angry with me. Let me explain everything. I am not faithless or to blame for what has happened. I am a miserable wretch who has displeased you without being able to help himself."

"Ah!" cried Bellissima, "Did I not see you flying through the air with the loveliest being imaginable? Was that against your will?"

"Indeed it was, Princess," he answered. "The wicked Fairy of the Desert, not content with chaining me to a rock, carried me off in her chariot to the other end of the earth, where I should even now be a captive but for the unexpected help of a friendly mermaid, who brought me here to rescue you, my Princess, from the unworthy hands that hold you. Do not refuse the aid of your most faithful lover."

So saying, he threw himself at her feet and held her by her robe. But, alas! In so doing he let fall the magic sword, and the Yellow Dwarf, who was crouching behind a lettuce, no sooner saw it than he sprang out and seized it, well knowing its wonderful power.

The Princess gave a cry of terror on seeing the Dwarf, but this only irritated the little monster. Muttering a few magical words he summoned two giants, who bound the King with great chains of iron.

"Now," said the Dwarf, "I am master of my rival's fate, but I will give him his life and permission to depart unharmed if you, Princess, will consent to marry me."

"Let me die a thousand times rather," cried the unhappy King.

"Alas!" cried the Princess, "Must you die? Could anything be more terrible?"

"That you should marry that little wretch would be far more terrible," answered the King.

"At least," continued she, "let us die together."

"Let me have the satisfaction of dying for you, my Princess," said he.

"Oh, no, no!" she cried, turning to the Dwarf, "Rather than that I will do as you wish."

"Cruel Princess!" said the King, "Would you make my life horrible to me by marrying another before my eyes?"

"Not so," replied the Yellow Dwarf, "you are a rival of whom I am too much afraid. You shall not see our marriage." So saying, in spite of Bellissima's tears and cries, he stabbed the King to the heart with the diamond sword.

The poor Princess, seeing her lover lying dead at her feet, could no longer live without him. She sank down by him and died of a broken heart.

So ended these unfortunate lovers, whom not even the Mermaid could help, because all the magic power had been lost with the diamond sword.

As to the wicked Dwarf, he preferred to see the Princess dead rather than married to the King of the Gold Mines, and the Fairy of the Desert, when she heard of the King's adventures, pulled down the grand monument which she had built, and was so angry at the trick that had been played her that she hated him as much as she had loved him before.

The kind Mermaid, grieved at the sad fate of the lovers, and caused them to be changed into two tall palm trees, which stand always side by side, whispering together of their faithful love and caressing one another with their interlacing branches.

Tales From Gallia

PRINCE FEATHERHEAD AND THE PRINCESS CELANDINE

This adaptation is taken from a story collected by Andrew Lang in his Green Fairy Book, published in 1892.

ONCE UPON A TIME THERE LIVED a King and Queen, who were the best creatures in the world, and so kind-hearted that they could not bear to see their subjects want for anything. The consequence was that they gradually gave away all their treasures, till they positively had nothing left to live upon. When this came to the ears of their neighbour, King Bruin, he promptly raised a large army and marched into their country. The poor King, having no means of defending his kingdom, was forced to disguise himself with a false beard. Carrying his only son, the little Prince Featherhead, in his arms, and accompanied only by the Queen, he made the best of his way into the wild country.

They were lucky enough to escape the soldiers of King Bruin, and at last, after unheard-of fatigues and adventures, they found themselves in a charming green valley, through which flowed a stream clear as crystal and overshadowed by beautiful trees. As they looked round them with delight, a voice said suddenly, "Fish, and see what you will catch."

Now the King had always loved fishing, and never went anywhere without a fish-hook or two in his pocket, so he drew one out hastily, and the Queen lent him her girdle to fasten it to, and it had hardly touched the water before it caught a big fish, which made them an excellent meal, and not before they needed it, for they had found nothing until then but a few wild berries and roots.

They thought that for the present they could not do better than stay in this delightful place, and the King set to work, and soon built a bower of branches to shelter them, and when it was finished the Queen was so charmed with it that she declared nothing was lacking to complete her happiness but a flock of sheep, which she and the little Prince might tend while the King fished. They soon found that the fish were not only abundant and easily caught, but also very beautiful, with glittering scales of every imaginable hue, and before long the King discovered that he could teach them to talk and whistle better than any parrot.

Then he determined to carry some to the nearest town and try to sell them, and as no one had ever before seen any like them the people flocked about him eagerly and bought all he had caught, so that presently not a house in the city was considered complete without a crystal bowl full of fish, and the King's customers were very particular about having them to match the rest of the furniture, and gave him a vast amount of trouble in choosing them. However, the money he obtained in this way enabled him to buy the Queen her flock of sheep, as well as many of the other things which go to make life pleasant, so that they never once regretted their lost kingdom.

Now it happened that the Fairy of the Beech-Woods lived in the lovely valley to which chance had led the poor fugitives, and it was she who had, in pity for their forlorn condition, sent the King such good luck to his fishing, and generally taken them under her protection. This she was all the more inclined to do as she loved children, and little Prince Featherhead, who never cried and grew prettier day by day, quite won her heart. She made the acquaintance of the King and the Queen without at first letting them know that she was a fairy, and they soon took a great fancy to her, and even trusted her with the precious Prince, whom she carried off to her palace, where she regaled him with cakes and tarts and every other good thing. This was the way she chose of making him fond of her, but afterwards, as he grew older, she spared no pains in educating and training him as a prince should be trained. But unfortunately, in spite of all her care, he grew so vain and frivolous that he quitted his peaceful country life in disgust, and rushed eagerly after all the foolish gaieties of the neighbouring town, where his handsome face and charming manners speedily made him popular. The King and Queen deeply regretted this alteration in their son, but did not know how to mend matters, since the good old Fairy had made him so self-willed.

Just at this time the Fairy of the Beech-Woods received a visit from an old friend of hers called Saradine, who rushed into her house so breathless with rage that she could hardly speak.

"Dear, dear! What is the matter?" said the Fairy of the Beech-Woods soothingly.

"The matter!" cried Saradine. "You shall soon hear all about it. You know that, not content with endowing Celandine, Princess of the Summer Islands, with everything she could desire to make her charming, I actually took the trouble to bring her up myself, and now what does she do but come to me with more coaxings and caresses than usual to beg a favour. And what do you suppose this favour turns out to be, when I have been cajoled into promising to grant it? Nothing more nor less than a request that I will take back all my gifts, 'since,' says my young madam, 'if I have the good fortune to please you, how am I to know that it is really I, myself? And that's how it will be all my life long, whenever I meet anybody. You see what a weariness my life will be to me under these circumstances, and yet I assure you I am not ungrateful to you for all your kindness!'

"I did all I could," continued Saradine, "to make her think better of it, but in vain, so after going through the usual ceremony for taking back my gifts, I'm come to you for a little peace and quietness. But, after all, I have not taken anything of consequence from this provoking Celandine. Nature had already made her so pretty, and given her such a ready wit of her own, that she will do perfectly well without me. However, I thought she deserved a little lesson, so to begin with I have whisked her off into the desert, and there left her!"

"What! All alone, and without any means of existence?" cried the kind-hearted old Fairy. "You had better hand her over to me. I don't think so very badly of her after all. I'll just cure her vanity by making her love someone better than herself. Really, when I come to consider of it, I declare the little minx has shown more spirit and originality in the matter than one expects of a princess."

Saradine willingly consented to this arrangement, and the old Fairy's first care was to smooth away all the difficulties which surrounded the Princess, and lead her by the mossy path overhung with trees to the bower of the King and Queen, who still pursued their peaceful life in the valley.

They were immensely surprised at her appearance, but her charming face, and the deplorably ragged condition to which the thorns and briers had reduced her once elegant attire, speedily won their compassion. They recognised her as a companion in misfortune, and the Queen welcomed her heartily, and begged her to share their simple repast. Celandine gracefully accepted their hospitality, and soon told them what had happened to her. The King was charmed with her spirit, while the Queen thought she had indeed been daring thus to go against the Fairy's wishes.

"Since it has ended in my meeting you," said the Princess, "I cannot regret the step I have taken, and if you will let me stay with you, I shall be perfectly happy."

The King and Queen were only too delighted to have this charming Princess in the place of Prince Featherhead, whom they saw but seldom, since the Fairy had provided him with a palace in the neighbouring town, where he lived in the greatest luxury, and did nothing but amuse himself from morning to night. So Celandine stayed, and helped the Queen to keep house, and very soon they loved her dearly. When the Fairy of the Beech-Woods came to them, they presented the Princess to her, and told her story, little thinking that the Fairy knew more about Celandine than they did. The old Fairy was equally delighted with her, and often invited her to visit her Leafy Palace, which was the most enchanting place that could be imagined, and full of treasures. Often she would say to the Princess, when showing her some wonderful thing:

"This will do for a wedding gift some day." And Celandine could not help thinking that it was to her that the Fairy meant to give the two blue wax-torches which burned without ever getting smaller, or the diamond from which more diamonds were continually growing, or the boat that sailed under water, or whatever beautiful or wonderful thing they might happen to be looking at. It is true that she never said so positively, but she certainly allowed the Princess to believe it, because she thought a little disappointment would be good for her.

But the person she really relied upon for curing Celandine of her vanity was Prince Featherhead. The old Fairy was not at all pleased with the way he had been going on for some time, but her heart was so soft towards him that she was unwilling to take him away from the pleasures he loved, except by offering him something better, which is not the most effectual mode of correction, though it is without doubt the most agreeable.

However, she did not even hint to the Princess that Featherhead was anything but absolutely perfect, and talked of him so much that when at last she announced that he was coming to visit her, Celandine made up her mind that this delightful Prince would be certain to fall in love with her at once, and was quite pleased at the idea. The old Fairy thought so too, but as this was not at all what she wished, she took care to throw such an enchantment over the Princess that she appeared to Featherhead quite ugly and awkward, though to everyone else she looked just as usual. So when he arrived at the Leafy Palace, more handsome and fascinating even than ever she had been led to expect, he hardly so much as glanced at the Princess, but bestowed all his attention upon the old Fairy, to whom he seemed to have a hundred things to say.

The Princess was immensely astonished at his indifference, and put on a cold and offended air, which, however, he did not seem to observe. Then as a last resource she exerted all her wit and gaiety to amuse him, but with no better success, for he was of an age to be more attracted by beauty than by anything else, and though he responded politely enough, it was evident that his thoughts were elsewhere. Celandine was deeply mortified, since for her part the Prince pleased her very well, and for the first time she bitterly regretted the fairy gifts she had been anxious to get rid of.

Prince Featherhead was almost equally puzzled, for he had heard nothing from the King and Queen but the praises of this charming Princess, and the fact that they had spoken of her as so very beautiful only confirmed his opinion that people who live in the country have no taste. He talked to them of his charming acquaintances in the town, the beauties he had admired, did admire, or thought he was going to admire, until Celandine, who heard it all, was ready to cry with vexation. The Fairy too was quite shocked at his conceit, and hit upon a plan for curing him of it. She sent to him by an unknown messenger a portrait of Princess Celandine as she really was, with this inscription, "All this beauty and sweetness, with a loving heart and a great kingdom, might have been yours but for your well-known fickleness."

This message made a great impression upon the Prince, but not so much as the portrait. He positively could not tear his eyes away from it, and exclaimed aloud that never, never had he seen anything so lovely and so graceful. Then he began to think that it was too absurd that he, the fascinating Featherhead, should fall in love with a portrait, and, to drive away the recollections of its haunting eyes, he rushed back to the town, but somehow everything seemed changed. The beauties no longer pleased him. Their witty speeches ceased to amuse, and indeed, for their parts, they found the Prince far less amiable than of yore, and were not sorry when he declared that, after all, a country life suited him best, and went back to the Leafy Palace.

Meanwhile, the Princess Celandine had been finding the time pass but slowly with the King and Queen, and was only too pleased when Featherhead reappeared. She at once noticed the change in him, and was deeply curious to find the reason of it. Far from avoiding her, he now sought her company and seemed to take pleasure in talking to her, and yet the Princess did not for a moment flatter herself with the idea that he was in love with her, though it did not take her long to decide that he certainly loved someone.

But one day the Princess, wandering sadly by the river, spied Prince Featherhead fast asleep in the shade of a tree, and stole nearer to enjoy the delight of gazing at his dear face unobserved. Judge of her astonishment when she saw that he was holding in his hand a portrait of herself! In vain did she puzzle over the apparent contradictoriness of his behaviour. Why did he cherish her portrait while he was so fatally indifferent to herself? At last she found an opportunity of asking him the name of the Princess whose picture he carried about with him always.

"Alas! How can I tell you?" replied he.

"Why should you not?" said the Princess timidly. "Surely there is nothing to prevent you."

"Nothing to prevent me!" repeated he, "When my utmost efforts have failed to discover the lovely original. Should I be so sad if I could but find her? But I do not even know her name."

More surprised than ever, the Princess asked to be allowed to see the portrait, and after examining it for a few minutes returned it, remarking shyly that at least the original had every cause to be satisfied with it.

"That means that you consider it flattered," said the Prince severely. "Really, Celandine, I thought better of you, and should have expected you to be above such contemptible jealousy. But all women are alike!"

"Indeed, I meant only that it was a good likeness," said the Princess meekly.

"Then you know the original," cried the Prince, throwing himself on his knees beside her. "Pray tell me at once who it is, and don't keep me in suspense!"

"Oh! Don't you see that it is meant for me?" cried Celandine.

The Prince sprang to his feet, hardly able to refrain from telling her that she must be blinded by vanity to suppose she resembled the lovely portrait even in the slightest degree, and after gazing at her for an instant with icy surprise, turned and left her without another word, and in a few hours quitted the Leafy Palace altogether.

Now the Princess was indeed unhappy, and could no longer bear to stay in a place where she had been so cruelly disdained. So, without even bidding farewell to the King and Queen, she left the valley behind her, and wandered sadly away, not caring where. After walking until she was weary, she saw before her a tiny house, and turned her slow steps towards it. The nearer she approached the more miserable it appeared, and at length she saw a little old woman sitting upon the door-step, who said grimly, "Here comes one of these fine beggars who are too idle to do anything but run about the country!"

"Alas, madam," said Celandine, with tears in her pretty eyes, "a sad fate forces me to ask you for shelter."

"Didn't I tell you what it would be?" growled the old hag. "From shelter we shall proceed to demand supper, and from supper money to take us on our way. Upon my word, if I could be sure of finding someone every day whose head was as soft as his heart, I wouldn't wish for a more agreeable life myself! But I have worked hard to build my house and secure a morsel to eat, and I suppose you think that I am to give away everything to the first passer-by who chooses to ask for it. Not at all! I wager that a fine lady like you has more money than I have. I must search her, and see if it is not so," she added, hobbling towards Celandine with the aid of her stick.

"Alas, madam," replied the Princess, "I only wish I had. I would give it to you with all the pleasure in life."

"But you are very smartly dressed for the kind of life you lead," continued the old woman.

"What!" cried the Princess, "Do you think I am come to beg of you?"

"I don't know about that," answered she, "but at any rate you don't seem to have come to bring me anything. But what is it that you do want? Shelter? Well, that does not cost much, but after that comes supper, and that I can't hear of. Oh dear no! Why, at your age one is always ready to eat, and now you have been walking, and I suppose you are ravenous?"

"Indeed no, madam," answered the poor Princess, "I am too sad to be hungry."

"Oh, well! If you will promise to go on being sad, you may stay for the night," said the old woman mockingly.

Thereupon she made the Princess sit down beside her, and began fingering her silken robe, while she muttered "Lace on top, lace underneath! This must have cost you a pretty penny! It would have been better to save enough to feed yourself, and not come begging to those who want all they have for themselves. Pray, what may you have paid for these fine clothes?"

"Alas, madam," answered the Princess, "I did not buy them, and I know nothing about money."

"What do you know, if I may ask?" said the old dame.

"Not much, but indeed I am very unhappy," cried Celandine, bursting into tears, "and if my services are any good to you…"

"Services!" interrupted the hag crossly. "One has to pay for services, and I am not above doing my own work."

"Madam, I will serve you for nothing," said the poor Princess, whose spirits were sinking lower and lower. "I will do anything you please. All I wish is to live quietly in this lonely spot."

"Oh! I know you are only trying to take me in," answered she, "and if I do let you serve me, is it fitting that you should be so much better dressed than I am? If I keep you, will you give me your clothes and wear some that I will provide you with? It is true that I am getting old and may want someone to take care of me some day."

"Oh, for pity's sake, do what you please with my clothes," cried poor Celandine miserably.

And the old woman hobbled off with great alacrity, and fetched a little bundle containing a wretched dress, such as the Princess had never even seen before, and nimbly skipped round, helping her to put it on instead of her own rich robe, with many exclamations of, "Saints! What a magnificent lining! And the width of it! It will make me four dresses at least. Why, child, I wonder you could walk under such a weight, and certainly in my house you would not have had room to turn round."

So saying, she folded up the robe, and put it by with great care, while she remarked to Celandine:

"That dress of mine certainly suits you to a marvel, be sure you take great care of it."

When supper-time came she went into the house, declining all the Princess's offers of assistance, and shortly afterwards brought out a very small dish, saying, "Now let us sup." Whereupon she handed Celandine a small piece of black bread and uncovered the dish, which contained two dried plums.

"We will have one between us," continued the old dame, "and as you are the visitor, you shall have the half which contains the stone, but be very careful that you don't swallow it, for I keep them against the winter, and you have no idea what a good fire they make. Now, you take my advice, which won't cost you anything, and remember that it is always more economical to buy fruit with stones on this account."

Celandine, absorbed in her own sad thoughts, did not even hear this prudent counsel, and quite forgot to eat her share of the plum, which delighted the old woman, who put it by carefully for her breakfast, saying, "I am very much pleased with you, and if you go on as you have begun, we shall do very well, and I can teach you many useful things which people don't generally know. For instance, look at my house! It is built entirely of the seeds of all the pears I have eaten in my life. Now, most people throw them away, and that only shows what a number of things are wasted for want of a little patience and ingenuity."

But Celandine did not find it possible to be interested in this and similar pieces of advice. And the old woman soon sent her to bed, for fear the night air might give her an appetite. She passed a sleepless night, but in the morning the old dame remarked, "I heard how well you slept. After such a night you cannot want any breakfast, so while I do my household tasks you had better stay in bed, since the more one sleeps the less one need eat, and as it is market-day I will go to town and buy a pennyworth of bread for the week's eating."

And so she chattered on, but poor Celandine did not hear or heed her. She wandered out into the desolate country to think over her sad fate. However, the good Fairy of the Beech-Woods did not want her to be starved, so she sent her an unlooked for relief in the shape of a beautiful white cow, which followed her back to the tiny house. When the old woman saw it her joy knew no bounds.

"Now we can have milk and cheese and butter!" cried she. "Ah, how good milk is! What a pity it is so ruinously expensive!"

So they made a little shelter of branches for the beautiful creature which was quite gentle, and followed Celandine about like a dog when she took it out every day to graze. One morning as she sat by a little brook, thinking sadly, she suddenly saw a young stranger approaching, and got up quickly, intending to avoid him. But Prince Featherhead, for it was he, perceiving her at the same moment, rushed towards her with every demonstration of joy, for he had recognised her, not as the Celandine whom he had slighted, but as the lovely Princess whom he had sought vainly for so long.

The fact was that the Fairy of the Beech-Woods, thinking she had been punished enough, had withdrawn the enchantment from her, and transferred it to Featherhead, thereby in an instant depriving him of the good looks which had done so much towards making him the fickle creature he was. Throwing himself down at the Princess's feet, he implored her to stay, and at least speak to him, and she at last consented, but only because he seemed to wish it so very much. After that he came every day in the hope of meeting her again, and often expressed his delight at being with her. But one day, when he had been begging Celandine to love him, she confided to him that it was quite impossible, since her heart was already entirely occupied by another.

"I have," said she, "the unhappiness of loving a Prince who is fickle, frivolous, proud, incapable of caring for anyone but himself, who has been spoilt by flattery, and, to crown all, who does not love me."

"But," cried Prince Featherhead, "surely you cannot care for so contemptible and worthless a creature as that."

"Alas, but I do care," answered the Princess, weeping.

"But where can his eyes be," said the Prince, "that your beauty makes no impression upon him? As for me, since I have possessed your portrait I have wandered over the whole world to find you, and, now we have met, I see that you are ten times lovelier than I could have imagined, and I would give all I own to win your love."

"My portrait?" cried Celandine with sudden interest. "Is it possible that Prince Featherhead can have parted with it?"

"He would part with his life sooner, lovely Princess," answered he, "I can assure you of that, for I am Prince Featherhead."

At the same moment the Fairy of the Beech-Woods took away the enchantment, and the happy Princess recognised her lover, now truly hers, for the trials they had both undergone had so changed and improved them that they were capable of a real love for each other. You may imagine how perfectly happy they were, and how much they had to hear and to tell. But at length it was time to go back to the little house, and as they went along Celandine remembered for the first time what a ragged old dress she was wearing, and what an odd appearance she must present. But the Prince declared that it became her vastly, and that he thought it most picturesque. When they reached the house the old woman received them very crossly.

"I declare," said she, "that it's perfectly true, wherever there is a girl you may be sure that a young man will appear before long! But don't imagine that I'm going to have you here! Not a bit of it, be off with you, my fine fellow!"

Prince Featherhead was inclined to be angry at this uncivil reception, but he was really too happy to care much, so he only demanded, on Celandine's behalf, that the old dame should give her back her own attire, that she might go away suitably dressed.

This request roused her to fury, since she had counted upon the Princess's fine robes to clothe her for the rest of her life, so that it was some time before the Prince could make himself heard to explain that he was willing to pay for them. The sight of a handful of gold pieces somewhat mollified her, however, and after making them both promise faithfully that on no consideration would they ask for the gold back again, she took the Princess into the house and grudgingly doled out to her just enough of her gay attire to make her presentable, while the rest she pretended to have lost. After this they found that they were very hungry, for one cannot live on love, any more than on air, and then the old woman's lamentations were louder than before.

"What!" she cried, "Feed people who were as happy as all that! Why, it was simply ruinous!"

But as the Prince began to look angry, she, with many sighs and mutterings, brought out a morsel of bread, a bowl of milk, and six plums, with which the lovers were well content, for as long as they could look at one another they really did not know what they were eating. It seemed as if they would go on for ever with their reminiscences, the Prince telling how he had wandered all over the world from beauty to beauty, always to be disappointed when he found that no one resembled the portrait, the Princess wondering how it was he could have been so long with her and yet never have recognised her, and over and over again pardoning him for his cold and haughty behaviour to her.

"For," she said, "you see, Featherhead, I love you, and love makes everything right! But we cannot stay here," she added, "so what are we to do?"

The Prince thought they had better find their way to the Fairy of the Beech-Woods and put themselves once more under her protection, and they had hardly agreed upon this course when two little chariots wreathed with jasmine and honeysuckle suddenly appeared, and, stepping into them, they were whirled away to the Leafy Palace. Just before they lost sight of the little house they heard loud cries and lamentations from the miserly old dame, and, looking round, perceived that the beautiful cow was vanishing in spite of her frantic efforts to hold it fast. And they afterwards heard that she spent the rest of her life in trying to put the handful of gold the Prince had thrown to her into her money-bag. For the Fairy, as a punishment for her avarice, caused it to slip out again as fast as she dropped it in.

The Fairy of the Beech-Woods ran to welcome the Prince and Princess with open arms, only too delighted to find them so much improved that she could, with a clear conscience, begin to spoil them again. Very soon the Fairy Saradine also arrived, bringing the King and Queen with her. Princess Celandine implored her pardon, which she graciously gave. Indeed the Princess was so charming she could refuse her nothing. She also restored to her the Summer Islands, and promised her protection in all things.

The Fairy of the Beech-Woods then informed the King and Queen that their subjects had chased King Bruin from the throne, and were waiting to welcome them back again, but they at once abdicated in favour of Prince Featherhead, declaring that nothing could induce them to forsake their peaceful life. The Fairies undertook to see the Prince and Princess established in their beautiful kingdoms. Their marriage took place the next day, and they lived happily ever afterwards, for Celandine was never vain and Featherhead was never fickle any more.

ROBIN REDBREAST

This adaptation is taken from a collection called Breton Legends, although the original author or collector remains unknown.

LONG, LONG AGO, ERE THE ACORNS were sown which have since furnished timber for the oldest vessels of the port of Brest, there lived in the parish of Guirek a poor widow called Ninorc'h Madek. Her father, who was very wealthy and of noble race, had left at his death a manor-house, with a farm, a mill, and a forge, twelve horses and twice as many oxen, twelve cows and ten times as many sheep, to say nothing of corn and flax.

But Ninorc'h was a helpless widow, and her brothers took the whole for themselves. Perrik, the eldest, kept the house, the farm, and the horses. Fanche, the second, took the mill and the cows, whilst the third, whose name was Riwal, had the oxen, the forge, and the sheep. Nothing was left for Ninorc'h but a doorless shed on the open heath, which had served to shelter the sick cattle.

However, as she was getting together her little matter of furniture, in order to take possession of her new abode, Fanche pretended to take pity upon her, and said, "Come, I will deal with you like a brother and a Christian. Here is a black cow. She has never come to much good, and, indeed, gives scarce milk enough to feed a new-born babe, but you may take her with you, if you will, and Mayflower can look after her upon the common."

Mayflower was the widow's daughter, now in her eleventh year, and had been called after the colourless blossom of the thickets from her unusually pale complexion.

So Ninorc'h went away with her pallid little girl, who led the poor lean cow by an old cord, and she sent them out upon the common together.

There Mayflower stayed all day, watching her black cow, which with much ado contrived to pick a little grass between the stones. She spent her time in making little crosses with blossoms of the broom, or in repeating aloud her Rosary and her favourite hymns.

One day, as she was singing the *Ave Maris Stella*, as she had heard it at Vespers in the church of Guirek, all at once she noticed a little bird perched upon one of the flower-crosses she had set in the earth. He was warbling sweetly, and turned his head from side to side, looking at her as if he longed to speak. Not a little surprised, she gently drew near and listened, but without being able to distinguish any meaning in his song. In vain he sang louder, flapped his wings, and fluttered about before Mayflower. Not a whit the wiser was she for all this, and yet such pleasure did she take in watching and listening to him, that night came on without her being able to think of anything else. At last the bird flew away, and when she looked up to see what had become of him, she saw the stars twinkling in the sky.

With all speed she started off to look for her cow, but to her dismay it was nowhere to be found upon the common. In vain she called aloud. In vain she beat the bushes, and in vain she went down into each hollow where the rainwater had formed a pool. At last she heard her mother's voice, calling her, as if some great misfortune had happened. All in a fright, she ran up to her, and there, at the edge of the heath, on the way homeward, she found the widow beside all that remained of the poor cow. All that was left were her horns and her bones, the latter well picked by the wolves, which had sallied forth from the neighbouring woods and made a meal of her.

At this sight Mayflower felt her blood run cold. She burst into tears, for she loved the black cow she had tended so long, and falling on her knees exclaimed, "Blessed Virgin, why did you not let me see the wolf? I would have scared him away with the sign of the cross, I would have repeated the charm that is taught to shepherd-boys who keep their flocks upon the mountains: 'Are you wolf, St. Hervé shend you! Are you Satan, God defend me!'"

The widow, who was a very saint for piety and resignation, seeing the sorrow of the little girl, sought to comfort her, saying, "It is not well to weep for the cow as for a fellow-creature, my poor child. If the wolves and wicked men conspire against us, the Lord God will be on our side. Come, then, help me up with my bundle of heather, and let us go home."

Mayflower did as she said, but sighed at every step, and the big tears trickled down her cheeks.

"My poor cow!" said she to herself, "My poor, good, gentle cow! And just, too, as she was beginning to fatten a little."

The little girl had no heart for supper, and many times awakened in the night, fancying that she heard the black cow lowing at the door. With very restlessness she rose before the dawn, and ran out upon the common, barefooted and but half-dressed. There, at the self-same spot, appeared the little bird again, perched as before on her broom-flower cross. Again he sang, and seemed to call her. But, alas, she was as little able as on the preceding evening to understand him, and was turning away in vexation, when she thought she saw a piece of gold glittering on the ground. To try what it really was, she moved it with her foot, but, lo, it was the gold-herb, and no sooner had she touched it than she distinctly understood the language of the little bird, saying in his warbling, "Mayflower, I wish you well. Mayflower, listen to me."

"Who are you?" said Mayflower, wondering within herself that she could understand the language of an unbaptised creature.

"I am Robin Redbreast," returned the bird. "It was I that followed the Saviour on His way to Calvary, and broke a thorn from the crown that was tearing His brow. To recompense this act, it was granted to me by God the Father that I should live until the day of judgment, and that every year I might bestow a fortune upon one poor girl. This year I have chosen you."

"Can this be true, Robin Redbreast?" cried Mayflower, in a transport of delight. "And shall I have a silver cross for my neck, and be able to wear wooden shoes?"

"A cross of gold shall you have, and silken slippers shall you wear, like a noble damsel," replied Robin Redbreast.

"But what must I do, dear kind Robin?" said the little maid.

"Only follow me."

It may well be supposed that Mayflower had no objection to make, so Robin Redbreast flew before, and she ran after him.

On they went, across the heath, through the copses, and over the fields of rye, till at last they came to the open downs over against the Seven Isles. There Robin stopped, and said to the little girl, "Do you see anything on the sands down there?"

"I see," replied Mayflower, "a great pair of beech shoes that the fire has never scorched, and a holly-staff that has not been hacked by the sickle."

"Put on the shoes, and take up the staff."

It was done.

"Now walk upon the sea to the first island, and go round it till you come to a rock on which grow sea-green rushes."

"What then?"

"Gather some of the rushes, and twist them into a cord."

"Well, and then?"

"Then strike the rock with the holly-staff, and there will come forth from it a cow. Make a halter of the rushen cord, and lead her home to console your mother for the one just lost."

All that Robin Redbreast had told her, Mayflower did. She walked upon the sea, she made the cord of rushes, she struck the rock, and there came out from it a cow, with eyes as soft as a stag-hound's, and a skin sleek as that of the mole that burrows in the meadows. Mayflower led her home to her poor mother, whose joy now was almost greater than her former sorrow.

But what were her sensations when she began to milk Mor Vyoc'h! (for so had Robin Redbreast named the creature). Behold, the milk flowed on and on beneath her fingers like water from a spring!

Ninorc'h had soon filled all the earthen vessels in the house, and then all those of wood, but still the milk flowed on.

"Now, holy Mother save us!" cried the widow, "certainly this beast has drunk of the waters of Languengar."

In fact, the milk of Mor Vyoc'h was inexhaustible, and she had already yielded enough to satisfy every babe in Cornouaille.

In a little time nothing was talked of throughout the country but the widow's cow, and people crowded from all parts to see it. The rector of Peros-Guirek came among the rest, to see whether it were not a snare of the evil one, but after he had laid his stole upon Mor Vyoc'h's head, he pronounced her clear of all suspicion.

Before long all the richest farmers were persuading Ninorc'h to sell her cow, each one bidding against the other for so invaluable a beast, her brother Perrik among the rest.

"Come," said he, "I am your brother. As a good Christian you must give me the preference. Let me have Mor Vyoc'h, and I will give you in exchange as many cows as it takes tailors to make a man."

"Is that your Christian dealing?" answered the widow. "Nine cows for Mor Vyoc'h! She is worth all the cows in the country, far and near. With her milk I could supply all the markets in the bishoprics of Tréguier and Cornouaille, from Dinan to Carhaix."

"Well, sister, only let me have her," replied Perrik, "and I will give up to you our father's farm, on which you were born, with all the fields, ploughs, and horses."

This proposal Ninorc'h accepted, and was forthwith put in possession, turning up a sod in the meadows, taking a draught of water from the well, and kindling a fire on the hearth, besides cutting a tuft of hair from the horses' tails in token of ownership. She then delivered Mor Vyoc'h to Perrik, who led her away to a house which he had at some distance, towards Menez-Brée.

That was a day of tears and sadness for Mayflower, and as at night she went the round of the stalls to see that all was right, she could not help again and again murmuring, as she filled the mangers, "Alas, Mor Vyoc'h is gone! I shall never see Mor Vyoc'h again."

With this lament still on her lips, she suddenly heard a lowing behind her, because, as by virtue of the gold-herb her ears were now open to the language of all animals. She distinctly made out these words, "Here I am again, my little mistress,"

Mayflower turned round in astonishment, and there indeed was Mor Vyoc'h.

"Oh, can this indeed be you?" cried the little girl. "And what, then, has brought you back?"

"I cannot belong to your uncle Perrik," said Mor Vyoc'h, "for my nature forbids me to remain with such as are not in a state of grace, so I am come back to be with you again as before."

"But then my mother must give back the farm, the fields, and all that she has received for you."

"Not so, for it was already hers by right, and had been unjustly taken from her by your uncle."

"But he will come to see if you are here, and will know you again."

"Go and gather three leaves of the cross-wort, and I will tell you what to do."

Mayflower went, and soon returned with the three leaves.

"Now," said Mor Vyoc'h, "pass those leaves over me, from my horns to my tail, and say 'St. Ronan of Ireland!' three times."

Mayflower did so, and as she called on the saint for the third time, lo, the cow became a beautiful horse. The little girl was lost in wonder.

"Now," said the creature to her, "your uncle Perrik cannot possibly know me again, for I am no longer Mor Vyoc'h, but Marc'h-Mor."

On hearing what had come to pass, the widow was greatly rejoiced, and early on the morrow proceeded to make trial of her horse with a load of corn for Tréguier. But guess her astonishment when she found that the more sacks were laid on Marc'h-Mor's back the longer it grew, so that he alone could carry as much wheat as all the horses in the parish.

The tale of the widow's wonderful horse was soon noised about the neighbourhood, and among the rest her brother Fanche heard of it. He therefore lost no time in proceeding to the farm, and when he had seen Marc'h-Mor, begged his sister to part with him, which, however, she would by no means consent to do till Fanche had offered her in exchange his cows and his mill, with all the pigs that he was fattening there.

The bargain concluded, Ninorc'h took possession of her new property, as she had done at the farm, and Fanche led away Marc'h-Mor.

But in the evening there he was again, and again Mayflower gathered three leaves of cross-wort, stroked him over with them three times from his ears to his tail, repeating each time St. Ronan of Ireland as she had done before to Mor Vyoc'h. And, lo, in a moment the horse changed into a sheep covered with wool as long as hemp, as red as scarlet, and as fine as dressed flax.

Full of admiration at this new miracle, the widow came to behold it, and no sooner was she within sight than she called to Mayflower, "Run and fetch a pair of shears, for the poor creature cannot bear this weight of wool."

But when she began to shear Mor-Vawd, she found the wool grew as fast as she cut it off, so that he alone far out-valued all the flocks of Arhèz.

Riwal, who chanced to come by at that moment, was witness of the wonder, and then and there parted with his forge, his sheep-walks, and all his sheep, to obtain possession of the wonderful sheep.

But see! As he was leading his new purchase home along the sea-shore, the sheep suddenly plunged in the water, swam to the smallest of the seven isles, and passed into a chasm of the rocks, which opened to receive it, and straight-way closed again.

This time Mayflower expected him back at the usual hour in vain. Neither that night nor on the morrow did he revisit the farm.

The little girl ran to the common. There she found Robin Redbreast, who thus spoke, before he flew away for ever, "I have been waiting for you, my little lady. The sheep is gone, and will return no more. Your uncles have been punished after their deserts. For you, you are now a rich heiress, and may wear a cross of gold and silken slippers, as I promised you. My work here is done, and I am about to fly away far from here. Only, remember always, that you have been poor, and that it was one of God's little birds that made you rich."

To prove her gratitude, Mayflower built a chapel on the heath, on that very spot where Robin Redbreast first addressed her. And the old men, from whom our fathers heard this tale, could remember lighting the altar-candles there when they were little boys.

THE FAIRIES

This adaptation is taken from Charles Perrault's book, Old-time Stories, published by Dodd, Mead & Company, New York in 1921.

ONCE UPON A TIME THERE LIVED a widow with two daughters. The elder was often mistaken for her mother, so like her was she both in nature and in looks, parent and child being so disagreeable and arrogant that no one could live with them.

The younger girl, who took after her father in the gentleness and sweetness of her disposition, was also one of the prettiest girls imaginable. The mother doted on the elder daughter, naturally enough, since she resembled her so closely, and disliked the younger one as intensely. She made the latter live in the kitchen and work hard from morning till night.

One of the poor child's many duties was to go twice a day and draw water from a spring a good half-mile away, bringing it back in a large pitcher. One day when she was at the spring an old woman came up and begged for a drink.

"Why, certainly, good mother," the pretty lass replied. Rinsing her pitcher, she drew some water from the cleanest part of the spring and handed it to the dame, lifting up the jug so that she might drink the more easily.

Now this old woman was a fairy, who had taken the form of a poor village dame to see just how far the girl's good nature would go. "You are so pretty," she said, when she had finished drinking, "and so polite, that I am determined to bestow a gift upon you. This is the boon I grant you. With every word that you utter there shall fall from your mouth either a flower or a precious stone."

When the girl reached home she was scolded by her mother for being so long in coming back from the spring.

"I am sorry to have been so long, mother," said the poor child.

As she spoke these words there fell from her mouth three roses, three pearls, and three diamonds.

"What's this?" cried her mother, "Did I see pearls and diamonds dropping out of your mouth? What does this mean, dear daughter?" (This was the first time she had ever addressed her daughter affectionately.)

The poor child told a simple tale of what had happened, and in speaking scattered diamonds right and left.

"Really," said her mother, "I must send my own child there. Come here, Fanchon. Look what comes out of your sister's mouth whenever she speaks! Wouldn't you like to be able to do the same? All you have to do is to go and draw some water at the spring, and when a poor woman asks you for a drink, give it her very nicely."

"Oh, indeed!" replied the ill-mannered girl, "I'm sure you would love to see me work so hard!"

"I tell you that you are to go," said her mother, "and to go this instant."

Very sulkily the girl went off, taking with her the best silver flagon in the house. No sooner had she reached the spring than she saw a lady, magnificently attired, who came towards her from the forest, and asked for a drink. This was the same fairy who had appeared to her sister, masquerading now as a princess in order to see how far this girl's ill-nature would carry her.

"Do you think I have come here just to get you a drink?" said the loutish damsel, arrogantly. "I suppose you think I brought a silver flagon here specially for that purpose. It's so likely, isn't it? Drink from the spring, if you want to!"

"You are not very polite," said the fairy, displaying no sign of anger. "Well, in return for your lack of courtesy I decree that for every word you utter a snake or a toad shall drop out of your mouth."

The moment her mother caught sight of her coming back she cried out, "Well, daughter?"

"Well, mother?" replied the rude girl. As she spoke a viper and a toad were spat out of her mouth.

"Gracious heavens!" cried her mother, "What do I see? Her sister is the cause of this, and I will make her pay for it!"

Off she ran to thrash the poor child, but the latter fled away and hid in the forest nearby. The king's son met her on his way home from hunting, and noticing how pretty she was inquired what she was doing all alone, and what she was weeping about.

"Alas, sir," she cried, "my mother has driven me from home!"

As she spoke the prince saw four or five pearls and as many diamonds fall from her mouth. He begged her to tell him how this came about, and she told him the whole story.

The king's son fell in love with her, and reflecting that such a gift as had been bestowed upon her was worth more than any dowry which another maiden might bring him, he took her to the palace of his royal father, and there married her.

As for the sister, she made herself so hateful that even her mother drove her out of the house. Nowhere could the wretched girl find anyone who would take her in, and at last she lay down in the forest and died.

Tales From Gallia

Tales From Gallia

THE SEVEN CONQUERORS OF THE QUEEN OF THE MISSISSIPPI

A Belgian Fairy Tale. This adaptation is taken from Edmund Dulac's collection called Edmund Dulac's Fairy Book, published by George H. Doran Company, New York in 1916.

ONCE UPON A TIME THERE WAS a boy who was ambitious. One day he said to his mother, "Give me a muffin and patch my trousers, for I am going to set out to win the Queen of the Mississippi."

So the mother gave him a muffin and patched his trousers, and the boy went off.

He had not gone very far when he came to a mountain path, on which was a great cross, beneath which stood a man holding a bow with an arrow fixed on the string.

This man looked down at the boy as if to say, "What are you doing here?"

The boy immediately answered his unspoken question by demanding, "Hello, friend! What are you doing there?"

"You see that fly on that cross?" said the man, pointing to a minute speck on one of its arms. "Wait then, and watch me! I will put out one of its eyes."

With this, while the boy watched, he drew his bow to the full, and let the arrow fly. It was a wonderful shot, for one of the eyes of the fly fell on the ground at the foot of the cross.

The boy was so taken with this, that he seemed to grow two whole years in half a minute. To look at him, you would have thought he was no longer a boy. He drew himself up proudly to his full height, and said in the voice of a young man, "Will you travel with me, my pippy?"

"Pardon?"

Then it was question and answer between them.

"Come, travel with me, my pippy."

"Oh! Where away? To old Mandalay?"

"But no, to the far Mississippi, Where a beautiful Queen holds sway, and I'll marry that Queen someday."

"I am yours! And the bounty?"

"Give it a name, I will pay."

Then the young man took his muffin, and, breaking off a little bit of it, handed it to the man with the bow and arrow. "Keep it," said he, "it's a pledge of good faith."

So they journeyed on together. When they had gone some distance, they came to a high field, and in the middle of this stood a man stock still, gazing at the sun. As soon as the young man saw him, he shouted out at the top of his voice, "Hi! What are you doing there, my good fellow?"

"I am just waiting for it to get a little more dazzling," replied the man, still keeping his eyes fixed on the midday sun.

As soon as the young man heard this he seemed to grow still more in stature. Indeed, he seemed to be almost a man.

"Will you travel with me?" he said.

"Pardon?"

Then it was question and answer between them.

"Come, travel with me, my pippy."

"Oh! Where away? To the land of Cathay?"

"But no, to the far Mississippi, Where a beautiful Queen holds sway, who has stolen my heart away."

"I am yours! And the bounty?"

"What you will, it's a pleasure to pay."

Then the young man took his muffin, and, breaking off a little bit of it, handed it to the man who gazed at the sun. "Keep it," said he, "it's a pledge of good faith."

"Hi, friend! Take the whole castle, with the Queen and all that it contains, on your shoulders!"

So they journeyed on together. When they had gone some distance further, they saw a man who had tied his legs together.

"Hello! What are you doing there, my friend?"

"I want to catch that hare over yonder, but unless I tied my legs together there would be no sport in it."

"Will you travel with me?"

"Pardon?"

"Will you travel with me, my pippy?"

"Oh! Where away? To Botany Bay?"

"But no, to the far Mississippi, where a Queen, tooral-ooral-i-ay, is waiting for what I'm to say."

"I am yours! And the bounty? Either here or in Botany Bay!"

Then the boy took his muffin, and, breaking off a little piece, handed it to him. "Keep it," said he, "it's a pledge of good faith."

So they journeyed on together. But they had travelled scarce a league when they met a man who was carrying ten great trees in his arms. And when the boy, who had grown into a young man, saw this, he was immediately full grown.

"Hi! my friend! What are you doing there?"

"My mother wants some wood," replied the man, picking a few branches off the trees and flinging them idly on the roadside, "so I am just taking her some."

"Will you travel with me?"

"Pardon?"

"Will you travel with me, my pippy?"

"Oh! Where away? To Rome or Pompeii?"

"But no, to the far Mississippi. There's a Queen of great beauty that way, and there's no one but Cupid to pay."

"I am yours! And the bounty?"

"Name your price, it shall be as you say."

Then the young man took his muffin, and, breaking off a little bit of it, handed it to the man who carried the trees. "Keep it," said he, "it's a pledge of good faith."

So they journeyed on together. They were still a long way from the Mississippi when they came across a man with a mouth large enough to swallow a river. When the boy, who had become a young man and was now full grown, set his eyes on him, his beard and moustache began to sprout.

"Will you travel with me?"

"Pardon?"

"Come, travel with me, my pippy. (Sing merry-ton-ton-ta-lay.) To the land of the far Mississippi where the crystalline fountains play. There's a Queen who will not say me nay."

"I am yours! But the bounty?"

"We're picking it up on the way."

Then the young man took his muffin, and, breaking off a little bit of it, handed it to the man with the mouth as large as a river. "'Keep it," said he, "it's a pledge of good faith."

So they journeyed on together. On and on they went until at last they came to a great hill-top, and there, standing on the crest of it, they looked down into an immense valley where they saw a man engaged in eating up the whole earth. As soon as he saw this gigantic meal going on, the boy, who had become a young man and was now full grown with moustache and beard, appeared like a knight errant. One could see that, from the spurs which had grown upon his heels.

"Hi! What are you doing there?"

"I am so terribly hungry that nothing less than the whole earth can appease my appetite."

"Will you travel with me?"

"Pardon?"

"Come, travel with me, my pippy."

"Oh! Where? Madras or Bombay?"

"But no, to that far Mississippi, which flows from the gates of the day, where a Queen all in purple array waits for me…"

"I am yours! And the bounty?"

"Wouldn't go in a twenty-ton dray!"

Then the young man took his muffin, and, breaking off a little bit, handed it to the man who was eating up the earth. "Keep it," said he, "it's a pledge of good faith."

They were still a long way from their destination when they came to a beautiful castle of burnished gold, surrounded by a very deep moat over which was a drawbridge, and on the bridge was a golden portcullis. As soon as they arrived, their leader rang the bell. When the door was opened, the travellers entered, and the hero asked to see the King.

"What do you want with the King?" replied an attendant, richly attired.

"I have come to ask for the hand of his daughter, the Queen of the Mississippi," said the hero.

"That is all very well, but consider well before you start on such an undertaking, for many have come as you have come and have lost their lives."

"That is nothing," they all replied. "We are not afraid!"

Then they were led before the Queen, and all were completely dazzled by her beauty. It was a long time before they realised that she was speaking to them. At last they understood her to say, "Here is my servant. See if you can eat more than he does."

And the servant sat down in front of a table covered with dishes crowded with large joints of meat. And behold, he ate the whole lot up.

"Oh! that is nothing at all," said the young hero. And, turning to the man who ate up the earth, he said, "Sit down there, my friend." Then turning again to the servant, he ordered him to bring in the biggest bull they could find.

They obeyed, and set it down in front of the man who ate the earth. And, in presence of the Queen, he swallowed the bull whole, head and tail and everything, and it was alive!

But the Queen said, "You have not won me yet!"

And then she called in a second servant and said, "Here is my servant. See if you can drink more than he can!"

And immediately the servant took hold of a whole cask of wine, and in one mouthful drank the whole lot up.

The young hero said, "That is nothing at all!" Then, turning to the man with a mouth as big as a river, he added, "Come here, my friend. Place yourself on your stomach on the moat, and drink well!"

And the man with the mouth as large as a river placed himself on his stomach, with his mouth to the water of the great moat outside, and in one second he had drunk up the whole moat, fishes and all, absolutely dry.

But the Queen still said they had not won her!

And she beckoned another servant. Then, turning to the young man, she said, "See if you can run better than he can. There," she said, "at the top of that high mountain, just near the sun, lives a hermit. Go and ask him what it is he wishes to say to me. Then come back and tell me."

"Oh! that is nothing at all," said the young hero. And, turning to the man who ran like a hare, he said, "Go to the top of the mountain and come back with the message."

And the man who ran like a hare was out of sight in a second, and before they could count three he had returned to the Queen with the message that the hermit was dead, which the Queen had known all the time.

And the young man said to the King, "You have submitted us to the test, and we have carried out all that you wished. We have now gained the Queen, and I am going to take her."

Then the King got very angry and called out all his soldiers.

The young man, hearing this, said to the man with the strong arms, "Hi, friend! Take the whole castle, with the Queen and all that it contains, on your shoulders!"

The man obeyed and they went on their way!

They had not gone a great distance when the man who had gazed at the sun cried out, "In the distance I can see that we are being pursued by an army. They want to take the Queen!"

The King and his army approached rapidly, and demanded the Queen.

Then the man of the strong arm killed the King and every one of his army with a single blow.

Then he departed with the Queen and the castle to the home of the young man, and as soon as they got there the hero married the Queen, and, with her and his mother, they lived very happily to a good old age.

Tales From Gallia

THE ADVENTURES OF COVAN THE BROWN-HAIRED

This adaptation is taken from a story collected by Andrew Lang in his Orange Fairy Book, published in 1906. The original is taken from Les Contes des Fees by Marie-Catherine Le Jumel de Barneville, Baroness d'Aulnoy, a French writer known for her fairy tales. When she termed her works contes de fées (fairy tales), she originated the term that is now generally used for the genre.

ON THE SHORES OF THE WEST, where the great hills stand with their feet in the sea, dwelt a goatherd and his wife, together with their three sons and one daughter. All day long the young men fished and hunted, while their sister took out the goats to pasture on the mountain, or stayed at home helping her mother and mending the nets.

For several years they all lived happily together, when one day, as the girl was out on the hill with the goats, the sun grew dark and an air cold as a thick white mist came creeping, creeping up from the sea. She rose with a shiver, and tried to call to her goats, but the voice died away in her throat, and strong arms seemed to hold her.

Loud were the wails in the hut by the sea when the hours passed on and the maiden came not. Many times the father and brothers jumped up, thinking they heard her steps, but in the thick darkness they could scarcely see their own hands, nor could they tell where the river lay, nor where the mountain rose up. One by one the goats came home, and at every bleat someone hurried to open the door, but no sound broke the stillness. Through the night no one slept, and when morning broke and the mist rolled back, they sought the maiden by sea and by land, but never a trace of her could be found anywhere.

Thus a year and a day slipped by, and at the end of it Gorla of the Flocks and his wife seemed suddenly to have grown old. Their sons too were sadder than before, for they loved their sister well, and had never ceased to mourn for her. At length Ardan the eldest spoke and said, "It is now a year and a day since our sister was taken from us, and we have waited in grief and patience for her to return. Surely some evil has befallen her, or she would have sent us a token to put our hearts at rest, and I have vowed to myself that my eyes shall not know sleep till, living or dead, I have found her."

"If you have vowed, then must you keep your vow," answered Gorla. "But better had it been if you had first asked your father's leave before you made it. Yet, since it is so, your mother will bake you a cake for you to carry with you on your journey. Who can tell how long it may be?"

So the mother arose and baked not one cake but two, a big one and a little one.

"Choose, my son," said she. "Will you have the little cake with your mother's blessing, or the big one without it, in that you have set aside your father and taken on yourself to make a vow?"

"I will have the large cake," answered the youth, "for what good would my mother's blessing do for me if I was dying of hunger?" And taking the big cake he went his way.

Straight on he strode, letting neither hill nor river hinder him. Swiftly he walked, swiftly as the wind that blew down the mountain. The eagles and the gulls looked on from their nests as he passed, leaving the deer behind him, but at length he stopped, for hunger had seized on him, and he could walk no more. Trembling with fatigue he sat himself on a rock and broke a piece off his cake.

"Spare me a morsel, Ardan son of Gorla," asked a raven, fluttering down towards him.

"Seek food elsewhere, O bearer of ill-news," answered Ardan son of Gorla, "it is but little I have for myself." And he stretched himself out for a few moments, then rose to his feet again. On and on went he till the little birds flew to their nests, and the brightness died out of the sky, and a darkness fell over the earth. On and on, and on, till at last he saw a beam of light streaming from a house and hastened towards it.

The door was opened and he entered, but paused when he beheld an old man lying on a bench by the fire, while seated opposite him was a maiden combing out the locks of her golden hair with a comb of silver.

"Welcome, fair youth," said the old man, turning his head. "Sit down and warm yourself, and tell me how fares the outer world. It is long since I have seen it."

"All my news is that I am seeking service," answered Ardan son of Gorla, "I have come from far since sunrise, and glad was I to see the rays of your lamp stream into the darkness."

"I need someone to herd my three dun cows, which are hornless," said the old man. "If, for the space of a year, you can bring them back to me each evening before the sun sets, I will make you payment that will satisfy your soul."

But here the girl looked up and answered quickly, "Ill will come of it if he listens to your offer."

"Counsel unsought is worth nothing," replied, Ardan, son of Gorla, rudely. "It would be little indeed that I am fit for if I cannot drive three cows out to pasture and keep them safe from the wolves that may come down from the mountains. Therefore, good father, I will take service with you at daybreak, and ask no payment till the new year dawns."

Next morning the bell of the deer was not heard amongst the fern before the maiden with the hair of gold had milked the cows, and led them in front of the cottage where the old man and Ardan son of Gorla awaited them.

"Let them wander where they will," he said to his servant, "and never seek to turn them from their way, for well they know the fields of good pasture. But take heed to follow always behind them, and suffer nothing that you see, and nought that you hear, to draw you into leaving them. Now go, and may wisdom go with you."

As he ceased speaking he touched one of the cows on her forehead, and she stepped along the path, with the two others one on each side. As he had been bidden, behind them came Ardan son of Gorla, rejoicing in his heart that work so easy had fallen to his lot. At the year's end, thought he, enough money would lie in his pocket to carry him into far countries where his sister might be, and, in the meanwhile, someone might come past who could give him tidings of her.

Thus he spoke to himself, when his eyes fell on a golden cock and a silver hen running swiftly along the grass in front of him. In a moment the words that the old man had uttered vanished from his mind and he gave chase. They were so near that he could almost seize their tails, yet each time he felt sure he could catch them his fingers closed on the empty air. At length he could run no more, and stopped to breathe, while the cock and hen went on as before. Then he remembered the cows, and, somewhat frightened, turned back to seek them. Luckily they had not strayed far, and were quietly feeding on the thick green grass.

Ardan son of Gorla was sitting under a tree, when he beheld a staff of gold and a staff of silver doubling themselves in strange ways on the meadow in front of him, and starting up he hastened towards them. He followed them till he was tired, but he could not catch them, though they seemed ever within his reach. When at last he gave up the quest his knees trembled beneath him for very weariness, and glad was he to see a tree growing close by lade with fruits of different sorts, of which he ate greedily.

The sun was by now low in the heavens, and the cows left off feeding, and turned their faces home again, followed by Ardan son of Gorla. At the door of their stable the maiden stood awaiting them, and saying nought to their herd, she sat down and began to milk. But it was not milk that flowed into her pail. Instead it was filled with a thin stream of water, and as she rose up from the last cow the old man appeared outside.

"Faithless one, you have betrayed your trust!" he said to Ardan son of Gorla. "Not even for one day could you keep true! Well, you shall have your reward at once, that others may take warning from you." And waving his wand he touched with it the chest of the youth, who became a pillar of stone.

Now Gorla of the Flocks and his wife were full of grief that they had lost a son as well as a daughter, for no tidings had come to them of Ardan their eldest born. At length, when two years and two days had passed since the maiden had led her goats to feed on the mountain and had been seen no more, Ruais, second son of Gorla, rose up one morning, and said, "Time is long without my sister and Ardan my brother. So I have vowed to seek them wherever they may be."

And his father answered, "Better it had been if you had first asked my consent and that of your mother, but as you have vowed so must you do."

Then he bade his wife make a cake, but instead she made two, and offered Ruais his choice, as she had done to Ardan. Like Ardan, Ruais chose the large, unblessed cake, and set forth on his way, doing always, though he knew it not, that which Ardan had done, so, needless is it to tell what befell him till he too stood, a pillar of stone, on the hill behind the cottage, so that all men might see the fate that awaited those who broke their faith.

Another year and a day passed by, when Covan the Brown-haired, youngest son of Gorla of the Flocks, one morning spake to his parents, saying. "It is more than three years since my sister left us. My brothers have also gone, no one know where, and of us four none remains but I. No, therefore, I long to seek them, and I pray you and my mother to place no hindrance in my way."

And his father answered, "Go, then, and take our blessing with you."

So the wife of Gorla of the Flocks baked two cakes, one large and one small, and Covan took the small one, and started on his quest. In the wood he felt hungry, for he had walked far, and he sat down to eat. Suddenly a voice behind him cried, "A bit for me! A bit for me!" And looking round he beheld the black raven of the wilderness.

"Yes, you shall have a bit," said Covan the Brown-haired, and breaking off a piece he stretched it upwards to the raven, who ate it greedily. Then Covan arose and went forward, till he saw the light from the cottage streaming before him, and glad was he, for night was at hand.

"Maybe I shall find some work there," he thought, "and at least I shall gain money to help me in my search, for who knows how far my sister and my brothers may have wandered?"

The door stood open and he entered, and the old man gave him welcome, and the golden-haired maiden likewise. As happened before, he was offered by the old man to herd his cows, and, as she had done to his brothers, the maiden counselled him to leave such work alone. But, instead of answering rudely, like both Ardan and Ruais, he thanked her, with courtesy, though he had no mind to heed her, and he listened to the warnings and words of his new master.

Next day he set forth at dawn with the dun cows in front of him, and followed patiently wherever they might lead him. On the way he saw the gold cock and silver hen, which ran even closer to him than they had done to his brothers. Sorely tempted, he longed to give them chase, but, remembering in time that he had been bidden to look neither to the right nor to the left, with a mighty effort he turned his eyes away. Then the gold and silver staffs seemed to spring from the earth before him, but this time also he overcame, and though the fruit from the magic tree almost touched his mouth, he brushed it aside and went steadily on.

That day the cows wandered father than ever they had done before, and never stopped till they had reached a moor where the heather was burning. The fire was fierce, but the cows took no heed, and walked steadily through it, Covan the Brown-haired following them. Next they plunged into a foaming river, and Covan plunged in after them, though the water came high above his waist. On the other side of the river lay a wide plain, and here the cows lay down, while Covan looked about him. Near him was a house built of yellow stone, and from it came sweet songs, and Covan listened, and his heart grew light within him.

While he was thus waiting there ran up to him a youth, scarcely able to speak so swiftly had he sped, and he cried aloud, "Hasten, hasten, Covan the Brown-haired, for your cows are in the corn, and you must drive them out!"

"Nay," said Covan smiling, "it had been easier for you to have driven them out than to come here to tell me." And he went on listening to the music.

Very soon the same youth returned and cried with panting breath, "Out upon you, Covan son of Gorla, that you stand there agape. For our dogs are chasing your cows, and you must drive them off!"

"Nay, then," answered Covan as before, "it had been easier for you to call off your dogs than to come here to tell me." And he stayed where he was till the music ceased.

Then he turned to look for the cows, and found them all lying in the place where he had left them, but when they saw Covan they rose up and walked homewards, taking a different path to that they had trod in the morning. This time they passed over a plain so bare that a pin could not have lain there unnoticed, yet Covan beheld with surprise a foal and its mother feeding there, both as fat as if they had pastured on the richest grass. Further on they crossed another plain, where the grass was thick and green, but on it were feeding a foal and its mother, so lean that you could have counted their ribs. And further again the path led them by the shores of a lake whereon were floating two boats, one full of gay and happy youths, journeying to the land of the Sun, and another with grim shapes clothed in black, travelling to the land of Night.

"What can these things mean?" said Covan to himself, as he followed his cows.

Darkness now fell, the wind howled, and torrents of rain poured upon them. Covan knew not how far they might yet have to go, or indeed if they were on the right road. He could not even see his cows, and his heart sank lest, after all, he should have failed to bring them safely back. What was he to do?

He waited thus, for he could go neither forwards nor backwards, till he felt a great friendly paw laid on his shoulder.

"My cave is just here," said the Dog of Maol-mor, of whom Covan son of Gorla had heard much. "Spend the night here, and you shall be fed on the flesh of lamb, and shall lay aside three-thirds of your weariness."

And Covan entered, and supped, and slept, and in the morning rose up a new man.

"Farewell, Covan," said the Dog of Maol-mor. "May success go with you, for you took what I had to give and did not mock me. So, when danger is your companion, wish for me, and I will not fail you."

At these words the Dog of Maol-mor disappeared into the forest, and Covan went to seek his cows, which were standing in the hollow where the darkness had come upon them.

At the sight of Covan the Brown-haired they walked onwards, Covan following ever behind them, and looking neither to the right nor to the left. All that day they walked, and when night fell they were in a barren plain, with only rocks for shelter.

"We must rest here as best we can," spoke Covan to the cows. And they bowed their heads and lay down in the place where they stood. Then came the black raven of Corri-nan-creag, whose eyes never closed, and whose wings never tired, and he fluttered before the face of Covan and told him that he knew of a cranny in the rock where there was food in plenty, and soft moss for a bed.

"Go with me there," he said to Covan, "and you shall lay aside three-thirds of your weariness, and depart in the morning refreshed," and Covan listened thankfully to his words, and at dawn he rose up to seek his cows.

"Farewell!" cried the black raven. "You trusted me, and took all I had to offer in return for the food you once gave me. So if in time to come you need a friend, wish for me, and I will not fail you."

As before, the cows were standing in the spot where he had left them, ready to set out. All that day they walked, on and on, and on, Covan son of Gorla walking behind them, till night fell while they were on the banks of a river.

"We can go no further," said Covan to the cows. And they began to eat the grass by the side of the stream, while Covan listened to them and longed for some supper also, for they had travelled far, and his limbs were weak under him. Then there was a swish of water at his feet, and out peeped the head of the famous otter Doran-donn of the stream.

"Trust to me and I will find you warmth and shelter," said Doran-donn, "and for food fish in plenty." And Covan went with him thankfully, and ate and rested, and laid aside three-thirds of his weariness. At sunrise he left his bed of dried sea-weed, which had floated up with the tide, and with a grateful heart bade farewell to Doran-donn.

"Because you trusted me and took what I had to offer, you have made me your friend, Covan," said Doran-donn. "And if you should be in danger, and need help from one who can swim a river or dive beneath a wave, call to me and I will come to you." Then he plunged into the stream, and was seen no more.

The cows were standing ready in the place where Covan had left them, and they journeyed on all that day, till, when night fell, they reached the cottage. Joyful indeed was the old man as the cows went into their stables, and he beheld the rich milk that flowed into the pail of the golden-haired maiden with the silver comb.

"You have done well indeed," he said to Covan son of Gorla. "And now, what would you have as a reward?"

"I want nothing for myself," answered Covan the Brown-haired, "but I ask you to give me back my brothers and my sister who have been lost to us for three years past. You are wise and know the lore of fairies and of witches, tell me where I can find them, and what I must do to bring them to life again."

The old man looked grave at the words of Covan.

"Yes, truly I know where they are," answered he, "and I say not that they may not be brought to life again. But the perils are great. Too great for you to overcome."

"Tell me what they are," said Covan again, "and I shall know better if I may overcome them."

"Listen, then, and judge. In the mountain yonder there dwells a roe, white of foot, with horns that branch like the antlers of a deer. On the lake that leads to the land of the Sun floats a duck whose body is green and whose neck is of gold. In the pool of Corri-Bui swims a salmon with a skin that shines like silver, and whose gills are red. Bring them all to me, and then you shall know where dwell your brothers and your sister!"

"Tomorrow at cock-crow I will begone!" answered Covan.

The way to the mountain lay straight before him, and when he had climbed high he caught sight of the roe with the white feet and the spotted sides, on the peak in front.

Full of hope he set out in pursuit of her, but by the time he had reached that peak she had left it and was to be seen on another. And so it always happened, and Covan's courage had well-nigh failed him, when the thought of the Dog of Maol-mor darted into his mind.

"Oh, that he was here!" he cried. And looking up he saw him.

"Why did you summon me?" asked the Dog of Maol-mor. And when Covan had told him of his trouble, and how the roe always led him further and further, the Dog only answered, "Fear nothing, for I will soon catch her for you." And in a short while he laid the roe unhurt at Covan's feet.

"What will you wish me to do with her?" said the Dog. And Covan answered, "The old man bade me bring her, and the duck with the golden neck, and the salmon with the silver sides, to his cottage. If I shall catch them, I know not. But carry the roe to the back of the cottage, and tether her so that she cannot escape."

"It shall be done," said the Dog of Maol-mor.

Then Covan sped to the lake which led to the land of the Sun, where the duck with the green body and the golden neck was swimming among the water-lilies.

"Surely I can catch him, good swimmer as I am," he said to himself. But, if he could swim well, the duck could swim better, and at length his strength failed him, and he was forced to seek the land.

"Oh that the black raven were here to help me!" he thought to himself. And in a moment the black raven was perched on his shoulder.

"How can I help you?" asked the raven. And Covan answered, "Catch the green duck that floats on the water." And the raven flew with his strong wings and picked him up in his strong beak, and in another moment the bird was laid at the feet of Covan.

This time it was easy for the young man to carry his prize, and after giving thanks to the raven for his aid, he went on to the river.

In the deep dark pool of which the old man had spoken the silver-sided salmon was lying under a rock.

"Surely I, good fisher as I am, can catch him," said Covan son of Gorla. And cutting a slender pole from a bush, he fastened a line to the end of it.

But cast with what skill he might, it availed nothing, for the salmon would not even look at the bait.

"I am beaten at last, unless the Doran-donn can deliver me," he cried. And as he spoke there was a swish of the water, and the face of the Doran-donn looked up at him.

"O catch me, I pray you, that salmon under the rock!" said Covan son of Gorla. And the Doran-donn dived, and laying hold of the salmon by his tail, bore it back to the place where Covan was standing.

"The roe, and the duck, and the salmon are here," said Covan to the old man, when he reached the cottage. And the old man smiled on him and bade him eat and drink, and after he hungered no more, he would speak with him.

And this was what the old man said, "You began well, my son, so things have gone well with you. You set store by your mother's blessing, therefore you have been blessed. You gave food to the raven when it hungered. You were true to the promise you had made to me, and did not suffer yourself to be turned aside by vain shows. You were skilled to perceive that the boy who tempted you to leave the temple was a teller of false tales, and took with a grateful heart what the poor had to offer you. Last of all, difficulties gave you courage, instead of lending you despair.

And now, as to your reward, you shall in truth take your sister home with you, and your brothers I will restore to life, but idle and unfaithful as they are their lot is to wander for ever. And so farewell, and may wisdom be with you."

"First tell me your name?" asked Covan softly.

"I am the Spirit of Age," said the old man.

THE WHITE INN

This adaptation is taken from a collection called Breton Legends, although the original author or collector remains unknown.

ONCE UPON A TIME THERE WAS an inn at Ponyou, known, from its appearance, as the White Inn. The people who kept it were both good and honest. They were known to be punctual at their Easter duties, and no one ever thought of counting money after them. It was at the White Inn that travellers would stop to sleep, and horses knew the place so well, that they would draw up of their own accord before the stable-door.

The headsman of the harvest had brought in short gloomy days, and one evening, as Floc'h the landlord was standing at the White-Inn door, a traveller, evidently of importance, and mounted on a splendid foreign steed, reined up his horse, and lifting his hand to his hat, said courteously, "I want a supper and a bed-chamber."

Floc'h drew first his pipe from his mouth, and then his hat from his head, and answered, "God bless you, sir. A supper you shall have, but as to a room, we cannot give it you, for we have now above, six muleteers on their way home to Redon, who have taken all the beds of the White Inn."

The traveller then said, "For God's sake, my good man, contrive for me to sleep somewhere. The very dogs have a kennel, and it is not fitting that Christians be without a bed in such weather as this."

"Sir stranger," said the host remorsefully, "I can only tell you that the inn is full, and we have no place for you but the red room."

"Well, give me that," replied the stranger.

But the landlord rubbed his forehead and looked grieved, for he could not let the traveller sleep in the red chamber.

"Since I have been at the White Inn," said he at last, "only two men have ever occupied that room, and on the morrow, black as had been their hair the night before, they rose with it snow-white."

The traveller looked full at the landlord.

"Then your house is haunted by the spirits from another world?" asked he.

"It is," faltered the landlord.

"Then God and the Blessed Virgin be merciful to me. I will sleep there, but make me a fire, and warm my bed, for I am cold."

The landlord did as he was ordered.

When the traveller had finished supper, he bade good night to all at table, and went up to the red chamber. The landlord and his wife trembled, and began to pray.

The stranger having reached his room began to look about him. It was a large flame-coloured chamber, with great shining stains upon the walls, that might well have been taken for the marks of fresh-spilt blood. At the further end there stood a four-post bed, surrounded by heavy curtains. The rest of the room was empty, and the mournful whistling of the wind came down the chimney and the corridors, and sounded like the cries of souls beseeching prayers.

The traveller, kneeling down, prayed silently to God, then fearlessly got into bed, and soon slept soundly.

But at the very moment when the hour of midnight sounded from a distant church-tower, he suddenly awoke, heard the curtain-rings sliding on their iron poles, and beheld them open at his right hand.

He was going to get out of bed, but his feet striking against something cold, he recoiled in terror.

There stood before him a coffin, with four lighted candles at the corners, and covered with a great black pall that glittered as with tears.

The stranger turned to try the other side of his bed, but the coffin instantly changed places, and barred his way out as before.

Five times he made an effort to escape, and every time the bier was there beneath his feet, with the candles and the funeral pall.

The traveller then knew it was a ghost, who had some boon to ask, and kneeling up in bed, he made the holy sign, and spoke, "Who are you, departed one? Speak. A Christian listens to you."

A voice answered from the coffin, "I am a traveller murdered here by those who kept this inn before its present owner. I died unprepared, and now I suffer in Purgatory."

"What needs there, suffering soul, to give you rest?"

"I want six Masses said at the church of our Lady of Folgoat, and also a pilgrimage made for my intention by some Christian to our Lady of Rumengol."

No sooner had these words been uttered than the lights went out, the curtains closed, and all was silence.

The stranger spent the night in prayer.

The next morning he told the landlord everything, and said, "My good friend, I am Monsieur de Rohan, of family as noble as the noblest now in Brittany. I will go and make the pilgrimage to Rumengol, and I will see that the six Masses shall be said. Trouble yourself no more, for this suffering soul shall rest in peace."

Within the short space of one month the red room had lost its crimson hue, and become white and cheerful as the others. No sound was heard there but the swallows twittering in the chimney, and nothing could be seen but a fair white bed, a crucifix, and a vessel of holy water.

The traveller had kept his word.

GRACIOSA AND PERCINET

This adaptation is taken from a story collected by Andrew Lang in his Orange Fairy Book, published in 1906. The original is taken from Les Contes des Fees by Marie-Catherine Le Jumel de Barneville, Baroness d'Aulnoy, a French writer known for her fairy tales. When she termed her works contes de fées (fairy tales), she originated the term that is now generally used for the genre.

ONCE UPON A TIME THERE LIVED a King and Queen who had one charming daughter. She was so graceful and pretty and clever that she was called Graciosa, and the Queen was so fond of her that she could think of nothing else.

Every day she gave the Princess a lovely new frock of gold brocade, or satin, or velvet, and when she was hungry she had bowls full of sugar-plums, and at least twenty pots of jam. Everybody said she was the happiest Princess in the world.

Now there lived at this same court a very rich old duchess whose name was Grumbly. She was more frightful than tongue can tell. Her hair was red as fire, and she had but one eye, and that not a pretty one! Her face was as broad as a full moon, and her mouth was so large that everybody who met her would have been afraid they were going to be eaten up, only she had no teeth. As she was as cross as she was ugly, she could not bear to hear everyone saying how pretty and how charming Graciosa was, so she presently went away from the court to her own castle, which was not far off. But if anybody who went to see her happened to mention the charming

Princess, she would cry angrily, "It's not true that she is lovely. I have more beauty in my little finger than she has in her whole body."

Soon after this, to the great grief of the Princess, the Queen was taken ill and died, and the King became so melancholy that for a whole year he shut himself up in his palace. At last his physicians, fearing that he would fall ill, ordered that he should go out and amuse himself, so a hunting party was arranged, but as it was very hot weather the King soon got tired, and said he would dismount and rest at a castle which they were passing.

This happened to be the Duchess Grumbly's castle, and when she heard that the King was coming she went out to meet him, and said that the cellar was the coolest place in the whole castle if he would condescend to come down into it. So down they went together, and the King seeing about two hundred great casks ranged side by side, asked if it was only for herself that she had this immense store of wine.

"Yes, sire," answered she, "it is for myself alone, but I shall be most happy to let you taste some of it. Which do you like, canary, St. Julien, champagne, hermitage sack, raisin, or cider?"

"Well," said the King, "since you are so kind as to ask me, I prefer champagne to anything else."

Then Duchess Grumbly took up a little hammer and tapped upon the cask twice, and out came at least a thousand crowns.

"What's the meaning of this?" said she smiling.

Then she tapped the next cask, and out came a bushel of gold pieces.

"I don't understand this at all," said the Duchess, smiling more than before.

Then she went on to the third cask, tap, tap, and out came such a stream of diamonds and pearls that the ground was covered with them.

"Ah!" she cried, "this is altogether beyond my comprehension, sire. Someone must have stolen my good wine and put all this rubbish in its place."

"Rubbish, do you call it, Madam Grumbly?" cried the King. "Rubbish! Why there is enough there to buy ten kingdoms."

"Well," said she, "you must know that all those casks are full of gold and jewels, and if you like to marry me it shall all be yours."

Now the King loved money more than anything else in the world, so he cried joyfully, "Marry you? Why with all my heart! Tomorrow if you like."

"But I make one condition," said the Duchess, "I must have entire control of your daughter to do as I please with her."

"Oh certainly, you shall have your own way. Let us shake hands upon the bargain," said the King.

So they shook hands and went up out of the cellar of treasure together, and the Duchess locked the door and gave the key to the King.

When he got back to his own palace Graciosa ran out to meet him, and asked if he had had good sport.

"I have caught a dove," answered he.

"Oh! Do give it to me," said the Princess, "and I will keep it and take care of it."

"I can hardly do that," said he, "for, to speak more plainly, I mean that I met the Duchess Grumbly, and have promised to marry her."

"And you call her a dove?" cried the Princess. "I should have called her a screech owl."

"Hold your tongue," said the King, very crossly. "I intend you to behave prettily to her. So now go and make yourself fit to be seen, as I am going to take you to visit her."

So the Princess went very sorrowfully to her own room, and her nurse, seeing her tears, asked what was vexing her.

"Alas! Who would not be vexed?" answered she, "for the King intends to marry again, and has chosen for his new bride my enemy, the hideous Duchess Grumbly."

"Oh, well!" answered the nurse, "You must remember that you are a Princess, and are expected to set a good example in making the best of whatever happens. You must promise me not to let the Duchess see how much you dislike her."

At first the Princess would not promise, but the nurse showed her so many good reasons for it that in the end she agreed to be amiable to her stepmother.

Then the nurse dressed her in a robe of pale green and gold brocade, and combed out her long fair hair till it floated round her like a golden mantle, and put on her head a crown of roses and jasmine with emerald leaves.

When she was ready nobody could have been prettier, but she still could not help looking sad.

Meanwhile the Duchess Grumbly was also occupied in attiring herself. She had one of her shoe heels made an inch or so higher than the other, that she might not limp so much, and put in a cunningly made glass eye in the place of the one she had lost. She dyed her red hair black, and painted her face. Then she put on a gorgeous robe of lilac satin lined with blue, and a yellow petticoat trimmed with violet ribbons, and because she had heard that queens always rode into their new dominions, she ordered a horse to be made ready for her to ride.

While Graciosa was waiting until the King should be ready to set out, she went down all alone through the garden into a little wood, where she sat down upon a mossy bank and began to think. And her thoughts were so doleful that very soon she began to cry, and she cried, and cried, and forgot all about going back to the palace, until she suddenly saw a handsome page standing before her. He was dressed in green, and the cap which he held in his hand was adorned with white plumes. When Graciosa looked at him he went down on one knee, and said to her:

"Princess, the King awaits you."

The Princess was surprised, and, if the truth must be told, very much delighted at the appearance of this charming page, whom she could not remember having seen before. Thinking he might belong to the household of the Duchess, she said, "How long have you been one of the King's pages?"

"I am not in the service of the King, madam," answered he, "but in yours."

"In mine?" said the Princess with great surprise. "Then how is it that I have never seen you before?"

"Ah, Princess!" said he, "I have never before dared to present myself to you, but now the King's marriage threatens you with so many dangers that I have resolved to tell you at once how much I love you already, and I trust that in time I may win your regard. I am Prince Percinet, of whose riches you may have heard, and whose fairy gift will, I hope, be of use to you in all your difficulties, if you will permit me to accompany you under this disguise."

"Ah, Percinet!" cried the Princess, "Is it really you? I have so often heard of you and wished to see you. If you will indeed be my friend, I shall not be afraid of that wicked old Duchess anymore."

So they went back to the palace together, and there Graciosa found a beautiful horse which Percinet had brought for her to ride. As it was very spirited he led it by the bridle, and this arrangement enabled him to turn and look at the Princess often, which he did not fail to do. Indeed, she was so pretty that it was a real pleasure to look at her.

When the horse which the Duchess was to ride appeared beside Graciosa"s, it looked no better than an old cart horse, and as to their trappings, there was simply no comparison between them, as the Princess's saddle and bridle were one glittering mass of diamonds. The King had so many other things to think of that he did not notice this, but all his courtiers were entirely taken up with admiring the Princess and her charming Page in green, who was more handsome and distinguished-looking than all the rest of the court put together.

When they met the Duchess Grumbly she was seated in an open carriage trying in vain to look dignified. The King and the Princess saluted her, and her horse was brought forward for her to mount. But when she saw Graciosa's she cried angrily, "If that child is to have a better horse than mine, I will go back to my own castle this very minute. What is the good of being a Queen if one is to be slighted like this?"

Upon this the King commanded Graciosa to dismount and to beg the Duchess to honour her by mounting her horse. The Princess obeyed in silence, and the Duchess, without looking at her or thanking her, scrambled up upon the beautiful horse, where she sat looking like a bundle of clothes, and eight officers had to hold her up for fear she should fall off.

Even then she was not satisfied, and was still grumbling and muttering, so they asked her what was the matter.

"I wish that Page in green to come and lead the horse, as he did when Graciosa rode it," said she very sharply.

And the King ordered the Page to come and lead the Queen's horse. Percinet and the Princess looked at one another, but said never a word, and then he did as the King commanded, and the procession started in great pomp. The Duchess was greatly elated, and as she sat there in state would not have wished to change places even with Graciosa. But at the moment when it was least expected the beautiful horse began to plunge and rear and kick, and finally to run away at such a pace that it was impossible to stop him.

At first the Duchess clung to the saddle, but she was very soon thrown off and fell in a heap among the stones and thorns, and there they found her, shaken to a jelly, and collected what was left of her as if she had been a broken glass. Her bonnet was here and her shoes there, her face was scratched, and her fine clothes were covered with mud. Never was a bride seen in such a dismal plight. They carried her back to the palace and put her to bed, but as soon as she recovered enough to be able to speak, she began to scold and rage, and declared that the whole affair was Graciosa's fault, that she had contrived it on purpose to try and get rid of her, and that if the King would not have her punished, she would go back to her castle and enjoy her riches by herself.

At this the King was terribly frightened, for he did not at all want to lose all those barrels of gold and jewels. So he hastened to appease the Duchess, and told her she might punish Graciosa in any way she pleased.

Thereupon she sent for Graciosa, who turned pale and trembled at the summons, for she guessed that it promised nothing agreeable for her. She looked all about for Percinet, but he was nowhere to be seen, so she had no choice but to go to the Duchess Grumbly's room. She had hardly got inside the door when she was seized by four waiting women, who looked so tall and strong and cruel that the Princess shuddered at the sight of them, and still more when she saw them arming themselves with great bundles of rods, and heard the Duchess call out to them from her bed to beat the Princess without mercy. Poor Graciosa wished miserably that Percinet could only know what was happening and come to rescue her.

But no sooner did they begin to beat her than she found, to her great relief, that the rods had changed to bundles of peacock's feathers, and though the Duchess's women went on till they were so tired that they could no longer raise their arms from their sides, yet she was not hurt in the least. However, the Duchess thought she must be black and blue after such a beating, so Graciosa, when she was released, pretended to feel very bad, and went away into her own room, where she told her nurse all that had happened, and then the nurse left her, and when the Princess turned round there stood Percinet beside her. She thanked him gratefully for helping her so cleverly, and they laughed and were very merry over the way they had taken in the Duchess and her waiting-maids, but Percinet advised her still to pretend to be ill for a few days, and after promising to come to her aid whenever she needed him, he disappeared as suddenly as he had come.

The Duchess was so delighted at the idea that Graciosa was really ill, that she herself recovered twice as fast as she would have done otherwise, and the wedding was held with great magnificence. Now as the King knew that, above all other things, the Queen loved to be told that she was beautiful, he ordered that her portrait should be painted, and that a tournament should be held, at which all the bravest knights of his court should maintain against all comers that Grumbly was the most beautiful princess in the world.

Numbers of knights came from far and wide to accept the challenge, and the hideous Queen sat in great state in a balcony hung with cloth of gold to watch the contests, and Graciosa had to stand up behind her, where her loveliness was so conspicuous that the combatants could not keep their eyes off her. But the Queen was so vain that she thought all their admiring glances were for herself, especially as, in spite of the badness of their cause, the King's knights were so brave that they were the victors in every combat.

However, when nearly all the strangers had been defeated, a young unknown knight presented himself. He carried a portrait, enclosed in a bow encrusted with diamonds, and he declared himself willing to maintain against them all that the Queen was the ugliest creature in the world, and that the Princess whose portrait he carried was the most beautiful.

So one by one the knights came out against him, and one by one he vanquished them all, and then he opened the box, and said that, to console them, he would show them the portrait of his Queen of Beauty, and when he did so everyone recognised the Princess Graciosa. The unknown knight then saluted her gracefully and retired, without telling his name to anybody. But Graciosa had no difficulty in guessing that it was Percinet.

As to the Queen, she was so furiously angry that she could hardly speak, but she soon recovered her voice, and overwhelmed Graciosa with a torrent of reproaches.

"What!" she said, "Do you dare to dispute with me for the prize of beauty, and expect me to endure this insult to my knights? But I will not bear it, proud Princess. I will have my revenge."

"I assure you, Madam," said the Princess, "that I had nothing to do with it and am quite willing that you shall be declared Queen of Beauty

"Ah! You are pleased to jest, popinjay!" said the Queen, "But it will be my turn soon!"

The King was speedily told what had happened, and how the Princess was in terror of the angry Queen, but he only said, "The Queen must do as she pleases. Graciosa belongs to her!"

The wicked Queen waited impatiently until night fell, and then she ordered her carriage to be brought. Graciosa, much against her will, was forced into it, and away they drove, and never stopped until they reached a great forest, a hundred leagues from the palace. This forest was so gloomy, and so full of lions, tigers, bears and wolves, that nobody dared pass through it even by daylight, and here they set down the unhappy Princess in the middle of the black night, and left her in spite of all her tears and entreaties. The Princess stood quite still at first from sheer bewilderment, but when the last sound of the retreating carriages died away in the distance she began to run aimlessly here and there, sometimes knocking herself against a tree, sometimes tripping over a stone, fearing every minute that she would be eaten up by the lions. Presently she was too tired to advance another step, so she threw herself down upon the ground and cried miserably, "Oh, Percinet! Where are you? Have you forgotten me altogether?"

She had hardly spoken when all the forest was lighted up with a sudden glow. Every tree seemed to be sending out a soft radiance, which was clearer than moonlight and softer than daylight, and at the end of a long avenue of trees opposite to her the Princess saw a palace of clear crystal which blazed like the sun. At that moment a slight sound behind her made her start round, and there stood Percinet himself.

"Did I frighten you, my Princess?" said he. "I come to bid you welcome to our fairy palace, in the name of the Queen, my mother, who is prepared to love you as much as I do."

The Princess joyfully mounted with him into a little sledge, drawn by two stags, which bounded off and drew them swiftly to the wonderful palace, where the Queen received her with the greatest kindness, and a splendid banquet was served at once. Graciosa was so happy to have found Percinet, and to have escaped from the gloomy forest and all its terrors, that she was very hungry and very merry, and they were a gay party. After supper they went into another lovely room, where the crystal walls were covered with pictures, and the Princess saw with great surprise that her own history was represented, even down to the moment when Percinet found her in the forest.

"Your painters must indeed be diligent," she said, pointing out the last picture to the Prince.

"They are obliged to be, for I will not have anything forgotten that happens to you," he answered.

When the Princess grew sleepy, twenty-four charming maidens put her to bed in the prettiest room she had ever seen, and then sang to her so sweetly that Graciosa's dreams were all of mermaids, and cool sea waves, and caverns, in which she wandered with Percinet, but when she woke up again her first thought was that, delightful as this fairy palace seemed to her, yet she could not stay in it, but must go back to her father.

When she had been dressed by the four-and-twenty maidens in a charming robe which the Queen had sent for her, and in which she looked prettier than ever, Prince Percinet came to see her, and was bitterly disappointed when she told him what she had been thinking. He begged her to consider again how unhappy the wicked Queen would make her, and how, if she would but marry him, all the fairy palace would be hers, and his one thought would be to please her.

But, in spite of everything he could say, the Princess was quite determined to go back, though he at last persuaded her to stay eight days, which were so full of pleasure and amusement that they passed like a few hours. On the last day, Graciosa, who had often felt anxious to know what was going on in her father's palace, said to Percinet that she was sure that he could find out for her, if he would, what reason the Queen had given her father for her sudden disappearance. Percinet at first offered to send his courier to find out, but the Princess said, "Oh! isn't there a quicker way of knowing than that?"

"Very well," said Percinet, "you shall see for yourself."

So up they went together to the top of a very high tower, which, like the rest of the castle, was built entirely of rock-crystal.

There the Prince held Graciosa's hand in his, and made her put the tip of her little finger into her mouth, and look towards the town, and immediately she saw the wicked Queen go to the King, and heard her say to him, "That miserable Princess is dead, and no great loss either. I have ordered that she shall be buried at once."

And then the Princess saw how she dressed up a log of wood and had it buried, and how the old King cried, and all the people murmured that the Queen had killed Graciosa with her cruelties, and that she ought to have her head cut off. When the Princess saw that the King was so sorry for her pretended death that he could neither eat nor drink, she cried, "Ah, Percinet! Take me back quickly if you love me."

And so, though he did not want to at all, he was obliged to promise that he would let her go.

"You may not regret me, Princess," he said sadly, "for I fear that you do not love me well enough, but I foresee that you will more than once regret that you left this fairy palace where we have been so happy."

But, in spite of all he could say, she bade farewell to the Queen, his mother, and prepared to set out, so Percinet, very unwillingly, brought the little sledge with the stags and she mounted beside him. But they had hardly gone twenty yards when a tremendous noise behind her made Graciosa look back, and she saw the palace of crystal fly into a million splinters, like the spray of a fountain, and vanish.

"Oh, Percinet!" she cried, "What has happened? The palace is gone."

"Yes," he answered, "my palace is a thing of the past, you will see it again, but not until after you have been buried."

"Now you are angry with me," said Graciosa in her most coaxing voice, "though after all I am more to be pitied than you are."

When they got near the palace the Prince made the sledge and themselves invisible, so the Princess got in unobserved, and ran up to the great hall where the King was sitting all by himself. At first he was very much startled by Graciosa's sudden appearance, but she told him how the Queen had left her out in the forest, and how she had caused a log of wood to be buried. The King, who did not know what to think, sent quickly and had it dug up, and sure enough it was as the Princess had said. Then he caressed Graciosa, and made her sit down to supper with him, and they were as happy as possible.

But someone had by this time told the wicked Queen that Graciosa had come back, and was at supper with the King, and in she flew in a terrible fury. The poor old King quite trembled before her, and when she declared that Graciosa was not the Princess at all, but a wicked impostor, and that if the King did not give her up at once she would go back to her own castle and never see him again, he had not a word to say, and really seemed to believe that it was not Graciosa after all. So the Queen in great triumph sent for her waiting women, who dragged the unhappy Princess away and shut her up in a garret. They took away all her jewels and her pretty dress, and gave her a rough cotton frock, wooden shoes, and a little cloth cap. There was some straw in a corner, which was all she had for a bed, and they gave her a very little bit of black bread to eat. In this miserable plight Graciosa did indeed regret the fairy palace, and she would have called

Percinet to her aid, only she felt sure he was still vexed with her for leaving him, and thought that she could not expect him to come.

Meanwhile the Queen had sent for an old Fairy, as malicious as herself, and said to her, "You must find me some task for this fine Princess which she cannot possibly do, for I mean to punish her, and if she does not do what I order, she will not be able to say that I am unjust."

So the old Fairy said she would think it over, and come again the next day. When she returned she brought with her a skein of thread, three times as big as herself, which was so fine that a breath of air would break it. It was so tangled that it was impossible to see the beginning or the end of it.

The Queen sent for Graciosa, and said to her, "Do you see this skein? Set your clumsy fingers to work upon it, for I must have it disentangled by sunset, and if you break a single thread it will be the worse for you." So saying she left her, locking the door behind her with three keys.

The Princess stood dismayed at the sight of the terrible skein. If she did but turn it over to see where to begin, she broke a thousand threads, and not one could she disentangle. At last she threw it into the middle of the floor, crying, "Oh, Percinet! This fatal skein will be the death of me if you will not forgive me and help me once more."

And immediately in came Percinet as easily as if he had all the keys in his own possession.

"Here I am, Princess, as much as ever at your service," said he, "though really you are not very kind to me."

Then he just stroked the skein with his wand, and all the broken threads joined themselves together, and the whole skein wound itself smoothly off in the most surprising manner, and the Prince, turning to Graciosa, asked if there was nothing else that she wished him to do for her, and if the time would never come when she would wish for him for his own sake.

"Don't be vexed with me, Percinet," she said. "I am unhappy enough without that."

"But why should you be unhappy, my Princess?" cried he. "Only come with me and we shall be as happy as the day is long together."

"But suppose you get tired of me?" said Graciosa.

The Prince was so grieved at this want of confidence that he left her without another word.

The wicked Queen was in such a hurry to punish Graciosa that she thought the sun would never set, and indeed it was before the appointed time that she came with her four Fairies, and as she fitted the three keys into the locks she said, "I'll venture to say that the idle minx has not done anything at all. She prefers to sit with her hands before her to keep them white."

But, as soon as she entered, Graciosa presented her with the ball of thread in perfect order, so that she had no fault to find, and could only pretend to discover that it was soiled, for which imaginary fault she gave Graciosa a blow on each cheek, that made her white and pink skin turn green and yellow. And then she sent her back to be locked into the garret once more.

Then the Queen sent for the Fairy again and scolded her furiously. "Don't make such a mistake again, find me something that it will be quite impossible for her to do," she said.

So the next day the Fairy appeared with a huge barrel full of the feathers of all sorts of birds. There were nightingales, canaries, goldfinches, linnets, tomtits, parrots, owls, sparrows, doves, ostriches, bustards, peacocks, larks, partridges, and everything else that you can think of. These feathers were all mixed up in such confusion that the birds themselves could not have chosen out their own. "Here," said the Fairy, "is a little task which it will take all your prisoner's skill and patience to accomplish. Tell her to pick out and lay in a separate heap the feathers of each bird. She would need to be a fairy to do it."

The Queen was more than delighted at the thought of the despair this task would cause the Princess. She sent for her, and with the same threats as before locked her up with the three keys, ordering that all the feathers should be sorted by sunset. Graciosa set to work at once, but before she had taken out a dozen feathers she found that it was perfectly impossible to know one from another.

"Ah, well," she sighed, "the Queen wishes to kill me, and if I must die I must. I cannot ask Percinet to help me again, for if he really loved me he would not wait till I called him, he would come without that."

"I am here, my Graciosa," cried Percinet, springing out of the barrel where he had been hiding. "How can you still doubt that I love you with all my heart?"

Then he gave three strokes of his wand upon the barrel, and all the feathers flew out in a cloud and settled down in neat little separate heaps all around the room.

"What should I do without you, Percinet?" said Graciosa gratefully. But still she could not quite make up her mind to go with him and leave her father's kingdom for ever, so she begged him to give her more time to think of it, and he had to go away disappointed once more.

When the wicked Queen came at sunset she was amazed and infuriated to find the task done. However, she complained that the heaps of feathers were badly arranged, and for that the Princess was beaten and sent back to her garret. Then the Queen sent for the Fairy once more, and scolded her until she was fairly terrified, and promised to go home and think of another task for Graciosa, worse than either of the others.

At the end of three days she came again, bringing with her a box.

"Tell your slave," said he, "to carry this wherever you please, but on no account to open it. She will not be able to help doing so, and then you will be quite satisfied with the result." So the Queen came to Graciosa, and said, "Carry this box to my castle, and place it upon the table in my own room. But I forbid you on pain of death to look at what it contains."

Graciosa set out, wearing her little cap and wooden shoes and the old cotton frock, but even in this disguise she was so beautiful that all the passers-by wondered who she could be. She had not gone far before the heat of the sun and the weight of the box tired her so much that she sat down to rest in the shade of a little wood which lay on one side of a green meadow. She was carefully holding the box upon her lap when she suddenly felt the greatest desire to open it.

"What could possibly happen if I did?" she said to herself. "I should not take anything out. I should only just see what was there."

And without farther hesitation she lifted the cover.

Instantly out came swarms of little men and women, no taller than her finger, and scattered themselves all over the meadow, singing and dancing, and playing the merriest games, so that at first Graciosa was delighted and watched them with much amusement. But presently, when she was rested and wished to go on her way, she found that, do what she would, she could not get them back into their box. If she chased them in the meadow they fled into the wood, and if she pursued them into the wood they dodged round trees and behind sprigs of moss, and with peals of elfin laughter scampered back again into the meadow.

At last, weary and terrified, she sat down and cried.

"It is my own fault," she said sadly. "Percinet, if you can still care for such an imprudent Princess, do come and help me once more."

Immediately Percinet stood before her.

"Ah, Princess!" he said, "but for the wicked Queen I fear you would never think of me at all."

"Indeed I should," said Graciosa, "I am not so ungrateful as you think. Only wait a little and I believe I shall love you quite dearly."

Percinet was pleased at this, and with one stroke of his wand compelled all the wilful little people to come back to their places in the box, and then rendering the Princess invisible he took her with him in his chariot to the castle.

When the Princess presented herself at the door, and said that the Queen had ordered her to place the box in her own room, the governor laughed heartily at the idea.

"No, no, my little shepherdess," said he, "that is not the place for you. No wooden shoes have ever been over that floor yet."

Then Graciosa begged him to give her a written message telling the Queen that he had refused to admit her. This he did, and she went back to Percinet, who was waiting for her, and they set out together for the palace. You may imagine that they did not go the shortest way, but the Princess did not find it too long, and before they parted she had promised that if the Queen was still cruel to her, and tried again to play her any spiteful trick, she would leave her and come to Percinet for ever.

When the Queen saw her returning she fell upon the Fairy, whom she had kept with her, and pulled her hair, and scratched her face, and would really have killed her if a Fairy could be killed. And when the Princess presented the letter and the box she threw them both upon the fire without opening them, and looked very much as if she would like to throw the Princess after them. However, what she really did do was to have a great hole as deep as a well dug in her garden, and the top of it covered with a flat stone. Then she went and walked near it, and said to Graciosa and all her ladies who were with her, "I am told that a great treasure lies under that stone, let us see if we can lift it."

So they all began to push and pull at it, and Graciosa among the others, which was just what the Queen wanted, for as soon as the stone was lifted high enough, she gave the Princess a push which sent her down to the bottom of the well, and then the stone was let fall again, and there she was a prisoner. Graciosa felt that now indeed she was hopelessly lost, surely not even Percinet could find her in the heart of the earth.

"This is like being buried alive," she said with a shudder. "Oh, Percinet! If you only knew how I am suffering for my want of trust in you! But how could I be sure that you would not be like other men and tire of me from the moment you were sure I loved you?"

As she spoke she suddenly saw a little door open, and the sunshine blazed into the dismal well. Graciosa did not hesitate an instant, but passed through into a charming garden. Flowers and fruit grew on every side. Fountains plashed, and birds sang in the branches overhead, and when she reached a great avenue of trees and looked up to see where it would lead her, she found herself close to the palace of crystal. Yes! There was no mistaking it, and the Queen and Percinet were coming to meet her.

"Ah, Princess!" said the Queen, "don't keep this poor Percinet in suspense any longer. You little guess the anxiety he has suffered while you were in the power of that miserable Queen."

The Princess kissed her gratefully, and promised to do as she wished in everything, and holding out her hand to Percinet, with a smile, she said, "Do you remember telling me that I should not see your palace again until I had been buried? I wonder if you guessed then that, when that happened, I should tell you that I love you with all my heart, and will marry you whenever you like?"

Prince Percinet joyfully took the hand that was given him, and, for fear the Princess should change her mind, the wedding was held at once with the greatest splendour, and Graciosa and Percinet lived happily ever after.

HISTORICAL NOTES

This section contains some brief biographical notes about the original collectors and their books featured in this collection. These notes have been adapted from those on Wikipedia.

Andrew Lang

Andrew Lang FBA was a Scottish poet, novelist, literary critic, and contributor to the field of anthropology. He is best known as a collector of folk and fairy tales. The Andrew Lang lectures at the University of St Andrews are named after him.

Lang was born on 31st March 1844 in Selkirk. He was the eldest of the eight children born to John Lang, the town clerk, and his wife Jane Plenderleath Sellar, who was the daughter of Patrick Sellar, factor to the first duke of Sutherland. On 17th April 1875, he married Leonora Blanche Alleyne, youngest daughter of C. T. Alleyne of Clifton and Barbados. She was (or should have been) variously credited as author, collaborator, or translator of Lang's Colour / Rainbow Fairy Books, which he edited.

He was educated at Selkirk Grammar School, Loretto School, and the Edinburgh Academy, as well as the University of St Andrews and Balliol College, Oxford, where he took a first class in the final classical schools in 1868, becoming a fellow and subsequently honorary fellow of Merton College. He soon made a reputation as one of the most able and versatile writers of the day as a journalist, poet, critic, and historian. In 1906, he was elected FBA.

He died of angina pectoris on 20th July 1912 at the Tor-na-Coille Hotel in Banchory, survived by his wife. He was buried in the cathedral precincts at

St Andrews, where a monument can be visited in the south-east corner of the 19th century section.

Lang is now chiefly known for his publications on folklore, mythology, and religion. The earliest of his publications is *Custom and Myth* (1884). In *Myth, Ritual and Religion* (1887) he explained the "irrational" elements of mythology as survivals from more primitive forms. Lang's *Making of Religion* was heavily influenced by the 18th century idea of the "noble savage", in it, he maintained the existence of high spiritual ideas among so-called "savage" races, drawing parallels with the contemporary interest in occult phenomena in England.

His *Blue Fairy Book* (1889) was a beautifully produced and illustrated edition of fairy tales that has become a classic. This was followed by many other collections of fairy tales, collectively known as *Andrew Lang's Fairy Books*. In the preface of the *Lilac Fairy Book* he credits his wife with translating and transcribing most of the stories in the collections.

Lang was one of the founders of "psychical research" and his other writings on anthropology include *The Book of Dreams and Ghosts* (1897), *Magic and Religion* (1901) and *The Secret of the Totem* (1905). He served as President of the Society for Psychical Research in 1911.

He collaborated with S. H. Butcher in a prose translation (1879) of Homer's *Odyssey*, and with E. Myers and Walter Leaf in a prose version (1883) of the *Iliad*, both still noted for their archaic but attractive style.

Lang's writings on Scottish history are characterised by a scholarly care for detail, a piquant literary style, and a gift for disentangling complicated questions. *The Mystery of Mary Stuart* (1901) was a consideration of the fresh light thrown on Mary, Queen of Scots, by the Lennox manuscripts in the University Library, Cambridge, approving of her and criticising her accusers.

Lang was active as a journalist in various ways, ranging from sparkling "leaders" for the Daily News to miscellaneous articles for the Morning Post, and for many years he was literary editor of Longman's Magazine.

Charles Perrault

Charles Perrault was born in Paris to a wealthy bourgeois family, the seventh child of Pierre Perrault and Paquette Le Clerc. He attended very good schools and studied law before embarking on a career in government service, following in the footsteps of his father and elder brother Jean.

He took part in the creation of the Academy of Sciences as well as the restoration of the Academy of Painting. In 1654, he moved in with his brother Pierre, who had purchased the position of chief tax collector of the city of Paris. When the Academy of Inscriptions and Belles-Lettres was founded in 1663, Perrault was appointed its secretary and served under Jean Baptiste Colbert, finance minister to King Louis XIV.

In 1668, Perrault wrote *La Peinture* to honour the king's first painter, Charles Le Brun. He also wrote *Courses de tetes et de bague* in 1670, written to commemorate the 1662 celebrations staged by Louis for his mistress, Louise-Françoise de La Baume le Blanc, duchesse de La Vallière.

In 1695, when he was 67, Perrault decided to dedicate himself to his children. In 1697 he published *Histoires ou Contes du Temps passé*, subtitled *Les Contes de ma Mère l'Oye*. These tales, based on French popular tradition, were very popular in sophisticated court circles. Its publication made him suddenly very widely known and he is often credited as the founder of the modern fairy tale genre. Naturally, his work reflects awareness of earlier fairy tales written in the salons, most notably by Marie-Catherine Le Jumel de Barneville, Baroness d'Aulnoy, who coined the phrase "fairy tale" and wrote tales as early as 1690.

Some of his popular stories, particularly *Cinderella* and *The Sleeping Beauty*, are still commonly told today in similar ways to that written by Perrault, while others have been revised over the years. For example, some versions of *Sleeping Beauty* published today are based partially on a Brothers Grimm tale, *Little Briar Rose*, a modified version of the Perrault story, although interestingly the Disney version is quite true to the original Perrault tale.

Perrault had written *Little Red Riding Hood* as a warning to readers about men preying on young girls walking through the forest. He concludes his fairy tale with a moral, cautioning women and young girls about the dangers of trusting men. He states, "Watch out if you haven't learned that tame wolves are the most dangerous of all".

He had actually published his collection under the name of his last son, born in 1678, Pierre Darmancourt, probably fearful of criticism. In the tales, he used images from around him, such as the Chateau Ussé for *The Sleeping Beauty*, and the Marquis of the Château d'Oiron as the model for the Marquis de Carabas in *Puss in Boots*. He ornamented his folktale subject matter with details, asides and subtext drawn from the world of fashion.

Following up on these tales, he translated the *Fabulae Centum* of the Latin poet Gabriele Faerno into French verse in 1699.

Charles Perrault died in Paris in 1703 at the age of 75.

Jeanne-Marie Le Prince de Beaumont

She was born in 1711 in Rouen, the daughter of Marie-Barbe Plantart and Jean-Baptiste Le Prince, and died in 1780. She lost her mother when she was only eleven. After that, she and her younger sister were mentored by two wealthy women who entered them into the convent school at Ernemont in Rouen. They were educated and then taught there from 1725 to 1735.

Subsequently, she obtained a prestigious position as a singing teacher to the children at the Court of the Duke of Lorraine, Stanisław Leszczyński, at Lunéville.

Her first marriage was in 1737 to the dancer Antoine Malter. Details of a second marriage to Grimard de Beaumont are unclear. However, it is known that she bore a daughter, named Elisabeth, by Beaumont.

In 1748, having separated from Beaumont in reaction to his marital infidelities, she left France to become a governess in London. She wrote several fairy tales, among them an abridged version of *Beauty and the Beast*, adapted from Gabrielle-Suzanne Barbot de Villeneuve's original. After a successful publishing career in England, she left that country in 1763 with her daughter Elisabeth and son-in-law Moreau. She lived first in Savoy, near the city of Annecy, then moved to Avallon near Dijon in 1774.

Her first work, the moralistic novel *Le Triomphe de la vérité*, was published in 1748. She published approximately seventy volumes during her literary career Most famous were the collections she called "magasins," instructional handbooks for parents and educators of students from childhood through adolescence. She was one of the first to include folk tales as moralist and educational tools in her writings.

Because of her relationship in London with the French spy Thomas Pichon (1700-1781), she is a character in a novel entitled *Crossings , A Thomas Pichon Novel*, by A. J. B. Johnston.

Comtesse de Sophie Ségur

Sophie Rostopchine, Countess of Ségur, born Sofiya Feodorovna Rostopchina on 1st August 1799 in Saint Petersburg, was a French writer of Russian birth and origin. She is best known today for her novel *Les Malheurs de Sophie*, intended for children.

Her father Count Fyodor Rostopchine was lieutenant-general and, later, Minister of Foreign Affairs for Russia. In 1812, he was governor of Moscow during the invasion of the Grande Armée under Napoleon I of France. While facts concerning the origin of the great fire of Moscow are disputed by historians, Sophie Rostopchine's father has been said by some to have organized the great fire which forced Napoleon to make a disastrous retreat.

In 1814 the Rostopchine family left Imperial Russia for exile, going first to the Duchy of Warsaw, then to the German Confederation and the Italian peninsula and finally in 1817 to France under the Bourbon Restoration. In France, the father established a salon, and his wife and daughter converted to Roman Catholicism from Russian Orthodoxy.

It was in her father's salon that Sophie Rostopchine met Eugène Henri Raymond, Count of Ségur, whom she married in July 1819. The marriage was largely an unhappy one, her husband was flighty, distant and poor until being made a Peer of France in 1830, and his infrequent conjugal visits to their château des Nouettes produced eight children, including the father of the historian Pierre de Ségur.

The Comtesse de Ségur wrote her first novel at the age of 58.

Marie-Catherine Le Jumel de Barneville, Baroness d'Aulnoy

Marie-Catherine Le Jumel de Barneville, Baroness d'Aulnoy (1650-1705), also known as Countess d'Aulnoy, was a French writer known for her fairy tales. When she termed her works *contes de fées*, she originated the term that is now generally used for the genre.

D'Aulnoy was born in Barneville-la-Bertran, in Normandy, as a member of the noble family of Le Jumel de Barneville. She was the niece of Marie Bruneau des Loges, the friend of François de Malherbe and of Jean-Louis Guez de Balzac. In 1666, she was given at the age of fifteen in an arranged marriage to a Parisian thirty years older, François de la Motte, Baron d'Aulnoy, of the household of the Duke of Vendôme. The baron was a freethinker and a known gambler.

In 1669, the Baron d'Aulnoy was accused of treason by two men who may have been the lovers of Baroness d'Aulnoy and her mother, who by a second marriage was the Marchioness de Gadagne. If found guilty, the verdict would have meant execution. The Baron d'Aulnoy spent three years in the Bastille before finally convincing the court of his innocence. The two men implicated in the accusation were executed instead. The Marchioness de Gadagne fled to England, and although a warrant was served for Baroness d'Aulnoy's arrest, she escaped from officers through a window and hid in a church.

It is possible she then worked as a spy for France before returning to Paris in 1685. The Marchioness de Gadagne stayed in Madrid financed by a pension from the Spanish King. Mme d'Aulnoy hosted salons in her home at rue Saint-Benoît that were frequented by leading aristocrats and princes, including her close friend, Saint-Evremond.

D'Aulnoy published twelve books including three pseudo-memoirs, two fairy tale collections and three "historical" novels. She contributed to the anthology *Recueil des plus belles pièces des poètes français* in 1692 and wrote a series of travel memoirs based on her supposed travels through court life in Madrid and London. And although her insights may have been plagiarized and invented, these stories later became her most popular works. She gained the reputation as a historian and recorder of tales from outside France, and was elected as a member of Paduan Accademia dei Ricovatri. The money she made from her writing helped raise her three daughters, not all produced during her time with the Baron d'Aulnoy .

Her most popular works were her fairy tales and adventure stories as told in *Les Contes des Fées* and *Contes Nouveaux, ou Les Fées à la Mode*. Unlike the folk tales of the Grimm Brothers, who were born some 135 years later than d'Aulnoy, she told her stories in a more conversational style, as they might be told in salons. Much of her writing created a world of animal brides and grooms, where love and happiness came to heroines after surmounting great obstacles. These stories were far from suitable for children and many English adaptations are very dissimilar to the original.

Katharine Pyle

Katharine Pyle (1863–1938) was an American artist, poet, and children's writer.

Born in Wilmington, Delaware, the youngest offspring of William Pyle and his wife Margaret, she was the sister of author and artist Howard Pyle. She was educated at the Women's Industrial School and the Drexel Institute, then studied at the Philadelphia School of Design for Women and the New York Art Students' League. She lived in Wilmington her whole life, except four years in New York during the 1890s.

Her art was exhibited at the World's Columbian Exposition in 1893. She found work as an illustrator no later than 1895, but her first major success occurred in 1898 with *The Counterpane Fairy*. Over the course of her career she wrote over 30 books and illustrated the works of others. Her works appeared in the Ladies' Home Journal and Harper's Bazaar. The Delaware Art Museum now has a substantial collection of her manuscripts.

Edmund Dulac

Edmund Dulac (1882-1953) was a French British naturalised magazine illustrator, book illustrator and stamp designer. Born in Toulouse he studied law but later turned to the study of art at the École des Beaux-Arts. He moved to London early in the 20th century and in 1905 received his first commission to illustrate the novels of the Brontë Sisters. During World War I, Dulac produced relief books and when after the war the deluxe children's book market shrank he turned to magazine illustrations among other ventures. He designed banknotes during World War II and postage stamps, most notably those that heralded the beginning of Queen Elizabeth II's reign.

Settling in London's Holland Park, the 22-year-old Frenchman was commissioned by the publisher J. M. Dent to illustrate *Jane Eyre* and nine other volumes of works by the Brontë sisters. He then became a regular contributor to The Pall Mall Magazine, and joined the London Sketch Club, which introduced him to the foremost book and magazine illustrators of the day. Through these he began an association with the Leicester Galleries and Hodder & Stoughton.

The gallery commissioned illustrations from Dulac which they sold in an annual exhibition, while publishing rights to the paintings were taken up by Hodder & Stoughton for reproduction in illustrated gift books, publishing one book a year. Books produced under this arrangement by Dulac include *Stories from The Arabian Nights* (1907) with 50 colour images, an edition of William Shakespeare's *The Tempest* (1908) with 40 colour illustrations, The Rubaiyat of Omar Khayyam (1909) with 20 colour images, *The Sleeping Beauty and Other Fairy Tales* (1910), *Stories from Hans Christian Andersen* (1911), *The Bells and Other Poems* by Edgar

Allan Poe (1912) with 28 colour images and many monotone illustrations, and *Princess Badoura* (1913).

Dulac became a naturalised British citizen on 17 February 1912.

During World War I he contributed to relief books, including *King Albert's Book* (1914), *Princess Mary's Gift Book*, and, unusually, his own *Edmund Dulac's Picture-Book* for the French Red Cross (1915) including 20 colour images. Hodder and Stoughton also published *The Dreamer of Dreams* (1915) including 6 colour images – a work composed by the then Queen of Romania.

Dulac's wife was Helen Beauclerk, author of *The Green Lacqueur Pavilion*, 1926, and *The Love of the Foolish Angel*, 1929, both of which books have his illustrations.

ABOUT THE EDITOR

I was born in 1962 into a predominantly sporting household – Dad being a good footballer, playing senior amateur and lower league professional football in England, as well as running a series of private businesses in partnership with mum, herself an accomplished medal winning dancer.

I obtained a degree in History from Leeds University before wandering rather haphazardly into the emerging world of business computing in the late nineteen-eighties.

A little like my sporting father, I followed a succession of amateur writing paths alongside my career in technology, including working as a freelance journalist and book reviewer, my one claim to fame being a by-line in a national newspaper in the UK, The Sunday People.

I also spent 10 years treading the boards, appearing all over the south of the UK in pantos and plays, in village halls and occasionally on the stage of a professional theatre or two.

Following the sporting theme, and a while after I hung up my own boots, I worked on live TV broadcasts for the BBC, ITV, TVNZ, EuroSport and others as a rugby "Stato", covering Heineken Cups, Six Nations, IRB World Sevens and IRB World Cups in the late '90's and early '00's.

You can find out more about my work at: www.boyonabench.com

ALSO BY CLIVE GILSON - *FICTION*

- Songs of Bliss
- Out of the walled Garden
- The Mechanic's Curse
- The Insomniac Booth
- A Solitude of Stars

AS EDITOR – *FIRESIDE TALES – Part 1, Europe*

- Tales from the Land of Dragons
- Tales from the Land of the Brave
- Tales from the Land of Saints and Scholars
- Tales from the Land of Hope and Glory
- Tales from Lands of Snow and Ice
- Tales from the Viking Isles
- Tales from the Forest Lands
- Tales from the Old Norse
- More Tales About Saints and Scholars
- More Tales About Hope and Glory
- More Tales About Snow and Ice
- Tales from the Land of Rabbits
- Tales Told by Bulls and Wolves
- Tales of Fire & Bronze
- Tales Told by the Samodivi
- Tales From The Land Of The Strigoi
- Tales Told By The Wind Mother
- Tales From Gallia
- Tales From Germania

Tales From Gallia

EDITOR – *FIRESIDE TALES – Part 2, North America*
- Okaraxta - Tales from the Great Plains
- Tibik-kìzis – Tales from the Great Lakes & Canada

Further North American & Native American collections will be published during late 2019 & 2020

 SOLITUDE

CPSIA information can be obtained
at www.ICGtesting.com
Printed in the USA
BVHW031802181121
621972BV00009B/74/J